Storm Constantine's Wraeththu Mythos

I0637162

Blood, the Phoenix and a Rose

An Alchymical Triptych

Acknowledgements

My thanks go to Wendy Darling and Bridgette Parker, who originally thought up the idea of 'harling farms' for their co-written Wraeththu Mythos novel 'Breeding Discontent'.

Thanks also to Louise Coquio and Ricardo Pinto for their reading and editorial comments.

Thanks always to Wendy for the alchemical processes of the major editing, and to Ruby for her wonderful artistic interpretations of my literary visions.

Wraeththu Mythos

Blood, the Phoenix and a Rose

An Alchymical Triptych

Storm Constantine

Stafford England

Blood, the Phoenix and a Rose: An Alchymical Triptych
By Storm Constantine
© 2016

http://www.stormconstantine.co.uk

ISBN 978-1-907737-75-6

IP0046

Cover art by Ruby
Cover design and interior layout by Storm Constantine
Edited by Wendy Darling

Set in Palatino Linotype

An Immanion Press Edition
http://www.immanion-press.com
info@immanion-press.com

Books by Storm Constantine

The Wraeththu Chronicles
*The Enchantments of Flesh and Spirit
*The Bewitchments of Love and Hate
*The Fulfilments of Fate and Desire
*The Wraeththu Chronicles (omnibus of trilogy)

The Wraeththu Histories
*The Wraiths of Will and Pleasure
*The Shades of Time and Memory
*The Ghosts of Blood and Innocence

The Alba Sulh Sequence (Wraeththu Mythos)
*The Hienama
*Student of Kyme
*The Moonshawl

The Artemis Cycle
*The Monstrous Regiment
*Aleph

The Grigori Books
*Stalking Tender Prey
*Scenting Hallowed Blood
*Stealing Sacred Fire

The Magravandias Chronicles:
*Sea Dragon Heir
*Crown of Silence
*The Way of Light

*Hermetech
*Burying the Shadow
*Sign for the Sacred
Calenture
*Thin Air

Silverheart (with Michael Moorcock)

Short Story Collections:
*The Thorn Boy and Other Dreams of Dark Desire
*Mythangelus
*Mythophidia
*Mytholumina
*Mythanimus
Splinters of Truth (NewCon Press)

Wraeththu Mythos Collections
(co-edited with Wendy Darling, including stories by the editors and other writers)
*ParaGenesis
*Para Imminence
*Para Kindred
*Para Animalia

Non-Fiction
*Sekhem Heka
*Grimoire Dehara: Kaimana
*Grimoire Dehara: Ulani (with Taylor Ellwood)
The Inward Revolution (with Deborah Benstead)
Egyptian Birth Signs (with Graham Phillips)
Bast and Sekhmet: Eyes of Ra (with Eloise Coquio)

*available as Immanion Press editions

Contents

Prima Materia
Introduction

The idea for Wraeththu, a race of androgynous beings who come to replace humanity, has its origins in the concept of the alchemical rebis – the divine hermaphrodite, the fruit of the *hieros gamos*, or sacred marriage between spirit and matter, represented as male and female in the form of a white queen and a red king. The rebis is the end product of the *magnum opus*, the Great Work, which is the alchemist's endeavour to transform base matter to gold.

While alchemy can be regarded as the transmuting of lead to gold in a literal sense – and perhaps the early alchemists did believe they could manipulate physical matter in that way – it more properly involves the inner purification and transformation of the alchemist themselves. The Great Work is life itself, and the alchemist's goal is to move towards enlightenment, wisdom and self-knowledge/awareness. The sacred androgyne is not concerned merely with sexuality, but the harmonious meld of male and female attributes in all senses, to create a greater being.

For humanity, the latest millennium has come and gone. Another milestone passed. Some wished for a kind of alchemical transformation for our species – the fabled Age of Aquarius – with a perceivable shift towards a more spiritual and harmonious state of being. Quite the opposite appears to have occurred, in a world fraught with greed, cruelty and pettiness, but who knows what alchemical processes are at work beneath the surface – the putrefaction, the breaking down – before the gold shines through?

Back in the late 1970s and early 1980s, when I was first working seriously on the Wraeththu Mythos, I was sickened by what I saw as the failings of the human race – intolerance and bigotry, all the savagery of division. In my fantasy world, humanity was wiped out and hara replaced them; androgynous beings of beauty, strength and intelligence. The first division was eliminated – that between the sexes. Having the attributes of both genders, I saw hara as free to express themselves in whatever manner they chose, and to whatever degree. Some might choose to veer towards the soume aspect (feminine), while others might be ouana prevalent (male), or these aspects could be emphasised upon a limitless scale at any time. Any har could host or 'spark' new life – harlings. Beyond their physical and emotional being – the physical being much improved and with the benefit of enhanced psychism - I envisioned hara would unite beyond creed or colour as they built their new civilisation. They seemed perfect to me, at first. But then, as I continued to write about them, I saw the Wraeththu were themselves transforming in the crucible of life. To fulfil their potential – to become gold – they must move beyond lingering human traits – the worst of human traits, that is.

Humanity could be said to resemble the hybrid offspring of angels and beasts. They are capable of the greatest acts of compassion and nobility, the most exquisite forms of art, the most eloquent expressions of spirituality, the most brilliant of creative thoughts and scientific breakthroughs, yet they also harbour a demon within, capable of inexpressible cruelty, selfishness, greed and violence, not to mention flagrant stupidity. Many have little regard for their home – the Earth – and wantonly damage the world that enables them to exist. Legends such as those of the Nephilim – the progeny of human women and fallen angels – echo these observations, perhaps because even the men and women of ancient times struggled to understand this strange dichotomy within their own kind.

As I was writing my first Wraeththu stories, which began when I was still in my teens, I thought that ridding the world of the human race would be the best thing for it. I imagined that a new advanced race could thrive in an environment free of such heartless, destructive predators. But as the mythos expanded, and I became wiser through age and experience, I came to realise that even though the hara I'd invented represented the evolution of humanity, the transformation wasn't done. Whatever first generation hara thought – or indeed the young writer who dreamed them up – they are in fact human, even if they are the next stage of evolution. The Wraeththu tribes sprang from terror, blood and violence in the death-throes of a failing civilisation. Their beginning was traumatic and often brutal. They too had to grow and learn how to make best use of their enhanced abilities and physical form. I saw eventually that what I was attempting to explore was humanity's second chance.

This book comprises three linked novellas – a tale of folded layers with an alchemical theme. Most of the story takes place during the earlier years of Wraeththu's development. For those who have read all my Mythos novels and stories, a few familiar faces will be found among these pages, but for new readers prior introductions to these characters aren't required. I suppose I'm still drawn to this formative era because it's more interesting to investigate than a future time when Wraeththu have reached their potential, live in harmony with the world, and conflicts have faded away. A beautiful world to live in, perhaps, but not the most exciting to read about. I think that if I ever venture into that future, it will be to take hara out of this world and into the realms of the ethers, the labyrinth of the otherlanes, but for now their evolution in this realm still intrigues me.

The chapters within the stories have titles that derive from alchemical terms and equipment. I've provided an appendix at the end of this book to explain them, but I feel the words alone conjure a feeling, which I trust encapsulate the ambience of the chapters. Those who know something of alchemy will perhaps intuit why and how I chose the titles.

Whenever I expand upon the Wraeththu Mythos, I always bear in mind that new readers don't want to be put off by a mass of canon, of which prior knowledge is essential to enjoy the tale. I want readers to be able to immerse themselves in the stories at whatever point they arrive. Therefore, I insert where necessary unobtrusive explanations for Wraeththu terms and traits, and provide a glossary at the end of the book to cover everything it would be too cumbersome to keep explaining in the text.

All that a newcomer to the world of hara needs to know is that the old humanity failed, and the new race that has arisen from the ashes must strive not to make the same mistakes; they must reach their full potential rather than squander it.

Hara are referred to as 'he', since back when I first started writing within the mythos, this pronoun seemed to me less gender specific than 'she'. A lot has changed in both culture and language since then, but to glue a new pronoun over all the stories would feel at best clunky and contrived. I ask readers to look beyond the loaded meaning of the male pronoun, and to read it as non-gender specific.

It fascinates me that while the idea of humans becoming androgynous was somewhat shocking when the first Wraeththu books went into print, nowadays gender has become a far more fluid concept and the subject is no longer taboo. Gender is no longer 'fixed' in the way it was, and people are freer to express their sexuality and gender in myriad ways. The idea of the true androgyne has left the pages of fiction and mythology to manifest in the world.

But I'm not writing mainstream fiction or trying to make an earnest political point – *Blood, the Phoenix and a Rose* is fantasy, full of magic, secrets and betrayal, and the tensions of relationships in a dangerous, rapidly-changing world. I hope you will be intrigued and entertained by this alchemical voyage.

Storm Constantine,
November 2016

"For I am the watery venomous serpent who lies buried at the earth's centre; I am the fiery dragon who flies through the air. I am the one thing necessary for the whole Opus. I am the spirit of metals, the fire which does not burn, the water which does not wet the hands. If you find the way to slay me you will find the philosophical mercury of the wise, even the White Stone beloved of the Philosophers. If you find the way to raise me up again, you will find the philosophical sulphur, that is, the Red Stone and Elixir of Life. Obey me and I will be your servant; free me and I will be your friend. Enslave me and I am a dangerous enemy; command me and I will make you mad; give me life and you will die."

— from *Mercurius: The Marriage of Heaven and Earth*,
By Patrick Harpur

"I am the true Green and Golden Lion without cares,
In me all the secrets of the Philosophers are hidden."

From 'Rosarium Philosophorum' or Rosary of the Philosophers, 1550

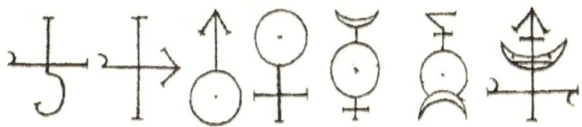

Song of the Cannibals

Nigredo

He came with the twilight, down the long, dusty road that led
from the darker cities to the sea. The day had been glorious; hot
and brilliant. Now evening was falling, balmy and secretive,
sewn with bats. The air smelled of flowery perfume – not
sweet, but somehow green – conjuring memories of the senses,
a wistful nostalgia. I can remember Ylisse leaning out from the
Amber Chamber window and saying, 'Look, Tambril, who is
that on the road?'

I looked. 'I don't know, perhaps a merchant of some kind.'

It was, in fact, quite unusual for somehar to seek Sallow
Gandaloi on foot. You could secure passage to the town of
Ferelithia from merchant parties, but the dusty avenue to
Gandaloi leaves the main coast road some five miles further
north. There is no reason whatever for anyhar to set foot upon
it unless they are coming here.

This is a beautiful house, a folly built by humans a long time
ago. Its high walls are pale cream; resting like a swan on lichen-
streaked cliffs above a cobalt ocean. The walls drink light; at
different times of day, they do not look white, but apricot or
deep golden. In the winter they may look blue, colder than
snow. The house is surrounded by a grassy plain that in the

15

distance rises into forested hills.

'I can smell honey,' Ylisse said, pleating his nose like a cat sniffing the air, 'and bitters, yes, bitters. Can you not smell it, Tam?'

No, I could not; I could smell only the late flowers, but then my nose has never been that acute.

That was the last I heard of the traveller until the following day. Sallow Gandaloi is a busy establishment, and I was engaged at that time in urgent work for Melisander, my employer and the keeper of this house. A year or so before, he'd had need of a new assistant, somehar who could write with a fair hand and whose words be understood, somehar who had no ties and could bind himself to Sallow Gandaloi, undistracted by family. Word of this position had come to me via friends, and I had applied hastily, been interviewed and considered acceptable. I moved into the spacious and comfortable apartment allotted for my use, spoke to the kitchen staff about my dietary requirements, (frankly, I eat almost anything), and considered myself fortunate.

Melisander kept me close to him for half a week, being keen to instruct me at length about his work as a historian of magic, with a particular interest in alchemy. Therefore, it took me a while to learn more about the household or explore the place.

My employer was a towering har, whose human ancestors had derived from the hot country of Olathe. His skin was of a bluish-black hue and velvetly matte. Unlike most hara, he wore his hair very short, perhaps because the shape of his head was a work of art and he was proud of it. His eyes were heavy-lidded, at first glance indicating indolence, but I soon learned his gaze was acutely penetrating, like a spike. He could see the shape of lies in a har's words, or so he told me, perhaps in case I was ever tempted to lie to him. I had no intention of doing so; the pay was too good. Sallow Gandaloi was relatively close to the vibrant town of Ferelithia, and few jobs of this relatively humble nature would involve such lavish accommodation for free.

Melisander studied old works by human cabalists and occultists. He rewrote them in the light of harish knowledge of such things. Alchemy in particular, with its emphasis on the rebis – the hermaphrodite – as a being of perfection, is of course widely studied by harish scholars. Humanity had often dreamed of its future self, or visualised it in symbols. Melisander had a vast library dedicated to the subject. Quite often he would be invited to teach in faraway places, or attend festivals to speak about his work, and occasionally to heal hara unfortunate enough to need mending and who could afford his services. Mostly, he told me, he sent his students on these latter errands, and only occasionally went himself. He was not a healer, he said, but a scholar, and if hara paid more attention to their own abilities they wouldn't need anyhar else to tend their hurts. He was impatient with what he considered to be stupidity or laziness.

On the first day I was introduced briefly to other members of the household – a full staff, essential because Melisander always had students in the house, even if his small flock of lesser teachers attended to the bulk of their education. Some of the students were the sons of influential hara, others individuals who had impressed Melisander in some way, so that he allowed them to stay and work for their lessons and their keep. Therefore a sizeable proportion of the household staff was also students. Of the teachers, several had been students who, once their studies were complete, hadn't wanted to move away and practice elsewhere. This was especially so with other Olathians, who appeared to worship their great teacher as a hero. But Melisander was a fair har, and occasionally generous, even if he did expect everyhar in Sallow Gandaloi to emulate his personal standards of excellence. I discovered very soon it was possible to maintain an illusion of this, since Melisander was often lost in his work and didn't really notice that much of what went on beyond his immediate environment.

On my third day in Sallow Gandaloi I was told about Gavensel. This was from Ylisse, with whom I was already building a friendship. Ylisse: an archetype of hara, being of the tiny kind, with bird-bones and that peculiar blond hair that is almost green. His skin too had a faint grassy tinge, especially in evening light. Flighty as a fey, mischievous, forgetful, somewhat shallow, but affectionate too in the way a cat can be.

'Gavensel will want to see you this evening,' he remarked.

This was in the late afternoon as he was showing me round the gardens, where summer seeds wafted on faint breezes, unwinding perfumes in the air. Melisander had dismissed me for the day, saying I should explore the house and gardens as there was much to see. I had a feeling he might set me a test about it the following morning.

'Who is Gavensel?' I asked, expecting this to be Melisander's chesnari or perhaps even a parent.

'Melisander's brother,' Ylisse said, in a tone it was particularly difficult to interpret. 'I think today he'll call for you. He'll want to meet you, because he likes us to believe he's equally in charge here.'

'Melisander didn't mention this har to me,' I said, remembering how my employer had listed by name, over considerable minutes, every single har who worked and studied in the establishment.

'Well, he wouldn't,' Ylisse replied. 'They're not much alike.'

'Explain,' I said. 'Arm me before the battle.'

Ylisse grinned. 'You don't need arming. Gavensel is not a frightening thing, rather the opposite. You'll pity him, if anything.'

'Is he... is there something *wrong* with him?'

'He's not mad or physically impaired,' Ylisse said, 'but rather... I don't know how to say it... fragile, maybe?'

'Oh.' I could imagine immediately why Melisander wouldn't mention somehar he no doubt considered to be a feeble relative; he would consider it his brother's own fault to be fragile.

The summons came before dinner, in that hour when the perfume of the day mingles with the scents of cooking, leading inexorably to the dark aromas of the night. Sounds change too at that time, becoming more sonorous: bird song shifts to the call of a har in the kitchen, to the clank of iron, the brittle rattle of crockery, and then, as the sun sinks low, there is the hymn of crickets, of breezes heard more keenly in the heavy summer tree-branches, and mournful calls amid the distant hills.

I was summoned to a high room beneath the eaves of Sallow Gandaloi; a chamber not cramped but constructed of strange angles so that the walls felt too close. The windows were narrow, thrown open to the fading sun. Candles gleamed upon the sills, their flames leaning into the room, away from the red light of evening. And here, caressed by gentle, shuddering gleams was Gavensel. For some moments, after the har who had guided me to this apartment had made introductions and departed, I stood staring. *This* was Melisander's brother?

The har before me was pale as milk, with the kind of skin that looked as if it might bruise easily, almost transparent. Of medium height, he had hair the colour of grey dust, and it appeared powdery in that light, as if half-cobwebbed. This hair fell to his thighs, almost obscenely abundant, folded and plaited and tasselled. He wore trousers and a tunic of soft, finely-pleated linen, dyed a purplish dove grey, that left his arms bare. His eyes, feverishly bright and pale sapphire, glistened from dark sockets. His lips were the same colour as his cheek, but perfectly formed, unexpectedly full. His face had high, bladed cheek-bones, a nose long and narrow and perhaps slightly too big for his face. Not in any way did he resemble Melisander, or appear to derive from the same stock, not even if some bizarre absence of pigmentation afflicted him.

Realising I must appear rude, I bowed my head and said, 'Tiahaar.'

Gavensel glided towards me a few steps and extended a hand. This I took hold of, not sure what to do with it. Kiss it? Shake it? Press it to my brow? I squeezed the hand briefly, then let go, noticing his fingers retract like the legs of a startled spider, hurry back towards his body.

'I like to meet everyhar,' he said in a voice of silver, 'who comes to Sallow Gandaloi.' He indicated chairs by a cold hearth. 'Please, be seated, have a drink before dinner.' He smiled, again feverishly, somehow eager to be liked.

I sat down, dumb with surprise. What *was* this creature? And why did Melisander keep him here, call him brother?

There was a table between us where two wooden goblets and a stone flagon stood. Gavensel poured us wine, passed me a goblet. I wasn't sure I'd want to drink wine from a wooden cup, but did so. It was the colour of water, bland, cool but not cold, perhaps diluted.

'Are you happy with your rooms?' Gavensel asked.

'Very happy,' I said.

'Good. I hope we will be friends.'

I didn't know what to say. He was like a harling.

'The last one,' he said, 'the last one my brother had as his assistant, he used to come to me twice a week, so I could recite my thoughts, and he would write them down. Sometimes these were poems. I'd like you to continue this work.'

I paused, then said, 'If Melisander is content for me to do this, then of course I will. I'm here for whatever task is given me.'

'Melisander and I own this house,' Gavensel said, and I heard a steel wire thread through his voice. 'The payment you receive, the bounty of our estate, is furnished by both of us.'

'My apologies. It was Melisander who interviewed me and offered me the job. He outlined my duties, but only those concerned with his own work.'

Gavensel regarded me for a few moments, then said, 'Yes, that is so. I should have sent for you on the first day, but...' He smiled again, coolly, while his eyes blazed febrile.

'When would you like me to start?' I asked, anxious to conclude this interview

'Tomorrow morning,' he said. 'After breakfast. I don't care

about the precise hour. I shall be here, waiting.'

I drained the dregs of my wine, having drunk it too quickly. Gavensel sat with his wrists resting upon the arms of his chair, watching me. From below we heard the vibrating clang of the gong that called the household to dinner, in their various appointed dining-rooms. Reprieve!

Gavensel said, 'You may go now. You must be hungry.'

I felt I should speak with Melisander about this development, rather than simply not turn up in his workrooms the following morning, so upon rising, and well before breakfast, I made my way there, knowing he'd already be working. Often he slept in an alcove of a lesser chamber, upon a couch that was covered in blankets of crimson and indigo with golden fringes.

Melisander raised his brows at me, perhaps a trifle surprised to see me so early. He must have sensed my agitation, though I sought to conceal it. 'Is everything all right, Tambril?'

'Yes... that is...' I didn't want to mention the word "brother", unsure why. 'Tiahaar Gavensel has requested I work for him this morning, and I thought it best to let you know.'

Melisander dropped his gaze, began sorting papers on his desk that were already neatly piled. 'Oh, very well. I don't have much for you today. Perhaps after lunch.' He glanced up at me. 'In future, should you receive any requests like this, simply send me a message through one of the staff. You don't have to come yourself.'

Perhaps you should have mentioned this would happen, I thought, not even bothering to keep that thought too heavily concealed, but if Melisander caught it, he did not reveal he had.

I was offered no explanation at all, merely dismissed.

From this point onwards, I attended Gavensel twice a week to take down his dictation in my strong, clear hand. I love to write; to me the forming of letters is like painting. I know my work is beautiful. When actually writing the words, I don't pay much attention to their meaning; it is the form that consumes me. Therefore, on the first occasion, when Gavensel asked me to read back to him what I'd written, I was surprised.

'My throat is long and it utters bright sound. There are eagles in my hair. I am their wings, and my eyes are their eyes. Ground below and ground above. Candle light in a cloud.'

And so on.

I found it nonsense, but Gavensel clearly considered his outpourings profound. Perhaps they were. I'm not a poet after all. He kept all the pages I wrote for him in a huge locked ottoman chest that was perhaps five hundred years old.

I never saw him outside of his apartment. As far as I knew, he never left the house. I felt uncomfortable in his presence, for I sensed a darkness in all that bruisable white. He seemed to me somehow incomplete, and perhaps Melisander called him brother to protect him, to keep him safely away from the world.

By contrast I enjoyed Melisander's company immensely. He had a wry sense of humour, which he allowed to emerge once we got to know each other. Like me, he loved shapes within language, and we'd pore over old documents, touching the faded letters with reverent fingers. 'The shape of a word is often its power,' he said to me. And he taught me some words that I might use in certain situations. He liked me, and this gave me prestige within the household. 'Tambril will see to it,' became a common response whenever somehar asked him to do something, especially tasks he found dull or annoying.

Sallow Gandaloi was full of life, even if much of it was hidden in walled gardens, in secluded rooms or the dark chambers of its two towers. There were sometimes conflicts, petty arguments, but nothing more serious than a topic to gossip about for a week or two. And yet, within this convivial hive, there was a dark pulsing bruise at its heart: Gavensel. I could sense him always, restless in his chambers, composing words, tossed by the storm of his own confused and confusing thoughts.

I asked – of course I asked – what other hara knew about

Gavensel and his relationship with Melisander. 'They were here before anyhar else,' I was told. 'They arrived together and then Melisander began his work, filled this house with hara he needed and wanted.'

Only the cook, apparently, (who had been in Sallow Gandaloi since the brothers first arrived), had ever been spoken to directly about Gavensel. This had concerned his diet, since certain foods affected him badly. He could eat nothing red, for example. But other than that, Melisander had never offered any explanation, and a stoniness came over him whenever Gavensel was mentioned by name that prevented hara from asking questions outright.

So, a mystery.

I asked Ylisse, 'Does Melisander ever visit Gavensel?'

My friend wrinkled his nose in his catlike way. 'If he does, he takes care nohar sees it.'

'Who keeps him company? What does he do when he's not dictating his words to me? Does he never write them down himself?'

'He summons hara sometimes to sit with him, or drink together as friends might. They converse, but they might as well be dolls sitting there.'

'Have you been to his rooms in that way?'

'Yes. Everyhar has. He doesn't have favourites. The selection is random and never falls often enough to hurt.'

From that I took that nohar enjoyed Gavensel's company. 'Why don't you want to know about him?' I asked. 'It's a secret so huge it fills the landscape here.'

Ylisse laughed. 'Everyhar asks about him at first – it's part of the ceremony of moving in. But you must reconcile yourself to never knowing. We have our duties to him and they are small; it takes little to fulfil them.'

It occurred to me also that Gavensel must have some arrangement with hara within the household concerning physical needs – aruna, which is our spiritual nourishment. Unless circumstances utterly prevent such intimacy, it's as essential to our well-being as eating or sleeping. Gavensel lived in a household full of hara. Urges must come to him, surely? I found it repugnant to think about how he might satisfy them. He was freakish. Could anyhar bear to touch him, never mind lose themselves in his being? I wondered how he'd come to be the way he was.

There had to be a tragic history. Perhaps Gavensel had suffered something so terrible it had ruined his mind. Or perhaps Melisander himself had damaged this 'brother' and – wracked by guilt and remorse – this was why he could not bear to see him or speak about him. I wondered too if Gavensel was dangerous, perhaps kept docile by medicines – he often seemed drugged to me. I realised that I was to some degree afraid of him. I was repulsed by his weird appearance, and yet at times he appeared ethereally beautiful. Sometimes, I *did* want to touch him, which even when it occurred seemed perverse. Other times the idea made me nauseous. In himself, he seemed devoid of sensuality, almost an automaton. Perhaps he was so damaged he had no arunic urges at all, and was estranged from all that was harish in that way. A ghost. The secret of Gavensel niggled at me, but Ylisse said it niggled at everyhar for a while, until it became so commonplace they forgot to notice it.

And yet the enigma of Gavensel never became invisible to me. Every time I visited him during that year, it was as if I met him anew, my memory erased. The shock of him never lessened.

And then, that day – a moving scribble of dark upon the road to Sallow Gandaloi. Standing with Ylisse at the window, the scents, the feeling of that day – those memories too have remained detailed in my mind.

I dreamed that night of footsteps upon the road, of a dark moving figure like a badly-drawn picture, scratched hastily upon a page. I stood at a high window, looking down at the road, and hara would come up beside me and comment on the approaching traveller. No matter how long I stood there watching, the figure never seemed to draw closer. Its details were not filled in, its edges flickered. And then I was in my bed asleep, but even in this dream sleep, I heard the footsteps, heard them enter the house, find their way along corridors and up stairs, coming at last to my door. Then I was awake in the dream and knew I was not alone in that room. I could see nothing, but was sick with fear. 'Show yourself,' I said, my voice tiny and uncommanding.

At this moment, I awoke for real, and morning light was coming in through my window, and morning sounds were waking the day.

After breakfast, I went to Gavensel's rooms, somewhat impatiently and annoyed. Melisander had a long, ancient document he wished me to transcribe and make copies of, since he needed them for a talk he was giving in Ferelithia the following week. Some of my friends had planned a trip into the hills in a few days' time, where we would relax and feast in the heart of nature, and I wanted to be free to join them. Now I would have to waste several hours taking down nonsense from the bleached lips of Gavensel instead of continuing my serious work. When I entered his sitting-room, he didn't notice my disgruntlement for he was preoccupied.

'Tambril, somehar came to Sallow Gandaloi last evening,' he said, the moment I stepped across the threshold.

I went to the desk I used and began to set out my pens and paper before I glanced up at him. He was agitated, restless. I nodded. 'Yes, I believe so.'

'Did you...' He stole closer to me, hunched in posture. 'Did you *see* them?'

'No, Tiahaar. I glimpsed the visitor only briefly from a window. I wouldn't call that *seeing* exactly.'

'Who is it?'

'I don't know, I'm sorry.'

Gavensel nodded vaguely, but I could sense a thousand thoughts tumbling behind those pale eyes of his. Was he afraid, intrigued? I could not tell; he was simply *affected*. Although we didn't have a regular stream of visitors to the house, they were not a rarity. Melisander was famous after all, and we also had need of produce, so traders came frequently. Then I remembered my dream and began to wonder. 'Do you think there's something *unusual* about this visitor, Tiahaar?'

Gavensel fixed me with a stare, probably because this was not a question he'd expect from me. He nodded, then shook his head, raked a hand through the opulent fall of his hair. 'Nothing, nothing, not yet time. Always thinking it is time.' He forced a smile after these odd words. 'Perhaps you should write that down.'

Later, I went to Melisander's workrooms. He wasn't alone when I entered the ante chamber. I heard him say, almost in a sigh, 'This is outstanding – beautiful!' Curious, I approached him quickly and found him leaning over his desk on which a large book lay open. A har stood with his back to me, dressed in a dark, dusty coat that reached almost to his ankles, still dressed – strangely – as if he had just arrived.

Melisander looked up. 'Tambril, come, look at this.'

The visitor turned and I saw his face. When hara say "my blood turned to ice", or "my blood ran cold", you translate the words as a feeling of shock or dread, perhaps both. But, at that moment, a silky numbness spread through my limbs that felt precisely like cold. I wanted to shiver, to back away. His eyes said, 'Betray nothing'; he did not need to speak or touch my mind.

'Good morning, Tiahaar,' I said to him, and moved my ice-stiffened body towards the table. What lay there appeared to be a very old book indeed; a treasure, apparently written by hand, with illustrations in vivid hues. The picture I saw was of a human male of the medieval era, in his laboratory, alchemical equipment about him. Within an alembic on the work table before him, something pressed against the glass with small hands. 'Amazing,' I said inadequately. 'Are you buying this book, Tiahaar?'

'It is offered for sale,' Melisander replied, which I took to mean there was some dispute over the price.

'How old is it?' I asked.

The visitor laughed softly, then spoke in a voice I knew so well, that even now could make me shiver with its glorious, ancient timbre. 'Tiahaar Melisander won't believe me when I tell him it is at most fifty years old.'

'A fake,' I said.

'Its worth doesn't lie in its age but its creation,' the visitor said, 'its origin.' He smiled at me, and at that moment a whisker of attention stroked my mind; I felt its humour, its sardonic joy. *Fancy finding you here.* He must have known, of course. I didn't for one moment believe this meeting to be coincidental. Dark of skin and eye; a crow of hara, yet not of Melisander's breed. His kind once came from the secret corners of the northern forests, where ancient *things* had survived human depredation and now again waxed strong. Hair like black feathers, teeth long and strong, yet a charming smile. I had to conceal that I knew him. For his part, that would not be difficult, for to deceive was his second nature. I thought quickly, tussled with the prospects, found a pattern: help him get what he wants then get rid of him. Any other course would simply bring me trouble.

I wouldn't risk a mind touch, because Melisander might catch it. I had to be loud, fill the atmosphere of the room. 'Are you going to buy it, Tiahaar?'

Melisander smiled at me. 'Perhaps you should examine it for me, Tam. See what you think.'

Gloves and tongs were laid out on the table for this purpose. I didn't want silence, so I gave a rather inane commentary as I turned the pages carefully. 'The folios do *appear* old, but upon close inspection you can see this is a created effect... Very well done though. Linen pages... The actual text? Hmmm. Reproductions from ancient works, I'd say. Without reading the text in full, I can't confirm whether it's a faithful copy.'

'That's my assessment also,' Melisander said.

I risked a glance at the visitor. 'Fifty years old, you say? Do you know its history?'

A cruel sickle of a smile. 'Not entirely. Only that it was removed from the ruins of Fulminir in Megalithica thirty years or so ago.'

'Looted,' I commented dryly.

The visitor inclined his head casually. 'Many treasures follow that road to reach the hands of collectors.'

This book, I felt, had passed through many hands. And yet – I let my fingers hover over a page – this might have once been owned by Ponclast himself, the archon of the fallen Varrs, who had delved into very dark areas of the occult seeking power. His library had been destroyed, as far as hara knew: looted, burned, trodden into the wet ashes of that cursed domain. If this book was genuine, it was priceless. But, given who had brought it here, it might be a double fake, not even what he claimed it to be. Still, if the contents were high quality, then perhaps this didn't matter. Melisander would have to decide for himself whether it was worth the asking price. Keeping my eyes on the book, I said, 'Hypersensory scans should reveal the truth of its origins, and this might repudiate the claims but, even so, I'd value the book on its own merit, for how it might enhance your collection. It is, at the very least, a work of art.'

'The jacket, of course, is made of *skin*,' said the visitor.

I closed the book. The material was leather. 'The majority of living creatures have skins,' I said.

He laughed. 'Indeed, but if this *has* come from Fulminir... well... draw your own conclusions.'

I glanced at Melisander and noticed his colour was peculiar, his bloom somehow dulled. He was uncomfortable, perhaps more than that. Was the mention of Fulminir the cause? Becoming aware of my attention, he made an effort to compose himself. 'I'd like to examine it at length,' he said to the book's keeper. 'Then decide.'

'Of course. I'd not expect you to commit yourself

immediately. I'm here merely because a colleague felt the book would interest you.'

'In the meantime,' Melisander said, ignoring this remark, 'my household is open to you.' He glanced at me. 'Tambril, would you find a room for Tiahaar Levvero, speak to the househara and the kitchen staff?'

So, a name. Not one I knew. 'Of course, Tiahaar.'

Melisander addressed the visitor. 'Please, let's dine together later.' He glanced at me. 'Perhaps you'd join us, Tambril?'

That surprised me: he'd never asked me to sit at his table before. 'Yes… 'If… if you wish it. Shall I inform the kitchens?'

'Do that.'

The corridors between Melisander's workrooms and the main body of the house were dark. Even at the height of day, lamps gleamed from the walls. In one of these tunnels, Levvero took hold of me, pushed me against a wall. I decided it best not to fight, let him say what he had to say and get it over with. 'Made a downy nest for yourself here, haven't you?' His tone was half contemptuous, half humorous. 'Scared I'll mess it up for you?'

I wrenched my arm free. 'Many years have passed since… I'm different now. I expect you are too.' I didn't believe that for an instant. 'You want to cheat my employer with that book? Do so. Get what you want and go. I don't want any more drama than that. And he won't hear from me what I know of you, *Sparn.*'

He laughed. 'Sparn. I've not used that name for over a decade. Call me Levvero, Tambril. It's who I am for the time being.' He put his head to one side. 'Have you lost your edge?'

'Let me find this room Melisander wants you to have,' I said, shoving past him.

'No.' He detained me again with a strong grip. 'Answer me. Have you really *no* idea what he has here?'

I stared at him, recognised in his eyes a hunger I knew too well and had hoped to forget. I suppose I knew instinctively to whom he must be referring. 'No,' I said. 'This is a house of learning. So far it contains no secrets. Quite the opposite, I'd say.'

But I suppose a glint must have been in my eyes too. 'Liar,' Levvero whispered, close to my ear, in a tone so reverent it sounded like a word of love.

'Suppose you tell me what I'm lying about?'

He pushed me away from him. 'Not yet. I'll let you think about it; let you think about how much you'll tell me.'

I had adored him once. Incredible.

Those of us who are first generation inevitably have history we'd rather keep buried. Nohar emerged from inception, and the blurred years after it, without shame and regrets. When I'd known Sparn back in Megalithica, in a world still reeling from its own traumatic transformation, we'd been proud of our tricksiness, of our ability to survive and prosper upon the ignorance, stupidity and fear of those less astute. Sparn's body, his face, his quick mind, even his glamorous heritage – all of them seductive – had cast a glamour over me. Only as the years advanced, and what it meant to be Wraeththu took root within me, had that glamour begun to harden and crack and inevitably splinter. To become truly har, I'd had to get away from Sparn. This was the only way I might evolve, stretch myself, take hold of freedom. When we were caught by Gelaming militia in the midst of one of our escapades, the opportunity had presented itself: *I'm so sorry, Tiahaara, but so afraid. Please help me escape that har who controls me. His name is Sparn...*

I'd had to pay for my crimes through repentance and a required donation of time, which hadn't been termed a sentence as I'd not been locked up. I'd been obliged to help with rebuilding, and had lifted shattered hara from the ruins, some of them without hope. Those experiences had taught me humility and compassion. I never regretted the decision to betray Sparn, but always, always, I feared he'd find me again.

And now, apparently, he had.

If I warned Melisander I'd open up a putrid wound, which could infect my life in Sallow Gandaloi, perhaps kill it. I had to keep the poison of Levvero contained. I hoped to every dehar I was wrong about what interested him here.

The dinner was harmless enough to begin with. Levvero encouraged Melisander to speak about his work – my employer's favourite topic – and eventually, when empty wine flagons crowded the table, he coaxed more interesting anecdotes out of him. We heard stories of stupid students, dangerous students, students who had fallen in love with him. We laughed. It became possible to believe that Levvero would sell Melisander an over-priced book that was undoubtedly a fake and move on.

Towards the end of the evening, Levvero drew out his weapon, a blade so thin it could barely be seen. He began to speak – carefully – of Megalithica. By this time, Melisander was happily intoxicated and his usual armour had been set aside.

'From your accent, Tambril, I'd say you came from Megalithica,' Levvero said.

Intoxication drained out of me immediately. My defences shot up: sharp barricades, one by one, in a row. 'Yes, when I was very young,' I answered. 'These territories are more to my liking, though.'

'And you, Tiahaar?' Levvero asked Melisander.

Melisander delivered one of his rather ophidian stares. 'Me?' He uttered a forlorn choked laugh. 'Oh, I had my days there, yes.'

Levvero refilled all our goblets. 'I expect some of your rare treasures came from there,' he said.

'In those days, you could walk into a private library where the roof was open to the weather,' Melisander said, 'so yes, I did some exploring and liberated a few items that would otherwise have been destroyed.'

Levvero nodded. 'Were you born in Megalithica?'

Of course, this was a rude and impudent question to ask of a har you barely knew. Melisander lowered his eyelids somewhat, inspected Levvero keenly, no longer appearing quite so drunk. 'Does this have any bearing on our business?'

Levvero raised his hands in an appeasing gesture. 'No, forgive me. I shouldn't have asked. I'm simply interested in first generation hara like ourselves.' He indicated the empty wine flagons. 'Sometimes, I forget the boundaries.'

Melisander nodded once, but I could tell that now he was alert. 'If you're that interested, I began my human life in the country now known as Olathe. My family moved to Megalithica, fleeing conflict. I was a small child.' And *that*, his eyes said, is all I will say on the subject. 'So, what of you, Tiahaar?'

Levvero laughed. 'Me? I'm from Jaddayoth, the land of wolves and vampires.'

This attempt to lighten the atmosphere failed; Levvero's enquiry had soured our evening. Melisander rose from the table. 'I must leave you,' he said. 'I have a lot to do tomorrow.'

I also got to my feet. 'As do I.'

Levvero leaned back in his chair, stared at me with narrowed eyes. A crow of hara, feathers and darkness. Surely he couldn't think...?

I made my exit hastily, ran to my room, locked the door, placed wards around the walls.

Albedo

The following morning, I began work early, determined not to be distracted so that I could concentrate on my task and be free for the *al fresco* trip later in the week. I hoped that today Melisander would come to a decision about the book and that Levvero would leave Sallow Gandaloi. I felt in my blood that his swift departure was crucial, and if he lingered, something bad would happen. I made good progress with my work, and by lunchtime was thinking I'd overestimated how long it would take. If I continued steadily, I should finish within two or three days. Therefore, when Gavensel's har, Obery, came to me in the mid-afternoon to inform me his employer wished to see me, I drooped in despair. 'This had better not take long,' I said crisply to the unfortunate har, who merely shrugged.

With long strides and a seethe inside me, I marched to Gavensel's apartment. I intended to say that I wasn't due to visit him today, and that my other work was pressing, thinking that if I allowed him to summon me whenever he pleased, this could become a bigger problem. But when I saw him, the words withered on my lips. 'Tiahaar,' I said, 'are you unwell?'

He sat stiffly in his chair beside the cold hearth, his eyes unfocused, as if he was caught in a psychic trance in which something horrifying was happening. After a moment, his gaze flicked to me and he shuddered into a likeness of normality. 'Oh, no, Tambril, no. I'm sorry. I was lost in my thoughts.'

'You seem… upset.'

'No, not that. Please… I'm sorry… I know I've called you away from your work, but… I would like to speak to you. I won't keep you long.' He gestured at the chair opposite his own and I sat down.

I put my hands between my knees and leaned forward in a posture of full attention. He said nothing, so I felt obliged to ask, 'What is it, Tiahaar?'

'The visitor,' he began. I must have rolled my eyes

involuntarily, because Gavensel frowned. 'You have seen him, spoken to him?'

'Briefly, yes.' I felt I had better explain my expression. 'He strikes me as an opportunist. I'm not convinced the book he wants Melisander to buy is a genuine relic, although it *is* very interesting.' A pause. 'Why?'

'He asked to see me.'

Again, that feeling of icy dread. 'And... did you allow that?'

'I had no reason not to... did I?'

In Gavensel's position, I would have worried more about the 'why' of the situation. Nohar spoke of Melisander's brother, and certainly not Melisander himself, so how did Levvero know of him? It was possible, of course, that he'd heard gossip in Ferelithia or another town close by. Gavensel was not a secret as such, and Levvero had always had more curiosity than was good for him. But I was aware I had to be very careful, limit damage, try to intuit what Levvero was up to and pre-empt him. 'I suppose not,' I said, and smiled in a manner designed to soothe. 'But from how you looked, it seems the meeting didn't go that well?'

Gavensel's shoulders drooped. 'Not badly, not that. I felt... it was just... I might have known him once.'

'I doubt that,' I said, more dryly than I intended, then added some oil to it. 'I know his type. What they used to call a wheeler-dealer, I think. And surely, Melisander would have recognised him too, if you *had* met before.'

Gavensel frowned again, nodding hesitantly. 'Yes, of course. I didn't think of that. Melisander.' He rubbed the ribbed skin between his brows as if to erase the frown, but it now seemed permanent. 'The old times... that is, the time before Sallow Gandaloi, I don't always remember it well. And that makes me feel uneasy, not remembering.'

I hesitated a moment, then said, 'Perhaps you should ask Melisander about it, to put your mind at rest.'

Gavensel flicked a glance at me. 'He might be... He might not like me asking. He says I should concentrate on now, not the past. I should write, and talk about interesting things with hara here... and yes, I should walk outside, but I find that...' He shook his head. 'I shouldn't speak like this, it's bad for me. I'm sorry.'

'Don't apologise,' I said. 'Personally, I don't think it's good to try and cover up something that isn't healed. Otherwise, it's like sewing up a wound that's infected deep inside.'

'Oh, it's not like that,' Gavensel said. 'I've made you think things you shouldn't.'

He was childlike, yet somehow, at that moment, incredibly ancient. I didn't think Melisander was dealing with Gavensel in the best way. In his position, I'd have paid for Gelaming help. He must be able to afford it, and it was rumoured Gelaming therapists could accomplish miracles, especially with casualties of the early days of Wraeththu history, which I was now convinced Gavensel most certainly was. But this was not my business. If I should bring the subject up with Melisander, it might go badly for me, and yet... It seemed cruel to let this har suffer, even if I didn't know the facts of his past.

'If the visitor makes you feel uncomfortable, don't see him,' I said. 'You're not obliged to.'

'Oh, it's not that. I liked seeing him.' He paused. 'Very much.'

Again, a freezing cascade crashed through me. 'You like him,' I said.

Gavensel tapped his chair arms with nervous fingers. 'Yes. I think I did. He told me I was a treasure.'

Right! I no longer cared what Melisander would think. I had to tell him about this, and if he was angry, so be it. Levvero should not be allowed near Gavensel. His interest could only presage a doom of some sort. But, a silky inner voice informed me: that would mean I'd have to confess to knowing Levvero. *Think,* I told myself. *Don't act impulsively.*

'I wouldn't see Tiahaar Levvero alone,' I said. 'Perhaps, if he visits you again, you should keep Obery with you.'

Gavensel nodded, still frowning, then looked at me

beseechingly. 'Would you… would *you* come… if I asked?'

By all the dehara, what toxic web was being spun for me here?
'I…'

'I would feel safer,' Gavensel interrupted. 'Please, Tambril. You are the only one here, the only one who *sees* me.'

'Well, I suppose so.'

He came to me, took my hands in his cool grip, which was surprisingly strong. 'Thank you!'

Significantly, over the course of that day and its night, Levvero kept away from me. I was unsettled to find I wasn't entirely happy about that; a feeling I had to change – forcibly. I'd seen hara witless in Levvero's control: I had once been one of them. He could enthral hara effortlessly, which was part of what made him so dangerous. You might find yourself doing something unspeakable without even realising what it was – what it *really* was. In his company, I had tormented, swindled, tortured, thieved, and occasionally killed, although usually it had been he who'd taken lives. What did he want with Gavensel? What did he *know* of Gavensel? Asking him direct would only incite him to mischief and initiate a game of taunting and pretence. I was trapped, horribly. But then, so was Gavensel. Fate had placed me here. Was this so that I might atone for my own past evils by saving a har from Levvero? When had I ever believed in the possibility of such redemption? The world was harsh and unforgiving. Evil ran unchecked within it, even to havens like Sallow Gandaloi. Still, I discovered the thorns of responsibility were pricking my conscience. I would have to wait, watch how events unfurled.

For two days nothing further occurred, other than my suspicions continuing to rise like a flood as to why Levvero had not concluded his business with Melisander and moved on. I couldn't believe my employer was taking this long to make up his mind about the book. Levvero avoided me, except when we met in Melisander's workrooms. Levvero was always hanging around there, and Melisander didn't seem to mind. The moment when my suspicions burst their banks came on the morning of the third day. I went to the workrooms early to pick up some documents and there he was, languid and half-dressed, with a self-satisfied smirk on his face, clearly having spent the night with Melisander. Perhaps this had been happening from the first day: I'd thought Gavensel was his target. I'd not considered he'd take this route to prolong his visit, but of course, once I knew, it made perfect sense. Lull Melisander into complacence so he wouldn't question Levvero's real reason for lingering. So much for Melisander's clear sight. The greatest of liars was now deceiving him effortlessly. Levvero was seducing them both, and I still didn't yet know the true point of it.

I was furious, worried, and incandescent with territorial jealousy. How dare this soiled fragment of my past turn up at Sallow Gandaloi and set about soiling that too. What could I do? I knew what Levvero was capable of – anything. I'd have to act carefully, inching my way to his riddance.

That afternoon, a summons came and I went to Gavensel's rooms aching with dread. When I arrived, Levvero was sitting by the empty hearth opposite Gavensel; they were laughing together. Seeing Gavensel somewhat illuminated made me wonder whether Levvero's presence was *all* bad. I'd never seen Gavensel that animated before and it made him appear normal, not so eerie.

'Tambril,' he said, smiling radiantly; less feverish now, simply more alive, 'Tiahaar Levvero says we should go outside, walk in the gardens.' From the look on his face, you'd suppose Levvero had proposed a trip to Immanion itself.

'Well... if you want to,' I said, packing my words with disapproval.

Levvero turned in his seat to look at me. 'You sound like a joy-gorger, Tiahaar. You *know* a walk in our fresh summer air would do Tiahaar Gavensel good.'

As if you care, I shot to him in mind-touch. He didn't respond, merely widened his grin.

I smiled in return. 'He doesn't need my permission, *Tiahaar*.'

Gavensel got to his feet. 'Let's go now. Before I change my mind.'

Obviously, he hadn't been outside for a long time, and I wondered if his apparent exhilaration was tempered with fear. Had to be, surely? I went to him and tucked his left hand into my right elbow. I wanted him to feel safe.

Our procession through the house predictably aroused curiosity in the other residents. Hara paused in their errands to stare, raise their eyebrows at me and pull quizzical faces. The ghost was down from the haunted room. He walked among us as if alive.

Outside the sky was powerful, summer-bright, but surging with immense clouds. Shadows writhed over the lawns, sunlight came in blasts.

'It's so big,' Gavensel said softly, as we made our way along paved walks towards the water gardens and the tamed groves. 'I'd forgotten how big.'

The sky, Sallow Gandaloi, the world itself? Perhaps all of it.

Once out of sight of the house, Levvero took hold of Gavensel's other arm. 'When did you last walk in daylight?' he asked.

'Only one of your kind could ask a question like that,' I said sweetly.

Gavensel flicked me a sharp glance, fearful.

'He's from Jaddayoth,' I said. 'Hara are vampires there. Generally, they can only come out at night.'

'Tiahaar Tambril is such a tease,' Levvero said, clearly revving himself up for play.

'Are there harish vampires?' Gavensel asked, in the voice of a harling scared of fairy tales.

Levvero's smile was by this time distinctly feral. 'Well if there are, we... I mean *they*... do not fear sunlight.'

'*You're* teasing me,' Gavensel said, but I could tell he was pleased about it.

I sighed. If only sunlight *could* burn Levvero to a blackened crisp.

Gavensel walked slowly, staring at everything, as if seeing the world for the first time. I noticed his breathing became shallow and fast. He was entranced, but also weakened in some way. Perhaps Melisander kept him indoors for good reason. Perhaps I'd be reprimanded for allowing Levvero to open the doors.

We came to a fountain surrounded by trees, where there were marble benches on a circular mosaic pavement of jet and verdigrisy tiles. Here, we paused and sat down – three of us on one bench. Somehow, Levvero had manoeuvred himself to be in the middle. The fountain was fairly modern, rather than a relic of human times. In a wide scalloped bowl of marble a sculpted har stood with raised arms. He held enormous conch shells. The water poured from them, over his hair, which clung wetly to his carved body; it bounced off his hips, spraying the tiles with droplets that evaporated almost instantly.

'I've never been here,' Gavensel said. 'It's *beautiful...* healing...' He laughed a little. 'That splashing sound... it soothes me. I could listen to it for hours. I've lived here for decades but have never seen this place.'

'Were you ill?' Levvero asked bluntly, carrying on before Gavensel could answer. 'I mean, you're clearly quite healthy now, but perhaps once...?'

'I...' Gavensel frowned.

Leave him be, I spat with a thought.

Levvero shrugged, answered as though I'd spoken aloud. 'I'm merely curious, wondering why nohar has suggested a walk like this before.' Criticisms dangled from his words.

'I never asked,' Gavensel said hastily, perhaps sensing that criticism also. 'I never wanted to.' He paused, then spoke in a firmer voice. 'Sallow Gandaloi is a sanctuary, not a prison.'

'Well, perhaps it's now time to enlarge the sanctuary,' Levvero said lightly, 'include the gardens.' He gestured widely with one arm. 'There are walls all around. You see? It's almost like being inside. Imagine how coming to this spot once a day would benefit you. Imagine seeing it in all its seasons.'

'Yes,' Gavensel said. 'But I could not come alone.'

'I'll come with you,' Levvero said.

I uttered a derisive snort. Levvero and Gavensel looked at me with disdain and surprise respectively.

'Well,' I said, 'how long are you planning on staying here, Levvero?'

'When I leave, *you* can be his companion,' he answered smoothly. 'Or is your timetable too busy?'

'Don't leave too soon,' Gavensel said to him.

I winced at this remark, wondering also how I could schedule a daily walk with Gavensel without too much inconvenience. There was no way I could allow Levvero to have Gavensel all to himself, and after he left Sallow Gandaloi, presuming he *would* leave, it would be cruel to deny Gavensel the freedom, health-promoting as it most certainly was. I felt that Levvero was right: Gavensel *should* widen his horizons. But of course there was so much about him we didn't know.

'The air makes me tired,' Gavensel said, 'the wideness of the sky, the heat, the glare, everything. Small doses... just that. At first.'

'Of course.' Levvero took Gavensel's right hand, pressed the back of it to his lips. Spots of carmine, like bruises, flared along Gavensel's cheek-bones. His eyes were too bright. He looked shocked. The moment seemed caught in amber, then we were all on our feet, heading back towards the house and Levvero was joking around, making Gavensel laugh. I walked behind them.

Levvero was adept at being terrifyingly *nice*, and while he was doing this, it wasn't an act. I knew this well from the past; his strategic seductions. He *did* have a benign aspect, even though this existed merely to facilitate his schemes. Therefore, it wouldn't be easy to counteract his charm. He had, for the moment, *become* this charming, caring har. I felt sick with anxiety. Whatever I tried now to confound him would make me look peevish, jealous, or spiteful. Clever Levvero.

Once back at the house, I found Melisander had left a message, asking me to go to him. I complied at once, wondering what was in store. I was almost disappointed when I found it was simply about work, although at the end of our short conversation about it, Melisander said, 'Tiahaar Levvero will be staying here for a while to help me go through my collections. I've accumulated so many items over the years, rooms full of them.'

This sounded to me like an excuse; he felt he had to justify Levvero's continued presence. 'I can help as well, if you like,' I said.

'Oh, well, I'm sure Levvero can handle it. He deals in artefacts and documents. Between us, he and I can decide what can be sold.'

If this was in fact true, no doubt Levvero would secure himself a juicy cut from the profits. 'Very well,' I said, unable to keep a breath of ice from my voice.

'He'll be useful to me,' Melisander continued, the least confident I'd ever heard him. 'He can bring me items of interest and sell others for me.'

By this time, a mounting anger had flattened my restraint somewhat, and I blurted out, 'You know he took Gavensel into the gardens today? I accompanied them. I thought I should.'

Melisander composed himself, became still, looked me in the eye. 'Everyhar is curious about Gavensel at first. You know that.' Unspoken, the last words: *but it will fade.*

'You're happy for him to go outside, then? I understand this is to become a daily practice.'

Melisander's gaze didn't even flicker. 'If Gavensel wishes to go outside, then it's appropriate. If anything, I applaud it.' He paused, clearly argued with himself for a moment. 'He's not helpless, Tambril, however he might appear. And...' He turned away from me. 'He's not confined here. He merely has his ways and preferences.'

Observed from within by a horrified part of myself, I tanked onwards: 'Will it be appropriate for me to accompany them on their walks? I'm thinking of the time when Tiahaar Levvero will no longer be here, and Gavensel might wish to continue the exercise. He's already said he doesn't want to go alone.'

'Do what you like,' Melisander said crisply, turning back to look at me coldly. 'As long as you keep up with your duties to me, your time is your own. If Gavensel has tasks for you, they're also obligations of your paid employment. I thought you understood that.'

Melisander was annoyed with me, and I was now furious with myself. I was playing into Levvero's hand, becoming part of his game, making myself the adversary, the nuisance. 'I apologise,' I said contritely. 'I was simply concerned.'

Melisander nodded, softening towards me. 'I understand. But, really, there's no need to be.'

Since that time, I've often wondered: Had he truly believed that? Or had he deluded himself? Or, perhaps, most importantly, had he in fact been powerless?

Before dinner that night, I managed to corner Levvero in his room. He didn't want to let me in, and kept me for some moments at the threshold before I barged past him. 'It's time you tell me what you're doing here,' I said.

He laughed. 'What business is that of yours?'

'Strange, a few days ago, you implied I was involved in some way, that I had information you wanted.'

He shrugged insouciantly, sat down on his bed. 'I hadn't expected to run into you here.'

'Liar. You knew only too well. I don't believe in such a stupendous coincidence.'

'Well, it is. I don't care what you believe. I'm here to trade, that's the simple truth of it.'

'Simple truth is a concept unknown to you,' I said. 'What do you want with Gavensel? It's obvious you're rooning

Melisander in order to have a reason to stay here, but he's not your target, is he?'

Levvero sighed, rolled his eyes. 'Just turn your back, Tambril. It'll pass you by. You were always so good at that – *not* seeing. I realise you have no information for me, so do yourself a favour and stay out of my way. Or...' He put his head to one side, dramatically placing a finger to his lips. 'Let me see... instead you could tell Melisander all about me, how you knew me, what your own history is. Hmm... somehow I don't think you'll do that, because I can embellish all the details. Melisander will never look at you in the same way again, will he? If, in fact, he lets you keep your job. The Gelaming keep records, we know they do. Your name could be found very easily, because like an idiot you never changed it. Tambril har Varr. That will go down well, won't it? Although, I suspect that during your job application the Varr part magically changed to something harmless like Unneah. Am I right?'

Yes, of course he was. However, we'd both been fugitives from the Varrs. We'd been incepted into that tribe, yes, but hadn't stayed with them for long, although we'd often used our connection with them to our advantage. Still, as Levvero had said, Tambril har Varr had a criminal record somewhere in Immanion. I'd confessed everything, in order to demonstrate how much I wanted rehabilitation, and a normal, sane life. Tambril har Unneah pretended to that.

'Ah, silence. Your little mind working so furiously hard.' Levvero laughed. 'You've not changed that much, Tambril. Still a sneaking creature, looking after yourself, dead of heart. For all my faults, at least I have emotions.'

'Not all emotions are noble,' I said, 'despite having them, you are still cruel. I know there's no point in me saying "don't hurt him", because you won't care. Just because I don't throw my feelings about like Natalia fireworks doesn't mean I can't tell the difference between right and wrong. If you have any decency, let that poor ruin of a har alone. What possible use can he be to you?'

'Well, that's for you to work out and brood over in silence, isn't it?' Levvero smiled sweetly. 'Now, get out. Play the game. Be nice. I'll be gone before you know it.'

I considered delivering a parting shot, but thought better of it. There might come a time when my own well-being had to be put behind somehar else's, but perhaps that fact should be concealed from Levvero. Let him think he had me neatly constrained.

Citrinitas

I'd forgotten that the following day I'd committed myself to accompanying my friends on the trip into the hills. I felt torn, knowing that, while I was away, Levvero would be intent on furthering his aims, whatever they were. But if I backed out of going, hara would want to know why, and that would open far too many cans of worms to untangle. What *was* it Levvero wanted from Gavensel? Was he a commodity of some kind? Had he once been well-known and was now in hiding here in Sallow Gandaloi? Was there a family somewhere looking for him? Could there, even, be a price on his head? There were so many possibilities. But whatever Gavensel's history was, he was safe here, cared for. So many of us had new lives. I'd worked for mine, others had suffered for theirs. The thought of Levvero and Gavensel alone together made me anxious, but I was in no position to police Gavensel's life. Unless I was careful, I was at risk of being excluded from it, and that was the worst outcome of all.

In the morning, I took the precaution of visiting Gavensel to explain my absence for the day. 'Perhaps Obery can go with you and Tiahaar Levvero on your walk today,' I said.

Gavensel appeared slightly confused. 'Oh, I… yes… maybe. I'll be fine,' he said. 'Go and have a good time, Tambril. You work very hard and deserve some fun. Please come and tell me about it later, if there's time.'

'Of course.' I intended to visit Gavensel's chamber at whatever hour I returned.

Gavensel drew closer and kissed my cheek. I jumped back involuntarily.

'You're shy!' he said, laughing. 'I meant that to thank you, for being my friend.' He sobered a little. 'I would never mean anything else, I promise.'

'That's… well… as long as you're all right.'

'I am.' He walked over to his window and said, 'They hung

them up by their hair, you know, hung them till they rotted and fell.'

'*What?!*'

He turned to look at me, frowning. 'I didn't say anything... Did I?'

'You... No, it was nothing. I'll see you later.' *Poor mad thing,* I thought, *with his crazy poetry.*

'Goodbye, Tambril.' He stood at the window, looking out, as if he'd shut down, the ghost of him elsewhere.

During the ride out to the hill forests, I was still anxious about what might be occurring back at Sallow Gandaloi, but once we'd found a place to spread out our feast, and the wine flasks had been opened, alcohol planed the edge from my concern. *Just let Levvero do what he's come to do. Ignore it,* I told myself. I pushed away thoughts of how when Levvero took an interest in hara's lives, disruption, if not ruin, was sure to follow. I didn't want to think about that. My life here was too easy. There was some discussion of Levvero among my friends, which I couldn't avoid. Most thought he was an attractive har and were eager to discuss his physical qualities. 'You've seen a lot of him, Tam,' somehar said. 'What do you think?'

'Not my type,' I answered, and then, to counter a somewhat incredulous silence, I laughed. 'I *know* that type. They are scorpions.'

'Oh, how do you mean?'

All of them had their attention on me.

I shrugged. 'Well, it's clear he's attempting to foist some faked artefact onto Melisander, no doubt with the plan to bring yet more to sell. He's nosing around the place to see what else he can profit from. He might look good, yes, but like you said, I've seen more of him than the rest of you. His beauty is his camouflage, a tool of his trade. What lies beneath isn't so appealing. I've come across his sort before. He's an opportunist, perhaps worse than that.'

'Strange how the most dangerous hara are the most

intriguing,' Ylisse said, and he flicked me a speculative glance. He might suspect I knew more of Levvero than I'd said, but he knew me well enough not to pry – at least, not yet.

'Well, dangerous or not, he can nose around me any time for opportunities,' somehar said.

Then they were all laughing, offering ever more salacious suggestions, and my involvement in the discussion was past. I felt like I'd avoided a blow.

Our trip was cut short by rain clouds that surged in from the sea. We had to ride back in a downpour and were drenched by the time we got home. Yet our spirits were still high, and we continued to drink in one of the communal sitting-rooms, far enough from the study areas so as not to disturb any of the scholars. By this time, I was quite drunk. I looked out upon the soaked gardens and, wondering whether Gavensel's walk had gone ahead, felt moved to go and visit him. Perhaps Levvero would be with him. I was intoxicated enough to be spoiling for a battle of words.

I slunk away from the by now raucous gathering, into the darkness of the house. Everywhere was strangely quiet, depressed by the weather. Reaching Gavensel's apartment, I knocked upon his door, leaning my head upon the wood. My inner voice, mostly gagged, protested in a muffled way, advising I leave at once, but as I said, it was muffled.

Obery opened the door to me. 'It's you,' he said, in a peculiar way.

'It is. May I come in?'

'As you please. He's not good.'

I found Gavensel in his sitting-room. Today a fire was burning in the hearth, but he wasn't sitting by it. He was standing at the window, staring at the moody sky.

'Tiahaar,' I said to attract his attention. This didn't work. I went to him, touched his shoulder. 'Gavensel, it's me. Are you all right?'

He shivered slightly, turned his head to me. His eyes

seemed unnaturally huge in his face. 'I remember the rain,' he said.

I can recall thinking, *he has been opened*. 'Old memories are coming back?'

He shook his head. 'Not exactly, but my *senses* are filled with recollections. There's a smell to go with the rain – ashes, I think. Something was burning.'

I took his arm. 'Come and sit down.'

'All right.'

He leaned on me like an invalid, having hardly any weight. I could feel that his body was hot, yet his hands were icy. I placed him in a chair. There was a knitted coat hanging among cloaks and shawls upon a row of hooks near the door. I took this and wrapped it around his shoulders. Obery had been right: he *wasn't* good. He seemed drugged.

'Did Tiahaar Levvero visit you today?' I asked.

Gavensel glanced at me furtively.

The message in that glance, ineptly hidden, sickened me. 'Did something happen?'

Gavensel said nothing, would not meet my eyes.

'Did he touch you?' I asked. The words were crude, but the alcohol I'd consumed was in charge. 'Gavensel, please tell me. I can see you're upset, and I'm your friend. You can speak to me about it.'

'He didn't *attack* me, Tambril.' A note of chill, almost haughtiness.

'I didn't say that.' I waited.

Gavensel tried to speak a couple of times, failed. Still I waited. Then he managed to say, 'He wanted to share breath with me.'

I was relieved it was only that. I was quite sure anything more intimate would have sent Gavensel spiralling into some kind of breakdown. He seemed that fragile. 'And did you?' I asked.

Gavensel closed his eyes for a moment. 'No, no, I've never...' He drew in his breath. 'I never have, with anyhar, nothing like that, ever.'

I stared at him; surprised, yet not. 'But... you *must* have.'

He shook his head. 'No.'

'But inception... althaia...'

He laughed dismally, 'Tambril, I wasn't incepted, I was *made*. Don't they call it pureborn?'

'But how do you...' I was reticent to address the obvious: hara, for the most part thrive on aruna. How could he manage without it, surrounded by so many others in this house?

Gavensel was clearly aware of my discomfort. 'Never mind it,' he said. 'I just *am*. Outside you all.'

'Different,' I said.

Gavensel made a weary gesture with his hands. 'Different, yes. You can call it that.' He exhaled through his nose. 'Yet now... I don't want to be that different. If a har I like asks to share breath with me, I want to do it.'

The spirit of alcohol took control of my wits and voice again. 'Gavensel, I hate to say this, but I don't think Levvero is the har to help you with this... *problem*.'

Gavensel stared at me. 'Why not?'

I pulled a face, not sure what to say. 'Well, he's... Aah, this is difficult!'

'Speak plainly. I won't break.'

'Very well... It's clear you're... well *something* must have happened to you in the past, and you're still recovering from that. If you've been estranged from hara – outside them as you described it – you need somehar sympathetic and selfless to guide...'

'Levvero is that,' Gavensel interrupted.

'He's not. Really, he's not.'

Hostility had crept into Gavensel's voice. 'How do you know that? He's never been anything but kind to me.'

I raised my hands. 'OK. I know you like him. My warning is instinctive, that's all. Levvero is a wanderer, who flits around the world. He might hurt you, even if unintentionally. You should be aware of that.'

Gavensel's hands were clasped whitely in his lap. Distress streamed from him. I felt cruel, even without telling him the whole truth. For some moments we sat in silence. I didn't know what to say, how to make it better. Then Gavensel raised his head. 'Help me,' he said. 'If you're truly my friend, help me.'

I had enough sense not to react strongly, to be cautious. 'In what way?' I dreaded he was about to ask me to speak to Levvero for him.

'Show me how it's done, how you share breath with a har and not get lost in it. I know enough to be aware you have to control it.'

I blinked at him. 'What?'

He made an odd hissing sound. 'But of course you don't want to. I don't blame you, Tambril. I know what I am.'

'No, I'm sorry. I meant... what do you mean exactly?' Actually, I was horrified.

'I can't say it any plainer than I did. You don't have to stall for time. Just say no.'

Could I do this? I wondered. If Levvero was searching for something within Gavensel, sharing breath with him would be the key to the vaults of his being. A way in. Yet Gavensel *could* be protected to a degree. 'You make your mind blank, utterly blank,' I said. 'Think of clouds, or water, something immense yet empty. He won't open himself to you fully, I'm sure of that, so he'll feed you images and sensations. You have to do the same, that's all. Think of the gardens, the fountain, think of *him*. Send him back to himself – the best flattery. Do you understand?'

'No. Words are not enough. Show me.'

At that moment, I recalled Melisander's words about Gavensel not being as helpless as he appeared. There was a strength to him now that I'd not seen before. Could I be dispassionate about this, like a hienama teaching arunic arts? At that point, I wished Gavensel had merely asked me to speak to Levvero for him.

'Am I really so hideous?' Gavensel said into the silence. 'No, don't answer. You don't have to.'

'Stand up,' I said.

I had to do it quickly, without thinking, like pulling out a splinter. The pain would be brief. When he got to his feet, I took him in my arms, put my mouth against his. Utterly blank. Then I thought of soaring birds, of the sky, the smell of rain – standard images and sensations. He was rigid against me for some moments, then slumped against me. I felt a current, like a stream of polluted air – his breath. *Control it,* I sent to him in mind touch. *Send me the fountain.*

The images were fractured, the smells and sounds mixed up, but it was a start. So easy to go with its flow, to open up, send greater birds flying. Images streamed from me. Immersed in the physical act, I wanted to share with him. Instinctively. *This is me.* That is the essential message of sharing breath, and also: *I trust you.*

Gavensel pulled away from me. 'Where is that place, Tam?' he asked. 'It's wonderful. Did you live there?'

'No.' I smiled, stroked his face. 'It's an idealised place, a *mind* place, but I *have* been there, many times.'

'Can I have one of those?'

'Of course. Invent it.'

'It's amazing. Seeing all those things, being part of you, like a memory. If that is sharing breath, what does aruna bring?'

I stepped away from him. 'It's less easy to control.'

He sat down, wouldn't look at me. 'What did you get from me?'

'The fountain,' I said. In fact, I'd not got very much at all. I didn't think he'd find it difficult to be blank. But of course that would only incite Levvero to explore, to push, to break through. What *was* hidden there inside?

'I can't do it, can I?' Gavensel said dully. 'You might as well just say so.'

'Everyhar can do it,' I said.

He leapt from his seat and was upon me before I could react. He took my face in his hands, not feeble now but powerful, potent. What he poured into me was like an immense and cosmic shout, the sound of universes colliding, smashing each other to atoms. There was a foul wind, strong enough to scour flesh from bones. A bellow of gigantic clarions, bigger than the earth, not thrilling, but deep and hollow and mournful, calling to dead to rise. I saw, for just a moment, a huge edifice of dark stone, bruised clouds roiling across the sky, and rain pelting down. Its acid cold burned my skin. I heard terrible screams and my nostrils filled with the stench of death. And while I was in this disgusting vision, something *sensed* me there. It sniffed and smelled me, began to slither closer. I knew if it found me, it was the end of everything, of souls and eternity.

'No!' I cried, pulling away. 'Don't ever... Gavensel, no!'

'Now I know,' he said, wiping his mouth. 'When I share breath, *that's* what I can give.'

'You must not,' I said, aware my whole body was trembling. 'Whatever that was... remember what I told you. Fountains, pretty skies, sweet scents and feelings. Not that.' I held out my shaking hands before me. They hurt. The backs of them were blistered, as if acidic rain had scorched them. *What are you?* I concealed this thought in a prison of steel, *my* thought, my reaction. But still, he could hear it now.

'I don't know,' he said. 'I don't know.'

Did Melisander know the truth of this har he called brother? Of course, he must do. I'd seen the past, some hideous event, in Gavensel's breath. Whatever it was, and no matter how deeply buried, it consumed his being: it had been the first thing to burst from him spontaneously. I didn't think it was right or moral to let that loose. I wondered then if the urge for aruna had been taken from him deliberately.

'Don't look so afraid, Tambril,' he said sadly. 'I *will* learn to control it. I can feel the way now.' He sat down again wearily. 'I'm sorry. I'm really sorry, but thank you.'

'Don't do it,' I said, my voice ragged. 'Gavensel, let the past stay buried. I think it's best.' Not for him, maybe, but for others.

He looked up at me. 'But I'm not sure it's possible,' he said, 'to put something like that back to sleep once it's awake.'

Rubedo

I think Gavensel called the rains to him that day, the boiling sky, the wrath of the ethers. After I left his apartment, I went to Ylisse's room, and was relieved to find him there. A storm broke within me too then. I fell on his bed and wept. This was unusual behaviour for me, and Ylisse knew it, yet he asked no questions, simply stroked my back. When the storm had subsided, he took me to a sweeter place, sent the darkness away. Afterwards, bathed in a drowsy arunic haze, I lay in his arms and told him some of what had happened, excluding my own history, and Levvero's. But I had to tell somehar about what I'd seen and felt in Gavensel's breath.

'That was not a sharing of breath but a sharing of death,' Ylisse said. 'If anyhar wants to go further with that, good luck to them. Do you think you should tell Melisander?'

'Are you joking? Could you really stand before that har and repeat what I've just told you?'

'No, I couldn't, but I thought *you* might.' We were still for a moment, then Ylisse said, 'Listen, the wolves of the air stalk the house tonight.'

The wind outside did have a voice; it *howled*. Rain threw itself against the windows as if to shatter them.

'He brought this,' I said.

'Gavensel? No. The storm started earlier, when we were out.'

'Possibly when Levvero asked for his kiss.'

'Now you're being fanciful, Tam. The storm is natural.'

I knew it wasn't.

I didn't realise it at first, but now I was bound to Gavensel. We were *in* each other. I was not the utterly heartless creature Levvero thought I was. Trust, compassion, generosity: I had given these freely to Gavensel, because it was my compulsion as a har to do so. He'd devoured them.

It was near midnight when I stole out of Ylisse's room. I left him sleeping and, obeying another compulsion, went down to Melisander's workrooms. I didn't know if he'd be there, but I wanted to see that book. Threads were weaving in my mind, below the surface. The rooms were in near darkness, with just a few dim lamps burning on the walls. There was nohar around. Melisander was most likely with Levvero elsewhere. I went to the main room, where I hoped the book was still on the work table. I'd seen it there yesterday, closed and waiting. And yes, there it was, clearer and sharper to my eyes than anything else in the room. Rain whipped the windows and the wind snarled at me through the fragile glass. I went to the desk and opened the book without hesitation.

The hermaphrodite was important in ancient alchemical lore; the fruit of the *hieros gamos*, the sacred marriage. Male and female combined. The higher being. Forged in the alembic, through weird transformations. A metaphor for human spiritual evolution, of course, which the mages craved and sought to achieve, but sometimes the transformation could go wrong. The exacting rituals, the deprivations of the flesh, the harsh disciplines, could drive a mind mad. In the alembic, the matter could decay, a horror be born.

I turned the pages, looked at the images of magical diagrams and equipment, incomprehensible formulae, humans of ancient times. Connections, connections. They were here; I was sure of this. *Had* the book come from Fulminir? Was it important that it had? I remembered the expression on Melisander's face at the mention of the name. *Of course.* He'd been there. He'd looted those ruins himself, and perhaps of something rather more than relics. The Fall of Fulminir – a great event in Wraeththu history. Armies had combined to assault it. The destruction of that great dark fortress, when the elements clashed, and the rain that fell upon the ashes was bile. And yes, by Aru, why had I not made the connection before? The captive hara they'd found there, some hung upon the walls by their own hair. I'd heard that from Gavensel's mouth, but at the time the information hadn't linked up in my mind with the historical facts.

So obvious now. The storm, the ashes, the fortress pelted with caustic rain: his memories. And what of Ponclast's mystical experiments, his quest for power? That too was documented, along with the horrors found by the liberators of Fulminir in its ruins. Ponclast had wanted an army greater than any other, hara more powerful than the Gelaming. In those days, harlings had been rare. There had been so much to learn about ourselves. Had Ponclast sought other ways to create life, beyond the crucible of creation in hara? Had he conjured his rebis, his sacred androgyne, in the alchemical crucible of etheric matter?

If Gavensel was a son of Ponclast, he was indeed a treasure beyond price. But how had Melisander come by him? The Parasilians and the Gelaming had thoroughly explored all of Fulminir, rescued captives, taken prisoners, buried the dead. If Melisander had been part of that force, and had taken Gavensel secretly, it would explain a lot. He was hidden in plain sight: an invalid brother, even though his skin was lich-pale, and he had, without doubt, no blood connection with Melisander. Still, stranger familial ties had been wrought in the early days. Nohar would really question it.

I closed the book, my hand still resting upon it. This had been Levvero's way in; perhaps a volume Ponclast's hienamas had created for him, a copy of ancient documents. If all I suspected was true, Melisander would of course have been interested in the book. Perhaps it could answer questions he'd been asking himself for decades. Clearly, Gavensel remembered very little of his own beginnings. Yet now, Levvero was poking at those hideous memories with a stick, making them scuttle and scramble to escape. I shuddered to think what the result might be.

Well, here it was: the nexus point. I had to tell Melisander what I knew, tell him everything, so Levvero could spring no surprises, and if I lost my job, my home and my friends, so be it. I would survive. I always had. I had friends elsewhere who knew my history. But I'd miss Sallow Gandaloi sorely. I realised I'd intended to stay for a very long time, perhaps always. Maybe, the best thing to do would be to confess to Melisander when Levvero was present, so he'd have no time to concoct lies, excuses and masks. He didn't really know me, not anymore. I could surprise *him*. I decided to sleep on it, ask the dehara for guidance, even though I generally paid them little heed. Ultimately, I'd be asking myself, hopefully a wiser, more evolved inner self, to make the right decision.

I left the workrooms and headed for my room, feeling strangely at peace, even though the worst of the storm was surely yet to come. I didn't relish seeing Melisander's expression once he knew the har he'd employed was a fiction.

In the darkness of the stairwell, I heard an unidentifiable sound. It resembled the call of an animal, not distress exactly – a cry of warning? It was partway between a huffing sound and a scream, ragged, not quite like a wild dog, or a big cat, but something of both. This sound echoed from high up in the house. Now came a low, chattering gibber, rising and falling in timbre like the wind outside. Then a series of angry yelps. None of these sounds were loud, but I heard them as if they were. My connection with him. *Of course.*

I hesitated for only a few moments, then sprang up the stairs and headed towards Gavensel's chambers. I didn't bother to knock on the door but went straight in. All was in darkness, and there was a hideous stink of shit and blood. 'Gavensel!' I was convinced he'd damaged himself horribly, was somewhere in the darkness bleeding to death.

I fumbled through the sitting room into the bedroom beyond, where again there was no light. The curtains were drawn against the night. I could do nothing in darkness, and felt around me frantically for the table near the window where I knew there was a lamp. Faint snuffling and shuffling came from the farthest corner, but I couldn't investigate until I could see properly. I tripped over what seemed to be broken furniture. After what felt like a quarter of an hour, but was probably only minutes, my hands found the curtains and pulled them open, which helped a little. I saw the lamp and the means to light it. The smell in the room was so foul I dreaded what I might find there. I broke the lamp's glass as I sought the wick, then lost several tinder sticks before managing to ignite one.

Light bloomed, unnaturally radiant after the darkness. There was indeed splintered furniture scattered around. All the coverings had been pulled from the bed and lay in a tangled mess beside it – bloodied. The bed itself was tilted, one or more of its legs had been fractured. 'Gavensel!' This time I hissed his name in a lower voice and heard movement on the far side of the room, which was still in shadow. Cautiously, I approached, carrying the lamp with me.

He was huddled in the corner of the walls. As the flickering glow touched him, he held up blood-streaked arms as if to protect himself from the light. 'Gavensel!' I put the lamp down on the floor and hurried to his side. What had he done to himself? His arms now were over his head, shaking, the fingers held out rigidly, slick with blood. 'It's me, Gavensel, how are you hurt? Where…?'

When he raised his head to me, I thought he'd blinded himself, for where his eyes should be was only darkness. Inky streams, poured down his face like thin tar. Then he blinked and I saw he still had eyes, but they were filled with oily black liquid, as if it had been thrown into his face. Where he was not black, he was red. He must've bitten his tongue, or his lips, right through.

'Tambril,' he said in a slurred voice and began to unwind like a serpent, slithering up the wall. He was like a corpse coming to life, no natural thing.

Swallowing fear and revulsion, I sought to examine him, seek injuries, but he struck out with one arm and hurled me away from him, so strongly I was thrown off my feet, backwards onto the floor. He towered over me from his corner, white as a lich, black as cold magma, red as terror, his hair wild rags to his thighs, his clothes hanging in ribbons from his body. Not only blood upon him, but gouts of the weird black liquid.

'What's happened?' I cried. 'Gavensel, let me help…'

He pointed at me, a dire prophet. 'Listen. The horses… the horses came. So tall, so heavy.' He shook his head wildly for a moment, his hands pulling at his hair. 'Crash and clash, crash and clash; harness and hooves. So loud. So tall. Came right into the room, to my corner. Black-skinned hara on them. Clothes of indigo and forest green. I remember them, you see? I remember… Some of them had emerald eyes.'

I lay on the floor gawping up at him, while his dark tears continued to fall. He opened his mouth wide, and it was similarly black. He spat and ink came out of him. I was relieved it didn't reach me.

'They found me, didn't they? Of course they found me. I couldn't hide, could I?' His voice took on a mimicking tone: "What is *that*?" "What *is* that?" they said.'

Gavensel took a few steps towards me, leaned down, put his nightmare face close to my own. He took hold of my arms, his nails digging into my skin.

'They nearly killed me. They *would* have killed me. They said so. "For the love of the gods, destroy it." That's what one said. Others agreed. It was because they found me feeding. I had to eat. I'd had nothing for so long. And it was there, just meat. But then, *he* came out from them. An angel. He came to stand before my corner and spread out his arms. They would have to get through him to reach me. Know what he said? "Brothers." That was it. He said, "Remember, we are *all* brothers. And any we find here are victims not enemies." They were arguing, shouting, everything hazy, but then I found he had put me on his horse. He carried me away… He owned me as brother.'

Gavensel laughed in an unspeakably hollow way. The laughter of a demon called into this world. He returned to his corner, stood there, not facing me. His voice, when he spoke, was unsettlingly casual. 'You know, I once read the ancient legends of this world. I know the stories of heroes. The witch blesses the hero so that he might not be killed by any pureborn har, who came from a hostling, but then...' He turned to me, his eyes blackly bloody, '...then there is me. I am pureborn, but have no hostling. The witch cursed that har rather than blessed him. I am the curse.' He stood rigid for a moment, before uttering a piercing scream of horror that seemed endless. Then he collapsed, like a suit of empty clothes, and lay motionless in a contorted heap before me.

That scream had been truly loud. Others heard it, came running.

When Melisander crossed the threshold to that room, the first thing he yelled at those who'd come with him was 'Find Levvero!'

He saw me cradling Gavensel in the corner and came over.

'I'll go,' somehar called.

'What?' Melisander turned to him. 'What are you doing?'

'Tiahaar Levvero? His room?'

'No, you idiot, in *here*!'

Hara looked at one another in confusion, but then began righting the room, searching among the broken chairs and cabinets, in the jumbled fall of the bed quilt and sheets.

'Stand him up,' Melisander said to me.

'He might be hurt,' I said. 'The blood...'

Melisander shook his head. He took one of Gavensel's arms, I took the other. He was as light as thistledown as we pulled him to his feet.

The blood wasn't Gavensel's. We soon found he wasn't injured externally at all, and they didn't find faeces anywhere in the room, despite the overpowering stink.

Melisander took Gavensel into the bathroom and cleaned him. After helping search the rooms for some minutes, I went to assist with the bath, thinking that perhaps Melisander might appreciate some support. Naked, Gavensel was thin as a rope. The inky fluid came off him in streams. He lay like a lifeless puppet in Melisander's hold.

'What do you think happened?' I asked with some trepidation. 'You think Levvero came here?' I already thought that was absolutely what had happened.

Melisander nodded, lips tight. 'It's my fault,' he said.

'Do you think... do you think Gavensel attacked him? The blood....'

Again Melisander nodded without looking at me.

'But we didn't find anything... The windows were closed. We checked everywhere.'

He ignored my remarks. 'Gavensel can't stay here. I'll take him to my room. Come with me, Tambril.'

I paused. 'Melisander, I think... and I must say it... that you should seek Gelaming aid now. I think that's what's best for Gavensel. I really do.'

Melisander nodded, his expression glum. 'I know, Tambril. I know. I will go to Ferelithia tomorrow, speak to the Immanion representatives there.'

'I know it's painful, but it's for the best.'

'Yes.'

Between us, we towelled Gavensel dry and dressed him in clean clothes. He seemed mindless now, and I wondered if he'd ever recover. I knew that his affliction was beyond our powers here in Sallow Gandaloi to deal with.

Melisander put Gavensel into his own bed, and beckoned for me to follow him to his sitting-room. Here, he poured us large glasses of Ferelithian yenayva mixed with diluted blackberry cordial, and we both drank in silence for a minute or so. Then Melisander sighed through his nose and rubbed his face. 'It's time you knew,' he said.

I shook my head. 'Not yet. There are things I'd like you to know first. Then you'll see that if something bad has happened to Levvero, it's entirely his own doing.'

By this time, Levvero's room had been searched. There was no sign of him, but his belongings were still there. If he'd been in a rush, however, he might've considered leaving them a sacrifice worth making. I like to think he'd realised he'd taken on more than he could handle and, once he'd unwittingly invoked the demon, had scarpered. That's possible, isn't it? But now was the time to peel off the mask, to reveal Sparn to my employer.

Melisander listened without comment as I told him my tale – merely the bare bones of my history, but enough. I told him also my suppositions about Gavensel. I expected some kind of indignant reaction, but at the end of my speech, Melisander only nodded, not smiling, but not angry either. He launched immediately into what he'd wanted to tell me. I don't think he'd been interested at all in my noble truth-telling.

'I couldn't let the Gelaming take him,' he said. 'That seemed wrong to me; he was so damaged. I thought I knew enough to heal him.' He sighed. 'You've guessed much of this story, Tambril, and Gavensel himself has told you more. How Ponclast created pearls, we don't know, perhaps never will, but he did. He followed what he thought were alchemical principles, perhaps forcing conceptions in some way, removing the pearls from their hosts, incubating them... I don't know.

'Gavensel was born to be a soldier, although you'd not think that to look at him. When I first saw him, he seemed only a broken creature, crouched in a corner, eating carrion because he was starving. There had long been legends that the higher echelons of the Varrs were cannibals. My companions believed that's what Gavensel was, but he was only hungry, I could see that. Feral, terrified, confused, not even sure what he was. I had to take him away, because he *was* a rare treasure. Even then, when he was in that state, I could see the ethereal being within.'

He shook his head. 'I made a choice – laid Gavensel over my saddle and rode away with him. He simply hung there like a limp doll, a clockwork thing that had wound down. I suppose, like a true fool and in a very strange way, I fell in love.

'My companions told me I was mad. I lost my phyle because of Gavensel, gave up my friends, became unthrist.' Melisander refilled his yenayva. 'I had to rear him, Tambril, wake him up as much as I could, teach him, rehabilitate him. I had to make something of my life so I had the means to support and hide him. Whatever initial yearnings I had for him faded. I made him my brother because he is. He is yours, too.' At this point Melisander rubbed his face once more, choked back tears.

I touched him reassuringly. 'You did the right thing,' I said, not sure if that was so. Really, I felt, he should have let the Gelaming take Gavensel. They'd have had the means to rehabilitate him properly. Perhaps.

Melisander snarled at me. 'No! I didn't do the right thing at all! Don't patronise me.' He softened. 'I'm sorry. I know you mean well, but... this night was going to happen all along. As time went on, my youthful dreams congealed into nightmares. I couldn't bear even to look at him, but kept my vow and looked after him, gave him all that I could. There were always *signs*, Tambril – hara didn't like to be near him. His behaviour was often peculiar – he escaped several times when we first moved here. Went out to hunt.'

I raised my brows in horror.

'Animals,' Melisander said dryly. 'I secured medicines for him – they helped.'

So my supposition about that had been correct.

'When he was... *normal*, he feared the colour of blood, would not eat meat, nor anything red, even vegetables of that shade.' Melisander drained his glass. 'I *know* that the true Gavensel is the fragile, fey thing you met, Tambril. That's who he's supposed to be, and that's what I sought to nurture, but... The truth was, I'd come to fear that, one day, he might remember everything and then... well...' He raised his arms expressively, shrugged.

I nodded; it all made sense to me. 'What do you think happened to Levvero? Couldn't he have simply run away scared?'

'I don't think we'll ever know,' Melisander said. He gave me a piercing glance. 'So, tell me. I know you must have your own theories – what did Levvero want with Gavensel?'

I stared back for a moment. 'Honestly? I think he saw Gavensel as a commodity to sell, but he was also intrigued about what demons might be evoked by waking Gavensel up to himself. Perhaps because, with that knowledge, he could up the price of the goods. Knowing Levvero as I did, I can't see any other reason for him coming here.'

Melisander nodded. 'It seems the simple answer. Perhaps too simple. Is it possible somehar sent him here as an agent, somehar else who wants Gavensel?'

'Entirely possible,' I said. 'You should mention this to the Gelaming, I think.'

Melisander grimaced. 'Yes. I don't like having to deal with them, but I've no choice now. Tambril, I think you have more experience of situations like this than I do. So please advise me now. How much do I tell the Gelaming about Levvero?'

I didn't bother to contest his opinion. 'Barest details. He was a trader who brought a book to you and who you suspect saw in Gavensel another item to sell. Before you could confirm these suspicions, Levvero left Sallow Gandaloi. You don't know where he went. If they want to know more about that, let them investigate by rummaging in Gavensel's ragged mind, but you know nothing yourself. If they pitched their greatest psychic at you, that's all they'll find, because it's the truth.'

Melisander shook his head at me. 'You're too good at this. And what do I say about how I met Gavensel?'

I gestured at him with my glass. 'The truth. Gavensel remembers some of his past now and that will come out during therapy. Why lie about it? You did what you thought was a good deed and it didn't end well. It was a long time ago. You were young. That's all there is to it.'

Melisander nodded. 'Somehar might come looking for Levvero.'

'Should that happen, you'll say what Levvero wanted you to think. You don't have to mention what happened tonight at all. Levvero simply left here because his business with the book was concluded. Gavensel will be gone from this house. Any pursuers can draw what conclusions they like from those facts. We can shield ourselves more than adequately from prying minds, I think.'

Melisander sighed deeply. 'Whatever Levvero wanted here, and whether he was trying to fulfil an order or not, one thing is certain: the work had a higher price attached to it than he imagined. Ponclast understood the cauldron of creation long before others who were more enlightened. He accessed the ethers like the Gelaming can, although that's not widely known. If Levvero tried to take aruna with Gavensel, only the dehara know what he might've opened up. For all we know, he could have been snatched from this reality.'

'A sad loss,' I said harshly, taking a sip of my drink.

Melisander managed a smile. 'I was blinded, as you once were. Levvero was the raven to me. I'd closed my heart for so long.'

'Yes, he was always an expert at spotting closed hearts, ripe for the breaking.'

Melisander took both my hands in his. 'So, we each have our histories, and this is a historic night.'

'And what now?' I asked.

Melisander closed his eyes, drew in his breath. 'We see what morning brings, clear the debris, tell hara that Levvero fled after an unfortunate encounter that was far from romantic... Do you think that will do?'

'The blood still needs to be explained. His mouth was red.' I paused. 'We can only say a tooth was knocked and the root bled. A blow to the face could cause that.'

'Sounds feasible, but it's not the truth. How did that blood get there... on his mouth...' Melisander swallowed thickly. '*In* it...'

I took a breath. 'I don't think he could have eaten an entire har in the time it took me to reach him.'

Melisander's glance was sharp. 'Unless he started a long time before you heard the noises.'

I grimaced. 'I don't want to believe that or even contemplate it. No, it's not possible. He's too... thin.'

'Perhaps he didn't feast alone.'

These far-fetched suppositions were getting too hideous. I had to end them. 'Well, perhaps he can be mended now,' I said. 'Are you truly willing to hand him over to the Gelaming?'

Melisander sighed. 'Not really, but don't worry, I won't change my mind about going to Ferelithia tomorrow. I'm concerned though that Gavensel will be terrified to leave here.'

'Given the state he's in, I wonder whether he'll even be aware.'

Melisander nodded glumly. 'You're right, and while part of me grieves, another will be relieved. I'm not proud of that part. I was cruel and foolish to think I could help him. Now, it might be too late.'

'You can't think that,' I said, knowing that what he needed was platitudes. 'This might go better than you think.'

'He stared at me directly. 'Sit up with me this night. Keep a vigil for him with me.'

'Of course.'

And so we drank to him, the ruin of Gavensel, a har who should never have been.

Gavensel has been gone some weeks now. Melisander rode to Ferelithia first thing in the morning and a party of Gelaming came back for Gavensel soon after. They gave Melisander information on how to keep track of Gavensel's treatment, and told him he could come to Immanion at any time to visit him. I don't think he'll take them up on that offer, though. Perhaps I'm wrong.

Sallow Gandaloi has more or less settled back to its usual routines. But there is a hole in its heart, where Gavensel used to be. Nohar goes to his rooms – Obery accompanied Gavensel to

Immanion, because he felt somehar should. Melisander was thankful to him for that. As for Levvero, nohar has come looking for him yet. The hara in the house have their own suppositions about what happened to him, but they care for Melisander enough to keep quiet. I've not yet told Ylisse what I know.

In the last hour before the dawn, on Gavensel's last night in Sallow Gandaloi, I went to the bed chamber where he lay and gazed upon him for some minutes. His arms were outside the quilt, set straight beside his body. He looked like a corpse, but – I had to admit – a fresh and beautiful corpse. In repose, he no longer appeared freakish, but simply ethereal, an illusion of the rebis, the perfect creation from *prima materia*. Perhaps he'll never wake up, living only in his own mind – I hope in a peaceful place.

Sometimes at sunset, out in the garden, I look up at the windows of Gavensel's chambers, which are now forever darkened. The shadows beyond the glass seem haunted; those windows are so different from all the others in the house. They are holes, sightless eyes. Gavensel is a ghost here. When I look up at those lightless panes, through which he gazed so often, I wonder whether one day I might catch a glimpse of him staring back.

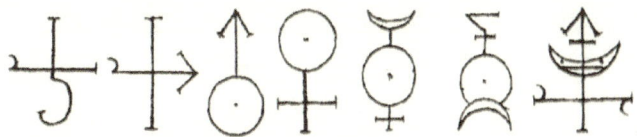

Half Sick of Shadows

Balsam of Soot

This broken swathe of land used to be a city. You can still see the ghosts of it, the places where buildings used to be. Stretching as far as I can see, a shattered plain, and in the distance the smudge of what remains stark against the sky.

Rain is falling and there is a gentle rumble of thunder, not a dramatic crash but rather the sound of some great monster dying. I can hear also the hiss of waves against the black cliffs some distance behind me, and feel in the shudder of my flesh the yawning drop to the hard rocks below.

There are stunted trees without leaf, and the rain falls from them, drop by perfect drop to the ground. Their piano notes complement the initial percussion against the skeletal branches. Rain is one of the most beautiful orchestras of nature. If you listen with stillness, you can hear a multitude of instruments within it.

The ruined road I follow is running with pure, clear water. If you look carefully, you can see the green is coming back, but it's a slow, hurting process here. Small weeds strain to thrive amid the cracked and crumbling concrete. Moss inches in a mollusc trail across the after-image of foundations. Life is a stubborn force. Humanity sought to suppress and destroy it, mostly in ignorance, but it refused to die. Unlike them.

I am walking slowly up the middle of the ghost road. I am empty of feeling. I am merely The Witness. This was the end of the world, says the narrator in my head, and this was where *we* started.

I know I'm dreaming and that I've had this dream many times, but when I have it, I can never remember how it ends. I have to keep following the road.

'Write it down,' my carers told me, and I did, but when I woke, the end had dissolved into rain, and this was all I could relate. The rain. The road. The empty landscape. They told me I was afraid of what I might find at journey's end. I don't forget it, as such, but bury it deep before I wake.

This forlorn place might exist solely in my mind, a metaphor for my ill-shaped self, or it might be a memory. This is what I had to find out.

Caput Mortuum

I have had more than one life – at least three. The first one was erased. My brother, Melisander, might once have told me what he knew about it but, as far as I was concerned, I never lived it. The second life *began* with Melisander, although its initial years were grainy and out of focus, like a bad photograph in poor light.

We left our home and started travelling. I assumed we must have lived in many places, and not for long. I knew I was pureborn, yet Melisander was not, which – I reasoned – must explain why his skin was black and mine as pale as wall plaster. I knew we couldn't be brothers in blood, because he was incepted, but he always told me we were related. We travelled, but I couldn't tell you where or when, or how long we stayed in places. I did know we derived from the great continent of Megalithica to the west, but at some point moved east across the ocean known as the Girdle of Tiamat, fetching up eventually in Ferelithia, a province of Almagabra. We settled in a beautiful but fairly isolated house named Sallow Gandaloi, which nestled in countryside near the ocean. These later years were clearer and revolved around that sanctuary where my brother hid me from the world. But it was not to be my haven forever. That time, too, ended.

When Melisander first sent me to hara of the Gelaming tribe and their house of healing, it was as if I'd just been born, reincarnated, and could remember glimpses of another life. There were certain constants in my mind, such as Sallow Gandaloi itself, and my brother, but other details didn't always remain. Sometimes, they might surface for an hour. All I knew was that something terrible must have happened; something so bad my brother had to be rid of me. He had surrendered me to hara who claimed they could mend the most broken minds. Melisander and I had been together all our lives, and he'd always protected me, so I could only think the worst. I must've killed somehar. That's the worst thing that can happen, isn't it?

So, where was this place? It was an airy and elegant house – or more accurately a complex – spreading over the top of a hill in the city of Immanion, capital of Almagabra and the Gelaming tribe. The name of the house was Reveriel, a fusion of reverence and dreams. But whatever its name, it was an asylum and its gates were locked.

The complex had terraces like skirts that flounced down the hillside, surrounded by walled gardens. Wings unfurled on every level, where hara lived, as if they were guests, not patients. Two other hara occupied my wing, but I didn't meet them until I'd settled in. Our collective rooms had a name – Pavonyx – which I believe derived from a word in some old language that means peacock.

When I woke up there, so began my third life. The first har I saw was Obery, who I remembered. He was my har in Sallow Gandaloi, an olive-skinned native of Ferelithia, who'd attended to my needs, fetched and carried, closed my drapes against the night. Now he stood beside my bed and the hazy light of early morning surrounded him.

'Good morning, Gavensel,' he said to me, as if I were waking on any ordinary day, and I hadn't been incarcerated far from home.

I looked around at the tasteful, clutter-free environment. 'What's happened to my room?' I asked.

'We're not at Sallow Gandaloi,' Obery said slowly, as if to make me understand this difficult concept. 'We're in Immanion.'

'Why? Where's Melisander?' I sat up and my brain lurched uncomfortably in my skull, so I had to lie down again.

'You've been very sick,' Obery murmured, putting a hand against my left shoulder. 'Melisander asked the Gelaming to care for you, so we came here.'

I knew those words: *Immanion, Gelaming*. They made me itch; I didn't like them.

'There's no need to be afraid,' Obery said. 'I'm here with you. You're not alone.'

'What's wrong with me?'

Obery didn't pause for an instant; he must've practiced his response for a long time before I woke. 'We're not exactly sure, but you suffered convulsions and went into a coma. Our healers couldn't make you better, so Melisander asked the Gelaming for help.'

'How long have we been here?'

'Around two weeks. You woke a few times before, but not fully. This time it's a real awakening. Don't you feel that?'

After breakfast on that morning, Tiahaar Rav Har Blansie came to see me and announced himself as the supervisor of this wing of the building – and my primary physician. He was a slim har of medium height, who made no effort to enhance his features cosmetically and therefore, lacking true beauty, appeared as bland as his name implied. He wasn't ill-favoured, but certainly not what I'd expected a Gelaming to be like, seeing as they're regarded as the most sophisticated and advanced of tribes. Har Blansie described efficiently what I could expect to happen during my stay. Mostly, this would be relaxation. My mind, when it was ready, would co-operate if it wasn't aggravated or bullied. My harish body was adept at self-mending, but needed to be left alone to do that. I must be a well-behaved passenger in it, make no fuss, let the flesh and bone examine itself, and allow the miraculous mechanisms in my head to identify faults in its streams, unblock dams.

'How long must I stay here?' I asked.

'We must first assess you,' Har Blansie replied smoothly.

'Yes, but… you must have *some* idea.'

He blinked slowly. 'Recovery is different for everyhar. I really can't yet say. But be prepared for a fairly long stay.'

I must have looked horrified.

'Reveriel is designed to be restorative,' Har Blansie said. 'Look on your time here as a holiday.'

'I see. In that case, I'd like to dictate poetry to Obery. I know this helps calm my mind, always has... I think. May I have writing materials for him?'

Har Blansie regarded me for a moment. 'Later on, certainly. For now, it's best you keep your mind as clear as you can. Indulge yourself in other ways. Enjoy food, a walk in the gardens, the sight of the sea. Let it all flow over you in waves of simple pleasure.'

There was nothing remotely sinister about Har Blansie, or what he said to me, yet even so, once he'd left my room, the air was paralysed. I felt I was on trial. But for what?

Remembering my past was like trying to recall one of those fleeting dreams you have between waking and sleep, which don't make sense, the details of which slide away to wisps before you can work out their meaning. An image might surface – gazing from my window at Sallow Gandaloi – but it would be isolated. I might remember saying, "Yes, that would work really well", but nothing beyond that, nonsense words out of context.

At first I was nervous of leaving my room; I could remember I had rarely left my chambers back home. Obery had little to do as far as my own needs were concerned, so on our second day in residence he offered his services to the house administrators, which they were happy to take up. There were times he must sit with me, but there were other times when I must be alone. By myself, during those first few days, I quickly became bored. The immense outside was threatening; I wasn't ready for that. There were no books for me to read and nothing to write with, and besides I felt Har Blansie would know if I even *tried* to make the music of words in my head. I felt watched.

A halian would come to me twice a day to direct agmara energy into me. Halians were lesser healers, somewhat below the physicians in rank, all of them willowy and graceful, looking *exactly* how I'd expected Gelaming to be. They appeared to have been recruited from all corners of the known harish world, so many different accents, different skins, different scents. I learned they attended to massage, agmara healing and sound therapy. Quiet, unobtrusive, these hara were like beautiful automata. They'd smile and speak softly, but seemed utterly devoid of personality. Close your eyes when one was with you and you couldn't feel them there.

I had a large room, divided by screens that I could place where I liked. The bed was low to the floor and covered in a milky green quilt that had an abstract design worked on it in silken white thread. There were paintings on the wall of seascapes, but restful ones. No angry waves, no sullen clouds, just light and space and the occasional gull thrown onto the canvas. The room was well-lit in the afternoon but relatively dark in the morning. The air, though, was always warm and I liked the dim wakings, after which I could go out onto my veranda and see the garden beyond gorging on the light. But that came later. Initially, I stood in the shadows of the room and stared out at all that radiant space, each day taking steps closer to the threshold.

Eventually – and it didn't take that long, because I was curious – I was able to step beyond the window-doors. I crossed the wooden veranda and stood bare-footed on the trimmed lawn. The garden stretched down the side of Pavonyx. There was a dark, knotted shrubbery to the left and a paved water garden to the right, with falls and fountains. Ahead of me a low wall faced the ocean. Reveriel was so high up that the city spread out below looked like a harling's toys. I might lean over the wall and pick something up; a little house, a tower with a bell, tiny hara like poppets who'd dance upon my hand. I felt as if I'd stepped into a magical landscape, the sky so immense above me, too big to understand, the grass like damp velvet beneath my naked feet. Something must wait for me in this enchanted place.

For a few days, I did what Har Blansie suggested. I stared at the wrinkle of the distant sea or at the oleanders by the edge of the lawn, where birds and insects went about their daily business. I stood at the wall to lean out over the folding terraces below, watching hara going about their lives. I could see halians and physicians in flowing robes of dark blue, and other hara, dressed in pale clothes, who I thought must be "guests" like me. They were all far away, lower down, as if I was trapped up here on this terrace and nohar could see me.

Then, one morning, I walked out onto my veranda, onto the lawn I now considered to be mine, and saw a strange figure moving in an odd, jerky way, along the path of pale stone that cut across the middle of the grass. I had seen nohar else since I arrived, but for the staff. I didn't realise at first it was even a har, thought I'd imagined it. This figure must have felt my scrutiny, because it stopped, wobbled a little, then turned to look at me. What a strange sight he was. Smaller than was usual for a har, somehow lopsided, his dull, brown hair a tangled thatch sticking up all over and around his shoulders. His face was small, the features pinched, almost simian. His clothes looked too big for him. We stared at one another, and then I raised a hand. He did likewise, then turned away and bustled off.

Later that day, I decided to extend my exploration of Reveriel, to walk up the passageway outside my room. Obery wasn't around; he liked to keep busy and I didn't detain him. All was quiet, no halians about. The corridor was not institutional, but like part of somehar's home. There were large ornamental ferns in tall pots, some benches with cushions, a patterned rug of gold and blue running down the centre of the floor. I passed open doors, saw a room where linen was kept, then a small and homely kitchen, then empty rooms with no guests, the beds bare as if hara had died on them and been cleaned away.

Finally, as in a harling's tale, I came to a room that shimmered with life – the door was open. The magic must surely lie beyond. I went to stand at the threshold; wary yet excited. Inside, a brown-skinned har was sitting on a black and white patterned mat on the floor, his back to me. He wore the pale tunic and trousers of a 'guest' and appeared to be meditating or at least deep in thought. I took a soft step backwards so as not to disturb him. Not soft enough. He jumped up and spun round, his body stooped into a defensive posture.

'Excuse me,' I said. 'I didn't mean to disturb you.'

'This is my room,' he said.

'I know.'

Like the har I'd seen on the lawn, he was strange. Not small or ill-composed, but with eyes far too large for his head, which stared at me wildly. I could see the whites of them all the way round and knew then he could be dangerous. The sides of his head were shaved, the long hair on top woven into long ragged braids. He was dark, but not of Melisander's kind. His features were sharper.

'I'm Gavensel,' I said.

His lips peeled back into a doglike snarl. 'Don't care who the fuck you are. Fuck off!'

'Goodbye, then.' Dazed, I went back to my room. This must be how it feels to be punched, I thought.

I knew the words he'd spat at me were a weapon, a defence. *Leave me be!* I knew also the profanity was an old one, from the human era, and in that way more insulting than it might have been. This was the first time in my life, which I could remember, I'd encountered such hostility.

Before my evening meal, Har Blansie came to see me and asked about my day. I told him.

'The har you saw in the garden is Grackle,' he said, 'and the other is Pazazil. They live on this wing too.'

'Am I supposed to…? Do we ever…?'

Har Blansie made a casual gesture with one hand. 'The residents are free to mingle, Gavensel, but be cautious. Some of our guests value privacy. Most of them had very traumatic experiences. Use your senses to discern when interaction is welcome.'

I didn't want to interact with either of the hara I'd met; one was deformed, the other insane. 'All right,' I said.

Obery came to me after dinner. Already, he'd made arrangements to eat with the other domestic staff – much like at home, I supposed. He made sure I was prepared for bed, turned down the soft lamps, extinguished the dish of burning oil. 'Do you need anything, Gavensel?'

'No.' I lay in my bed, looking up at him, wondering what it would be like if Obery could actually sleep for me, and I could go somewhere else while he did it.

After he'd gone, I counted to a thousand slowly, imagining each number as a different colour. Then I held my breath for a while, listening to the sounds of the night – occasional nightingale song from the gardens, a distant hiss that might be the ocean, an odd snatch of music and laughter from the streets below Reveriel. Closer to, I could hear the building breathing very softly; I decided it was a kindly place, but also a little stupid. Restless, I got out of bed and put on my dressing-robe. Obery had plaited my hair into a long rope, which I put over my shoulder. If needs be, I could strangle somehar with it.

I walked down the corridor beyond my door, but on the side opposite the har Pazazil's room. I had yet to see what lay beyond that point. There were a few more rooms – one was a library, where I was pleased to see books were stacked, even if untidily. I looked into several therapy rooms the physicians and halians must use, and afterwards found a sitting-room that overlooked the garden, its outer wall made completely of glass doors. There were low sofas here and slightly more colour than in the other rooms – ethnic designs I could perceive even by moonlight.

A voice from the shadows startled me. 'Your loved ones can come into this room.'

I turned to see that what I'd taken to be a tatty rug thrown over one of the sofas was actually Grackle. 'A visiting room,' I said, to cover my surprise.

He sat up, hugging his knees, his odd little head to one side. 'I call it a waiting room, 'cos I wait in it. I wait for them. They haven't come yet, but they will.'

I sat down in a chair across from him, leaned forwards. 'Your family.'

He nodded. 'All my sons.'

He didn't look capable of hosting – or even sparking – pearls to me, but I said, 'They'll come soon, I expect.'

'Have you come here to wait too?'

'No, I'm just looking around. I haven't been here long.'

'Night's the best time, yes. There's nohar else here, then. It's just ours for a while, like it's our own house.'

I smiled at that. 'Yes.'

'Why did they put you in here?'

I drew back from him, surprised by the directness of the question, wondering whether it was in fact allowed.

He wrinkled up his face. 'Oh, sorry… was that rude? I'll tell you why I'm here. We're *supposed* to talk.' He paused, no doubt remembering instructions. 'Will that be OK?'

'I don't mind.'

'When I was young, I was chosen to be a hostling.' His eyes squinted with pride, his pointed chin thrust out.

'Chosen?'

'Oh yes… It was our honour to host the pearls that would make an army for the Varrs. Only…' He frowned, faltered, losing his words.

I stared at this strange creature, thinking about what he'd said. I couldn't remember ever being intimate with a har, yet this one had perhaps had too much of that.

'How many… pearls?' I asked.

He shrugged. 'I can't really remember, to tell the truth. So much happened. But I run it round a lot in my head, recapture the days, and think maybe it was five.'

'Five! Most hara are lucky to have one.'

'It was my calling. We were taught how to do it.'

'Didn't you mind it?'

He blinked. 'Oh, we all *minded.* Every son who left us was like a death. That was the price of our calling. But then, when everything went wrong, and the Gelaming fought with the Varrs, we were forgotten and nearly all starved. Uigenna bandits attacked us. Many died. I was hurt and very ill. But then the Gelaming found us and they were kind. I'm all right now.'

Which is why you're still here, I thought, harshly. 'That's good. My name is Gavensel. I'm guessing you're Grackle.'

'Yes, we were all named for birds in our homestead. My name isn't very pretty, but...' He laughed, 'then I'm not either.' His smile twisted into a grimace. 'I was, once. But...'

'Pretty on the outside doesn't mean pretty on the inside,' I said, thinking of myself. Melisander had often called me beautiful, but an over-abundance of hair can cover many defects. I'd always thought my nose too long and my mouth too wide for my face, and there's a fine line between gracefully slim and skeletal – easy to fall on the wrong side of it.

'I like you,' Grackle said. 'You're not like the other one. He's mean sometimes. But it's only because he's so sad. You can't do anything, though. He won't let you near enough.'

I guessed this little scrap of a har, this professional hostling, had tried. 'He shouted at me,' I said. 'Is he violent?'

Grackle shook his head. 'No, only to himself.'

If Grackle could be direct, I decided to be so too. 'If you're better, why are you still here?'

'I'm better physically,' he answered simply, without embarrassment, 'but I can't live outside in the world. I get frightened easily, and sometimes my head is too full of mist to work properly. There's nowhere else for me to go.'

'Unless one of your sons comes,' I said.

He nodded vigorously. 'That's what I'm waiting for. The Gelaming might be able to find them. They found records in the homestead, but many had been burned because we needed fuel. We couldn't understand them ourselves – there were codes.'

My knowledge of history was scanty, but I knew enough to guess that if Grackle had bred soldiers it was likely most of them – if not all – were dead. *Varrs...* I knew that word. Perhaps Melisander and I had been Varrs too once. I knew we'd come from Megalithica many years ago. I wondered how long Grackle had been here, but was reluctant to ask.

We sat in silence, looking out at the stars through the open windows. I occupied wholly the present moment. The air smelled of jasmine and was warm like a bath. A scops owl crooned in a cypress tree. I realised that talking to Grackle had left me feeling different. I was content. How huge that feeling is, and yet how small.

The following morning, Har Blansie came to ask me about my dreams. I couldn't remember any. I held onto the wonderful feeling I'd experienced in the sitting room with Grackle, as if everything in the world was fine and as it should be. Better to fill my mind with that than unsettling dreams. I decided not to tell Har Blansie about my meeting with Grackle. This was a possession I could keep to myself for a time.

Dreams, Har Blansie told me, are the cleansing system of the soul. Within them, I could examine from a distance events and hara who made me afraid or uncomfortable.

I dreamed always of the same place, that devastated landscape, and there were never other living beings in it.

'Today,' Har Blansie said, 'we'll begin your path-working, which is rather like having waking dreams. Another har will guide you in this, a hienama named Typhis Har Aquillon. I think you should take Obery with you.'

Hienamas, in this place, were physicians of the mind and soul. It was time to enter the darkness.

Obery walked with me to a room down the corridor, which Har Blansie had told me was known as a helrumian – Gelaming-speak for a therapy room. I felt anxious and clenched-up. We entered the designated room, which was virtually empty, but for two chairs, a few rugs and cushions on the floor. Gauzy drapes shifted languorously at the long windows. Wooden wind-chimes tonked among the curtains.

A har was seated on one of the chairs, near the centre of the room. He didn't look to me like a hienama, being somewhat stiff of posture. He was dressed in a long, fairly tight-fitting robe of dark blue, sashed widely with black at the waist. His skin was olive-coloured, his hair and eyes black. The curl of his hair and the brightness in his eyes suggested he would be a cheerful har, but he was actually sombre and had rather a long face, like a horse. He indicated I should find a comfortable place to lie down among the cushions, while Obery must sit nearby.

Har Aquillon had notes of my dreams, what little I'd already told Har Blansie, and I knew we'd have to begin with that awful, dark place. Perhaps I could walk through this part quickly, find something better beyond. I could make that happen, couldn't I? I didn't voice any of this, but remained meek and amenable. I remembered then Melisander once saying to me, 'How well you hide your true nature, Ven. Did I teach you that?'

I had reached for his face, touched the beautiful planes of him, and said...

No, it was gone, but the face of my brother remained. Would he visit me soon?

Har Aquillon took me walking into my dreams. Very soon, it really was as if I was asleep, and if anything the details of my environment were clearer. There was a stark splendour to this landscape. The anger of the sea behind me was thrilling. I was drawn to gaze upon it, but Har Aquillon kept me to the path, his voice firm yet soft, compelling – lovely, in fact. I noticed, as I walked, that some of the rain drops were blood, starkly crimson against the blacks and greys, the occasional deep greens, of the scene. The sky overhead was bilious with dark clouds, but there were areas of wan yellow within them, occasional coughs of weak lightning.

I walked until I could go no further and was pacing in place upon the ghost road. 'This is the end of the path,' I murmured.

'It's not,' Aquillon replied. 'But simply stand there a while. The gate is invisible. You can peer beyond it.'

The landscape ahead was too dark to penetrate. Something immense massed against the unsettled sky. A sheet of lightning retched down and I saw it then; a fortress rearing against the clouds. Terrifying and wondrous. Was it real or a symbol? I supposed I had to tell Har Aquillon what I saw, mainly because I wondered what he'd say about it.

'Walk towards it,' he said.

'I can't.' (More than that – I didn't want to.)

'Just take one step. You can do that.'

I could, but it was a choice. If I took that one step, then others would surely follow, if not now then another time. My psyche shrank and convulsed at the idea of it. 'Not today,' I said and opened my eyes. When I looked at Har Aquillon he seemed faintly surprised.

'You have a strong will,' he said, and smiled then, transforming himself into a different creature.

I didn't reply to that. 'I don't like visiting that place,' I said. 'Is there no other way?'

Har Aquillon drew in his breath through his nose, for a second considered humouring me – I could sense that plainly – then said, 'Tiahaar – Gavensel, if I may call you that – the landscape and fortress represent a key in a locked door. Beyond that door lies freedom. Your past is hidden, even from you. You don't need me to tell you it must be painful, and you might've locked a door upon it because, if you hadn't, you'd have lost yourself completely. But here... among us... it's safe to open the lock. Maybe only one click at a time. Today you learned you can cross a boundary. That's a single click.'

'What if I open the lock and then go mad? I might kill you.'

Har Aquillon laughed. 'I'd knock you out before that happens.'

It was a joke, of course. What he would do, and what I could see so clearly in his mind, was fire at me an arrow of agmara energy, so strong it would make me swoon, no matter how maddened I was.

After the session was concluded, I told Obery I'd return to my room alone, as I suspected he was itching to be back with all his new friends among the staff. I could tell he loved Immanion and was grateful to me that my madness had enabled him to move there.

I realised, as I wandered slowly along the corridor, that all my life the har I'd presented to others had been merely my puppet. They all thought I was delicate, fey and simple, but just because my memory was bad didn't mean I was the naïve, mooncalf harling I often pretended to be. And yet I had chosen to be that, because it had saved me a lot of trouble in the long run.

I passed the kitchen and heard laughter, glanced in to see who was there. I saw Grackle and Pazazil, squeezing lemons at the table. They looked like friends. I watched them for maybe half a minute before they registered my presence. Pazazil looked at me with his wide stare and said, 'It's the Lady of Shalott.'

'Don't call him that,' Grackle snapped, his face reddening.

I went into the room. 'What does it mean?'

'Tatty Bird likes poetry,' Pazazil drawled. 'He reads the human books in the library. He said you're the Lady of Shalott. That's a woman, incidentally.'

'Oh. Why am I like her, Grackle?'

He shrugged awkwardly. I felt sorry for his discomfort, even though these two had been gossiping about me. 'Just... tragic,' he said, not looking at me.

'Died,' Pazazil added gleefully.

'Tragic and dead,' I said coolly, then realised this statement didn't fit my persona. I was supposed to be fluttery and confused by this point.

'Floated dead in a boat down a river, her hair all around her,' Pazazil continued. 'Such a pretty image. You find the

Lady pretty, Grack?'

'Will you just shut up?' Grackle said. 'Why do you have to be so vile? You were fine before he came in. You're putting on an act. Stupid!'

'I'll leave you to it, then,' I said, backing out of the room.

'It's one of his good days,' Grackle said to me as I walked away.

Bizarrely, the exchange had cheered me.

Flowers of Sulphur

I had the dream that night and got to the point where I could walk no further, except of course I was perfectly capable of going as far as I wished. I put one toe over the invisible mark and the sky did not fall, nor did the great fortress rumble towards me in a ravenous cloud of smashing masonry, roaring as it came.

I did glance to my side, at one of the straggling shrubs, and noted the delicate pearls of blood that had formed on its trembling leaves. These beads were the most intense and beautiful red, shadowed dark at their edges, with a small eye of light on top, just a pinprick gleam. I wanted to fashion a necklace of these blood-beads that would hang to my knees. Or I would put them into my dusty-grey hair. I am a creature of grey and white. The red beads would stand out well.

This was obviously not the kind of internal monologue my carers wanted me to have.

At this point, I awoke, realising I'd been quite aware in my dream and had known I was sleeping. My room was darker than normal and I perceived a slight chill. There was also a peculiar smell, like burning hair or cloth. A spot deep within my skull, but above my right eye, was throbbing sharply.

I sat up and the quilt fell from me. At the end of my bed, or just beyond it, I saw an oblong of glittering black, around my own height. This didn't sparkle like crystal or even like sunlight on water; the glitter itself was composed of black. And the black of this object was not merely a colour but a substance – heavy as clay, fluid as ink, gaseous like a cloud. While the black was in some way solid, I knew it was also a portal, but whether it went out or in I couldn't say. It was both an invitation and an announcement – calling to me and warning me. I couldn't make up my mind whether I was afraid, challenged, or simply intrigued. All three, I suppose. What I saw, I realised, was not an object native to this world. But should I know of it? Was it an aspect of my past and that landscape I walked in dreams?

As I gazed at the black, wondering what to do, I saw a white hand and arm emerge from it. These were long and thin, and felt around, as if inspecting the room. The hand raised palmwards towards me and its fingers went back like the legs of a threatened spider. Fingers don't naturally bend back that far.

'I see you,' I said. 'Know that I see you.'

The hand lowered and I expected more of the being to which they belonged to emerge from the black. The air prickled, as if feathers tickled my skin. The throbbing in my head was sharper. I got out of bed and walked naked to the black. I could, if I wanted to, fall forwards into it. Close to, I could perceive its dark sparkles clearly. The hand and arm dangled from the object's centre, not moving now.

I reached out impulsively and took hold of the hand. It wasn't cold, or dead, or ghostly, but a real hand in my hold. It didn't return the pressure of my grip, but hung there limply. Then, in an instant, it yanked itself away, withdrew into the portal, which condensed swiftly into a black spark that popped out of existence.

I stared, dazed, at the place where it had been. The pain in my skull had gone completely.

I didn't think I'd get back to sleep after that episode, and didn't want to wake anyhar to tell them about it – *that* could wait till morning – so pulled on my dressing-robe and made my way to the library. Har Blansie might have forbidden me to write but he'd not mentioned anything about reading. I assumed that was acceptable. I could take some books back to my room. But once among the plump sofas that filled nearly the entire room, and surrounded by those comforting, untidy shelves, I wanted to remain there. I remembered the poem Pazazil had mentioned and searched the shelves. Dawn was beginning to creep across the sky – such wondrous light – and eventually rays began to paw their way into the room. There weren't many poetry books and, of those, few were ancient, but then I found it and read the first two verses of the poem.

> On either side the river lie
> Long fields of barley and of rye,
> That clothe the wold and meet the sky;
> And thro' the field the road runs by
> To many-tower'd Camelot;
> And up and down the people go,
> Gazing where the lilies blow
> Round an island there below,
> The island of Shalott.
>
> Willows whiten, aspens quiver,
> Little breezes dusk and shiver
> Thro' the wave that runs for ever
> By the island in the river
> Flowing down to Camelot.
> Four grey walls, and four grey towers,
> Overlook a space of flowers,
> And the silent isle imbowers
> The Lady of Shalott.

I closed the book then, somewhat breathless, my fingers still marking the page. I had to sit down in one of the chairs, close my eyes for some moments. I recognised the place in the poem, I knew the words. Sallow Gandaloi was Camelot, but also Shalott, like two different places super-imposed over each other.

The silent isle embowers...

I had looked down from a tower upon the world, upon the gardens, the space of flowers, and the fields and road beyond.

I read on, paused again at some lines that made me shudder in recognition.

But who hath seen her wave her hand?
Or at the casement seen her stand?
Or is she known in all the land,
The Lady of Shalott?

And more...

There she weaves by night and day
A magic web with colours gay.
She has heard a whisper say,
A curse is on her if she stay
To look down to Camelot.
She knows not what the curse may be,
And so she weaveth steadily,
And little other care hath she,
The Lady of Shalott.

And moving thro' a mirror clear
That hangs before her all the year,
Shadows of the world appear.

By this time I was tingling all over; a delicious and unnerving feeling. Hadn't the poems I'd written been my weaving? And hadn't I always felt as if I were under a curse, which had kept me to my rooms, made me fear the outdoors? Through my puppet mask, hadn't I always gazed upon the world as if through a mirror?

More lines stilled my breath.

But in her web she still delights
To weave the mirror's magic sights,
For often thro' the silent nights
A funeral, with plumes and lights,
And music, went to Camelot:
Or when the moon was overhead,
Came two young lovers lately wed;

> *"I am half sick of shadows," said*
> *The Lady of Shalott.*

Even as I'd written my poems, and enjoyed my love affair with beautiful words, hadn't I envied those around me in Sallow Gandaloi – those who'd come to my chambers to pretend to be friends, but who'd really been desperate for the afternoon to end? Melisander had sent them, and they'd been resentful, seeing it only as part of their job, for which they were paid. And I *had* seen them in the garden, chesnari in moonlight, embracing and laughing, with moths and starlight in their hair. In truth, I'd hated them, become sick of my shadow life. I read on.

> *A bow-shot from her bower-eaves,*
> *He rode between the barley-sheaves,*
> *The sun came dazzling thro' the leaves,*
> *And flamed upon the brazen greaves*
> *Of bold Sir Lancelot.*

Now I turned the open book on its front in my lap. *He rode between the barley sheaves...* No, not ridden, *walked*. Somehar had come. And his garments had not shone but had been black as crows, like the strange portal I'd seen. I was almost afraid to read on, remembering Pazazil's words of death.

> *From underneath his helmet flow'd*
> *His coal-black curls as on he rode,*
> *As he rode down to Camelot.*
> *From the bank and from the river*
> *He flash'd into the crystal mirror...*
>
> *She left the web, she left the loom,*
> *She made three paces thro' the room,*
> *She saw the water-lily bloom,*
> *She saw the helmet and the plume,*

She look'd down to Camelot.
Out flew the web and floated wide;
The mirror crack'd from side to side;
"The curse is come upon me," cried
The Lady of Shalott.

My eyes were blurred with tears. This was a fairy-tale of my life, surely? The mirror had cracked and a doom had come, so terrible it had been buried too deep to be found, in unhallowed ground sown with salt. I had to read to the end, however dreadful it might be.

Lying, robed in snowy white
That loosely flew to left and right -
The leaves upon her falling light -
Thro' the noises of the night
She floated down to Camelot:
And as the boat-head wound along
The willowy hills and fields among,
They heard her singing her last song.
The Lady of Shalott.

But I hadn't died – somehar else had, I was sure of it. Clever Grackle, how sensitive he was. Had he seen all that in me? Poor little scrap, his sons torn from him, sons bred to kill. I shuddered. There were two more verses. In the last one, the court of Camelot goes to inspect the dead body that has floated in.

Who is this? and what is here?
And in the lighted palace near
Died the sound of royal cheer;
And they cross'd themselves for fear,
All the knights at Camelot:
But Lancelot mused a little space;
He said, "She has a lovely face;

God in his mercy lend her grace.
The Lady of Shalott."

They were afraid, even though she was dead, and the one who'd doomed her had merely noticed casually that her face was lovely. She – and her fate – had meant nothing to him.

The poem filled me with emotion – anger of behalf of the Lady, scorn and hatred for Lancelot, disdain for the stupid people who'd lived nearby and had never bothered to *know* her, never *helped* her. She'd just been an object of fear to be shunned. I wanted to throw the book at the wall, and only its antique value prevented me. Instead I wept bitterly, consumed by my soume aspect, that woman within me, the Lady of Shalott.

Somehar came to my side and said, 'You'll get tears all over the leather,' and removed the book from my lap. I didn't want to look up or say anything and whoever it was just stood there, waiting.

Eventually, I stopped, exactly like a tap being turned off. The feeling had drained out. I looked up at the har beside me and saw Pazazil.

'If you insist on squawking like a newly-hatched harling, can you do it more quietly?' he said in a manner that was both pleasant and insolent. 'You woke me up.'

'No I didn't.'

He shrugged. 'Well, I was awake, then.'

'I read that poem Grackle likes,' I said.

'Yeah, gathered that. Strummed some nerves, did it?'

'Could say that.' I rubbed at my wet face. 'Is Grackle particularly psychic?'

'Has honed senses to sniff out distress,' Pazazil said. 'Must've helped him look after the hatchlings, but that was forever frustrated, so his ability is as taut as an unreleased orgasm.'

'Quaint,' I said coldly.

Pazazil shrugged. 'Well, feels like that to me. And now you

can't unhear what I said so it'll feel like that to you.' He threw himself down in a chair opposite me, one leg over its arm. 'I reckon they keep him here to help hara like us, like they keep dogs and cats in sanatoriums for the physically fucked, in the hope it stops hara dying. Know what I mean?'

'Maybe. He said he had no other place to go.'

Pazazil's lips and nose stretched into a sneer. 'Oh, there *are* other places, once the treatment's over, where the non-perfects can live together, be discreetly monitored. Grackle's our pet we can hug when the black hounds of our insanity get too fierce.'

'I see... Still, he was right about the poem.'

Pazazil pulled a scornful face. 'Please don't *tell* me about it.'

'Didn't intend to.' I paused. 'So, what are you like on a bad day?'

Pazazil laughed. 'You don't wanna see, but will probably have no choice.' He got to his feet. 'G'night.'

'It's morning.'

'Whatever.'

Grackle, I know, is named for a bird. Pazazil must be a kind of demon. And me... I think Gavensel sounds like a herb, magical in nature. *He fled to where gavensel grew, near waters old and swamp-fire blue...*

They can't stop me creating poetry even if it's bad.

All that day I wondered about the portal I'd seen, wondering if I *had* still been half asleep, or if it had been a hallucination or else somehow real. I wondered about it as I ate my breakfast, and as I walked down the corridor to a helrumian where a halian with narrow hands gave me a full body massage while humming.

In the afternoon, I'd be seeing Typhis Har Aquillon and recognised within myself a strong desire not to co-operate with him. It wasn't that I wanted to remain as I was, or never go home, but that these Gelaming took it for granted they could interfere with my mind and that I should be grateful. What if I wanted to heal myself, as we hara are supposed to be able to do? I wasn't deformed like Grackle, or angry like Pazazil. I was in control of myself and always had been, really. I had functioned well considering... considering *what*?

Oh, poke at that sore place, Gavensel! The rain, the shattered landscape, the fortress. Dream symbols or literal pictures? What was the worst that could have happened to me in the past? Physical damage, torture, something like what had happened to Grackle? Had I been one of Grackle's sons, bred to kill? Had Melisander found me in a ring of corpses, hara I had slaughtered? Yet how could a soulless murderer turn into the Lady of Shalott?

I went to Har Aquillon submissive. I obeyed his words and wandered my inner landscape looking at potential necklaces on the foliage. I told him I was afraid of the fortress, which wasn't true, and actually I couldn't see it very well that day. I wanted to keep it from Har Aquillon and had drawn a shutter over it. I went into long descriptions of the clouds and sensed the hienama fidgeting.

Realising I should satisfy him in some way, I mentioned malformed shadows at the edge of my vision that were staggering or crawling over the ruins. That sounded suitably gruesome and eerie, something for him to write notes about. As I was giving him the spookiest details I could imagine, I saw the black had manifested in the landscape, just to my right side. At once a needle of pain lanced through my head. I didn't speak about what I saw, simply stared, willing whatever was observing me from the other side to come through. 'Coward!' I said in my vision. The black popped out of existence and the pain flowed away. Had the thing within the black been intimidated by me? I doubted it. Perhaps the manifestation was irrelevant, merely some fragment of information from the past that didn't mean anything.

Before Har Aquillon ended our session I had a clear flashback. Not to the fortress or anything like it, but to Sallow Gandaloi. I remembered a har and his name – Tambril. He'd been the nearest I'd had to a friend and had worked for my brother. There was another with us, but he was a shadow – I suspected it might be my Knight of Doom. I didn't want to poke that part of the recollection too sharply. I needed to observe what was coming to me before it faded. We were walking through the house out into the gardens. The light splashed over me, blinding. The world felt far too big, as if it were a great devouring mouth attached to a bottomless stomach. I was cripplingly nervous, light-headed – and yes, afraid. I realised I never felt like that now. The recollection ended there. Something had changed in me, but only I knew it.

As I went back to my room, I decided there were certain things I must do.

First, I questioned Obery at dinner time. 'Have I changed to you?' I asked.

Obery appeared both furtive and surprised. 'Well, you seem better.'

'That's not what I meant. Tell me the truth.'

He shrugged awkwardly. 'You seem more… *here,*' he said.

'What was I like before?'

'You were somewhere else,' he answered simply.

'Were hara afraid of me?'

Obery squirmed. I empathised with his uneasiness but I had to know. I suppose his reaction was answer enough. 'You were distant, not quite with us,' he said at last.

'Who died?' I demanded.

His eyes went almost as wide as Pazazil's. 'Nohar,' he said awkwardly, 'not that we know of. Please don't ask me about this. It's not my place to answer these questions and your carers won't like it if I do.'

'They're not here. They won't see or hear.'

'You *think*?' Obery said, a more confident tone entering his voice.

I nodded, paused, then said 'Thank you.'

Obery began clearing away my dishes. 'You *are* better,' he said, then leaned closer and whispered to me. 'You were given medicines. That's all I can say.'

He left me then to digest that information along with my dinner.

I waited until well past midnight before making my way to the visiting room. I didn't know whether Grackle would be there, but if he wasn't, I'd find his room and wake him. Yet there he was, lying on a sofa, gazing at the stars. I greeted him and sat down on a chair. He stared at me for a moment. 'What is it, Gavensel?'

'Will you help me?' I asked.

He sat up. 'In what way?'

'What would you do,' I said 'if one of your sons came to you here, and you found out his mind had been damaged by what he'd been made to do?'

'You're not one of my sons,' Grackle said flatly.

'It was a hypothetical question.'

He put his head to one side. 'I'd put my hands upon him in love. I'd breathe over him and blow the badness away.'

That wasn't quite what I'd had in mind. 'How much did you know of the Varrs? Tell me what you remember of the time before you came here.'

'Well, I *was* Varr,' he said. 'When I lived in Megalithica, I knew the names of our leaders, the war leader Terzian and our archon Ponclast. I knew that we were at war with the Gelaming who wanted to take our land and enslave us.'

'But you were enslaved anyway.'

'I *know*. You asked what I remembered and that was what I used to think, what I'd been taught.'

'Did you ever see a huge black fortress in a burned landscape?'

He stuck out his lower lip, shook his head uncertainly.

'This is important, Grackle. Please think about it.'

He sighed. 'Gavensel, I was taken to the homestead when I was very young, before feybraiha. I knew no other life than that, but...' He screwed up his face and was silent for a few moments. 'One of the hara who came to me, who sparked one of my pearls, he liked to talk. Perhaps needed to.'

'And?' I prompted impatiently.

'He talked of a black fortress once. He felt proud to have been there, but I knew that wasn't all of it. He couldn't let himself think what he really felt. I could smell it, though, and it was like carrion. It was like blood running down the drains of the delivery rooms. I'm sorry. I can't remember any more, but I felt sick when he talked about it.'

I nodded. 'Thank you. Now tell me what you see in me.'

He stared. 'I...'

'Is that black fortress in *me*, Grackle?'

He shook his head. 'I don't want to look that closely.'

'I'm not just the Lady of Shalott! I want to find out everything, but not from these hara here. From myself. From a friend... you.'

'Oh, well...'

My instincts had been right. He was pleased I'd referred to him as a friend.

'I *can* look, although I probably shouldn't.'

'That's OK. This is between us and, whatever happens, nohar will hear about it from me.'

He nodded, drew in his breath, then narrowed his eyes, and his gaze became unfocused. I sat with him in silence for over a minute, having to remind myself to breathe.

Grackle drew in his breath. 'Yes,' he said. 'Yes, you were there.'

I let my breath go, as if we were one set of lungs. 'Tell me more.'

'I can't really.' His eyes were still closed. 'I see that place, like a black and white drawing. It is grand and beautiful, yet also dark and horrifying. Bad things happen there. Life means so little. It's a place without love.' He writhed in his seat. 'I don't want to see any more of it...'

'Then stop,' I said.

He shook his head, did not open his eyes, but his brow was

deeply furrowed now. 'Not yet. I can remain where I am, at the threshold. What is this place to you?'

'I see it in my dreams and in my path-working with Har Aquillon, but it's like looking at a painting. I don't know what happened there.'

'Decisions were made,' Grackle said, his voice becoming fainter, 'decisions that affected everyhar. The Varrs... it wasn't just the Gelaming they fought... wanted to eradicate all other tribes. They were like humans... hated what was new about hara. Sought to destroy it. It was like...' His whole face pleated with distress and his voice became louder, harder. 'The tribe was like a bad birth, a deformed thing, a throwback to the old race, all its hatred and greed and bigotry and fear given life in new flesh.' He blinked, came out of the trance abruptly. 'You were created in that fortress.'

'Stop *now*,' I said. 'Really. I've heard enough for the moment, and I think you've seen enough too.'

Grackle sighed. His eyes were red and watering. 'OK, but that last stuff just came to me. I had to tell you. I've broken it now, the link.' He peered at me for a few seconds. 'I think you were much like me. I don't mean a hostling, although it *could* be that. But you had... a purpose.'

'A soldier then...'

Grackle shook his head. 'No... I feel strongly that soldiers weren't bred at the fortress. They came from the homesteads that were created as... well... *har farms*. Your purpose must have been something else.'

'You said I was created there. What did you mean exactly? Born? Conditioned? What?'

Grackle was quiet for a moment, then said, 'It's odd, Gavensel, and I don't want you to read too much into it, because my vision was fragmented, but I got this feeling you weren't made in the way harlings usually are. I don't know why I think that – I simply *feel* it. That place...' He shuddered. 'You *started* there, definitely. That's all I can say.'

I considered what he'd told me, then said, 'I want to know

everything, yet there's a danger… I might be a monster, kept in a tower of ignorance for a good reason.'

'Yes, that's possible,' Grackle said. 'But the truth might be better than a half-life. I *feel* there is – or could be – a good future for you. You're strong enough to step up out of the ruins. I'll never do that.'

'I think you already have,' I said. 'You're still what you were raised to be, that's for sure, but through your own choice. Except now your offspring are great hulking anomalies like Pazazil and me. You bring light. You *are* nourishment. I've felt it.'

Grackle laughed. 'Thanks, if that's a compliment.'

'It is.'

'Neither of you could be described as great and hulking, though.'

'OK, *lurching*, then.' I went to sit beside him and he leaned against me. That felt strange because I rarely touched anyhar, but I didn't pull away.

'You don't lurch, you glide,' Grackle said softly, 'like a pale ghost, and yet you are so strong and *real*.'

'Listen, Grackle,' I said, more to break his train of thought than to express my own, 'you said the Varrs were monstrous, but you were Varr, as were all those other hostlings you lived with. You weren't monsters, and I'm sure most other Varrs weren't. They were just ordinary, trying to survive. The leaders were at fault, surely?'

'I know. I didn't mean… the words just came. Varr as a *thing* was what I meant, like an entity in itself.' He stroked my arm. 'And the fact you can think like that means you're not a monster either.'

I hoped that to be true.

Over the next couple of weeks, my dreams of the fortress continued. Nothing ever happened, other than me walking through that landscape. I always woke before I could reach the fortress itself. The black portal did not reappear. Then one night I awoke to see a har standing in my room. He was close against the wall, in a corner, pale and thin, staring at me. He looked sick. I was aware of a high-pitched whistling in my head and the dart of pain slit through me again.

'What are you doing here?' I demanded and he shrank away from me. 'Don't be afraid.'

I got out of bed and put on my robe, meaning to guide this lost har back to where he'd come from, imagining he was another guest of Reveriel. But as I drew near to him, I saw that his hair, which was as long as mine, rose vertically from his head, like weed under water. He glowed a little, the detail of him slightly blurred.

'Are you a ghost?' I asked him. 'Are you a dream?'

Tentatively, he put out a hand to me, his eyes beseeching.

'It's all right,' I murmured. 'You're safe. Let me help you.' I reached out to touch him, but he shook his head sadly and sank backwards through the wall.

The next night, there were three of them, and they weren't standing in a corner. They were hanging from the ceiling by their hair and were beyond staring at me, or doing anything else.

Spirit of Vitriol

In the morning, I went looking for Grackle and found him eating his breakfast at the round wooden table on the jade-marble terrace beyond the sitting room. There were five pinewood chairs around the table, and it had become our habit to meet there every day to talk or eat our meals. Pazazil had begun to join us more often, perhaps because he was becoming used to me.

I sat down opposite Grackle. 'Listen to this,' I said.

About half-way through my account, Pazazil sauntered out to join us. I stopped speaking, but clearly he'd heard enough already.

'Those hanging hara are from your black fortress,' he said, standing behind Grackle to pick up a partly-eaten bread roll from his plate. Pazazil tore the roll in two and stuffed half into his mouth. 'Would put money on that.' Wet breadcrumbs sprayed the table.

I stared hard and meaningfully at Grackle.

He shrugged, blushed a little. 'I'm sorry... I tell him everything.'

'I didn't think you were interested,' I said coldly to Pazazil.

'Oh, I'm interested enough.' He sat down and grinned at me. 'I just don't *care*.' After a silence he said, 'Well, everyhar likes a good ghost story.'

I drew in my breath, resigned to tolerate his presence. 'I don't think they're ghosts,' I said, 'more like... reminders. *Bookmarks*. Do you know of this fortress, Pazazil?'

He shrugged. 'No. I'm not from Megalithica. I collected my madness elsewhere.'

I realised at this point it would have been useful to keep my carers abreast of what I'd been experiencing, because they might know more of Megalithica than Grackle and Pazazil could tell me. There might also be other residents of Reveriel who'd been there and experienced first-hand what I dreamed about.

That afternoon with Har Aquillon I decided to be blunt. As I settled myself on the cushions, I noticed him yawn, and then wondered about his life, what he did when he wasn't working. He had friends, a home, perhaps a family. He had opinions and preferences. He was not a cypher, and I must appeal to the side of him he left at home every day.

'Typhis?' I said.

He was as usual sitting on a chair, so was slightly higher than me. Now he glanced down, almost furtively. I never addressed him by his first name. 'What is it, Gavensel?'

'The fortress I see in dreams and visions is real. I think I must go there.'

His eyes widened. 'Might I ask why and how you came to this decision?'

I realised then I must break a promise. 'As you must know, Grackle is extremely sensitive. I asked him to look into me and he said the place was real. I believe him, so I suppose it's all a question of whether you do.'

Har Aquillon adopted a stern expression. 'Gavensel, that was irresponsible. Guests here should not experiment in that way. Remember that Grackle too has…'

'Oh, be quiet!' I said, in a low, even voice. I sat up. 'We both know there's not much wrong with Grackle now. He's still here because he's useful to you. I expect there have been others before *me* he's looked into.'

Har Aquillon drew in a long breath through his nose. 'What I meant was that whatever lies hidden in that fortress might be too much for Grackle to bear. You must be aware of that.'

'Yes. But I made him stop when he became uncomfortable.' There was a silence. 'Well?'

The hienama didn't answer immediately and I realised with a genuine jolt of shock that he knew *exactly* what my fortress was. I could smell this truth pouring from him. I could see the veil across his eyes. When I was lying down, walking along those inner paths, I never saw his face. Now, I could.

He crossed his legs, smoothed the fabric of his robe. 'I think it would be better if you discovered this place's true nature for yourself before confronting it in reality.'

'Perhaps I should call its ghosts through more forcefully,' I said. 'Shall we do that today?'

'Its ghosts?'

'I've seen several of them in my room at night, also what appears to be a black portal.'

Har Aquillon didn't hide his displeasure; his tone became sharper. 'Why haven't you told me or Tiahaar Blansie this?'

I shrugged. 'I didn't consider it necessary, then.'

He made a gesture with both hands. 'But we're your carers. We're trying to help you. Don't you trust us?'

'It's not a question of trust,' I said. 'I had my own thinking to do. Now I've told you. As I've been truthful to you, will you grant me the same courtesy?'

He opened his mouth a little, filtering his words before he spoke.

I sighed impatiently. 'Please don't fabricate some meaningless response, Typhis. You *know* what I see in my dreams. Just tell me.'

'It is Fulminir,' he said.

I took the word into me, tasted it, experienced it. There was a familiarity to its shape but no immediate unlocking of doors. 'Tell me about it. Don't worry, I'm not as frail as I look. This is my camouflage. I'd have thought you'd have realised that before.'

Har Aquillon stared at me for some seconds. 'Very well. Fulminir was the seat of the Varrish leaders back in the days following the Devastation. Part of it had been constructed by humans as a military facility, but Ponclast, the Varr archon, embellished the original buildings. It became a symbol of his power, a dark beacon, if you like.'

'A *black fortress*,' I said. 'Do you know my connection with it?'

Har Aquillon didn't hesitate. 'Your brother told us he found you there, during the fall of Fulminir, when the Gelaming besieged it.'

'He's Gelaming, then?' The idea somehow appalled me, as if Melisander had told me a terrible lie.

Har Aquillon shook his head. 'Melisander belonged to a phyle of the Varrs that defected to the Gelaming and was recruited into their army. He has never, as far as I know, been officially affiliated to any tribe since, although would be able to call himself Gelaming, should he wish or need to. In any case, Melisander was present at Fulminir as part of the Gelaming assault force, and rescued you, believing you to be a slave.'

'I see.' I pondered these words. Why couldn't I remember that? Being rescued from slavery in a black fortress didn't seem a thing so terrible it must be hidden from my conscious mind. 'Typhis, Grackle had more to say. He had the suspicion I wasn't created in the way a harling normally would be. Do you know about this too?'

Har Aquillon straightened up in his chair. 'No. What else did he say?'

'He couldn't divine any more than that. I can't decide what it means.'

'Harlings can only be created one way,' Har Aquillon said. 'Two hara – one to host and one to spark. Perhaps what Grackle picked up on was the Varrs' foul tendency to brutalise other hara.' He frowned, then sighed through his nose. 'We wanted to believe harlings could only be made by enlightened hara, in spiritual love. What we found after the Varrs were vanquished informed us otherwise. Harlings can be created through violation. It's not a pleasant thought, Gavensel, but I think you might have to accept that's the case with your conception.'

'I see.'

Har Aquillon leaned towards me a little. 'Please tell me what you're feeling and thinking.'

'I'm not sure. I'm searching for thoughts and feelings, if you must know. I don't feel much at all.' I frowned. 'Why was the information you *did* have kept from me?'

'Even Melisander doesn't know what you went through in Fulminir,' Har Aquillon said smoothly. 'But there *was* fallout. With...'

'What do you mean, *fallout*?' I interrupted.

'Your behaviour was erratic,' Har Aquillon replied. 'Sometimes you became manic.'

'Which Melisander attempted to control with medicines.'

Har Aquillon nodded, made a gesture. 'Well, he's an alchemist, isn't he? That would have seemed to him the best way. Anyway, I was going to say, with hindsight, Melisander now accepts he should have handed you to the Gelaming at Fulminir, but for whatever reason he decided to try and help you himself. He wasn't trained to deal with such a situation. He might've made things worse, without realising it.'

'Perhaps he didn't want me to spend my life in a place like this,' I said bitterly.

Har Aquillon raised his brows. 'Are you unhappy or uncomfortable here?' he asked.

'It's very nice,' I said, 'but it's still a house of lunatics, isn't it? Can I just walk out of here now and go into town, get a job, rent a nice apartment by the ocean?'

Har Aquillon leaned back in his seat. 'So... tell me, Gavensel. Tell me why you think you're here.'

I stared at him. 'Obviously, I killed somehar. I'm dangerous, and perhaps the worst sort of dangerous in that I look pathetically weak.'

He twitched a smile. 'That is *animal* camouflage, isn't it? Extremely effective for a predator.'

'I meant it, and you make fun.'

He looked contrite, yet was still smiling. 'I'm sorry, that was in poor taste. Perhaps I'm not as observant as I like to think.'

I drew in a breath, then asked, 'You must tell me now, Typhis. *Did* I kill somehar?'

He didn't react physically to this, and his voice remained even. 'You seem obsessed with this idea. What do you think?'

'I'm asking *you*, because you know the answer.'

'There's no concrete evidence to suggest such a thing.'

'That's an evasive reply.'

His expression was gentle. 'That's the way it has to be, Gavensel. You're here to remember, not to be told. I'm not being obtuse on purpose. My only aim is to help you heal.'

I thought for a few moments. 'The evidence is I had some kind of *episode*, after which I was unconscious and remained so for quite some time. From what I've learned, I think this must mean I became manic, perhaps violent, despite whatever tranquillising philtres Melisander was giving me. I want to know what triggered that mania. There must be a trigger, because the har I think myself to be couldn't harm anyhar or any*thing*.' I got to my feet, went to sit in the only other chair in the room, my back to the window. Har Aquillon wouldn't be able to see my face that well now. 'You tell *me* why I'm here. Tell me why Melisander had to accept he couldn't help me anymore.'

Har Aquillon laced his hands in his lap, put his head to one side. 'As I said, you must remember that yourself,' he said. 'I'm here merely to guide you.'

'Then we begin with the ghosts,' I said. 'Today we go into the fortress.'

Har Aquillon considered. 'All right. But take things slowly. We don't want a breakthrough to become a breakdown. Retreat the moment you feel discomfort.'

I couldn't imagine *not* feeling discomfort entering that place but agreed to his condition.

I slipped into a meditative state quickly, as if my mind was now eager to confront whatever was buried alive within. As usual, the sky above the fortress was dark and thunderous, stitched with skeins of lightning. This time, there was no rain, only the heaviness of it, unshed. I stood facing the fortress from perhaps two hundred yards away. The landscape was desolate; I could feel its memories pressing upon me like an insistent hand.

Stop hiding from me, I told the secrets within the landscape. *I'm here to see.*

In an instant, I was in the midst of a crowd, and was for some moments disorientated and dizzy. I struggled to the side of the road, leaned upon the wall of a half-fallen house. This was too real. I had to regulate my breathing as I would in reality. Soon, I was calm enough to carry on.

Gleaming black horses, bearing Varrish warriors, trotted heavily up and down the ghost road, which now looked new, whole. Sitting erect on their mounts, the Varrs were grim-faced and neatly attired in black leather armour, embellished with silver.

There were high-sided carts upon the road too, hauled by mules, laden with produce – vegetables, slaughtered meat, logs and planks of wood. The sky wasn't as dramatically gloomy as I was used to, but still overcast. The road was lined by dwellings, reclaimed human buildings, scorched with spiny graffiti. Hara were engaged in mundane tasks all around me, costumed like actors to appear fierce and tribal. None appeared to notice me.

I walked up to the monstrous arch that led into the fortress. Spikes gored down from it like fangs. There were corpses hanging upon the walls to either side of that hungry maw, whether human or hara I could not tell, for they were partly devoured: crows clustered thickly upon them. A faint carrion stench was eclipsed by the smoke from immense braziers upon which aromatic woods and resins were being burned.

Hara who looked like primitive hienamas were tending these censers; they were dressed in torn, diaphanous robes and – in this respect, *unlike* hienamas – yelled lascivious greetings at the passing warriors, who ignored them. The hienamas wore cosmetics on their faces, but in an exaggerated way. Their skins were powdered dead white; smears of thick soot plastered around their eyes, their lips daubed with deep crimson paint that turned their mouths to bloody gashes. On those whose chests were bare, black circles were painted, perhaps to imitate female breasts. I knew then, could remember it almost, that this was how the early Varrs dealt with their soume aspect – made a parody of it, a caricature of femininity.

The inner courtyard was packed with hara and haphazardly placed stalls, hara behind them selling produce of many different kinds, although the majority of them were heaped with scavenged items from the ravaged human cities. The hara who filled this area were gaudily yet brutally decorated, their skins pierced with spikes and rings, their faces made to look like skulls or demon masks. These were not Varrs – I could remember that too. They were Uigenna, vassals of the Varrs. They clustered in swaggering groups, and sometimes squabbles broke out among them, and there'd be a brief eruption of violence, accompanied by screeching that sounded like eagles. Once, an arc of blood splashed against the awning of a stall.

I passed beneath another arch into the interior of the fortress itself and crossed a vast, high-ceilinged chamber, its air heavy with smoke from burning sconces on the walls. The floor was of dark flag-stones, greasy underfoot, yet in places covered by reed matting. This space was also filled with hara, apparently from several different tribes. There were sandy-robed Kakkahaar with hair to their knees, weaving illusions for fascinated onlookers. Slithering Colurastes with shifting, serpent locks, wound through the crowd, attempting to appear mysterious and dangerous. I even saw representatives of the Sulh, dressed in black robes, some with their faces hidden behind masks of coins and shells and peculiar head-dresses of sticks and feathers.

This eclectic gathering comprised Ponclast's minions and accomplices. He shunned all that was soume within himself, banned it in his warriors, yet delved into magic, gathered to him hara adept in its disciplines, who themselves were not sexually sundered, who were whole not halved. I knew – I suppose *remembered* – the hostlings of the Varrs did not frequent these public areas of Fulminir. They were hidden away, performing their function in private; that is, enduring the Varrs' efforts to learn how to breed and, when this was successful, to bear the pearls and care for the harlings who came from them.

I could remember fragments now, but nothing personal. Had this chaotic heart of Varrish rule been my home? I couldn't yet imagine it.

The fortress was a warren, a labyrinth, a hive. It was constructed entirely of black stone, its walls hung with the huge war banners of the Varrs, from which crudely-drawn white eyes stared and painted skulls leered – not harish eyes or skulls but stylised designed that were suggestively demonic. Across the entrance hall was a wide staircase. The stairs were thoroughfares, hara trailing up and down in endless streams. Some were accompanied by animals – hawks or kestrels on their leathered arms, cougars and hounds at their sides. One har who passed me appeared to be covered in bees.

I climbed to the first floor, and here there were boards of polished wood underfoot, stained black. A vast mezzanine held yet more crowds that milled amid entertainers, magicians and scryers. I had the feeling that Fulminir went on forever, and if you tried to explore every corner you would keep finding new stairways, new corridors, new rooms, perhaps even a forest or a cave at its core.

But the heart, of course, was a throne room, which was Ponclast's chamber of audience. This was in the centre of the complex on the second floor. I was drawn inexorably to it, and passed between its towering open doors. Here, fields of rugs were strewn, woven of wool and silk in deep, jewel hues. There was no furniture, but for the imposing basalt throne at the far end, carved with stylised wolves and eagles, and an immense fireplace on the right hand wall, where flames gulped ravenously at felled trees. The cavernous room before me was empty, but for a small group of hara standing around the throne, where nohar sat.

I drew closer, saw him then, taller than the others, his black hair hacked short: Ponclast, leaders of Varrs. I *knew* him, recognised him, but not from his appearance. His features were fine, which surprised me, but there was no softness to him. He smouldered with repressed and mangled impulses, a slowly-incandescing volcano that would one day erupt and *destroy* everything. He talked in a low voice with the hara around him, some of them military leaders, I assumed, and a smattering of sycophants from other tribes seeking his favour and, through this, protection from his brutality. I walked right up to him, to his side, could hear the creak of his leather armour. He was far taller than me. He smelled of the outside, of smoke and crushed leaves, and faintly of blood. He could not, or would not, see me, so I extended a tendril of myself, an etheric limb, and reached inside him, touched him in a place he refused to acknowledge. I saw him flinch, glance furtively around himself.

You can't see me, but perhaps you can hear me, I sent to him in mind touch.

His self-control was so strong he was able to maintain the appearance of conversation with the others, while asking me: *What are you?*

A har. I was made here.

Ponclast did not respond to this, but after a few moments, he said to his companions, 'You must excuse me for a few minutes, Tiahaara.' To me, he sent a silent command: *Follow.*

We left the towering chamber, passing into one of the anterooms behind the throne. Here, the air smelled nuttily musty, of old wood, and there stood a table spread with maps and other documents. Ponclast leaned against the table, folded his arms. 'Well then, show yourself, harling of Fulminir.'

'I am showing myself,' I said aloud, 'but perhaps you just can't see me.'

'What is your business with me?'

'To discover my origins.'

He frowned. 'Were you abducted, or are you dead, a ghost without memories?'

'I'm not dead. I'm in trance somewhere else, somewhere in

the future. In my time, this place, the heart of your empire, is only a ruin.'

His nostrils flared. 'Indeed. I think it's more likely you were sent by my enemies to unsettle me.' He laughed. 'Pathetic Gelaming ploy. Do you think me so stupid? A bodiless voice uttering dooms!'

'It doesn't matter whether you believe me or not. I'd like a question answered. Are you amenable?'

'You must know that depends on the question.'

'Naturally. I am pureborn, but not in the usual way. I believe I was *created* here, for a purpose. Could this be true?'

Ponclast squinted at the place where I was standing, where my voice was coming from. 'My enemies would give much to learn the answer to a question like that.'

'You no longer have enemies,' I said. 'In fact, at the present moment, I'm being treated in a Gelaming infirmary. What I was created for means little to them now, but it means a lot to me. I need to know, because so much is hidden within me.'

'Come with me,' he said.

He left the room by another exit, so as not to re-enter the great hall. He led me back to the mezzanine on the first floor, hara parting ahead of him like mist before a flame. Eventually, he came to a har who was conjuring coloured sparks and smokes in the air, along with exclamations from spectators. Ponclast said, 'Azvith, here! Now!'

The har, a Kakkahaar by the looks of his enveloping sand-coloured robe, obeyed. He bowed. 'Lord,' he said in an unctuous voice, with a tone of smothered contempt. Perhaps he was a prisoner here.

'Come!' Ponclast snapped, and led us to a secluded place, a balcony that hung from the outer wall, where an acrid wind blew.

'An entity is with me, or claims to be,' Ponclast said coldly to the Kakkahaar. 'Perceive it, if you'd be so kind.'

The Kakkahaar looked at me, for a moment blankly, then wove a series of symbols on the air, which apparently revealed me to him. 'Yes,' he said. 'There *is* a har's essence at your side.'

'What is he? Gelaming sent?'

'Varrish,' the Kakkahaar replied. 'He has not been sent. He's visiting of his own accord.' The har paused, then spoke, again with that edgy tone: part envy, part disdain. 'He is an offspring of yours, I believe.'

This information was an unpleasant shock to me, but I remained quiet.

Ponclast drew in his breath impatiently. 'Make him visible to me.'

'That is hardly down to me,' the Kakkahaar protested mildly.

'May I speak with *you*?' I asked the Kakkahaar.

The har flicked a glance at Ponclast, who nodded once.

'What was the intention of my creation?'

'That's difficult to say for sure, Spirit,' said the Kakkahaar, 'since you don't yet exist. Let me explain something to you. Your sire has many allies, and some of them are wise. In their transformation from the base pattern – humanity – secrets of the past were revealed to them. My kind were given the faculty to relearn ancient knowledge that humanity had forgotten. With our help, His Greatness, Lord Ponclast, will enhance the Varrs to be superior. He will meld the essences of the tribes to create the best of all.'

I felt he was trying to imply something to me clandestinely in that little speech. 'I was bred to be a warrior?' I asked.

The Kakkahaar paused for a moment, narrowed his eyes. 'Ah. I see now. Yes. You were *conceived* in a har, Spirit, but did not grow in him. As for your purpose, it's sound to assume you were made for war.'

'What do you mean, not grown in a har?' Ponclast said. 'Explain.'

Again, the Kakkahaar bowed to him. 'Be patient, Lord. What this manifestation means is that you will achieve success in your endeavours.'

'Yet he spoke to me of Fulminir in ruins.'

'Perhaps your seat of power will change,' the Kakkahaar said carefully. 'Immanion, maybe?'

Ponclast stared, his eyes unfocused, clearly mulling over this choice thought. Then he nodded. 'Then the direction we must take is the creation of harlings in a new way, as this ghost suggests. Start work on it, Azvith! Give it your full attention. Make it real.'

These words jolted me from my trance, and this had to be a blessing because I didn't want that monster to learn any more from me. I opened my eyes to the tranquil ambience of the helrumian, my flesh chilled to ice, even in that balmy Almagabran air. Had I, through an impulsive craving to know the truth, created myself? I lay gasping on the cushions, barely able to suck air into my lungs, so that Har Aquillon was moved to kneel beside me, put a hand upon my shoulder. 'Gavensel, breathe deeply,' he said softly. I felt the heat of healing energy pouring from his palm. 'Breathe with me,' he said.

It took several minutes for me to feel normal again.

Har Aquillon summoned a halian to bring me hot tea, that most basic yet effective of restorative fluids. As I sat sipping it, he asked me, 'Are you able now to speak of what you learned?'

I nodded. 'Yes. Ponclast sired me.' I wondered whether this would change Har Aquillon's opinion of me, but he appeared to pick up this thought and appeared only to be interested by this news, not disgusted.

'That might explain how you could speak with him so easily in trance. Tell me all that you saw.'

He wrote notes all the time I was speaking, becoming visibly excited by the detail of my recollections. At the end of it, he said, 'This is astounding. It's possible your essence actually went back there, didn't simply visualise the past.'

'I don't know. It *felt* real.'

'Well, we must continue when you feel strong enough.'

'Tomorrow,' I said.

Har Aquillon pursed his lips. 'No, leave it three days,

Gavensel. Assimilate what you've learned. Don't push yourself too hard.'

I opened my mouth to protest but Har Aquillon silenced me before a single sound came out.

'I mean it. And no delving around on your own. What you've experienced isn't just a dream, Gavensel. You might be hurt – physically. We can't take that risk. I understand your eagerness, but please be sensible, and patient.'

'All right. I'll wait.'

'Write it all down, before the memory fades.' He smiled. 'We've made real progress today.'

Ens Veneris

I had promised Grackle and Pazazil I would tell them what happened that afternoon, but couldn't face it. I needed to be alone. The evening came in on blue wings of cloud. The moon was dark. I began to write up the experiences of the afternoon, but the words seemed flat, barely describing all I'd felt and seen. The fact I was related to Ponclast so closely was horrible. Was it any wonder then that dark urges might lurk inside me? I wondered whether I had ever ridden at Ponclast's side, fought hara, been as brutal and cruel as he had been. I could sense now another har inside me, the one with the memories. Or was it even a har?

Something slithered like a great serpent deep within my mind, and I was scared it might be aware I was remembering things. I tried not to think about it, but this simply made the impressions stronger. Sallow Gandaloi, and what had happened to me there, was the key. I was haunted by the idea that an earlier version of me had forced its way up through the layers of my sealed memories and had pushed me aside, rendered me senseless. This idea refused to be dismissed, no matter how hard I tried to conjure other explanations. I didn't want it to be true. I couldn't bear the thought that the Lady of Shalott could be something worse than a simple murderer.

Obery brought me a light meal around seven o'clock. I could barely eat, picked at the food, which was tasteless to me. I knew Obery noticed my unease, but he didn't say anything and didn't remain with me for long. Alone once more, I craved the outside, the air, the night sounds, but didn't want to come across my fellow guests. If only there was some other place to go.

I sat on the bed to finish my notes. I was annoyed that the words didn't sing how I liked them to, but I knew Har Aquillon was right and that the bare facts should be recorded before my memory faded. *Ponclast's blood in my veins...* I wrote that sentence down dozens of times but could not draw its sting.

A couple of hours after Obery had removed my mostly untouched meal, somehar came to my room. I'd shut the door, which we rarely do. They knocked – several times. This couldn't be a physician or a halian; they would knock once and walk in.

'Gavensel!'

It was Pazazil.

I put my notebook beneath the bed and went to stand on my side of the door. 'Not now,' I said.

'I want to come in.'

'Why?'

'Tell me what happened.'

'Is Grackle with you?'

'No.'

I realised I wanted to talk to somehar now, and decided Pazazil's caustic nature would be more bearable than Grackle's smothering concern. I opened the door and looked out. 'I know its name,' I said, 'the fortress is Fulminir.'

Pazazil stared at me with his round, feral eyes. 'They told you?'

'Yes. It's a ruin now.'

Pazazil put his hands upon my shoulders and pushed me backwards into the room, slowly, carefully, like moving something on wheels. 'By all means, come in,' I said.

He stared at me, still holding onto my shoulders.

'Let go, or there'll be trouble,' I said, in a flat voice.

'Probably.' He took my face in his hands and kissed me.

I stood rigid, unsure how to react. I remembered, then, once asking my friend Tambril how hara shared breath, because I didn't know how it was done. Pazazil gave me no breath, no intimate visions, only his living warmth. This was not unpleasant.

He pulled away from me. 'You see – no invasion, no sharing. It's quite safe.'

'You've been practicing,' I said and backed away from him. 'That was rather presumptuous of you.'

He shrugged. 'Couldn't resist it, sorry. I wondered what it would be like.'

'Stimulating, as you discovered.' I sat down on my bed. 'Do you want to know what I found out, or not?'

'Sure.' He sat down on a floor cushion, looking up at me.

'I was found in Fulminir, a long time ago.' I pondered for a moment. 'That means of course, I must be quite old. This afternoon, I actually visited the place in trance, went back in time.'

Pazazil pantomimed shock. 'Seriously?'

'Yes, I spoke with Ponclast, saw Fulminir. If it *was* merely a vision, it was incredibly realistic.'

'What was it like?'

I told him as much as I could remember but left out anything concerning my own creation and connection with Ponclast. I wasn't ready to reveal that to anyhar else.

'If your experience wasn't real, that was unbelievably sharp memory,' Pazazil said.

I was relieved he was prepared to believe me and didn't scoff. 'It couldn't just be memory, though, could it? I spoke with hara as me, not an earlier self.'

Pazazil stuck out his lower lip. 'True... If so, that's incredible.'

I nodded. 'Yes, I know. I've never experienced anything like it... that I can remember. I was Varr, Pazazil. I lived in Fulminir, the fortress of the archon, Ponclast.'

'Even I've heard of *him*,' Pazazil said. 'Remembered fondly as a murderous lunatic, I believe?'

I grimaced. 'Yes. I'd like to say that was Gelaming propaganda, but it wasn't. What I've learned is that Ponclast saw Wraeththu as an abomination, the curse of humanity's folly, not a cure for it. He couldn't allow himself to be whole. He separated his hara into genders, or tried to. His idea of evolution was... different.'

'Would never have worked,' Pazazil said. 'Once the pureborns came, with their clear minds.'

There was a silence, then I dared to say: 'Can I ask – are you pureborn?'

'No.' Pazazil scowled. 'I'm stunted… like you.'

'Thank you.'

He shrugged. 'No offence. Hara like us are obsolete. We were merely mechanisms to get the whole thing going.'

'Interesting way to look at it.'

'But probably correct.'

I took in a breath. 'Pazazil, I *am* pureborn, but perhaps not in a natural way.'

He raised his brows. 'What do you mean?'

'I think it's likely I was *made* differently, perhaps not conceived in the manner harlings usually are.'

Pazazil thought over this implausible idea for a moment. 'Maybe you came from somehar like Grackle.'

I dragged my hands through my hair. 'It doesn't feel quite like that. I can't explain…'

Pazazil's eyes were narrowed. 'But the Gelaming must *know*, surely? They went over the Varrish sites in Megalithica methodically.'

'How do you know that?'

He grinned. 'I'm not *entirely* without education. Besides, they did that in my country too.'

I sighed. 'They do know a lot, but Har Aquillon insists I rediscover my memories rather than hear it all from him. I see his point. There's a reason I locked it all away. It was bad. His concern is whether I'm ready yet to find out.'

Pazazil pulled a face. 'What's the worst that can happen?'

'Something I feel very strongly – losing my reason, becoming something else. I can imagine it, almost *remember* it. I'm afraid I might not come back from that. Maybe it's some freakish kind of psychic inception, and once it's turned on, my purpose is revealed. I rise up and roar and devour the world.'

Pazazil laughed at what he no doubt thought was the

absurdity of that idea.

'How long have you been here?' I asked sharply.

He shrugged. 'A couple of years, maybe. Can't remember.'

'How did you end up here?'

He looked away from me, picked at the embroidery on the cushion beneath him. 'The reason anyhar does. The brokenness becomes inconvenient to others. Where I lived...' He took a breath, looked me in the eye once more. 'It took some time for anything like civilisation to grow anew. I was in the midst of factions at war, preserving the legacy of the past. We were God's vengeance on the world, his army. None of us cared if we lived or died. No longer human – merely *things*. We were simply muscles of the tribe, limbs to carry it about, organs to keep it healthy. Wait...' He put his head to one side. 'Since when did this become *my* therapy session?'

'It's not,' I said. 'I'm simply trying to view the whole in context, that's all. How I fit into things.'

'From what I know of the Varrs, I imagine your creation and life in that fortress were more *civilised* than what I experienced. Ponclast at least had a vision. He created order, of a sort.'

'I suppose the Gelaming came and found you,' I said.

He nodded. 'Them and their allies. Not all hara in my part of the world were like us. Some were more like the Gelaming, a tribe known as the Obliviata. When it became possible, that is when communication opened up again between countries, they sought aid to bring peace to their lands. Their inexorable compassion dismantled the limbs and organs of tribes like mine. Now I'm a muscle without a body.' He grinned, then sobered. 'I remember it all, Gavensel. You remember nothing. I envy you that, and wonder now whether clawing through the debris to haul those dead memories out is the right thing to do.'

'It's probably not,' I said, 'but it's the *only* thing to do. Maybe some of us aren't meant to find peace.'

'Perhaps not, but we can find islands sometimes, where peace lives for an hour.' He fell silent and this hung between us for several moments. Then he gave me a strange kind of stare.

'Let's roon, Gavensel, find that kind of island.'

I blinked at him, astounded he could be so direct. I'd given him no signals. 'What? I don't think I ever have. It might be dangerous.'

'I doubt it. On all counts. You can't *remember* anything. If you don't do it with me, eventually they'll send a halian to you, because aruna is healing, but that's like rooning a stuffed toy. Really.'

I knew the idea was hazardous, because alarms were tingling in every cell. Small tongues of lightning flickered in my head, flashes of images. But maybe this was the only way – grasp a head of the hydra, hope the others wouldn't bite too hard. I got down from the bed and knelt in front of him. 'All right. But be alert... Don't let down your guard...'

He shook his head. 'I never do.'

'What did they call you?' I asked. '...those you were close to. Pazazil is a long word to take to bed.'

'Zil,' he answered. 'And you?'

'Ven.'

I wanted to observe, so was submissive to him. I felt this was the best way to remain in control. He wept, but didn't realise I saw. I had wanted this closeness once... with somehar. My Knight of Doom presumably. I remembered I'd asked Tambril obliquely to show aruna to me, but he'd recoiled, pretended he hadn't understood. Only the broken can bear to touch the broken. The expression in Tambril's eyes had appalled me. Not even disgust, something worse. Yet here was this har, tangled up in me, weeping into my shoulder because I'd agreed to our intimacy.

He whispered to me, 'Don't let go. Keep it physical, then the demons can't scratch through.'

My body didn't object to this procedure; the sensations were pleasant. And yet I was detached. The observer within me was calm; there was no danger. I could sense the island Zil had spoken of – beautiful, tranquil, even the air was soporific.

Moving in harmony with him was like walking along the edge of a perfect shore, warm wavelets sizzling over our feet. Eventually, of course, things became less controlled and I suppose I did let go to some degree, uttering cries, trying to ride the crest of the tsunami that plundered through my flesh. The island was drowned, and as the tide receded, all we could do was gasp for breath, surprised to find ourselves alive.

I didn't want more that night. The experience had been at once shattering and enlightening. I would never see Pazazil in the same way again. And it seemed my fears had been groundless. I could have *this* – what all other hara had. I was normal in this respect. He lay beside me, drowsing, and I leaned on my elbow, supporting my head on my hand, watching him. His skin, dark, but not black like Melisander's, more the colour of polished oak. I could imagine him adorned with a wide collar of gold and lapis lazuli, his eyes outlined with kohl – a king. He ruled a hot, ancient land where lions haunted the desert, lions who were gods. In this bubble of time, we were like any other hara, caught in the tail of a dream, languorous and content.

The following day, a halian named Tarice, who had become my regular healer, came to me after breakfast and massaged my body with his impersonal yet expert touch. He told me my energy felt far healthier. 'What have you been up to?' he asked lightly. Despite what Pazazil had implied, I wasn't sure whether I was supposed to take aruna with my fellow guests, so didn't say anything about that.

I met the others – who I must now refer to as friends, I suppose – for lunch on our terrace. I was surprised by the hunger that ignited within me at the sight of Pazazil. I enjoyed the simmering glances we exchanged, the secret smiles. I repeated some of my story to Grackle, who then chattered on, as he always did. I'm not sure if he sensed what crackled between Pazazil and me. I was due to see Har Aquillon that afternoon, but before I went to his helrumian I dragged Pazazil in among the drapes at the sitting-room windows. He became Zil again, then, *mine*. Enfolded in gauzy cloth, I sought to devour him with a kiss. Such appetite; it was astounding. Perhaps my body was making up for lost time.

'Later,' he said to me, nipping my neck.

'I'll come to you.'

He grinned, kissed me briefly. 'OK.'

I composed myself as best I could and went to my hienama.

Like Tarice, Har Aquillon noticed a change in me, but didn't for one moment intuit the cause. 'We're on the right road,' he said. 'You were wise to initiate the process yesterday. Thank you for that.' He laughed. 'But this is what we do here – work together. It's just I'm not used to seeing such remarkable results so swiftly.'

'Does this mean I'll be out of here soon?' I asked, only half meaning it.

'I can't say, but it does mean there's progress. There might be bumps in the road ahead, so let's be cautious. Your core energy has been vitalised, Gavensel, far more than before.'

I smiled. 'So the stagnant pool has become a bubbling spring.'

He nodded. 'You are growing. I have an opinion if you'd care to hear it – my own, not official.'

'Tell me.'

'I think that when Melisander found you, there had been a shutdown of some kind within you. He deduced that himself, of course. But whatever the real you was – and is – it was hidden beneath layers of defences in your mind, particularly the dominant personality you fabricated as a survival mechanism. This much is part of your case history. Some might consider part of you is gone forever, irrecoverable, damaged beyond repair. Our aim here is to help hara in that condition to recreate themselves, so they're able to function in the outside world. They make themselves anew, with our help, into a har that doesn't need the parts they have lost. What emerges from

Reveriel might not be the same har who walked into it.'

'That sounds… a little sinister,' I said.

Har Aquillon nodded. 'I understand why you think that, but we've had horrific cases here over the years. For some, it's the only option – a patching up, a…' He raised his arms expressively. '…a broken machine that's somehow made to work.' He smiled, with real sincerity. 'You'll be pleased to know I don't think that's the option for you. I believe what we're doing now, in our sessions, is more like clearing an overgrown garden of rubble and weeds. I don't think you're lost. ' He raised a hand. 'But that's not official, not yet. Har Blansie will sit in on your next pathworking session. I want him to see for himself.'

'So, in your opinion, I'll eventually have a life like any other har?'

'I don't want to raise your hopes too high but at this moment I think there's a strong likelihood that will be the case.'

I sat for some moments in silence – no doubt Har Aquillon thought I was mulling over his words. In fact, the first thing I thought about was Pazazil. Could we have a proper relationship and one day walk out of Reveriel together? Was this the magic I'd sensed waiting for me here? 'Thank you for telling me your thoughts, Typhis,' I said. 'It's encouraging.'

In fact, Har Aquillon appeared to be more excited and pleased than I was.

For the next few days, I spent most of my time with Pazazil. I craved his presence, not just his body and a physical connection between us, but the whole of him. This wasn't simply the product of emotion, but something else. We were like food to one another. During this time, I shrank from taking any active role in aruna, and couldn't decide exactly why I felt that way. There was a sense within me of the uncanny stillness that reigns before a storm erupts, a stillness that is oppressive. An instinct within me wanted me to remain passive until I'd faced the storm, walked through it. I knew Fulminir still had much to show me. The third day came too soon, and yet I was relieved when it arrived.

Lunafaction

When I reached the helrumian that afternoon, I found both Har Aquillon and Har Blansie there, the latter asking immediately if I was happy for him to be present; I gave my consent.

I didn't want to take up from where I'd left off three days before, but rather wanted to go forward to my own creation, the story behind it. I felt sure that once the facts were known my carers would better understand how to help me. I'd also know how to help myself.

For some time, it was difficult for me to return to Fulminir. The images were broken up in my head with weird etheric static. Eventually, Har Aquillon's hypnotic voice guided me successfully. Har Blansie infused me with agmara to help clear the way. The reality I knew fell away and I was inside the fortress, invisible within its vast bulk and febrile activity.

I found myself in a different area to the one I'd visited before. The sense of crowds was still there, but this time distant. I stood in a creaking, high-ceilinged corridor, where the light was dimly crimson. At the far end, a window to the outside shone like a white star. A har came out of a doorway right next to me, so close I flinched away, but he didn't see me. This creature was ethereal, lovely, and I realised he must be a hostling. Though beautiful, and somehow regal, his stare was blank. He was clothed in a sheer robe of ruby gauze, and I felt that beneath it there were scars. As he swayed in an intoxicated way down the corridor, I entered the room he had come from.

This chamber was sumptuous, a nest of seduction. But despite the warm lighting from crimson-shaded lamps, and the fume of burning sandalwood, the atmosphere was cold and dank. On a huge bed strewn with furs and tapestried coverings sat another har, dwarfed by the high-ceilinged chamber. He looked very young, his hair hanging round him like a dark shawl. He was hunched up, awkward, hugging his knees. Occasionally, he shuddered and I sensed he was swallowing tears, forcing himself not to give in to terror and weep. Was this the har who'd manifested in my room? He looked similar, but then every terrified, emaciated har of this type looked the same to me: huge eyes, abundant hair, a thin body. I went right up to him but he gave no sign of seeing me. I spoke. Still no reaction. Now, I was truly a ghost. He was clawing at his forearms, and I heard him mutter: 'Don't, don't, you're alive, alive. Just keep living.'

The feeling in my heart was so heavy I had no words to describe it fully. Grief, horror, despair, pity? All of those and more. I sensed this har awaited a terrible fate, was powerless to stop it, and could find solace only in reminding himself he wasn't dead. I wanted to give comfort and actually sat down beside him, tried to put an arm around his shoulders, but I had no substance. Not even my feelings could reach into his pain.

Presently, two hara came to the doorway. One was another of acutely soume aspect, whose waist-length dark brown hair was a complication of braids, his garment a stiff robe of dark purple with a high collar that spread behind his head like wings. He had an air of authority about him, and held a slate onto which was attached a sheaf of papers. The har with him was Ponclast. They came towards the bed.

I wanted to leave that room at once. I knew what would happen; I didn't have to observe it. But when I went to the threshold I couldn't pass through. It was as if some higher power forced me to remain, be witness.

'Where's this one from, Vashti?' Ponclast asked, in a conversational tone. 'What tribe?'

The other flicked through his papers. 'He was picked up in Sooth, to the north. Unneah. Our mindscans confirmed he is suitable material. This is the one I selected especially for you.'

'Good. Administer the elixir then and let's get started.' They might as well have been discussing some menial task.

The har on the bed made a small show of protest as the one named Vashti took hold of his hair with one hand, forced back his head. With the other hand, and with practiced speed, he emptied the contents of a vial into the har's gaping mouth.

'He has some spirit,' Ponclast said, with approval.

'He is perfect,' Vashti said.

They conversed then for a few minutes about something utterly commonplace – the decoration of a room and Vashti's requirements from the fortress stores – while the elixir took effect. The har on the bed leaned over the side of it, vomited.

Vashti glanced at him. 'Don't worry about that, Lord,' he said to Ponclast, who had raised a disapproving eyebrow. 'Some take it that way.'

'Is he ready?'

'A moment, please.' Vashti again lifted the har's head by his hair, and peered into his eyes. 'Yes, Lord.'

I turned my face to the wall, but I could hear them. *Pelki: hateful!* I thought. How can harlings come from that? At the start, the victim made little noise, then there were sounds of distress, then pleading, finally hoarse cries of agony. From Ponclast, there was no sound at all. From the side of my vision, I saw Vashti cross to the window, gaze out, his arms hugging his slate-board to his chest, patiently waiting for this procedure to be completed, perhaps thinking about the rooms he wished to improve. The light from outside was colourless, cold. Vashti looked as if he was posing for a portrait. Did he have any compassion? Had he hardened himself to what was happening in that room in order to survive? Or was he like Ponclast, a creature of frozen cruelty?

The har being assaulted had fallen silent now, and I couldn't help but glance behind me. Ponclast was still busy at him, and there was a film of mist around them. I turned away again, rested my forehead against the wall, which felt utterly real. I could smell the mustiness of it. I could hear the shudder of my breath. Finally, Ponclast uttered a grunt and a sigh and said, 'Done, Vashti. He opened well. You made a good choice.'

I turned again. Ponclast was standing beside the bed, adjusting his clothing. Vashti crossed from the window, flicked the unconscious har's clothing back into place. 'I'm glad he was satisfactory.'

'I need more like that.'

'I know. We'll find them.' He stroked the har's head. 'Congratulations, Tiahaar. You are blessed. You will host a pearl for the mightiest of hara.'

I saw the har's eyes were open now, staring. I don't know if he heard those words. I wondered if he was still grateful simply to be alive.

I was ready to leave the path-working now, shaken by what I'd witnessed. But as tried to surface to normal consciousness, the room reeled about me, colours sliding into one another. I couldn't wake. I was spinning, caught in a vortex. Occasionally, the spin slowed down and I caught glimpses of that violated har in this room. He stood at the window in dull light, sat at a table picking at food, lay on the bed while other hara pampered his body. He walked about, like a caged cat, pacing, pacing, clutching his belly.

Time spun onwards, that treacherous web. And then came a moment when the room stopped spinning completely, and the har was on his knees on the rugs, screaming, his pale robe turning red from the hips down. They came running then, spread-eagled him where he lay, wouldn't let him writhe, held him down. One of the hara was Vashti. He gave sharp orders I couldn't hear, but I saw the flash of a blade. They gave the har on the floor a wedge of wood to bite on and his cries were muffled by it. I saw their hands, greasy with blood, pull something from his opened belly.

I knew. Of course I knew. The barely-formed pearl they harvested from that tortured frame was mine.

And still I wasn't released. My surroundings spun around me once more and I was dragged to a bizarre, high-ceilinged workshop, filled with mystifying equipment of glass and metal. I saw my pearl developing in an aludel, a Hermetic vase swimming with nutrients and arcane fluids.

Time sped forward. Hienamas chanted to me as I grew. Smokes were fanned over me, substances injected directly through the leathery skin of the pearl. A rebis, child of the alembic, nurtured by alchemical matter. The hienamas called something into me and I grew in both this world and somewhere else. I couldn't see that place but I felt it, sensed the formless entities slithering through its voids and channels. The pearl changed colour from yellow to red to black. Occasionally pinprick portals would open around it, perhaps not visible to the eyes of those who observed and supervised my growth. Fronds emerged from the portals, penetrated the leather of the pearl, fed me with substances unknown in our reality.

The hienamas wished to create a har who would fight for the Varrs in a way that no enemy could prepare for; the unseen forces who co-operated with this process had their own aspirations. I could sense this, as an observer, but couldn't tell then what their purpose was.

Time moved on, until the skin of pearl became brittle and cracked. When I hatched from it, my consciousness moved partly into this historical self. The images I received from him were abrupt and fragmented, as if sometimes he was able to blind and deafen me. After the hatching, the hienamas gave me raw and bleeding meat to chew. Then I was taken to a kind of nursery where there were other harlings, but they were not like me. They were normal. But eventually my true brothers joined me, others created as I had been, and the normal harlings were taken away. The nursery was not a friendly place. They made us fight for our meals sometimes. Although at other times, they held us close as harlings should be held and murmured soft words. Ponclast never came, never saw his sons. He simply made them, as he might fashion a golem from earth and will. We were told we were special.

All of this I observed impartially – knowing I was both a witness and a participant – but unaffected by the cruelty I experienced.

The years spiralled on.

My training began when I was very young, maybe five or six years old. I was taught to use traditional weapons, to not fear a kill. We were given friends, of a sort, perhaps harlings our own age from the homesteads, who weren't deemed suitable to be fighters. But ultimately we had to murder those friends, without feeling. Our actions were for the good of the tribe. That was our only purpose for existence.

At feybraiha, a har was sent to me. I was soume for him, and then later ouana, during which I tore out his throat. They allowed me to devour some of my kill as a reward. One of my trainers told me, 'You are a Succubus. This is your calling.'

Other hara were given to me, prisoners of war, or those who'd fallen out of favour. I looked upon these episodes as treats, could not see my prey as beings with thoughts and feelings, with lives. They were simply there to be killed in the way I'd been taught, lulled with the syrup of soume, slaughtered with the blade of ouana. I wasn't sundered, but was hardly a healthy whole.

Time thundered forward.

They sent my brothers and me out into the mists of the world, along roads, through forests, into the camps of enemies, or those they did not trust. We were the Succubi, alluring and deadly, melting away after our tasks were done, as quietly as we'd arrived, in the mist.

Just once, Ponclast had me sit at an evening meal, where he was entertaining another har. There was only the three of us. I'd been trained to turn on the charm when I needed to. I could converse with wit, beguile a har with glances and smiles. That night, before the guest arrived, Ponclast ordered me to be quiet – use my eyes alone to bewitch. This I did. The guest complimented me, and joked about how I did not speak, surely the best kind of soume-har.

'He is yours,' Ponclast said. 'For tonight.'

'Are you sure?' this har said. 'I mean he's a jewel, uncanny… and if he is *yours*, my lord, I wouldn't presume…'

Ponclast smiled. 'No, take him with my gratitude. Look on

him as payment for all you've done.'

This included delivery of intelligence to the Gelaming, a betrayal which the unfortunate har believed he'd kept concealed.

I killed him slowly as my father had instructed me to do. He did not stay to watch. Others came to clear up the remains.

During all these experiences I was never truly myself – my kind were kept tractable with intoxicants. I didn't question anything. I'd been born into that life, knew no other. I observed the hideous details of my early years unfold with utter detachment. And yet I perceived that a fair and compassionate personality, the one I now believed myself to be, lived within that earlier, brutal self; some remnant of my hostling perhaps, a prisoner within the flesh. He could do nothing to change his circumstances and his existence wasn't noticed by the prevailing, interloping self. Most of the time he slept, because it was horrific to be awake.

I understood now how I'd been formed. The hienamas had called something into my pearl, some incomprehensible life form from the ethers. They knew so little then, but were arrogant and thought they were in control. They never were, but the fruit of their ignorance was not harvested fully for decades and is part of a story far greater than mine. I – and my brothers – were merely part of the first chapter of that history. I felt compassion now for my younger self trapped within that body. Outwardly, I was recognisable: the shawl of dusty grey hair, the cold eyes in that delicate face with its long elegant nose and wide mouth. Beautiful, in its way, I suppose. A glorious, deceitful mask.

As a young har, the 'active' me never wondered about the hostling in whose body he'd been made – such relationships were meaningless for my kind. We were aware of when hara of the household fell out of favour, and some of the captured hostlings often did rebel, usually by trying to kill themselves. These were then taken to a chamber where the hostlings were supposed to relax, which meant getting so drunk and drugged they didn't care about anything.

The miscreants were hung upon the walls by their hair. The other hostlings were required to throw things at them, to cut them with blades, to violate them with whatever implements were to hand, to spit upon their bodies, to claw at them. I was there when this happened a few times, although generally the Succubi kept away from the hostlings. We were of higher rank than them. Still, some of us liked to watch the punishings. Bets were made on how long it would take these hara to die. Often, the more compassionate (or bravest) among the hostlings waited until most of the others were asleep, and then crept to the miscreants, slit a vein or administered poison. This wasn't condoned, but was strangely never punished. I assume this was to give those wretches the illusion of having some control over their lives.

At some point my own hostling must have been hung upon that wall. I might even have witnessed his suffering without realising who he was. In his delirium, had he called out to his harlings, clutching at the one relationship in the Varrish world that might have compassion attached to it? Had he, in his ravings, found me in the future?

Eventually, history rolled round to the point when the Gelaming laid siege to Fulminir. Warfare between the Varrs and their enemies, at this crucial point, was never destined to be conventional. Otherworldly powers clashed and splashed. The sky broke over us. Our food rotted away, our water turned to poison. After some weeks, the Gelaming brought in their greatest weapon, an entity forged from the fires of Grissecon. And that was the end of it. Fulminir shattered and fell, and the Gelaming rode in with their allies to liberate or incarcerate the survivors, as appropriate.

There was a gap here in my recollection. I remembered the exploding sky and a strange kind of acceleration, as if I was flying, but then, suddenly, I was crouched in ruins, little more than a wounded animal. I hadn't been able to feed, and was dehydrated. All I could drink was blood and what I could find of that, from those still living or recently dead, only made me thirstier. As the powers of Fulminir were destroyed, so something was destroyed in me too. I was partially released. But not entirely. I can remember a vague sensation of fear, but not really knowing what that feeling was.

I somehow came to be alone. I clawed my way through the alchemical workshops where I, and others like me, had been grown. I wasn't sure for what I searched, but my rummaging was frantic. I think maybe I was looking for an escape route. I smashed my way through locked doors, and found myself eventually in a small, round chamber that was dark, but for the faintest burn of indigo light. A shifting oval of this light shivered in the centre of the room. I approached it, one hand held before me. The indigo turned to black: a hole. Sometimes, we had used portals like this to reach our targets.

I can't say what thoughts and impulses went through that earlier me. He reached out to the portal, perhaps prayed for help of some kind. I think though that all he got was a brief glimpse of his future: my room at Reveriel, grasping the hand of a self he was yet to be.

When Melisander found me, I was as broken as the splintered halls of Fulminir. He saw only a victim, feeding on carrion in a ruin. He felt he had a duty to free me, to care for me. He would have been wiser to cut off my head or, as the calmer of his companions suggested, hand me to the Gelaming. Some part of me, the survivor, perhaps even the soume-succubus bred to kill, took on the mantle of what would best secure my survival, and I became that fey, damaged creature, an object to be pitied, locked in a tower, gazing at the world through a mirror, until it cracked from side to side.

I found myself awake and once again breathing in the perfumed air of Immanion. I couldn't hear properly because a singing static fizzed in my head. Har Blansie raised my head, gave me water. I found out later I'd been out for nearly three hours.

One of the things I learned in my visions of Fulminir was why the Gelaming were obsessed with being evolved, tolerant, wise, kind, compassionate – or being seen that way. It was because all they found in that place was too much to bear; the complete opposite of such noble qualities. They found the ultimate warping of harish potential. They found cruelty – *evil*. If the Varrish vision of Wraeththu had taken root, the Devastation would have been for nothing. The world would have carried on suffering as before, only with more potent tyrants in control.

I felt so weak and disorientated that Har Blansie and Har Aquillon virtually had to carry me back to my room. My halian Tarice came to me, gave me healing as I lay on my bed, stroked my back and arms until I felt drowsy although I couldn't fall asleep. 'Do you want a philtre, Gavensel?' he murmured. 'To make you sleep?'

'No,' I said. 'When it's right for me to drop off, I will.'

He smiled at me. 'I'll stay nearby. If you need me, call my name in your head.'

I nodded. 'Thank you.' I just wanted him to leave. Then I remembered Pazazil. 'Wait...'

Tarice paused at the door. 'Yes?'

'Please, take a message to my... friends, to Pazazil and Grackle. Explain I can't see them tonight, that I'm resting.'

Tarice inclined his perfect head. 'Of course.'

I lay in darkness, aware of the utter silence of my room. There would be no more manifestations there. Was I cured now? Was it all over? Was the only consequence to assimilate what I knew? I still couldn't *feel* that the har I'd seen grow and become a monster was me. Perhaps it was best I never did feel that. All the time my suspicions – my dread – had been right; I *had* killed. And I had to face the possibility that a fraction of that entity survived in hiding within me. But that creature wasn't me. Surely, it was as much a mask as the fragile ghost of Sallow Gandaloi had been? I had ripped the mask of the ghost in two. I must believe I had the power to destroy this other mask too.

As for my hostling, the emotions his fate conjured in me were too deep and complicated to understand. Yet. I found myself praying to Aruhani, dehar of aruna, life and death, of hostlings. 'Sweet Aru, in your mercy, glance back in time and grant him a swift death.' My throat was swollen and sore with grief I couldn't release, my eyes scalding with unshed tears.

Mercurius Vitae

Sleep restored me. Although aftershocks of the previous day still juddered through me, I felt well enough by morning to meet the others at what had become our regular dining-table. When I stepped cautiously from the shadows of the building, they were already sitting there in the sun-soaked garden. They got to their feet at the sight of me. Almost at once, Grackle scurried over to take me in his arms. Pazazil only watched from a distance, his face inscrutable.

'Tarice said you were resting,' Grackle babbled, 'but I knew – felt – it was more than that. All afternoon yesterday I felt sick. I could barely breathe. You saw terrible things, didn't you?'

I disentangled myself from him, patted his shoulder. 'Yes, it was vile but I'm glad I did it. I know the truth now.'

I glanced at Pazazil, but he was still unreadable, perhaps wary now. 'What truth did you learn?' he asked.

'I was like Grackle's sons,' I said, 'bred as a soldier.'

'*Made*?' Pazazil asked.

I didn't hesitate. 'My pearl was taken from my hostling's body early. From what I perceived, this was because he was miscarrying. The pearl was tended outside his body. That's how I was made.'

'There, you see,' Grackle said. 'The truth isn't as bad as you thought.'

'You don't look like a soldier to me,' Pazazil said.

'I was barely more than a harling when Fulminir fell,' I said, needled by the challenge in his voice, and I could hear the defensive tone in mine. 'Melisander took me half dead from the ruins. My life with him changed me.'

Nothing I said was untrue exactly. Pazazil nodded, but I could tell he knew there was more to it than that. At that moment, though, I felt that telling them everything would simply feed a prurient desire to hear about gruesome things happening to somehar else. Ultimately, my history was not their business.

But there were aspects I *could* speak of – how the hostlings lived, for example. Grackle wanted to hear about that, of course, but I censored my words, keeping the worst from him. I explained that the har I'd seen in my room was almost certainly my hostling, perhaps an entity created by my mind rather than his actual ghost, and that the black portal was a link to my past.

While I spoke, Pazazil watched me covertly. Eventually, I risked sending a mind touch, hoping Grackle wouldn't pick up on it. *May I see you later, alone?*

The answer took a while to come. He wasn't sure. But eventually I heard the single word: *yes.*

I had wondered whether what I'd witnessed in Fulminir, the warped forms of aruna, the soullessness of it, would affect how I felt about intimacy with hara now. And yet, as the day went on and the sun dreamed slowly as it travelled above the land, desire ignited within me, the promise of my later meeting with Pazazil. When I'd been with him before, it was as if I'd taken aruna for the first time. All that had happened in my early years was gone from me; those memories I had disinterred belonged to a har who had died in Fulminir. He wasn't me. *He wasn't me.*

The sun went down in blood, and the deepening sky was hooked upon a paring of the moon. Beyond my window the ocean glowed distantly and the stars looked on coldly. I felt like an animal, perhaps a horse, some proud and high-stepping creature, who might, under certain circumstances, breathe fire. The sensations within me were interesting. My heart beat fast, my breath was shallow. I felt light-headed, eager, excited. Could it really just be aruna – or the promise of it – that made a har feel like this?

I wore only my dressing-robe and let my hair hang loose. I went to his room, found him sitting naked on the wide windowsill. He looked fraught, perhaps wondering himself why he felt the way he did. Every day of our lives, our clever bodies follow a variety of procedures to relieve themselves of pressure. I thought that this was simply another procedure, but still, the imperative was strong. Perhaps, *then*, I should have realised.

'Zil, you are quite beautiful,' I said, standing over him.

'Only quite?'

There were no more words; the hunger was too great. The first part, too, was quite beautiful. We did share breath, but in an abstract synesthetic way. I could hear what he saw, smell what he heard. I was soume for him as before, an act so far removed from anything I'd glimpsed in Fulminir it might be a different thing altogether. We didn't speak of what I'd been through. We barely spoke at all, or, if we did, it was only with our hands and eyes.

Then came the moment when he pulled me onto him – *opened* beneath me. There was a faint wariness in his eyes that spoke of historical hurts of his own. There was sadness too. *Oh, Zil, flower of a scorching land, beauty of the lion-haunted desert, the ancient indigo sky. Temple of the east.* I believed I'd find sanctuary in that temple; cool, scented darkness, the murmur of priests behind veils of incense, the shivery percussion of sistra. And it was that. It *was*. But only for a time.

For then the wild horse reared up, breathing fire. I felt a chill, bitter power rise from another universe deep within my body, a hole into this world from a void. This force had sentience – will. All life was its enemy. The very worst of the masculine, condensed. My body was a weapon, irresistible as steel. Black tears oozed from my eyes, fell onto Zil. I stared at the inky puddle in the hollow of his throat, wondering if it was blood. Then, there was no more thought. I knew what I had to do, what I was *here* to do. Complete the task.

I punched Zil's face, appalled, helpless, a passenger in this carriage of hate. I knew I would kill him, perhaps worse, expel his very soul from this world... And I couldn't help him – or myself.

But Zil had been forged in potent fires. He shook his head,

suddenly focused. He bucked his body to free himself, kicked out with both feet, wriggled away, and then attacked me in return. I was unused to fighting, no matter how instinctual it appeared to be. My body remembered the moves, but hadn't executed them for decades. We struggled, clawed, furniture crashing around us. There were no words, not even a shout, just the ragged gasp of our breath. Eventually, he knocked me out and, from what I saw of myself later, continued to thrash me for some time after I was no longer a threat. He must've stopped only when the halians came running, alerted by the reverberations of conflict through Pavonyx, and pulled him off me.

They locked me in my room. I was kept unconscious for two days, hienamas and halians fussing about. Sometimes, I was outside my body and could see them beetling round me. Zil had made quite a mess of me. My face was almost entirely purple and grotesquely swollen. Several ribs had been cracked, muscles torn in my shoulders. Severe bruising and trauma to my torso, the organs within. Being har, it wouldn't take my body that long to right itself, but I knew I'd feel the ghosts of his blows for a long time to come.

When I came back to full wakefulness, I was alone. Presumably I wasn't supposed to wake at precisely that moment. I went to look at myself in the mirror, numb. They'd plaited my hair, quite tightly, back from my face. I looked bony, raw, some weird creature of an alien species. I appraised myself for some minutes, then went to try the door, found it locked. I hit it with the palms of my hands and presently Har Blansie and Har Aquillon came together, along with Tarice, presumably as backup.

'It's gone,' I told them. 'Whatever it was, it's gone.'

'Hush,' Har Blansie murmured, taking hold of one of my arms. 'Sit down. Let's look at you.'

I obeyed, sat on the bed, and subjected myself to their inspection.

'Ouana is the trigger,' I said. 'Well, it *was*. I didn't *think*. I should have done. That's what made me kill… before.'

Nohar commented on my explanation.

'Do you need something for the pain?' Har Blansie asked.

'No. Is… Pazazil all right?'

'Yes,' Har Blansie said.

'I was made to be an assassin,' I said. 'My fault. Should have remembered!' I punched the bed. 'It's because I've not been with any har since Melisander found me."

'Gavensel,' Har Blansie said evenly. 'Is that true? Calm yourself. Think.'

I stared at him, wondering what he meant, and then the lines whispered in my head:

Out flew the web and floated wide;
The mirror crack'd from side to side;
"The curse is come upon me," cried
The Lady of Shalott.

I put my head in my hands.

'Do you remember now?' Har Aquillon enquired.

'Levvero,' I said.

The mirror had cracked and fallen, and behind it there had been a door, a portal to some unimaginable *other* place. I remembered Levvero, a crow of hara, coming to Sallow Gandaloi. He'd sought to steal me away, either sensing or knowing what I was. He would have sold me, I think. I'd seen that in him, during his final moments. So confident was he. Seduction in mind. Unprepared for the consequences.

'What happened to him?' Har Aquillon asked in barely more than a whisper. 'No body was ever found.'

I choked out a laugh. 'Body? He invoked death and it came. Death took him away, through a black portal.'

I didn't have clear memories of this event, simply wisps, impressions. I remembered vaguely a struggle, not knowing what was happening. I thought I'd been expelled from my body, and in a way I had. Sharply, though, came the recollection that I'd taken my portion, as I'd been used to do. I could taste him again, now. I didn't tell them that.

'Perhaps this was why the Lady of Shalott was locked up too,' I said.

'What?' Har Blansie asked.

I shook my head. 'Nothing.' I swallowed, inhaled deeply. 'What will happen to me now? Must I be punished?'

Har Blansie shifted a little beside me. 'Gavensel, as Melisander always believed – and still does – you were a victim as much as those you were sent to kill. We're wholly confident your rehabilitation can be absolute and permanent, but this could – and probably will – involve having to expel the remains of whatever etheric influence inhabited your body.'

'It's gone... It's...'

Har Blansie put a hand upon my shoulder. 'Gavensel, please, hush. I know how badly you want that to be true, but face reality. This entity has slept within you for so long, apparently surfacing only twice in all that time. There is a trigger, yes. We know what this is now, but you can't go through life avoiding half of your nature. Do you really want that?'

I shook my head; a chastened harling.

'As you mentioned to Typhis a few days ago,' Har Blansie continued, 'we think the next step of your treatment should be that you go to Megalithica and see Fulminir for yourself. Perhaps in this place you may be cleansed. Typhis will go with you. Are you agreeable to that?'

I paused. 'Yes,' I said feebly. 'If you think I should.'

'Don't retreat,' Har Blansie said, more firmly. 'You're not the limpid invalid wafting around Sallow Gandaloi. You're Gavensel, the har you've begun to get to know here in Reveriel. That's what you should build upon. Now. Answer me again. Are you agreeable to going to Megalithica with Typhis?'

'Yes. I'm agreeable. I want to go.'

'Good.'

I looked Har Blansie in the eye, conjuring the self I must learn always to be. 'Can I see Pazazil?'

He held my gaze. 'No, Gavensel. That's not possible.'

'Will you tell me why?' I thought it was simply a punishment.

Har Blansie drew in his breath. 'You have to understand that Pazazil is in some respects more damaged than you ever were. He hides much of his past, as you did. It was unwise of you to take aruna together, since it's always the key that unlocks many doors, however barricaded they might be. However, we don't discourage intimacy between our guests. Generally, it's therapeutic. In this case, knowing the history as we did, we didn't warn you sufficiently, and that was an oversight on our part.'

'You mean you didn't think me capable, nor Pazazil.'

Har Aquillon smiled ruefully. 'Yes, you could say that. We're equally responsible for what happened. Pazazil has gone back to a dark place and needs to recover now. It won't help him to see you.'

I nodded. 'I see.' I stood up. 'Can I bathe, please?'

'Of course,' Har Aquillon said.

'And bring me scissors...'

'Gavensel,' Har Blansie began, 'I don't think...'

'I won't *harm* myself, if that's what you're worried about. Please do as I ask. I just want to cut my hair. It's symbolic.'

There was some fuss over finding me a dressing-robe, since my own had been ruined during my fight with Pazazil. They had burned it. Tarice went to find me some scissors. I complied with all their requests, smiled at them, but once all was ready, I broke away from them and ran down the corridor to Pazazil's room, hoping to all the dehara he was there and he was: sitting on his meditation mat, staring out at the sky.

'Zil...' I meant to apologise, but what words could I use for that? I wanted it all to be made right.

He turned, saw me, leapt to his feet. He was nowhere near as damaged – physically – as I was.

I held out my hands to him.

He turned his back. 'Get out. Now.'

'Zil...'

'Get out!' He kicked a chair, sent it flying. 'Fuck off, you freak! Just fuck off!'

I did so.

The bathroom was decorated in different shades of green – tiles, foliage, lighting. Water poured down the walls. The entire floor was running wet. There were waterfalls at each corner, spilling over serpentine boulders. I stood under one of these, still in my robe, and let the blood-hot liquid crash over me. Then I picked up the scissors. I debated whether to hack my hair off at the roots, but considered that too dramatic, and instead sliced off the plait at shoulder length, which took some time, as if it didn't want to be cut away. But eventually it lay there on the floor before me like a dead snake. I wasn't *that*, no fey and beauteous thing. That was part of the illusion, the puppet.

I went to sit against one of the walls, the scissors still in my hand. Water ran down over me. Without the weight of all that hair I thought I might float towards the ceiling but the water held me down. I couldn't tell if I was weeping or not, but doubted I actually could, now.

After some time, Grackle edged into the room. He looked frightened, perhaps remembering the hara who'd come to him back in that factory they'd called a homestead. I didn't speak, just stared at him.

'Gavensel, can I come in?' he asked. I noticed him looking at the scissors, so I threw them into the middle of the room. He flinched.

'Come in,' I said. 'You're quite safe, little bird.'

He sidled towards me, hunkered down some feet away. 'Gavensel, I'm so so sorry...'

'What for?'

He shook his head, put one hand to his face, across his eyes, shuddered with difficult sobs.

'He hates me,' I said.

Gavensel's weeping monkey features twisted with concern, with *love*. 'You hurt him,' he said, explanation enough.

I put my hands against my face, concentrated on the warm streams that flowed down my fingers. There was no going back from this, only forwards, to that grim place, where I had been forged and fashioned. The worst thing was I felt utterly, clinically *cured*, but I couldn't deny my carers' suspicions. Just because I felt exorcised didn't mean I was. Still, now I knew *what* I was, and I wasn't mad.

'The precise reason I am here,' I said, lowering my hands, 'is because I killed a har.'

Grackle stared at me.

'As I killed him, I saw what he was, and that in many ways he deserved no other fate, but he invoked a demon and was sucked away from this world, sucked inside out, I expect.'

Grackle shuffled towards me, holding out his arms. I nodded and allowed him to embrace me. That made him cry again.

I sighed. 'I can never go home,' I said. 'I know that now. Melisander doesn't know this har I am, and he feared the other one. He won't want me back.'

Grackle had the sense not to try and contest my words. He merely held me, silent. I thought of his sons, the love they'd been denied. All those dead harlings.

After some minutes, I pushed Grackle away gently and got to my feet. There was nothing else to say.

'Gavensel,' Grackle said, still standing by the raining wall.

I turned at the threshold.

'He will not be good for a while now, but give him time. These things pass.'

I sniffed an unconvincing laugh, went from him.

Solifaction

I wasn't prepared to wait for another session with the therapists, not this time. If that demon was still coiled within I wanted to know *now*. I wanted to challenge and fight it. If it was always to be a part of me, there'd never be a normal life in my future. I'd be doomed to remain here in Reveriel, half a har. That wasn't a life. My battle, when it came, must be to the death – one way or another.

That night, I resolved to invoke my demon. This was, of course, a reckless thing to do. There would be nohar there to strike me down. My door would no doubt be locked. I might not be able to ask for help, might transform into something hideous, break free of the room... These thoughts didn't concern me. I was shaken and stupid, grieving over Pazazil, horrified at the truths I'd discovered, fearful for the future. Selfish. I might have put everyhar in Pavonyx at risk, never mind other inhabitants of Reveriel. Unfortunately, I was good at deception, and presented a meek, passive face to my carers. Even though they turned a key on me, they left me alone. Perhaps that was stupid of them, too.

At midnight, in the dreaming silence of the moon, I sat naked in the centre of my room, having positioned a mirror that usually hung upon the wall before me, propped on a chair. I knew 'The Lady of Shalott' by heart now and sat in the blue owl-light, chanting lines of it I thought relevant. This was my invocation to soume, the Lady.

> She knows not what the curse may be,
> And so she weaveth steadily,
> And little other care hath she,
> The Lady of Shalott.

I needed to evoke soume within me, and what other way than through images of Pazazil, our times together? I basked in those intoxicating thoughts for a while, until glimpses of Levvero intruded, the har who'd flashed his eyes at me to break a spell. I stared at myself in the mirror and remembered that silly creature, the me who'd languished at the window of his chamber in Sallow Gandaloi, believing a har could love him.

And I was glad those thoughts overshadowed the memories of Pazazil, because if I was to feel rage, it should not be against him. Levvero! Vain, confident, cold of heart. Thought he could woo me, lie to me, steal me away to sell to somehar else. Somehar who'd known what I was, who wanted what lay hidden within me. Levvero had been so careless he hadn't guarded his thoughts sufficiently. He'd indulged himself, thought he'd enjoy my seduction, eat all the fruits he could grab. Fool. He'd paid in blood. How wrong he'd been about me. I wasn't sorry about what I'd done to him. I'd do it again, in an instant.

Resentment and anger bubbled inside me. The demon twitched within this toxic brew, uncoiling, rising, sniffing. The temperature in the room dropped. It was time.

"I am half sick of shadows," said
The Lady of Shalott.

I murmured the words repeatedly, building them in strength, until I was spitting them out, like the poison of a serpent. I stared into the mirror, willing myself to see that I was no languid, dreamy thing, but a potent, predatory beast. I raked my hands through my chopped hair, shook my head, snarled, condensing all the energy in my body into ouana, the masculine aspect. In this form, I might be twenty feet high, with razor claws and a snout full of sabre teeth.

The demon flexed.

I could feel it, seeping into every cell of me, becoming stronger. Hungry and focused.

I leapt to my feet and hissed:

Out flew the web and floated wide;
The mirror crack'd from side to side;
"The curse is come upon me," cried
The Lady of Shalott.

The air in the room was freezing now; it was difficult to draw breath as if I attempted to take solid ice into my lungs. My ragged breath steamed. I stood silent for some moments, the air vibrating around me.

'Come on,' I murmured. 'Come out. I know you're there.'

And there he was, in the mirror before me, a shimmering bluish outline of a har that gradually became denser. I could not see myself in the glass. The demon looked like me and yet not. He was brutish, his features twisted. His hair had not been cut but was fashioned into spikes and quills. His nails were a carrion bird's talons.

'Do you have a name?' I asked this sneering vision.

'Gavensel,' it replied and then simpered coyly, fluttering its eyelids.

Even as this abomination spoke, knowledge awoke within me that I'd snatched from the conversations I'd heard at festival times, of the dehara, our gods. I knew what to say. 'I detach that label from you, in the name of Agave, dehar of will.'

The demon laughed. 'You seem to think I'll be diminished by your absence. This is not so. You were merely one of the beasts who fed me. There are others, in all times and all places.'

'I banish you in the name of Aruhani, dehar of aruna, life and death!'

Again, that sickening simper. 'You are not so sweet now, Gavensel. Look at you. Such a priggish, pointless creature. You'll suffer more from my departure than I will.'

'I cast you out in the name of Miyacala, dehar of wisdom and knowledge.'

The demon stepped out of the mirror, stood before me. 'And what must you invoke now? Shall I tell you I love you, so you call upon Lunil to wash away such an ugly feeling?'

I would not flinch, *must* not. 'I banish you in the name of Lunil, dehar of the strongest magics and of compassion.'

The demon sighed. 'How sad. We had such times together, Gavensel, such times.'

'Just go,' I said, 'in the name of the Aghama, the star and your master.'

'No master of mine,' the demon replied.

'Perhaps not, but *I* am your master.'

The demon put its head to one side, a coquettish gesture. 'Are you really? It's more a case of you are the lady who does my bidding and I the lord who smites.'

'No, you are separate,' I said. 'I am both lord and lady, and they are equally capable of forcing you out.'

The demon stared at me for some moments, half-smiling. 'It's amusing you believe that so fully.'

'Belief is a strong force in this world,' I said. 'But you know that.'

The demon sighed and shimmered, and I could see myself through it. I knew it would leave, simply because to fight would be too much bother, and after all I was har and the fight would not be that simple.

'Very well,' said the demon. 'Have your desire, but know I do not leave because you force me to. I leave of my own choice. Besides you've been of no interest for decades. I was summoned back for a brief but happy interlude. You'll be relieved to know you're like all the others now. Insufferable and dreary. This is my parting gift: I leave you to your incurable and tedious mortality.' It laughed cruelly. 'God in his mercy lend you grace, Lady of Shalott.'

With these words, the creature stepped back into the mirror, which at once became cobwebbed with cracks. After a moment it burst, showering me with splinters, yet not one of them cut me.

The temperature in the room became warm again, the air was breathable. I was short of breath, motes of light pulsing before my eyes, and had to lie down on the bed. I knew the creature I'd banished wasn't a demon in the literal sense; it was an entity from beyond this reality, a parasite. It only had power over me when I was weak with fear. I didn't fear it now. Also, I suspected that when a host became aware of this psychic tick's presence, its control lessened. And yet perhaps we would be forever connected, like estranged relatives, disgust on both sides. If this must be, I could tolerate it, as long as the fiend could no longer use me as a vehicle. I must work on being so strong this couldn't happen – ever.

The day had dawned and it was cold and wet. The battle was over, the bodies being cleared from the field. Somehar had won and it was done. But the victory was hollow.

The following morning, I confessed to my carers the action I'd taken. They weren't as angry as I'd expected, but perhaps only because I'd been successful. However, they still thought I should go to Fulminir and enter trance there – to be sure the link was sufficiently severed. I agreed. Demons can lie, after all.

The night before Har Aquillon and I went to Megalithica, I dreamed of the hara hung up by their hair. The roof had gone from the ruined chamber where I found them, and icy rain was stabbing down through the blackened spikes of rafters. The floor was covered in viscous puddles and the smell of burning was strong – meat, cloth, hair.

Most of the victims were long dead and rotting, but one was still alive. I heard pitiful sounds, saw the body twisting slightly on its hook. There were crates lying around, a table, some broken chairs. Somehow I made a ladder of these things. This I scrambled up, with bits of it tumbling away, but I reached him, took out the scissors I had in the pocket of my coat and cut him free. He fell heavily into my arms, and we both crashed down through the splintering crates.

Lying in the debris, he clung to me and whispered, 'I knew… if I waited… you'd come for me. My son…' He reached out with bloody fingers to touch my face. I took that chilled hand in mine, kissed it.

He was gone.

I woke up, sobbing uncontrollably, as if I were retching, but there was nothing to bring up. 'Grackle,' I said, 'Grackle.'

But, of course, that had not been my hostling's name.

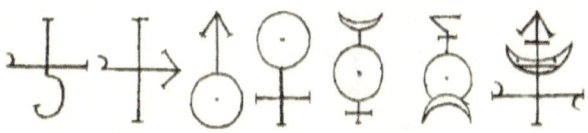

A Pyramid of Lions

Calcination

'Let me in, Vashti. Why won't you let me in?'

The voice came again this morning, not long past dawn. It's been a while since I heard it and I've never been sure if it's real. The wind in the apple trees, the dawnsong of starlings, the scuttle of mice in the walls, the creak of the old gate: Could these conspire to make words?

Whether the voice is real or not, I know whose it is. I did deny him, a long time ago. I did what I had to do, and nothing I was capable of would have saved him anyway – not for long. Everything in our world was horrific or sad. Some of us were simply more adept than others at looking out for ourselves, at surviving.

And here I sit in my wooden house: safe, alive, alone.

Don't think I haven't paid for those gifts. I gave part of my soul for them. But I don't regret that. It's pointless to feel bitterness and remorse, because the monster we faced, and which ruled us, was so powerful that nohar could fight it. We could only dodge and hide, wear masks, learn to smile in the face of dread, not flinch, carry on.

Perhaps the ghost knows I could never save him, but maybe I can at last let him in. The only way to do that is to tell it as it happened, for the truth has been warped over the years. The past is both better and worse than memory and hearsay.

I was born in the homestead named Ashen Weald, the spawn of a professional hostling whose sole function was to produce pearls. The place was essentially a farm. This was in the days before hara understood their reproductive processes. Harlings were at that time rare, and it was believed they could only be created under precise conditions, between hara who were spiritually close. But the Varr tribe had learned that nature and spirit could be manipulated. Offspring didn't have to be rare, nor even that special.

Once a year, hara came from Fulminir to take a ripened batch of harlings away and allocate them to various functions within the Varrish military. A few, of course, remained behind, destined to become hostlings themselves, being considered unfit for any other purpose. Of these, some were sent to other homesteads. We understood that more were being established continually.

Maybe I was born under a strange moon, but I always knew I was different. I individuated and became self-aware before harlings normally did so. Even when very small, I felt that every other har around me was asleep, going through the motions of being awake – living – whereas I was incapable of sleep. Later, once I'd had time to think about it more, and had learned words to describe what I intuited, I believed they slept because they were too weak to face the reality of their lives. But I was cursed with open eyes. If ever I tried to discuss my ideas with anyhar – and I did persist with this futile endeavour for a short while after I learned to think and talk – they would change the subject, or look through me as if I wasn't there. I realised then what they were and what I was.

I knew also I had no desire to become a hostling. The way to ensure this seemed obvious – simply don't be like them. They were all weirdly childlike; they would chatter and preen each other, believing themselves blessed, sacred even. Flowers in their hair and witless smiles on their faces, waiting for the hara sent by the military to impregnate them, as if this was a privilege, some romantic prospect to be cherished, even though they had no choice but to submit to a har they didn't know, and would never see again, and who no doubt thought nothing of them, *or* what had been created. I despised the hostlings for their wilful stupidity. The cows in our fields had more freedom. The single difference was that the hostlings weren't occasionally slaughtered to be eaten.

The only other choice available to homestead harlings was to join the warrior class. This didn't appeal to me either – seemed to be little more than a death sentence, since our tribe was constantly at war. The mere fact the homesteads existed, churning out livestock, must mean that fighters had a shorter life expectancy than a cow. I knew I must find another way.

For the first few years of my life, I wrestled with this dilemma, because I was aware the day would arrive when they'd judge me. I must decide by then what I wanted to be, because my life would depend on it, even though I lacked the experience and knowledge to make an informed decision. I would have to create a function for myself that our keepers would value – a function that didn't simply involve breeding or fighting, but which displayed patriotic loyalty to my tribe. That must mean, I supposed, rising to become a keeper myself, or a guardian – the hara who protected and defended Ashen Weald and its boundaries – but I hadn't seen such promotions among homestead-bred hara, ever.

My harlinghood wasn't all bad. Those who cared for us weren't deliberately cruel – such treatment might taint the livestock, after all. (Don't they say that the meat of an animal that dies in fear tastes foul? Perhaps those conceived in fear are tainted in a different way.) We had long summers, an idyllic bucolic lifestyle. We were well-fed and well-groomed, vigorously healthy. The homestead was surrounded by fields – for cattle, sheep and the growing of crops. The main house had, in the human era, been first a rich family's home, then a school and finally some kind of business institution. It had been abandoned for around five years when the Varrs chose it to be a homestead. It was enormous and sometimes frightening. Within its many rooms, you often felt that you might open a door and find yourself in a different era.

Behind the house and its sprawl of outbuildings lay a dark placid lake with an island in its centre. A wide, drowsy river ran nearby, and beyond this our protective forest crept; thick and dark and breathing. I can't say I didn't enjoy playing in the landscape there – it was beautiful, vast and sentient. Never since have summer trees seemed so heavy, so real, nor skies so clear and high.

I pretended to be friends with my peers, cawing with laughter like a little rook, tumbling around with them in the skirts of the woodland, the edge of the lake and the entirety of the wide fields. (The guardians observed us always.) But inside I was always only watching my companions. I could tell who would stay at Ashen Weald and who would leave. I fancied I even knew who'd die first, out there in the warrior's world.

There were a couple of harlings of whom I sensed I might become fond, but they were gentle, pretty creatures, and I had to scour that feeling from me because I knew their fate. Even when so tiny, I was weirdly *old*. I felt and thought things my playmates didn't. I might have been a prodigy, if I'd been born into a tribe other than the Varrs. I kept away from those I feared to love and forgot their names, because this seemed the best way to detach myself. But even now I remember their faces, their soft smiles, their hair. They would become hostling stock, kept almost constantly in pearl, allowed no proper relationships with other hara. And they'd never be *real* hostlings, because their young would be taken from them, reared separately.

In our schooling, we were taught that Wraeththu were vastly superior to the all-but-extinct human race that had ravaged the world. One of our advantages was that harlings were not as helpless as human children had been. We didn't need a mother's milk. We matured more quickly. We were designed to be self-sufficient if necessary, to survive alone from an early age. With this in mind, and in order to prevent inconvenient attachments between parent and offspring, homestead harlings were raised together in a nursery – a house within the grounds – cared for by hara who did not produce pearls themselves. But even so, we heard the hoarse cries – like cows lamenting for their calves – when harlings were removed from the main house. Some hostlings were quiet about it, accepting with cauterised numbness the way things were. But others could never make themselves numb. Their mourning cries made all of us tense and uncomfortable, although I don't think any of us really cared for whoever was grieving.

I had no idea who'd carried my pearl and refused to think about it. The hostlings were all the same. They had a custom, a sort of group ritual, for when the harlings were taken away from them, which happened very soon after hatching. These rites were not prohibited, even if they weren't overtly supported. Our keepers no doubt believed such customs helped keep the hostlings sane and working. Even an animal mourns lost offspring, and some hostlings grieved as if for a death – they needed the ritual more than others. Such a har would wear white, daub ash on his face and body, and tie up his hair into severe knots. He would trail out like a ghost into the fields and lie down there. After dark, the others would creep out to sing over him. His body would be strewn with torn petals, as if he were about to be put into the earth. Perhaps a part of him perished, every time, until all that was left was an unburied corpse, still breathing. Whenever I witnessed or could hear these ceremonies, I vowed I would not suffer that fate – I would die first, and in a clean, proper manner.

I was always very well-behaved and hid my real self. I realised this camouflage would have to be my road out of Ashen Weald. Some of the harlings played up, tried to rebel, and were swiftly quashed. Discipline was generally fair but sometimes harsh, when the keepers felt it necessary. I knew from the start that only an idiot would make themselves visible to the keepers in that way. The intransigent signed their own death warrants –

they would no doubt be the first to be taken as warriors, given a front line role wherever they were sent to fight. Appearing to be amenable allowed much more freedom.

You might ask why I didn't simply run away. Shouldn't escape attempts have been common at the homestead? But then why don't cows wander away from the fields? Apart from the fact that they don't know any better than to stay there, the answer is that they would be rounded up and brought back, and also, out in the endless, merciless landscape of forests and mountains, there are dangers with which cows are not equipped to cope. So it was with us. You can be sure I did think about walking out of Ashen Weald – quite a lot – but realised I wouldn't know how to feed and defend myself or find shelter. Homestead harlings were taught that wild hara and savage animals lurked beyond the boundaries of our safe domain, and that we must not venture deep into the forest, because unspeakable things would happen to us. We were far from Fulminir, or any other node of civilisation. The country was vast and empty, and there were not enough hara to fill it in the way that humans had. In order to escape, I would need the cooperation of older hara, who were familiar with the world beyond the wilderness and how to survive in it.

I began offering my services to the keepers, rather than going out to play with my companions every day. This began when I was not much past three years old. Other harlings offered to work too, but I started far sooner than those my own age, and never to seek approval or favour like the others did. I didn't crave attention, (quite the opposite), but simply got on with the tasks allocated to me. I made myself useful, helping in the kitchens or the dairy, assisting the carers who looked after the youngest harlings, never allowing myself to become attached to anyhar or anything. Obedient, swift, economical in movement and thought: I felt I faced a wall that was three feet thick, which I needed to chip my way through using only my fingernails, but I was patient.

I acquired the reputation of being 'sensible' and as I grew older was given more responsibility. In my mind, I refused to have a name, because these were handed out at hatching, and revolved around a theme. I learned it was the same with all homesteads – harlings named for flowers, birds, gems, creatures, and so on. I saw the names as chains, dark spells that had power to enslave. Even now, I realise, some part of me fears them because I'm reluctant to remember them. When others said the name I'd been given, I divested it of meaning; it was nothing more than a noise that commanded my attention. Privately I referred to myself as 'This One' and to others as 'That One', waiting, always waiting, for the day of escape.

Feybraiha in the homestead was also an occasion for ritual, but with lavish celebration rather than misery. At this time, when adulthood stole upon us, we took our first aruna. The keepers didn't want us growing up afraid of this aspect of life, because for hostlings it was part of their calling and they had to be comfortable doing it so they became proficient at creating pearls. The keepers attempted to instil within us a sense of our great purpose, whatever role was chosen for us in the future. To become adult was a time of reverence, because soon we would take our places within the tribe, in order to ensure its triumph. We were taught how most other tribes were our enemies, the result of humanity's weakness and folly. Humankind had condemned the earth, made Wraeththu happen. It was up to the Varrs to right the wrongs, to live how humans should have lived and take up the opportunities they had squandered.

During our precise and narrow education, we learned that human children had taken on a single gender in the womb of their mothers – became a half. For Varrs, this happened long after birth and not in a physical way, for in our bodies we would be forever whole. But, in our minds and hearts, we must follow the path most suited to our psyches, aware always we still possessed that complement within us, upon which we could call should circumstances demand it. I always sensed this *sundering* was an imposition – *wrong* – but having no knowledge of how hara in other tribes lived supposed it must be normal. Essentially we had to choose a prevailing gender – or rather this choice was made for us. I didn't know what I was, only that I had unswerving determination concerning what I should *not* be. I suppose, essentially, I didn't want to be a slave, and was alone among my peers in realising this was exactly what they all were. I didn't learn the word slave for quite some time, but I knew the feeling of it.

Feybraiha came for me in the mid-summer. Beneath a bloated moon strange urges filled my body. This was to be the first of many battles, I felt. I knew, because it was alluded to in poetic metaphor during our schooling, that first aruna helped the keepers determine our future roles. I had to strive to keep that decision uncertain, but how? I had asked careful questions about it, but the answers had been vague, perhaps because our teachers guarded against any harling becoming too involved in decisions about themselves, such as trying to influence outcomes.

Because we were born in batches, feybraiha came upon my friends at the same time. They became excited and hyperactive. A few became melancholy, which was regarded as illness and treated as such. One har disappeared and we were told his feybraiha symptoms had made him so sick he'd had to be taken to an infirmary elsewhere. Whether this was true I never found out, but he didn't return to Ashen Weald. At the same time, we were told not to go near the lake for a couple of days; some excuse about a dead animal contaminating the water. I wondered if they'd found him drowned, but there'd been no sign he'd felt that desperate. For one brief moment I thought I should have noticed his distress, spoken to him, but if he'd felt anything like I did he'd kept his own secrets.

One of our teachers, a har named Jacx, summoned me to a private meeting, during which he informed me he would be the one to guide me through feybraiha. I decided at once I was lucky, because of all of them Jacx seemed the most remote, a dour survivor. When he spoke of aruna and duty, it was without passion or belief. He recited a script. He lacked the zeal I had sensed in others, who looked up to our leaders as if they were gods, and our appointed roles as some kind of holy calling. I said nothing to Jacx about my concerns, merely bowed my head politely yet without meekness.

When he came to me in the night, I soon realised – from the incision aruna made in his psychic defences – that he had long ago lost all hope, and had done what he had to do to survive. He had closed his heart to what he had to face every day of his life. He felt nothing for me, not even pity. I sensed it had once taken great effort to squash his natural compassion, but in that I recognised somehar similar to me.

This is what he taught me: not the swooning caprices of aruna, but how to be cold and apart in a stronger way than before. Because he helped me in this manner, I have always remembered his name. He showed me what to do, and throughout the experience I copied him exactly, down to the nothingness within. He didn't remark upon this, although at the end he stared at me for several seconds, his expression inscrutable. I didn't say anything and neither did he. I knew that to question or make suggestions would mark me as troublesome. I wondered what decision he'd come to and hoped he wasn't sure about it.

After Jacx had left, I went outside, into the quadrangle of garden beyond my dormitory wing, which had once been part of the domestic quarters and was on the ground floor. Nohar stirred as I crept from my room and along the corridor to the door. Once in the night air, I could see, beyond the great arch that led to the main driveway, homestead guardians patrolling, with their mastiffs at their sides. To them, I was nothing more than a shadow on the ground. My body was sore but my heart was elated. I felt, in some way, I'd scored a victory. In the darkness between two walls, where the cold moon couldn't reach, I smeared the earth with my blood, thanked it. *Now take me further,* I thought.

Now that I was adult, the days of play were curtailed. I was already used to working so this didn't make much difference to me. Anyhar older than my 'batch' in the homestead was a keeper, a guardian or a hostling, but for us the day of judgement was yet to come. The mood among my peers was that of nervous anticipation, because we all knew hara from Fulminir would arrive before the end of summer. Some of my friends were already sure of their futures, because it was obvious to anyhar what their role must be. Some I think were afraid but didn't voice it. I sensed this fear most in those who'd have to leave the homestead to fight. The minority who were sure they'd be hostlings didn't think there was anything to worry about; they'd be safe. Incarceration and safety or freedom and danger? Was I the only one to crave freedom and safety? Didn't it occur to any of them there could be an alternative to the judgement that would be cast upon them?

On the day before the Fulminir party arrived, we decorated the homestead with garlands of flowers and wreaths of woven barley. There would be a feast, a celebration during which the newly-adult would sit in the same dining-room as the guests. At the end of the evening, the judgements would be made and afterwards the Fulminians would go to the hostlings, and a new batch of harlings would be conceived.

Late morning, my friends and I gathered beside the road that led south to await the guests. We held baskets of strawberries to offer immediate refreshment. A cloud of dust billowed in the distance from which eventually our visitors emerged. They rode in black, high-sided carriages, or else upon black horses alongside them. I remember thinking they were oddly silent. They passed through us, almost as if they were ghosts, although a couple reached down to take the fruit. A few smiled at us, but most did not. We were only livestock, after all. The windows of the carriages were veiled.

My friends, undiscouraged by the apparent lack of delight at the sight of us, ran behind the party all the way back to the house, some of them singing. We poured through the open gates. In our absence the rest of our household had gathered upon the driveway – hostlings, keepers and harlings. The harlings looked at us with a kind of awe, poor little fools. The high-keeper of Ashen Weald stepped forward to greet the visitors. I refuse to remember his name or even his face. Farmer. Market time. That's all I need to recall.

The Fulminians dismounted and one important-looking har went to open the door of the largest carriage. From this another har emerged, clearly of high rank. He looked surprisingly young and was not particularly tall; guards surrounded him like a high wall. His lion-coloured hair was short but styled around his face. He possessed a contained sense of power and confidence. He was announced as Lordra Averen and later I learned he was a favourite of the archon. (Lordra was a rank given to those in our leaders' immediate circle.) But from the moment I looked upon his hands and his posture, and noted the languor of his expression, I could see he was not a warrior and certainly not a hostling. This, perhaps, was my template. I knew that for the first time in my life I must actively curry favour with another, not simply make myself useful. For the first time, I must be noticed fully and in a different way to how my friends were seen.

While I was mulling over these thoughts and wondering what I must do, another carriage was opened. From this a har stepped down, followed by three companions. He must be a hostling, I thought, for he was dressed in ornate robes of a red so dark it was almost black, and his face was painted. His hair was a dark river – a magnificent fall – that splashed from his head to the floor. I'd never seen such a creature; he wore his beauty like a mantle – it simply hung from him, disregarded. He took us all in with a single circling inspection, his eyes never resting upon any of us for long. His companions, similar though less striking hara, hovered around him, whispering behind their hands to one another. The rest of the Fulminians ignored him, but I could see he did not care about that. He was Averen's, I assumed. Had he once come from a place like Ashen Weald? I had no desire to be like him, though. It was Averen's role I wanted.

We went indoors to prepare for the evening, while the guests were taken into the high-keeper's spacious apartments to refresh themselves and rest. In a few hours my destiny would be decided. I would leave Ashen Weald or stay. What must I do? I rarely felt anxiety, but it pressed upon me in those hours. I was convinced my whole future depended upon my actions that night.

As I made my way downstairs, having successfully disentangled myself from my friends, I came upon Jacx in the shadows at the top of the hall, looking down. He was a lean, ascetic har, who was always expressionless. Now, he looked like a ghost observing the living. Below us, hara had gathered and were standing around, talking to one another. Somehar played the old piano that stood beneath the curving arm of the stairs. The notes echoed upwards, turning sinister in the darkness. As I passed him, Jacx put a hand upon my arm. 'Rest a while,' he said.

I ducked my head, 'Tiahaar.'

For some moments there was silence, then Jacx said, 'We are not permitted here to choose for a har any role other than hostling or warrior.'

I said nothing, afraid he was testing me and that I might betray myself.

Jacx took his hand from me. 'What seems a long time ago, I too faced a forked road, but in my case I could choose which I would follow. I knew that in order to survive I must be adept at playing games, at influencing how others saw me.'

My face flamed, my gaze was fixed upon the carpet.

Jacx fell silent, then said softly, 'Look at me.'

Reluctantly, I did so. 'I danced for a har,' he said. 'Not a dance of seduction or of war, but of my whole being. With my body and my art, I exclaimed "Look at me!" And he saw.' Jacx smiled, but sadly. I had never seen him smile before. 'Sometimes we have to be brave and not fear to look a fool. Do not care what others think. Do always what you have to. Dance when it's needed – in all of its many forms and meanings. We live in difficult times, and I pray to the Aghama that we survive to see better.'

He turned and walked away from me towards the upper reaches of the house. I stood for some moments unable to move, unsure of what I'd just heard. A wave of cold retched through me: *he knew.* And yet he had not seemed to condemn – quite the opposite.

After the meal, the hostlings would perform for the visitors with dance and acrobatics. Some would sing. They were trained in these arts to help set the mood when hara came to make them with pearl. The dance of the hostlings would take place in the gardens, beneath the gaze of the moon. A couple of rooms had been provided for them on the ground floor where they might prepare themselves for the performance. I'd escaped the dining room easily, since I'd managed to find a seat so far from the glittering guests nohar knew or cared if I was there or not. There'd been no opportunity to make myself noticed in the right way, but I was aware that time was slipping too quickly through the glass. Now, I wandered around the chambers where the hostlings preened, drawn there almost against my will, and watched them carefully. They were lovely creatures, chosen for their physical beauty and their gentle natures. I sensed and was appalled by their innate desire to please.

Pedigree cows, I thought.

I walked unseen among them, for they did not know me and I chose not to know them. They no doubt considered me weird and best not examined too closely. What must I do to make Averen notice me? Would a hostling be sent to him? Somehow, I couldn't image that. And I was hardly equipped to be a devastating seducer. Wouldn't I, to some degree, have to believe in what I was doing to be convincing at that? Then I remembered Jacx's words. He couldn't mean *this*, surely? I let my hands trail over the spillings of beads and diaphanous fabric that lolled across chairs and tables.

Do not fear to look a fool...

No, I couldn't. Could I? But as a little harling I'd been taught to dance – we all had been. I could be more convincing at that than at seduction.

'What are you doing?' somehar demanded.

I glanced up to see a hostling staring at me. He didn't appear hostile, only curious. 'I was thinking,' I said, 'that I might dance.'

He smiled, reached out to touch my face from which I flinched away. 'Sweet foal,' he said, 'the judgement has already been made, one way or the other.'

'That's not why I wish to dance.'

He raised his brows. 'Oh!' A pause. 'I am...' he began, and I knew he intended to tell me his slave-name.

'No,' I said, putting my fingers against his lips. 'Just help me dress.'

He clasped my fingers in his hands. 'You want to stay with us,' he said, faintly feverish. 'Can't we then be friends?'

I saw in his face a most horrible yearning. He wondered whether I could be his son, and whether – if I stayed at the homestead – he might pretend that anyway. Perhaps he did this every time the judgement was made. He was a strange-looking har, though pretty in his way, with a charming almost monkey-like face.

I pulled my hand from his hold. 'I don't want to stay,' I said, impulsively, to squash his thoughts rather than to reveal a truth. I regretted my words at once. 'But please... help me.'

My appeal reached inside him. He smiled with his entire face, like a light turning on, and then he was truly beautiful. 'You want to impress. I see. But this must not be a roon-dance.'

'No, not that.'

'Let's see, then.'

He dressed me, quite simply, in a garment that was a knotted leather harness from the waist up, and a skirt of strings of wooden beads that reached to the floor, but would fly out if I spun round. Beneath it I wore trousers of soft brown leather that clung like a second skin. Once my helper had dressed me, he bade me sit before a mirror. I didn't like looking at myself. I wasn't classically beautiful in the way hara can be; my face was square and angular with wide cheekbones. My lips were full but not quite wide enough, my eyes heavy-lidded and – I thought – a shade too large. This gave me an owlish look. I always wore my hair in a plait, but my attendant hostling said this was too severe and unbraided it. He pulled some of it back from my face and confined it with varnished apple tree twigs, embellished with tiny green beads like the sweat of sap. He did not paint my face, perhaps because this would accentuate my features unflatteringly. He did, however, give me the feathered mask of an owl to wear. I wasn't sure whether to be angry or amused by that.

Others had come to watch as he'd worked on me, thinking it quite a novelty an unjudged har wished to dance. As far as I knew it wasn't forbidden, but neither was it encouraged. I had no idea what the outcome of this would be. The judgements would take place after the entertainment. Before then, Averen must notice me and judge me differently.

I listened to the hostlings' gossip – mainly it was of the har whose name was Sashtri, he who'd travelled with Lordra Averen. Apparently, he was famous. The hostlings speculated that they too might one day catch the eye of a high-ranking har and be whisked away to a life of privilege and romance. I was convinced by now that Tiahaar Sashtri had come from somewhere quite different to a homestead and no amount of alluring behaviour would transform my housemates' fates to his. Did that apply to me too? I mustn't let my conviction waver. This was my only chance.

My helper stood back to appraise his work and appeared to

be happy with it. It was clear the other hostlings hoped my dance would unsettle the high-keeper. He wasn't loved by them, because they held him responsible for their continual grief, even if he did profess the sundering of hostling and harling was for their own good – the offspring belonged to the tribe rather than the bodies who bore them.

'What is it you hope to achieve?' a hostling asked, somewhat sourly.

I stared him in the eye. 'I will dance as both warrior and hostling, which is what we all are anyway.'

The hostling uttered a scoffing laugh. 'Won't make a difference,' he said, folding his arms defensively. 'You're not unique. Don't you realise others have tried it before?'

I shrugged. 'But I haven't tried it before.'

The har sneered. 'You're wasting your time. You're the same as everyhar else. By the end of tonight, you'll know that.'

I ignored him. My helper pressed something into my hands, which was concealed in the sleeves of his costume. 'Here,' he whispered. 'It's only a toy, but use it as a tool.'

My hands closed about an ornamental knife, a fragile, pretty thing that wouldn't even cut a strawberry. But it was at least a symbol.

Then he handed me a large glass of sheh. 'For courage,' he said.

I drank, took its autumnal burn right into me.

In the gardens, there was a circular lawn surrounded by a high yew hedge, which was used often for seasonal ceremonies. In the centre was a shallow fire pit, surrounded by grey stones. Here, a bonfire lay waiting to be lit. Benches had been provided for the audience and set around the edge, as well as globes of burning oil that emitted a soft illumination. We walked out there ahead of the audience, along with a troupe of musicians. The hostlings barely spoke and held each other's hands. I walked beside my helper, and the back of his left hand brushed against me, but I would not clasp it. We passed beneath the arched opening in the hedge and stationed ourselves along the far side of the lawn. We were enveloped in dark, hooded cloaks, so were virtually invisible against the dense foliage. I stood off to the right side, my heart determined to remind me how painfully hard it could beat, and thus within this reminder the threat that it might stop. I must be insane. This wouldn't work. At best I'd be thought an idiot and sent off to fight. Hostlings didn't have initiative or tried to challenge tradition. Ironically, by dancing among them, I would seal off the avenue to become one.

After a few minutes, the audience arrived. Averen and Sashtri walked arm in arm through the arch in the hedge, followed by their adoring minions. Averen was much shorter than Sashtri, yet this did not appear to discomfort him. I envied their tranquil confidence, their absolute sureness of their position in life and their worthiness to deserve it.

The rest of the Fulminians came after them, followed by the entire household, who were allowed to watch the entertainment. The high-keeper and his staff guided hara to their allocated seats, and arranged the harlings to sit cross-legged on the grass in front.

Once everyhar had settled, the fire was lit. Presently the music started up; at first this was only the chime of a single bell, then a fluttering of notes on a harp, followed at last by the drums. A dozen of the hostlings peeled away from their companions, casting off the concealing cloaks. They became at once magical, enthralling, their arms twisting on the air, their bodies moving like liquid. The costumes they wore, though diaphanous and floating, were dyed the colours of the deep forest and of the night sky. Stars glimmered upon them, or the eyes of beasts in the brambles – gems and beads that caught the firelight and the cold glow of the moon.

Beneath the hood of my cloak, I looked dimly upon the Fulminians seated on the front row, just above the harlings. Within hours, these hara would be taking the hostlings to their beds. Suddenly, the whole performance seemed tawdry and obscene. I wanted to run away, but to do so now would only draw attention to myself. The dancing hostlings were shadows, sinuous and weirdly powerful in that pagan setting of night and fire and sky. Witches beneath the moon, experiencing for these scant hours how it felt to have control. I would remember this conjuration of power; it might be useful.

The drumming intensified and by this time the flames roared high. More hostlings now cast off their cloaks and joined the dance. They wove a complex pattern with their bodies, shadows against the flames, like leaves upon the wind, lifting and falling, never touching, never quite landing on the earth. I sensed how this – *this* – could be a mighty force, but the dancers didn't realise it.

Eventually, there was only me left standing in the shadow of the hedge. My helper hostling turned to me, blown away from the others for a moment. He beckoned. I went to him, some instinct within telling me not to cast off the cloak. It became part of my performance. Even though I had learned how to dance at an early age, I had never done so for pleasure, but my muscles remembered what to do. I had an urge to whirl and create power, build it up. The hostlings achieved this instinctively, making the audience giddy, forcing those greedy Fulminians to pant for their reward.

The hostlings made space for me, spinning around, until a few came close and tore off my cloak. I dropped to one knee, my hands braced against the grass. I was the owl-har, poised for flight, ready to rise then swoop down upon the vulnerable body of my prey. I could almost feel wings growing from my back.

The drums were building to a climax. The power circled.

I leapt into the air, imagining those ghost wings spreading wide.

I threw the knife.

The feeble blade arced glittering through the air and pierced the dew-damp lawn between Lordra Averen's feet.

Averen jumped up, and immediately his guards swarmed

around him. I landed upon the damp grass.

The music faltered, stopped. Hara came running to grab hold of me.

Chaos. They thought me an assassin. I would be killed.

Roughly, they seized me, dragged me forward. The hostlings were uttering strange, fluting cries at my back. The household appeared to be frozen in time, some with hands to their mouths, others shocked and wide-eyed. Perhaps they feared my behaviour would reflect badly on them all.

'What...' Averen said, with no panic in his voice, '...is going on?'

I didn't know what to say. What had I been thinking? I hadn't thought it through. Now I was helpless.

There was a moment's stasis, then the high-keeper moved forward to speak, no doubt to utter orders, but before he could do so I heard laughter. It was Sashtri. The high-keeper took a step back, clearly unsure what to do. Sashtri stood up and began to clap his hands. 'A superb performance,' he said.

Averen glanced at him. 'He attacked us.'

Sashtri gestured at a minion who, obeying his command, went to retrieve the ornamental knife from the grass. This was handed to Sashtri, who examined it. 'Averen, this is not a weapon. The worst it could do is snap against your skin and give you a splinter.'

'The intention...'

'Oh shush.' Sashtri came to stand before me, lush and tall. 'Did you seek to harm Lordra Averen?' he asked.

I shook my head.

'But this was not part of the usual performance.'

Again I shook my head.

'What is your name?'

I stared up at his wondrous face, which was alight with humour. I could barely find the words. 'This One,' I said.

He raised his brows, stared at me for a moment. 'You have no name?'

'I am This One.'

'Hmph.' Sashtri drew in his breath and returned to his seat. He gestured at the high-keeper who stood looking mortified a short distance from him. 'Bring This One to me later.'

The high-keeper glanced at Averen, perhaps seeking confirmation. Averen merely made a languid gesture with one hand. 'Do as he says. His word is my word.'

Sashtri spoke the high-keeper's name and the har bowed to him. 'Make no judgement on This One,' he said, pointing at me.

I had the feeling Sashtri rarely involved himself in Averen's work nor made requests of this type, but when he did take notice and did speak, he was obeyed without question. I had aimed the silly knife at the wrong har, yet still it had struck the right target. But the night was not yet over.

I was taken indoors and made to wait in my room, where I sat holding the owl mask in my hands, staring at it. I didn't have to wait very long. Perhaps Sashtri was too intrigued to delay our meeting.

He had been housed on the first floor, among rooms I never had reason to enter. His chamber was lit by amber light, a flattering, blurring glow. He stood in the centre of this room, alone. Although he was lean, he appeared voluptuous – a quality that came from within. 'Well,' he said, 'just what have we here?'

'I meant no offence,' I said, pathetically.

He approached me and looked me up and down. 'You *do* have a name, harling. Why don't you want me to know it?'

'I am known by a word. It's not my name.'

He narrowed his eyes. 'You are brave,' he said. 'And perhaps desperate.' He paused. 'If I am to take you away with me, you must give yourself a proper name. You sound simple calling yourself This One. What name would you like?'

I barely took in the latter half of this speech. 'You'll take me?'

'Of course. That *was* the point of it all, wasn't it?'

'How... how did you know?'

'Because hara like you have limited options. This isn't a fairy-story, harling. I don't go to all judgements of calling with Averen, but when I do, if I see the need, I assist. I regard this as the least I can do for those less privileged than myself.'

'Oh... thank you.'

'You're welcome. Now, a name.'

I looked up at him. 'I want *your* name.'

He laughed. 'But you are not like me.'

'Are you a hostling?'

'Gods forbid, no!'

'Then I want your name.' I have no idea what prompted these insane words. I felt possessed.

Sashtri narrowed his eyes, a cat's smile. 'There isn't room for two of us in Fulminir. You must choose.'

Strangely, I knew at once. 'Vashti,' I said.

'I approve,' Sashtri said. 'Welcome to our staff, Tiahaar Vashti.'

I bowed my head to him. 'Thank you, Tiahaar. I can't express how...'

'Then don't,' Sashtri said. 'You took a gamble. You won. Thank Fate for its co-operation.'

I was leaving Ashen Weald. I would not be sent to fight. I was going to work in Fulminir, and this magnificent har was my saviour and patron.

Sashtri said he wanted me for his staff, and the high-keeper had to abide by that request. I don't suppose he cared what happened to me, anyway. The next morning, once this news became known, some of my friends looked at me with anger, others with respect, a few with sadness. When I climbed into Sashtri's carriage, I saw Jacx, tall at the back of the crowd. I nodded to him and he offered me a grim smile, raised his hand to me. 'Thank you,' I mouthed silently. He turned and went into the house.

Dissolution

In the dusky light of the jolting carriage, and beneath the slit-eyed observation of the companions, Sashtri said to me, 'You don't have a purpose in life yet, Vashti, but you must use your wits to acquire one. You will work for me, but I'd advise you to aim higher than that. The Varrs are very busy and there are opportunities to take, if your eyes are open to see them.'

'You never said that to me,' one of the companions wheedled, a sting in his voice. 'Do you think so poorly of me?'

Sashtri glanced at him. 'Not at all. But you have no killing instinct, Zevvi, which is why it's best you stay close to me rather than hunt further afield.'

I imagined then – and later found out I was correct – that Sashtri's mission in life was to save hara. Some he had to keep by him because they were vulnerable, others he educated and sent on to chart their own paths. He was not sentimental or nurturing like a hostling would be. He could, when provoked, be deadly. Once, some years after I left the homestead, and after some incident that had annoyed us, I said to him, 'You could go to the Gelaming, you know. You could have gone a long time ago. They would welcome you.'

He'd laughed. 'And who'd pull the shivering puppies from beneath the thundering hooves then, Vashti?'

I believe he suffered some guilt because he'd come out of inception glorious, and this had enabled him to find a comfortable niche within the Varrish hierarchy. He knew what the alternatives might have been. So he stayed, and he rescued, and everyhar in his circle laughed indulgently at this, as if it were some amusing little hobby. He and Averen were not chesna; they were a team who worked together to survive and thrive. We all believed, at that time, that Ponclast and Terzian would be victors in the war to claim this land for the Varrs. We felt we had to make our nests within the tribe watertight and secure.

Fulminir was the core-hive of the Varrs and enemies could not touch it. Gelaming were the only tribe that could be termed a threat – other tribes were too disorganised and too small to be troublesome. Any that *might* have been a problem had been annexed: the addled Uigenna, the original Wraeththu tribe, whose remaining hara bordered on lunatic, and the sinister Kakkahaar, who were amoral and dedicated to honing their natural abilities in questionable ways. Hara of other tribes haunted the chambers and corridors of Fulminir, some as allies, some as slaves, and yet others because they were curious or drawn to power. *I* was drawn to power. Fulminir's walls ran with it like sweat, they stunk of it: the beating heart of the tribe.

While not beautiful, Fulminir was in those days majestic. It was sturdy, massive and indestructible, a strange mixture of architectural styles old and new. It wasn't a single edifice but a complex with a cyclopean fortress at its heart. In its early days, it had been a stronghold-city of the human leaders in Megalithica and even then had not faltered in its task of defence. Disease had taken the last of its human inhabitants, and any who survived that epidemic had fled. Then Fulminir had opened its doors to new owners, for without living beings to enliven its energy, and living hands to maintain it, any building falls into decay. Fulminir was alive; from the first moment, and forever afterwards, I could sense its attention all around me.

The Varrs made changes to Fulminir to reflect the egregore of the tribe. War banners hung in the fortress's immense atrium. Victims of war hung from the walls of the courtyards where once gentle fountains had played and people had come to relax – fountains that were now dry, like eyes that had wept so much they could no longer do so. The rooms in every part of it had been scoured of functional furniture and redecorated in the severe yet weirdly baroque style of the Varrs. The walls were covered with panelling ripped from churches, or from old houses: layer upon layer of items from the dead eras of the past. Fulminir was a scavenger's vision of glory. There was a wing dedicated to hostlings, although the hara who lived there were not like homestead hostlings. These had a more specific purpose that I didn't discover for some time.

At Ashen Weald we'd only been vaguely aware of tribe politics, which were condensed into Varr equals good and Gelaming equals bad. The Gelaming wanted this country, which by right belonged to the Varrs, who had developed from the Uigenna, the proto-tribe. Even in Fulminir those not directly involved with defence didn't often speak of it, but one time Sashtri said to me, perhaps after I'd suggested he should have gone to the Gelaming, 'The Varrs believe they own this land because they were created here. Ponclast was Uigenna once, you know, as was Terzian. They formed the Varrs because the Uigenna lacked strong leadership. The Gelaming would have rounded them up eventually. But ironically, the Gelaming were also formed by a har from the Uigenna, or so it's said. He's rumoured to be the first Wraeththu of all. So, you have to ask yourself, who *does* have more right to rule here?'

'The ones who win,' I answered.

Sashtri nodded and smiled. 'I see you have an astute grasp of politics.'

The lesser Varrs, those who weren't grand warriors or high-ranking advisors, believed the Gelaming offered immense riches and a life of luxury to its tribe members, but they wouldn't take just anyhar. You could reach them only by magical means and had to undertake peculiar trials to be accepted. I suppose when you had to pass daily the bodies of enemies and traitors rotting on the garden walls, these fancies helped keep you sane. We were supposed to hate the Gelaming, but I knew I wasn't alone in imagining these hara as heroic and exceptional. I suppose to us they weren't real, but figments of a romantic dream.

On the day I arrived at Fulminir, an ocean of cold rain thrashed from a bruised mauve sky. The outer courts were muddy and filled with hara selling all kinds of produce, some freshly-made, but mostly scavenged from the dead human towns nearby and the ruins of a vast city beyond them. My only impression was of the immense size of the complex and how the cruel downpour seemed part of it, its dressing.

Most of Ponclast's staff, apart from his military leaders and council of advisors, were squirreled away deep inside the main fortress, some with living quarters that had no windows. But Sashtri and Averen, being favourites, lived in a spacious apartment of fifteen rooms, high on the western wall, which had a terraced balcony. This overlooked an ornamental lake beyond the stronghold's walls, created by the men who'd once owned the building. Magpies strutted along the terrace, made tame by Sashtri's bribes of titbits. They took liberties, sometimes attacking hara who didn't offer them food.

As a contrast to the dramatic decor of indigo, crimson and black beyond the apartment walls, Sashtri had fashioned his living space to be calming – a pocket of serene *elsewhere* within the cruel heart of the Varrs. Colours were muted and pale, not, he said, because he favoured those hues, but because it was essential, given what roared outside. He would not let that in. Once the doors were closed it was possible to believe you were not in Fulminir. If you didn't go out to the edge of the balcony, but gazed from inside through the long narrow windows, you could believe you were in isolated countryside. Most of the old city beyond Fulminir had already been eaten by nature, gulped down, so that the green could undulate slowly, sated, over the ugliness of the past. This had created a weird and beautiful topography.

At first, Sashtri gave me trivial jobs to do, allowing me to settle in. I didn't want to venture beyond his sanctuary, half afraid somehar would recognise undesirable tendencies in me, and drag me away to an unspeakable fate. Daily, I marvelled at my luck, with a reverence that was almost spiritual. An agency beyond the everyday world had saved me; Sashtri was merely its instrument. I savoured every moment of being alive. Sashtri encouraged me to educate myself and invited me to read the books in his library – volumes that had been looted and restored from the wreckage of human habitation. I was especially fond of the books on ancient mythology and sat up far too late at night immersing myself in the old legends. I felt the stories were parables of universal truths. The humans who'd written these books couldn't have been that much different from us. Once the supply of these books had been exhausted, I moved on to history, and found disturbing parallels there. Had anything really changed in the world? Weren't *we* supposed to have changed it?

After a couple of weeks, I became an assistant to Marenne, Sashtri's head of household, at first helping to maintain the apartment, but later, once my confidence grew, delivering messages and running errands. I would go down to the makeshift markets in the outer courts of the stronghold and buy the items on the lists I was given. I learned to haggle. I learned to recognise hara and greet them with familiarity. I saw hara around me, who, in the midst of Ponclast's little empire, were neither warriors nor hostlings. They were simply themselves, in a colourful diversity of personalities and traits.

During this time I first became aware of hara who Sashtri told me were known as Vigilants. They were not leather-clad militia but rather like priests, dressed in robes of umber and orange. I saw these individuals gliding around Fulminir, sometimes alone or sometimes in pairs, and at first, until investigation informed me otherwise, imagined they were hienamas of some kind. In fact, they were a division of the stronghold guard and their purpose was to oversee the inhabitants. Like all tyrants, Ponclast had a streak of paranoia concerning his own followers.

But despite this disturbing aspect of security, I came to feel safe there, as did most of the hara who lived within Fulminir's walls. It was neither lovely nor soothing, but it was strong, and you couldn't help but perceive a protective nature pulsing from it. To me, it became Valhalla, Olympus; impregnable. Fulminir had once failed in its purpose and its inhabitants had died or fled. I was sure the stones of the place would not let that happen again. Perhaps these impressions were simply emanations from the soul of Ponclast – who I'm sure regarded Fulminir as an extension of his physical body.

I did not see the archon, never mind meet him, for at least three months. Sometimes I would hear the long unearthly bellow of horns, which sounded as if they were blown deep in the earth. I asked Marenne what this sound was and he explained it was the tusk-call of Ponclast's personal guard, escorting him back to the fortress. To me, it was the sound of doom, dark gods coming up through the ground from the underworld. Yet it thrilled me.

Winter was approaching, and often by the time I got to the market, it was nearly dark and torches had been lit. One afternoon, the moan of the horns started up, and hara became skittish around me. I knew Ponclast had been away, dealing with some skirmish or another, but now he was returning. Fulminir rose upon its hackles, opened its eyes. The torches burned brighter.

I waited, because I knew the party would pass through this section of the market, since it was close to the main gates. I was excited. Everyhar was. Rooks circled the high walls, uttering their music of war, and presently the gates groaned open. A company of black horses trotted beneath the arch, harness jangling, ridden by beautiful yet stern warriors. And in their midst the Lord Rook, Ponclast himself. His black hair was short, like a cap of feathers, his face strong and sculpted, but I noticed his finely-drawn lips and brows. Handsome, I suppose you'd call it. He was dressed as a typical Varr warrior in black leather, but with a vivid crimson cloak wrapped around him, looped at the neck. Beside him rode a fair-haired har, equally arresting. This, I thought, must be Terzian, he who stood at Ponclast's right hand.

Like everyhar else, I put a fist to my breast and bowed as this company rode past.

After they had gone, and a strange stillness had fallen over the stalls, I hurried home. I felt compelled to go into Sashtri's sitting room and say, 'I saw Ponclast.'

He smiled, somewhat sourly. 'I can see that,' he said. 'Break the glamour, Vashti. See through it. That might save your life one day.'

His tone embarrassed me and this must have been obvious.

Sashtri laughed. 'Don't be ashamed. We all felt like that once. Our beloved archon weaves a magic spell, which you must recognise and resist. Bow down to the master magician and do as he wills, but only while wearing a mask.'

I thought of Jacx then. 'Keep dancing,' I said.

'Quite.' He straightened in his chair. 'Anyway, what have you brought me? Something interesting, I hope.'

I always tried to find unusual things at the market for Sashtri because it amused him – trinkets from the past. Sashtri was compiling a wall of history as he visualised it. I think he put much of his pain and frustration into it. That day, I had come across a beautiful marcasite watch that no longer worked. Only a couple of the stones were missing. 'It doesn't tell the time,' I said, 'but it's beautiful enough to wear as a bracelet.'

Sashtri held it before his face. 'Marcasite is made from an essence of iron,' he said. 'Dark and lovely yet strong.'

'Like you,' I said.

He put the watch down on a table, stared at it. 'It doesn't work,' he said. And for a moment he was melancholy, but that never lasted long. He wouldn't indulge himself in that way. 'It's wonderful, Vashti. Thank you.'

He never wore that watch, but hung it upon the wall with his other precious memorabilia, surrounded by a photograph of a dog and a child, a pair of women's long silk gloves, an antique gun.

I wanted to meet Ponclast, hear his voice. Despite Sashtri's warnings, he intrigued me. It wasn't his physical appearance or the aura of power he wore, but simply the fact he was top of the pile: a lion standing proud and fierce upon a pyramid of lions. I dreamed of this image and was haunted by it. What had made Ponclast? How had he come to be so powerful? Could I too aspire to such greatness and the freedom it gave? In his position, would I be a kind leader and forbid the forced breeding of hara for war? Or would I then see it as a means to ensure my rule? Does such power inevitably corrupt? I was still young. These questions gnawed at me.

I utilised all the skills I'd learned at Ashen Weald to further my position within Sashtri's household, which inevitably didn't go down too well with the more vulnerable of Sashtri's rescued hara, who were jealous. Averen was rarely seen. He had nothing to do with the staff or anything domestic. When Ponclast was in residence he often didn't even come home at night. He had been given the title Procurator, with the emphasis on the second syllable: Cure. It seemed ironic. He oversaw communities and took from them hara he felt would augment Ponclast's army. This included visiting the breeding facilities. When making his choices, he rejected hara of unstable temperament, those who were frightened, those who were lost. It was important his hara too were lions, and he was the pride leader who sat licking his paws on top of this lesser pyramid.

At the midwinter festival, Averen was to celebrate his birthday with a party, which Sashtri and his hara would organise. This would not be a huge affair with hundreds of guests, but held within the apartment, attended by thirty or so significant hara. Among them would be Ponclast. The household, predictably, was thrown into mild hysteria at the prospect. Ponclast rarely made personal visits to his hara. As I'd manoeuvred my way towards being indispensable and eminently useful I would be helping to organise and service this party.

Birthdays for first generation hara did not mean celebrating the day of their human birth but that of their inception, their rebirth. Averen, though appearing very young, was not. Sashtri said to me dryly, 'Averen has to be forced to hold parties. He sees no point celebrating...' Whatever else he was about to say he thought better of uttering. 'The theme will be purple and silver, but the purple of the peacock, deep and vibrant.'

Marenne was happy for me to assume responsibility for the decoration of the apartment, since he was busy with the other arrangements. I had boughs of evergreen brought in, as we'd always done in the homestead, and sent hara out to scour the scavenger markets for decorations in the required colours. There were hardly any human buildings left unforaged in the near vicinity, so the markets were our only resource. Some merchants traded with the secretive, scavenging hara who still lived in the city ruins, which were said to go down into the earth for miles. There were rich pickings there, even if they were somewhat dangerous to acquire. My agents did well, assisted by Sashtri's apparently bottomless purse. One set of decorations, I was told, had been taken from a shuttered house, where life had ended at the winter festival humans had called Christmas. Festive garlands had still hung from the walls, glass baubles upon a withered tree. Bones clad in rags had lain upon the floor. I hesitated for a few moments at the symbolism of this, and whether using these items might incur bad luck, but ultimately decided they were safe. They had, after all, persisted long after their previous owners were dust.

Sashtri was pleased with the results, which I'd deliberately made Gothic and rather a departure from the usual ambience of these rooms. Thick garlands of holly and yew hung upon the walls, the berries sprayed with a paint of silver blended with royal purple pigment. Ribbons hung down, artfully tattered. Other garlands of ivy and fir were made to look dusty and old, as if ripped from a tomb, with swags of purple silk behind them. And leaves were strewn upon the floors, the decaying remnants of autumn, damp and pungent, the essential fragrance of the season.

Terzian did not attend the party, since he'd gone home to spend the festival at his estate in Galhea. Ponclast came alone. I thought he must have dozens of hara who catered for his physical needs, in all senses, but he had no consort at his side, which was unusual in a leader. Even in those barbarous days, a chesnari represented foundation and certainty, especially so if there was a harling from the union. Some said Terzian was his chesnari, unacknowledged, and perhaps this was true, but Terzian had another life elsewhere. I wondered why Ponclast hadn't found a har like Sashtri to be his complement, a bauble perhaps, but also shrewd and intelligent. Why hadn't he chosen Sashtri himself, come to think of it? Perhaps he preferred to be alone.

When Ponclast arrived, I was at the door offering hot, spiced sheh to guests. Averen was nearby. He came to take a glass from my tray and said to Ponclast, 'This one here threw a knife at me once. Now he serves my guests.'

Ponclast gave me a look that could strip flesh from bone. 'I hope he no longer harbours that tendency. Skewered guests might be awkward.'

'Sashtri likes him,' Averen said. 'He threw the knife to make an impression in order to escape the homesteads. It didn't hit me, but accurately pierced the ground at my feet.'

'Commendable,' Ponclast said to me. I felt I might wither beneath that gaze, the strength that pulsed from him. 'If you know you're worth more than where you find yourself, you should work for better, whatever it takes.'

I ducked my head but smiled to show I was not wholly tamed. I was surprised, though, that Averen had felt moved to explain me to Ponclast. He appeared barely to notice me nowadays.

I was surprised too when Ponclast spoke to me again, once Averen made to lead him further into the gathering. 'Did you keep the knife?' he asked.

I ducked my head again, 'No, lord. It was only a toy, a symbol, not a weapon.'

'Symbols are important. You should have kept it to remind yourself of how life can change and through such small agencies. What is your name?'

'Vashti.'

He nodded once and walked away. I had to lean against the wall.

I found out the next morning that Sashtri had asked Averen to make the introduction. Sashtri summoned me to his sitting room, where the winter light sliced hard and bright through the windows. 'I've been thinking about your future,' he said. 'You know a lot about the homesteads, don't you?'

I shrugged but not with disrespect. 'I know about the one I came from.'

'Then you could be of use to Averen. I will recommend you join his personal staff.'

'No!' I exclaimed and Sashtri raised his brows. 'I mean... I don't want to leave your service, Tiahaar.'

Sashtri made a dismissive gesture with one hand. 'Don't fret, Vashti. You may keep your room, which you will continue to use when you're in residence. You will become my friend and not simply my employee. Will that suit you?'

I nodded. 'I'm sorry... yes, of course. Whatever you want me to do.'

Sashtri sighed impatiently. 'It's not a case of what I want, but securing a future for you. I believe you'll be a good judge of hara, and will assist Averen in making his selections. Also, perhaps it's now time for a third choice other than hostling or warrior to be introduced – for hara who might have other benefits for our tribe. Hara who are like you.'

'It would be better,' I said cautiously.

'At one time it was essential that warriors were bred and trained who weren't first generation lunatics. The Uigenna are too crazy to last and lack discipline. The Varrs are now more secure in their territory and different hara may rise to prominence. Hara who use their minds, and who act through wisdom and experience. The Gelaming are thought to brag about their art and science, and so should we. But for that we need artists and those with scientific minds. At my suggestion,

Averen has relayed these ideas to Ponclast's higher staff and they weren't met with displeasure. What do you think?'

'You're probably right.' This was all I could think of to say. Sashtri expected me to be pleased about this, but I simply didn't care. I'd made the effort to escape Ashen Weald. Fate had helped me. If others were awake and astute enough to make similar plans they'd earn their freedom. If they were dozing cows, they wouldn't. I had no desire to help Averen sift through docile livestock and – in the case of the warrior class – yapping dogs, in the hope of finding hara of worth. But I could appreciate this would be a promotion, and I must take it.

'I told Averen that Ponclast must be made aware of you,' Sashtri said. 'If you want true freedom, he must like, trust and need you.'

I frowned. 'What is it you see in me, tiahaar? I'm adept only in self-preservation.'

Sashtri laughed. 'And that makes you creative. Take my advice: to be safe, be needed.' He smiled tightly.

Separation

My employment in Averen's staff began shortly into the New Year. At that time, there were no homesteads to visit, although some would have hara ready for inspection in the spring. I learned there were over thirty of these establishments in the surrounding area. They weren't positioned too closely together in case the Gelaming should hear of them and decide to interfere. They were known publicly as regular farms and most had been running for over a decade. Now there were batches of harlings from them every year. I realised that at one time somehar had come up with the idea for these appalling places and had suggested it to Ponclast. Somehow, I didn't credit he'd thought of it himself. But homesteads were not the only resource. Varr territory was occupied by other tribes, subservient to them, and over the years they had begun to breed. Tithes were paid in flesh, but this was regarded as a privilege by the parents of those selected, as if their sons were not being sent to be trained as dispensable killers but merely to be educated at a good academy. If they were loyal, Varrish warriors were well cared for, indulged even. I could appreciate there were worse lives to live.

Very soon I realised I possessed a gift that made me good at my job. I could tell which hara would produce the best offspring. This quality wasn't obvious, and not a part of their physical appearance or build, or even their psyches. It was something else, something deep. I could smell it. Strength. Potential. The flowering of possibility.

'What makes you so sure?' Averen once asked me.

'You'll see,' I answered, '*if* you bother to track my suggestions. Naturally, this will take years.'

When we travelled, Averen expected me to take aruna with him. I didn't mind this, as he wasn't sentimental or overpowering. After our unions, we'd discuss our work. He trusted me – I became to him too more than an employee. One night he touched my face and said, 'If Sashtri hadn't seen the

186

truth in you, we wouldn't be here now.'

'He was meant to see the truth,' I said.

'One day we'll drive the Gelaming out completely, seal our borders against their sneaking incursions,' Averen said. 'Then hara like you, and Sashtri, and me – we'll have laid our strong foundations. We'll have all we desire.'

'Serve the master,' I said.

'As long as he remains the Ponclast we know, yes. I have little doubt that will change.'

We had no idea what the future would hold, how Thiede, leader of the Gelaming, was building his tribe from carefully-chosen hara all over the world – not bred but found, willing volunteers of all races and cultures. Thiede did not resort to force or fear. The hara he discovered possessed skills learned in earlier human lives, or else quick minds that could recapture knowledge in danger of being lost. He no doubt flattered his recruits, made them feel special – the best. Some were proficient in the arts of warfare, others in the arts of magic and healing. Yet more became shrewd politicians who could negotiate with other tribes to build alliances of which the Varrs could only dream. Thiede knew what should be kept of the human era and what should be discarded. He played a long game. We had no idea a day would come when he'd release his perfect creatures upon us and no matter how carefully hara like Averen and I sought to improve our tribe, we'd not be able to best the Gelaming when they were ready.

That summer, Averen and I went to Ashen Weald. Sashtri did not accompany us and we took no personal staff, but for the warrior guard who would service the hostlings. When our carriage sprang onto the road that led to the homestead, and the young hara came to greet us, my heart turned to iron. I wouldn't look at them, and drew curtains over the windows. Averen inspected me in the sepia gloom. 'Don't think of it,' he said.

I didn't answer.

Eventually, we were in front of the main house and the household was arranged there to receive us. I stepped down from Averen's carriage, dressed in close-fitting black leather, with my hair long and loose: Varr yet not of the standard template. I stared straight into the high-keeper's face. 'Do you know me?' I asked him.

He bowed his head. 'No, Tiahaar. Forgive me if I should.'

None of them knew me, yet I felt I looked the same, even if I had grown taller since I'd left them. I know now it was because they didn't look too closely. I could walk around that place like a lord, like Ponclast. Hara shrank from me, bowed, ducked, touched their hearts in gestures of respect. I wanted to find Jacx and thank him, but discovered he'd moved to a different facility. Or this is what I was told. And there was another I wished to see.

I went to the hostlings' quarters and threw them into panic. It wasn't yet their time; my visit was irregular. But I was there to find my saviour. I owed him.

Following a hostling's nervous instructions, I found my har in the courtyard beyond the kitchens, sitting on a stone bench by the old well with several companions. They were laughing together, weaving garlands of flowers, not a care in the world. I watched them from the darkness of a doorway for some moments. My saviour appeared happy, silly little creature. When I emerged from the building and the hostlings caught sight of me, they froze at once like frightened does. I said to my saviour, 'Do you remember me, Tiahaar?'

He flushed. 'Forgive me... I have seen many.'

'That's not what I meant. It's been so little time since we last met. Only a year. You gave me a chance at life. You gave me a wooden knife.'

His eyes widened. 'It's you?'

'Yes. You see? This is what you enabled. Now I will repay you. Come away with me to Fulminir. I'll find you a secure position.'

His flush faded. He glanced at his friends for support, but

they only turned their faces away, terrified. 'My lord... Tiahaar... your offer is... I don't deserve it, but more than that...' He shook his head. 'This is my home. Please don't make me leave.'

I stared at him. 'Is this what you want? To be kept like a cow and made to breed? Don't you *want* freedom?'

His eyes filled with tears. 'Lord, I'm nohar. This is my life. But I'm your servant. I must please you.' He held up his hands as if they must be tied, so I might drag him away at the end of a rope.

I turned from him – in both disgust and disappointment – and walked back into the house.

A har ran after me. In the shadow of a domestic passageway, with the metallic chink of pans echoing nearby, he caught hold of my arm. I recognised him at once: the hostling who'd been sharp with me while my saviour had dressed me for my fateful dance.

'He might be a fool, but I'm not,' he said. 'Take me.'

I stared at him. 'No.'

He staggered back as if I'd punched him. He didn't ask me twice.

Would Sashtri have taken that brave har? Most likely. He was kind at heart. But I was angry, not simply because my saviour had refused my offer but because his life in Ashen Weald had made him the har who must refuse. This place was an abomination. Let the other, who had mocked me, rot there.

By the time I regretted that decision, it was far too late to change it.

I continued to work for Averen for around six years, becoming closer to him and – in a different way – to Sashtri. He knew I took aruna with Averen and did not care. Sashtri had his own lovers and was so discreet none of us knew who they were. As Averen had once said to me, the three of us were allied to secure our positions. There were reports the Gelaming were building settlements further south, which were shrouded in unnatural mist, not of this world. It was said they rode horses that could fly. Some said Thiede had built an entire city by magic, which was on the other side of the great ocean and had become the capital of his tribe. The Gelaming could cross that ocean in an instant, by sorcery. I didn't believe these rumours and thought it likely the Gelaming were responsible for their propagation, in order to instil fear and uncertainty. My friends and I agreed that these hara wanted to appear greater than the Varrs and fool us into thinking they wielded strong forces we could not counter. I had never set eyes upon a Gelaming, and over the years my impression of them had changed. I now imagined them to be preening, pompous creatures, who believed they occupied the moral high ground, while in fact they were stealing that ground from others.

Occasionally I would cross Ponclast's path – usually at official meetings to which I accompanied Averen and where I would take notes for him. Ponclast always glanced at me speculatively, which was unnerving and more than a little sinister. I sensed he pondered me, perhaps wondering if I was a threat. Often I felt he was on the verge of saying something to me, and while I dreaded that one day he'd decide to do so, I also yearned for such a day.

Even though I was eager to rise in rank, I never conformed. I didn't hack off my hair or emphasise the ouana side of my nature, as many of Ponclast's immediate staff tended to do. I always wore my hair in loose, curling ropes, yet adopted the close-fitting, black leather uniform of the others, which I knew a few found confusing. Was I soume or ouana prevalent? It was inconceivable to some I could be both, and to others, who weren't so blind, but who were afraid to emulate me, it was perhaps folly. Yet I was never reprimanded. I was simply Vashti, Averen's irreplaceable if somewhat eccentric aide.

The Varrs had become closer to the Kakkahaar, who were formidable scryers and could to some degree monitor the Gelaming's movements. We learned that Thiede's hara were massing forces in Megalithica, but discreetly. There were no overt settlements or camps. They perhaps had agents among us, but none were smoked out – although quite a few suspected hara were executed, who were no doubt innocent of any wrongdoing. The Kakkahaar advised Ponclast that he should also bolster his forces and eventually go south to confront the invaders.

Then something unaccountable happened.

Ponclast was not a har given to strange whims and fancies. He believed concentrated will could affect change, which explained magic, but he would never be a har to conjure spirits before a fire, or dance in the smoke of incense. He had others who did such things for him. Yet he did have a dream that affected him to such a degree his friends and advisors were shaken by it. He claimed to have been shown a way to strengthen the tribe through supernatural means.

This was the kind of talk you'd expect from a Sulh or a Unneah, perhaps even from the more flamboyant of the Kakkahaar, but not a Varr and especially not our archon. The rumour, when it broke out, was quickly quashed. We weren't allowed to discuss the matter, and to do so would be regarded as treason against the leadership.

Nohar really knew what was going on, but Fulminir was alert and wary. The walls cracked and groaned in the night.

Averen was summoned to a meeting to which I was not invited. Only the highest-ranking Lordra were present, along with the leaders of the resident Kakkahaar. Sashtri and I sat together in his sitting-room while the meeting took place. It was as if we held our breaths, although our lungs still worked mechanically.

'This could be *them*,' Sashtri murmured. I had never seen him unnerved before and reached for one of his hands.

'Ponclast is no fool,' I said. 'He wouldn't be taken in by Gelaming tricks.'

'Feel it, Vashti,' Sashtri said, glancing around the room. 'Something is about to happen. Even the walls feel it. What's coming? It's too soon. I'm not ready for it, but I wonder if we should try to leave.'

I squeezed his hand. 'Leave? No, I don't think we should do that.'

'Go and see if there's news.'

'They won't let me in.'

'Doesn't matter. Somehar might've heard something. Go to the war chamber. Wait outside if necessary. Just *be* there.'

Reluctantly, I did as he asked, convinced there would be nothing to hear. Ponclast's staff would release any news when it was deemed appropriate. Rumours would not leak out.

I thought the best place to start would be in the kitchen area that serviced the chamber. If hara had been providing refreshments, they might've heard something. But as I suspected, nohar had learned anything – voices had fallen silent as food and drink had been dispensed. Hara in the kitchen were too afraid even to discuss the matter, and worked in tense, unnatural silence. A Vigilant haunted the room, walking slowly around it. Heads were kept low. My presence seemed a crass intrusion, so I wandered outside and stood before the massive closed door. The hallway had been cleared of other hara and lay in eerie stillness. There weren't even any guards, which was unusual.

After I had waited some minutes, the door opened a little and Averen came out. His eyes widened in surprise when he saw me. 'How did you know I wanted you?' he snapped.

'How do you think?' I countered, although bewildered by his words.

He laughed. 'Well, you're here and it saves me having somehar summon you.' He gestured back towards the chamber. 'Come in. They're waiting.'

I crossed that threshold, aware it marked a change in my life. Beyond it was a long, polished table, hara sitting around it. They all stared at me, none cordially, and some with resentment. Ponclast sat at the head of the table, before a stained glass window of which he seemed to be a part, radiating colour. That window, and the living icon at its heart, dominated the room. I felt disorientated, as if I'd been sucked into a different reality. I bowed from the waist, then kept my head lowered and murmured, 'Tiahaara, how might I serve you?'

'His arrival was quick,' somehar said sourly.

'Vashti's senses are sharp,' Averen replied, his voice light. 'He sensed I wanted him and he came.'

'A convenient faculty,' somehar else said.

'Probably trying to eavesdrop,' said another. 'I know this type – cunning. Soume-shrew.'

I couldn't see the hara who spoke, as my head was still bowed, but I heard the blades in their words. These were potential enemies, even if at the moment they were simply bullies. Now it seemed I must dance again.

'If you *are* so prescient,' Ponclast said, his tone neutral, 'do you know why you are here?'

'No, lord.'

'But you knew to come here.'

'I'm attuned to my Lordra's wishes. I am his servant.'

'Good. Now I wish you to work for me.'

I raised my head abruptly, couldn't help it, my gaze colliding with his serpent stare. I couldn't speak. What was this?

Ponclast laughed. 'The prospect doesn't please you. Perhaps you've gleaned an inkling of what's afoot, but you've no need for concern. I have a specific purpose for you, as advised by your master.'

I shook my head in what I hoped appeared to be genuine contrition. 'You must excuse my reaction, lord. I'm simply surprised I can be of use to you.'

'That has yet to be seen, but Averen thinks well of you and your... abilities.'

I touched my breast with my right hand. 'I'll be honoured to serve you, lord, in whatever capacity.'

'I'm told you're good at sniffing out stock. Now you must

use that sense to its full capacity, for the sake of your tribe. I want you, har, to choose for me a specific kind of breeder. You will work with the Kakkahaar and act on their advice.'

I glanced at Averen whose expression was inscrutable. He offered me nothing by way of support.

A tall Kakkahaar got to his feet. He was dressed in a sand-coloured robe, which was embellished with embroidery of arcane sigils in green and gold. His eyes were slanted, yet not in the Oriental way. His skin was golden yet weirdly dusty, as if he'd just slithered up through the sand of his tribal territory. He looked to me like Death. 'I am Azvith. Tomorrow morning, early, I'll send a har to bring you to my studio. Then I shall tell you my requirements.'

I bowed my head once more. 'I'll be ready, Lordra.'

Visiting the homesteads to quicken pearls was considered beneath the dignity of the highest-ranking Varrs. Therefore, to facilitate the breeding of top-class hara, they had their own complement of hostlings within Fulminir itself. These prize specimens of harish beauty occupied a sprawling set of rooms high up in the north side of Fulminir, where windows overlooked the green sculptures that had once been a city. I was now ordered to augment this pristine collection of livestock, because simply quickening pearls within them wouldn't be enough to realise Ponclast's vision.

He'd dreamed that one of his sons had visited him and had informed him he was a har of greater strength and ability than any before him. He had crossed time to speak to his father, and offered the information he had not been born of a har. In the dream, Ponclast saw an array of alchemical equipment with harlings growing with them – breeding alembics. It was this idea he'd related to Azvith and his colleagues. Could this be done? Was there some magical principle that could be utilised to create hara greater than those naturally born?

Azvith, being a har full of curiosity, and lacking any code of morality or ethics, had liked the idea and was eager to find out.

He was a strange creature, who could not have been of a great age, but seemed to be, at least in his mind. He had the look of the ancient magi I saw in the books on alchemy he possessed, but was handsome as hara usually are. I'm certain only a particular kind of har is drawn to the Kakkahaar tribe; they perform a specific function within Wraeththu as a whole. This has never diminished, even if eventually it became more respectable.

Following the instructions I'd been given, I went to Azvith's studio on the morning after my interview with Ponclast and his advisors. The Kakkahaar's workplace was a series of high-ceilinged connected rooms, where every available space was filled with equipment, books, dried plants, stuffed animals, withered animal parts, insect wings and limbs, metallic objects of various shapes and sizes, and a jumble of other items I couldn't even identify. How he could work in such chaos I had no idea. Never mind the creation of super-hara; my fingers itched to get tidying. Azvith did have assistants, but they were very similar to him and didn't seem to notice the mess.

On the first day, Azvith explained to me the ideas he'd had. 'There are realms beyond our own familiar world,' he told me. 'We know that hara may access these realms, because the Gelaming already do so. We've experimented ourselves in opening portals, but although we may have tantalising glimpses, we certainly can't travel through them. Not yet. These realms thrive with life beyond our current level of comprehension; some of it, I believe, is bodiless. But this is not to say such entities can't be clothed in flesh. I'm convinced that many reports of hauntings and possessions stem from the incursion of these beings into our material world. My plan, following the visionary ideas in our archon's dream, is to do this very thing. Incite a more potent form of life to enter a developing pearl.'

His words appalled me. It wasn't so much I cared about the fate of hostlings and harlings, but was afraid of what might happen if he was successful. 'Why would other-realm entities wish to enter bodies in this world?' I asked.

Azvith shrugged, as if this did not matter, but indulged me with a reply. 'Curiosity, perhaps, or entertainment, or simply to research, as we do.'

'Or to... frighten hara, wreak havoc.'

Azvith smiled as if discussing the antics of a playful puppy. 'Perhaps that too.'

I could only question the wisdom of attempting to coax such an entity into the fabric of a pearl. What would be born of it? However, the idea sounded too far-fetched to be feasible. Let Azvith go along with Ponclast's outrageous suggestion and play at being a god if he wanted to – I doubted much would come of it.

'We'll need the best hara for this experiment,' Azvith told me. 'Averen claims you have a highly-developed sense for finding the best stock for hosting. Now, we must go further. We must find *superlative* stock.'

Obviously, this task would not fill all my working day. I'd only have to look over hara who were brought in by Averen's staff. In the meantime, I'd be helping in the studio. I offered to clean the place. Azvith looked at me in perplexity. 'Well, I suppose so... I don't have much else for you to do immediately.'

'I could catalogue your equipment and store it in an orderly fashion,' I said.

'Why? I never have trouble finding anything.'

'I'd like to do this. I hate standing idle.'

'Oh, very well, but don't lose or break anything.'

As I sorted and sifted, with Azvith regularly coming to check I wasn't damaging his precious possessions, I learned the purpose of the stranger objects in his collection. Most were alchemical vessels, used for transmuting one substance into another. This idea would come to play a great part in the project.

Azvith told me that the majority of the Lordra were sceptical of Ponclast's vision, but nohar would dare speak against it.

Azvith, however, thought the idea had merit and wasn't beyond his powers to realise. The first batch of hara came in and I inspected them as required. As I'd expected, none of them could be termed 'inferior', but only a couple possessed the special quality I looked for. Azvith arranged for two of Ponclast's closest aides to quicken pearls within these hara. Once this was accomplished, Azvith had the hostlings brought to the studio and into one of the chambers he'd set aside for the project. Here, he had the hostling lie on a table and injected a concoction of substances through their bellies into the pearls that rested within the cauldron of creation. He felt this would attract otherworld entities to investigate the developing hara and hopefully enter into it. To aid this, he created around the table small portals to the ethers, almost like baiting a trap. But the experiments did not go well at the start; the harlings within the pearls died or hatched deformed. The hostlings were made ill – and of course it's very difficult to make a har ill for any length of time.

While the project progressed very slowly, the studio became a neat workplace where hara could find exactly what they wanted straight away. Azvith even rediscovered items he'd forgotten he had and grudgingly approved of my work.

Even though I rather came to like Azvith and his absent-minded quirkiness, (which disguised a very sharp mind), I knew that the work I assisted with now was worse than what had taken place in Ashen Weald. Azvith was meddling with the stuff of creation, using hara's bodies with no consideration for how it might affect them. The hostlings had no choice in this matter; they weren't volunteers. But they were given instruction swiftly by those already in residence on how to survive. Survival meant compliance.

A couple of months after my new employment began, I received a summons from Ponclast himself. He came often to the studio to talk with Azvith about the project and I assumed he wished to grill me for more details. Azvith told him as little as possible. I knew he didn't like our great archon, because he made a poor job of disguising his feelings.

I went to Ponclast's chamber in the early evening and was surprised to find I was expected to dine with him. This also put me on edge. I was to be buttered up for something. It might not be good.

Ponclast came into the dining room dressed more informally than I'd ever seen. He wore a robe of deep crimson and black, which softened his movements somehow and made him appear more dangerous. 'Have sheh,' he said to me and gestured at an unseen servant who emerged from a corner and handed me a glass. This was warm to the touch, as if the har had held it for some time. I drank the contents in one gulp. The har would not meet my eye. He took the glass and departed.

'I have another task for you,' Ponclast said.

I bowed. 'What is your wish, lord?'

'This will take a few months out of your schedule, which is unavoidable. You will host a pearl for me.'

I blinked at him. 'Me?'

'What better stock than yourself? Don't you agree? This won't be an alchemical creation, but the usual kind. I need no heir, but find myself desiring family. I want the Gelaming to have something else to fear about me.' He punctuated his next words with abrupt gestures of his hands. 'The sons of Ponclast.'

'A mighty company,' I said.

He smiled. 'Such is my plan. We have to start with one, and I must observe his development, decide if this experiment should be taken further. I have sifted the options and have decided the most adequate har for the task is you.'

My guts twisted in a presentiment of pain but somehow I managed to remain composed. 'As you wish, lord.'

He laughed. 'Look at you. How often you wish you had a real knife in your hands! You don't fool me, but I know you're a survivor and won't swerve from your path of self-preservation. Grit your teeth and do this. I don't ask you to be a hostling in the traditional sense. Just carry the pearl for me, and once it's done you need not think of it again.'

'I...'

He gestured with one hand to silence me. 'Don't feel it necessary to make some mewing sounds about loving and raising a son, because you think you should. I know you, Vashti. I know what you've made of yourself. I wouldn't be speaking to you otherwise.'

'If you know me, lord, then you're aware that even though I'm able to select hara for pearl-bearing, I've never done this myself nor have been trained in the techniques of quickening. I feel obliged to mention this.'

'I know the techniques,' he said. 'Now, we'll eat, drink, then later see to this business. Don't worry. I don't expect you to spawn an army of sons for me. Just the first. After that, you'll select the hostlings. Anyway, that's for the future. My hara have prepared us a feast, so let's enjoy it. Please, sit down.'

As I sat there across from him, barely able to eat, I realised this was what I'd wanted all along. Not the harling – that was irrelevant – but to work my way into the confidence of the most powerful har in my world. Now I would taste that power fully, take it into me, and apparently shape some of it into new life. He was right. I didn't care about the pearl we would make. I'd make no demands of him, have no expectations. I'd be loyal. I knew he'd never take a chesnari. But some things I'd make sure of: He would trust me. He would *need* me. He would keep me close to him. And as long as he held power I would be safe.

Eventually, these warming thoughts enabled me to eat.

It's interesting to note, in the light of all that happened afterwards, that Ponclast was never the soulless creature he liked to present to the world. Like me, he hid his true self well, but it's hard to remain detached during aruna. I'd learned how to do so, and I've no doubt Ponclast was equally familiar with this technique, but that night we showed a little of ourselves to one another. This sealed my future in Fulminir. I learned, in just the slightest glimpse of a memory, that once he'd been violated and so physically damaged, soume was forever after repulsive to him. This explained a lot. I never discovered the circumstances surrounding this pelki, this attack, but I knew it lodged deep in the core of his being and contributed greatly to who he'd become. Part of him hated Wraeththu; being har had made him vulnerable to such an attack. Therefore, he hated himself, his physical body. But that body had needs. Taking aruna as ouana allowed him control, even at those moments when we most let go. But despite his armouring, he was sensual, passionate.

Perhaps he believed he pleasured me to make me quicken, but I know he enjoyed our union and wanted me to enjoy it too. At times I still couldn't believe it was happening and yet it was incredibly real. First, he dealt with the lust, had me on the table, among the remains of our meal. He was the first har I'd ever truly wanted. His touch ignited me. His breath was hot, like demon fire, and conjured flame within me too. This was no hasty act – he knew how to prolong aruna and tormented me with it. The release, when he eventually allowed it, was so forceful it was painful.

And then, more wine, more food. We sat upon the floor to pick at the scattered meal. I wrapped my naked body in the table cloth. For those hours, we were ordinary hara, partaking in simple delights. We shared breath as we stumbled blindly to his bed chamber and there, upon his bed, he became almost reverent, stroking my body, studying it. Carefully, he opened me up, until I was delirious. When he entered me, I didn't perceive an ouana-lim but some kind of ceremonial instrument. I felt something within me give way and something within him take advantage of that. So it was done.

Ponclast did not want our plan kept secret, although we were both aware it might cause difficulties for me among his hara. We talked of this in the blue hours of the predawn before we slept.

'Years ago, I suffered for being a favourite,' he said. 'I think you know something of that.'

I nodded, remembering the fleeting glimpse of his pain I'd experienced during aruna.

'Don't feel shame in keeping me informed,' he said. 'I don't want you damaged.'

The jostling for position within Fulminir was intense, and feuds easily kindled. Ponclast's longest-standing allies would not take kindly to me – a young, untried interloper – suddenly having influence over the archon. Because they would know I did. But neither would any of them have wanted to undertake the task I had accepted so willingly. Eventually, they would look upon me as a necessary nuisance, and later still some would grudgingly come to respect me. They all feared Ponclast too much to harm me – at least physically.

He let me sleep in his bed until an hour past dawn, then woke me and sent me home, but he sealed our farewell with a kiss, his hand on my belly. I felt as if I'd reached the moment I'd striven for since the day I'd understood I wanted to be free. While ironically, it would make a hostling of me – that type I so despised – I'd learned that no function was exempt from being a tool for progression.

Sashtri and Averen were pleased about this development, seeing it as yet another way to cement our relationship with Ponclast. They had brought me to him, and he'd rewarded them for that.

Sashtri said to me, 'Your body is a vehicle. Look on it only as that.' He put his head to one side. 'I think I know you, Vashti, but I hope that deep within there isn't some part of you bonding with that pearl.'

'Believe me, I know not to do that,' I said, and then told him more about my early life, the sad ceremonies I'd witnessed, the grief. 'There is nothing useful in feeling like that.'

'I wonder, though,' Sashtri said, 'why he balks so much at taking a consort, somehar at his side to produce and raise sons. A family. Terzian has a consort, as do the other Lordra. Is he afraid, perhaps, they'd steal some of his power?'

'I don't think it's that,'

I kept Ponclast's confidence. I never revealed what I'd learned about his past.

He said he'd wanted me for this one purpose, yet after that first night he summoned me once a week or so to take aruna with him. I was aware that was the excuse, anyway. He liked my company. He asked me about the homesteads and I told him, making no suggestion of improving the hostlings' lives or anything like that. I wasn't Sashtri. I was determined to be careful at all times, because our meetings felt as if they were spun of fragile glass. I had to guard against shatterings. I did not try to make him love me, nor kindled such feelings for him. He must trust me, always, and I would move around him so lightly and gracefully I'd never break the glass.

When it became obvious I'd reached the latter stage of pearl-bearing, Ponclast no longer summoned me. I was temporarily unfit to take aruna and I suspect the sight of a har exhibiting such overt soume characteristics discomforted him. But he did send me gifts, delicacies that had come from far communities, ancient books, a real knife. He did not insult me with flowers or scent, such as the soume-oriented were expected to enjoy.

Sashtri was with me when I dropped the pearl. He had procured potent philtres that dulled my pain and it was over relatively quickly. A har came and wrapped the pearl in a towel. He carried it away. For some minutes I was aware of an unsettling emptiness within me, but Sashtri was prepared for that too and offered me another of his medicines. This enabled me to close the shutters of feeling. I turned over and went to sleep.

I did think of that pearl over the following weeks; it was impossible not to. But I knew it was foolish to harbour any fantasies about it. Ponclast had been clear in his demands of me. I was to have no part in the raising of a harling. If I had any wistful yearnings, I squashed them with the thought that my son would have the most privileged of upbringings. He would never be a simple warrior nor forced to breed. He would be a

Lordra and perhaps one day, when he was grown, I might be allowed to know him. Until then, I tidied away my feelings and locked a door upon them. Such feelings could make a har weak.

Once I was fully recovered, Averen came to see me and told me I'd been allocated an apartment of my own. This was a direct order from Ponclast apparently. I imagined the grumbling amongst this advisors and cronies that was no doubt taking place because of it. I was sorry to leave Averen and Sashtri's household, but also pleased to have my own space, so I could choose my own staff. Some of Sashtri's hara got on my nerves.

My new quarters were nowhere as large as Averen's and Sashtri's apartment but consisted of seven rooms. I was also allocated two hara as staff, with the understanding I could change them if I found them unsuitable. Fortunately, I found no fault with them. I was pleased to find the apartment had windows, albeit looking over the central garden of Fulminir, which nowadays wasn't much of a garden at all. I wondered who had lived in my rooms before and what had happened to them, but they'd left no impressions behind. Perhaps the place had been empty for a while. I didn't emulate Sashtri's muted decorations, but allowed free rein to the interior designer who was sent to me. So the rooms became very red, but not particularly black. They were softened with gold and amber.

On the second night after I'd moved in, Ponclast visited me unannounced, which was uncharacteristic. I could have been out, or had other visitors. Previously, I'd always been summoned to him like a servant. He asked how I was and told me the pearl had been pronounced healthy, its passenger forming well. This was the first of only two times he ever mentioned our son to me. He thanked me for fulfilling my work so well.

'I would do anything for you,' I said.

'I know that,' he snapped back, and in his tone I heard, like a muffled voice in a far room, a faint and wistful longing that I might accommodate his requirements through affection and not through expediency. I don't think he realised he'd let that sliver of feeling show to me, but I was curiously touched. I went to him, reached up to take his face in my hands, pulled him to me to share breath. This lasted for some minutes and afterwards neither of us said a word about it.

'Would you like something to drink?' I asked him.

'Not this time,' he said. 'I must go. I hope you like these rooms.'

'Very much,' I said. 'Thank you.'

And that was it; our romantic moment.

The Kakkahaar chose a name for Ponclast's son: Gahrazel. I had closed down my feelings for him so efficiently, I never felt that he was partly mine even on the rare occasions I caught sight of him, although he was similar to me in appearance. He never knew me. Even after Fulminir fell we had no opportunity to meet. He didn't live that long.

Conjunction

Sethra was not a homestead har, but had been born free. A scouting crew had found him during one of their regular inspections of Unneah communities in the Longmaw Mounds, a hilly wilderness some miles from Fulminir. I knew from the moment I saw him that here was treasure. The crew-leader, Vert, had summoned me to the holding pens to inspect the stock he'd brought in. He noticed me paying attention to this har and said, 'He ran, or tried to. Down the hill like a hare.'

He *was* like a hare, softly brown and quivering, but with ancient knowledge in those deep pool eyes. He might shape-shift into something quite different.

I experienced a sense of hesitation, as if I could easily say, 'No, not this one, there's something not quite right. Just let him go.' I could have done that, but curiosity shouldered this thought aside. I wanted to know him.

When he saw me and met my gaze, he drew his shoulders back, even though he was afraid. He knew what I represented, I suppose, and perhaps recognised his own Lordra Averen in me. But I was neither that, nor compassionate Shastri. He was mistaken to look for release in my direction. Still when a har inspects you with keen attention, as I certainly did during those moments, you *know* they're to be a part of your future for good or ill. *He* knew. The pattern of our destiny unrolled before us; we had only to weave it, then.

Sethra was not the most beautiful of hara, but he was arresting. There was a wistfulness within him that shone through his skin, which made you feel a strange yearning for something you'd forgotten. But that's not to say he was naturally melancholy. He could be mischievous and his laugh, surprisingly, was deep and often described as dirty. And yet I experienced an intangible sense he was a doomed, fey creature, and that part of him was aware of that. He had tried to run, but not fast enough. His doom had caught up with him.

I went close to him in the room that was like a cell, but was merely an anteroom, and murmured, 'You should not have run, Tiahaar. I suspect you can make yourself invisible in a crowd, should you choose to. Why did you run?'

He looked at me steadily. 'Because I dreamed I'd be taken, and in the dream I was pulled from a crowd. I thought I could escape this fate, but I was wrong.'

'Yes.' I smiled, no doubt a rather gruesome sight for a har in his position. 'Still, you will be well cared for here, and if you cooperate, live a life of relative luxury, which is denied most hara beyond the walls of this fortress. I advise you to comply and do what you must to survive.'

'Like you did,' he said, and there was no fear in his eyes then at all. Oh yes, he *knew*.

I stared back. 'Yes, exactly like that. Who knows where it might lead?'

He raised his gaze above my shoulder, said no more. I turned to the crew-leader at the threshold, nodded to him. 'Fine,' I said and went out into the corridor beyond.

I didn't see Sethra for two more days, but only because I willed myself not to seek him out. The settlement he'd been taken from would do all they could to appease the Varrs. When inspections were made and hara taken for various purposes, they would never complain, but no doubt simply thanked their gods it hadn't been them, this time. They knew some hara were taken to be warriors, and the most beautiful to amuse the warriors or become hostlings. I wondered what Sethra's parents thought of his abduction. He wasn't of the warrior type, nor particularly lovely in a soume-prevalent manner. Did they worry over what his fate might be?

The following evening, I entertained the crew-leader, Vert, in my apartment to find out more about Sethra. 'What drew you to him?' I asked as we sat at the dining table.

'Why do you care?' Vert responded, helping himself to more of my sheh. 'He's just another, isn't he?'

'Surely we were both "just another" at one time?'

Vert shrugged. 'I suppose so, but this one...' He shook his head. 'Oh, I could smell him out. I've learned to recognise what you look for, Vashti. But in all honesty, now I've seen more of him, I don't think he's that special. I was drawn to him, as you put it, because instead of waiting there with the others, he decided to bolt. What else could I think but that he ran for a reason, had something to hide? So I chased the little hare and brought him down. Now he's yours for whatever you want him for.' Vert narrowed his eyes. 'What *is* this? Has Vashti the Frozen been pricked by a hot thorn? Will he melt a little?'

I laughed. 'How absurd! I was simply intrigued. You know we're on the lookout for a certain type of har.'

Vert dared to reach over the table and touch my shoulder. 'What for, Vashti? What are you doing, hidden away in your dark chambers?'

'Helping to secure your future,' I said. His touch could not melt me. I could barely feel it. Still, I took him to my bed around an hour later.

The friendship between Sethra and me was forged from his initial scorn and my unquellable attraction to him. He was bright, so quickly decided there was little point in being difficult. Like I once had, he clearly decided that in order to engineer an escape he needed to blend in, not draw the wrong kind of attention. Where else to start but with the har who, for whatever reason, seemed interested in him?

When I saw him for the second time, it was in the hostlings' quarters. I'd gone there on the pretext of examining the newcomers for Azvith. The hara who lived in those rooms weren't treated cruelly, but were pampered, even if they had their own complement of Vigilants to observe them. Yet despite their fairly comfortable lives, they still had a function they must fulfil. Now, following our archon's peculiar dream, that function had taken a darker turn.

I'd requested that Sethra be kept separate from the others for the time being, because I wanted to explain his purpose to him myself. I didn't trust the hara there, as they tended to tease newcomers. Anyhar who was markedly different would be singled out for such treatment, I was sure. What I didn't account for back then was that Sethra's difference endeared him to others rather than incurred their derision.

I was led by Nethenya, the head of the hostling house, to one of the smaller sitting-rooms. The narrow window had a limited view, so the room was not often used. Nethenya unlocked the door to let me in and departed.

Sethra sat hugging his knees in the cramped window-seat, looking out, perhaps in the direction of his old home. He had been dressed in a flimsy robe of cobalt blue that shifted restlessly about him. He appeared at ease in this costume, as he'd appear in anything he wore. The gift of natural grace. I looked at him for some moments before he decided he should turn his head to me. In that scant time I fancied I saw his future, the pearls he'd produce. I felt he wouldn't grieve, not this one. But I could also see that his apparent indifference to his circumstances was gulping up his energy. He was near exhaustion; soon the façade would crumble. I didn't want that to happen.

'Tiahaar,' I said, moving towards him.

He ducked his head, said nothing, but got to his feet.

'Do you understand why you've been brought here?'

He lifted a handful of his robe in one fist, squeezed it. 'I think that's pretty clear.'

'You're mistaken. Come for a walk with me. I'll explain.'

Conjuring curious glances from any staff we passed, I led him down rarely-trodden passageways and stairs to one of the courtyard gardens, a barely-visited place that somehar clearly loved and cared for – I don't know who. It was overgrown, but artfully so. I found a bench in a shaded bower and here I told Sethra his purpose.

At first he didn't believe me. 'That's... mad,' he said at last. 'Few hara can make harlings, even when they want to. How can pearls be made to order?'

'Discipline of the mind and body,' I said. 'It's not that difficult if you manipulate the circumstances.'

'And you *procure* hara for this… procedure.'

'No, they are procured for me. I'm part of the team, that's all.'

He sighed, shook his head. 'Is there no depth you hara won't sink to?'

I ignored the insult. 'If you're wise, that's how you'll see yourself too.'

'Part of the team…'

'Yes.'

He laughed in a hollow way.

'It's your choice,' I said. 'Think about how so many hara have none at all. This might seem grotesque to you, but look on what's happened as an opportunity – a chance. You might not be able to choose your path at this moment, but you can certainly choose how you walk it.'

'So I let my body be abused and hope my mind can remain sane.'

'Essentially.'

'And become the walking dead.' He reached out and put one hand flat on my chest. 'Strange, you are warm and you breathe.'

I pushed his hand away.

'Ah, you can still feel *something*,' he said.

'You'll have some time to adjust, before anything is demanded of you. I'll make sure of it.'

'I suppose I should thank you, but I can't force those words out.'

I laughed coldly. 'Don't thank me, thank Fate. Make the most of this situation. Learn to dance, in all of its many forms and meanings.'

He stared at me strangely, then gazed at the ground, again shaking his head.

Shortly afterwards, we returned indoors, and I directed a har to take Sethra back to his room.

I dreamed of him most nights. Sometimes we conversed – and I couldn't remember a word upon waking. Sometimes we were about to take aruna, but something always happened at the last moment to prevent it: hara came upon us, or our surroundings collapsed through disasters both natural and otherwise. I realised I wanted him, and in a different way to how I'd wanted Ponclast. Why? What was it about Sethra that clawed through my icy armour and curled fingers around my heart? I knew he wasn't manipulating my feelings. If there was bewitchment, it was entirely of my own conjuring. During the next few weeks, I met with him regularly to talk about the work, and tried to impress upon him how he could – and must – remain detached. I delayed his introduction into the project, and was aware hara were beginning to notice my interest in him. Sometimes, when I talked to him, I feared I was babbling, betraying my image of being cool and constrained.

One day he said to me, 'It's as if you're uttering warnings all the time, as if you're afraid for me. If that's the case, why not let me go? You have that power, don't you?'

'Hara would question it,' I answered. 'They would wonder why I let you go and inevitably either bring you back or kill you.'

'So you've cemented my fate by taking an interest in me.'

I held his gaze. 'Sethra…' There was a brief, intense silence.

Then he grinned without humour. 'I see… Poor you. You don't just take what you want, do you? I suppose that means you must really love me.'

I felt heat pulse in my face and neck, even if it didn't show in an outward blush. 'Don't say such things. Hara have died for far less in this place.'

'For love of you?'

'Don't be ridiculous. I mean generally.'

'Imagining they can have influence?'

'Can't you just accept I want to help you? Stop twisting what I say.'

'At the moment, I'm finding it hard to care. I'm already

dead, despite all you've said to me about chances and opportunities.'

'I don't love you,' I said.

He didn't respond to that. 'Are we done for today?'

Sethra made me feel my age – young. Whatever magic he possessed, in his company I found it hard to maintain the ice-har image I'd created. Of course, he was right. I'd been infected by love. What makes this happen? It's an affliction that strikes suddenly and devastatingly – one of the few diseases to which hara can fall victim. When it strikes, you lose all reason; the world becomes a different place, furnished with the fevered imaginings of the mentally ill.

I told nohar of these feelings, but I agonised over what to do about them. I held onto enough sense to realise I was in danger. Nohar fell in love with a hostling. They belonged to the archon and were allowed no chesnari. There were Vigilants aplenty in the hostling house, because of course they were all beautiful and a temptation to any har who saw them. I knew I should simply order Sethra to be sent to one of the homesteads. Never see him again. But while I might convince myself in bed at night to issue that order, come morning I couldn't force myself to do it. The situation wasn't helped by the fact that Ponclast was away during this time. I didn't even have his overwhelming presence to distract me. Averen too was absent and Vert, to whom I occasionally resorted for physical release, wasn't interesting enough to extinguish my desire. I was too embarrassed to go to Sashtri for advice, who I knew would suggest something drastic and final, because to him self-preservation came before all other considerations. We couldn't help ourselves – or others – if we were weakened. Once, I'd felt the same way.

I kept away from Sethra for a few days, until he sent me a message through one of the hara who served the hostlings. I was aghast he could be so indiscreet. The har who'd carried the note would no doubt have read it and subsequently report the contents to all he knew. The message simply read: 'It wasn't a criticism. I'm bored without your teaching. I'll behave now.'

Delicious gossip indeed. I was relieved it wasn't more explicit.

I shouldn't have responded in any way. I should have given an order for his removal from Fulminir. But I didn't. I instructed one of my house-hara to bring Sethra to me, on the pretext that I had further instructions for him and was too busy to go to the hostling house myself. I trusted my staff, because I treated them well enough to ensure their loyalty *and* their silence. Being part of my household gave them rank and privilege they didn't want to lose, but even so my actions were unwise.

He arrived at my threshold wearing a tapestried coat over his robe of diaphanous twilight. His eyes were dusked with kohl. I realised he had become lovely to me, not merely intriguing. The sight of him flooded me with relief and longing. We stared at one another for some moments, while my house-hara fled like spooked cats to the farthest corners of my chambers. Of course, they knew.

He came into the room, took off his coat and threw it onto a sofa. His eyes said to me, *You know why I'm here. Why delude yourself any longer?*

Had he decided in the sleepless early hours of morning that he must get closer to me? Did he have any feeling for me, or was this simply an act of self-preservation? Had I taught him too well?

We didn't even exchange a greeting. Hunger was met with hunger, or appeared to be. In fact, I remember very little of what actually happened between us that first time. It was a fever dream.

He didn't return to the hostlings' quarters for two days. Everyhar must have known why, yet I didn't care. Inevitably, we spent most of our time in bed, our limbs tangled, coiling like snakes, being ouana and soume for one another, becoming delirious, until it seemed we were merely one creature. I had never experienced the depth of feeling Sethra conjured in me. Previously, even with Ponclast, aruna had been merely a function. Now I understood its true power. I dissolved into this other har. I told him I loved him, that he had bewitched me and knew it, even though that was a lie. I had bewitched myself with him, as if he was a magical drug.

'You're a mystery to me,' he said, 'like a creature of infinite layers. Perhaps one day I'll find the har hidden deep inside, if I venture through one layer at a time. Only a fool would love a har like you, so perhaps I should call my feelings something else.'

Those days seemed endless, yet over too soon. Eventually, doubts and fears niggled at me enough to make me say, 'You must go home now, Sethra. There will be talk. Tell them I've been training you.' We were lying in bed, from which we'd barely moved.

He stared at me for some moments, then said, 'You could make it so there can't be talk, couldn't you?'

'Not easily,' I said. 'We have to be cautious, very cautious.'

'I don't want to go.'

'You must.'

He sat up. 'Is it that you've sated yourself? Now, I'm dismissed?'

'Sethra, no… it's not like that at all. I have to be careful. You've no idea.'

'Are you not allowed friends?' he snapped. 'Is *he* your only one? Yes, there is always talk, Vashti. They *all* love to talk about you.'

I was shocked, because for two days we'd been united in bliss. There had been no mention of my association with Ponclast. Now, Sethra's anger conjured an uncomfortable swimming sensation within me, as if I was being sucked down a tumultuous river, too fast to save myself. I wanted to say – plead – *did you mean none of what you said to me?* Fortunately, I wasn't too far gone in my delusions. 'He makes no restrictions on me,' I said. 'I simply work for him.'

'Of course.' Sethra uttered a cold laugh. 'Very well. I understand.' He got out of bed, stood looking down at me. 'You told me to aim high. You're the highest I can reach. If you're free to do so, help me as your friends helped you.' For a few moments longer he maintained that stony, aloof stance, then it crumbled. He turned away from me and wept, all the while trying to control himself and failing. Eventually, he was able to say, 'If you can't help me, then it would be kinder to kill me. I don't want to be like those sad, frightened creatures I live with.'

I'd spoken to him about freedom. The truth was none of us were free, no matter how far we clambered up the pyramid, our feet in lions' mouths and on a ladder of claws. Still, I could give him a position on my household staff, if nothing else. I must speak to Sashtri.

'I'll have somehar take you home, Sethra,' I said. 'Let me think about this. I'll do what I can.'

He dressed himself, his movements jerky and stiff, far from his usual grace. 'It's not my home, but I'll go.'

'We mustn't part like this.'

He turned to me, his eyes like black fire, as he pulled on his coat. 'That's easy for you to say. You're not the one being sent back to the breeding pool. If you truly love me, how can you even bear that?'

'I've protected you. You know that.'

'But for how long?' He shook his head. 'It can't last like this, can it? Is this just a game to you, or a romantic play? How does it end?' He would not kiss me, or even let me near him. 'Goodbye, Vashti. You don't have to call a guard for me. I know the way and have nowhere else to go.'

Love made a fool of him too. I let him go, unaccompanied. He could have escaped then, if he'd wanted to.

After he'd gone, the room felt desolate and cold. I knew, deep within, that he'd delivered an ultimatum without uttering the words. If I couldn't give him some kind of freedom, the only way I'd have him in future was by force.

I couldn't eat breakfast, but gulped down some coffee, which tasted bitter as bile. Then I went to see Sashtri.

I told him everything, because he couldn't advise me unless he knew the facts. His face was impassive as he listened. At the end of my story, I said, 'I've never loved before, Sashtri, not in this way. I never thought such a finer feeling would – or could – be part of my life.'

Vashti drew in his breath through his nose. 'What do you truly want, Vashti?'

I held his gaze. 'I want to take him as my chesnari.'

He sighed, sadly. 'I thought so.' For a moment he was silent, then leaned towards me, narrowed his eyes. 'Don't you *know* what you've become?'

'I don't know what you mean.'

He smiled a little. 'You're still so young, and you haven't kept your eyes open. Ponclast might deceive himself, but not others. Ask yourself this: Would you dare to stand before him and ask if you could take this Sethra as a consort?'

'Must I ask him? Are we not free in these matters?'

'Some are,' Sashtri said. 'Not you. Remember that Ponclast owns the hostlings. He owns you too, but it's more than that.'

'What do you mean? Just say it.'

'He *visits* you, Vashti. He confides in you. No har who's ever shared his bed has had such privileges, except perhaps for Terzian. And the fact is you share that bed far more than any har has before. He would never admit to having feelings for you, even to himself, and that makes the whole situation more dangerous. You can't risk the consequences. You really can't.'

I wondered how this could have happened when I'd tried so hard to be detached and not to be the kind of har an archon might love. Clearly, I didn't know him very well. 'Then what must I do?'

'Do what's best for both you and Sethra. End it. Ensure that har fulfils the purpose he was brought here for. Hara are talking, Vashti. When Ponclast returns, those who resent you will use this against you, because they know only too well in what high regard he holds you. Some hate that. If you truly love Sethra, and want to protect him, hand him to Ponclast for his breeding project. That will silence all gossip and guarantee Sethra's safety. You can say, quite legitimately, you were testing the goods to see if the quality they promised was authentic. You must state you were preparing Sethra for your archon.'

Had I expected any other reaction? Not really. The air had become hard around me, as if I were encased in diamond. I couldn't speak for some seconds, but eventually managed, 'I must send him away, then.'

'Too late,' Sashtri said. 'You should have done that at the start. I wish you'd come to me sooner.'

The horror of it all silenced me.

Sashtri reached to touch my arm. 'Vashti, I'm sorry, but you know there's a price we must pay for security. Averen and I are lucky, but then our relationship was no threat to anyhar and we were never in love, never *mad* in that way.' He paused. 'You know what you must do to survive,' he said gently. 'You always have. You just didn't expect it would be something like this.'

'This will break him,' I said in a voice that sounded rusty from disuse. 'I don't know how I'll tell him.'

'You'll tell him nothing,' Sashtri said. 'Don't see him alone again, Vashti. I mean it.'

'He'll hate me.'

'Then allow him that armour. You'll stay here with me until Ponclast returns. This will be soon.'

'It sounds like you're placing me under arrest.'

'In a way, I am. I don't trust the madness of love. Let me protect you from it.'

Vashti summoned one of his hara and asked him to fetch his medicine box and a glass of water. The box was an antique made of mahogany, which unfolded to reveal many small compartments, each containing a tiny bottle. Sashtri lifted one out, and infused the water with three drops of a moss green colour, which swirled within the liquid until the colour all but disappeared. 'The Kakkahaar taught me to control pain,' he said. 'It comes in many guises. I helped you with the pearl. Now I'll help your sick heart.'

I stared at the glass, knowing it was poison, but still I drank it.

The tincture was so strong it made a living statue of me. Sashtri kept me medicated for three days, during which I functioned normally and appeared normal to other hara. Inside, I was empty, so without feeling I couldn't even appreciate the most basic sensual pleasures, such as exquisite food or a scented bath. At the end of this time, Ponclast returned to Fulminir.

We had yet to see successful results from Azvith's experiments on pearls. He'd spoken to me about it, confessing he felt he had not yet cracked the code. Pearls, by the time they left the body of their hostling were perhaps too fully-formed to be altered in the way he envisioned. He'd been mulling over the idea of introducing more potent substances into the pearls while they were still in the hostling's body, but believed there would be risks. No har yet fully understood the process of harish reproduction, only that it was nothing like that of humanity, and might well take place partly beyond the physical body.

I didn't want to subject Sethra to Azvith's experiments, because now they were taking a more dangerous path. Yet I knew Sashtri had spoken the truth as he understood it. I'd been careless, allowed too many hara to witness my interest in Sethra. I mulled over what Sashtri had said and many obvious truths became clearer. Love had blinded me to them. It was no secret Ponclast's advisors were wary of me; they were suspicious of my influence and dismayed he made scant effort to hide his fondness for me. He allowed me by him in public.

He directed questions to me at the meetings he asked me to attend. His hara saw that I'd wheedled my way in. As far as they were concerned, I was a jumped-up concubine who should have been kept in his place, an underling who provided a trivial service.

In the light of all this, I should have realised for myself that some hara would now be waiting to drip their venom into Ponclast's ear. The results of that could be catastrophic for both Sethra and me. I must do what I could to limit damage. I had no idea, though, how quickly I would have to act, how little time I'd have to formulate a plan.

Ponclast summoned me the first night he was home. I felt this was fortunate as I could begin groundwork immediately before others could get to him. As I walked to his quarters, I considered suggesting a role other than hostling for Sethra, but knew this was risky. Once my enemies had served Ponclast their gossip, any suggestions of mine would inevitably take on a sinister meaning.

Ponclast had been absent visiting the most powerful of his phyle leaders, all the way down to the tribe's southern limits. Beyond that were rogue tribes, splintered phyles that had not prospered, or simply gangs of unthrist bandits, as dangerous as rabid bears. There was an ocean of unnatural mist and swathes of shattered land and, hidden somewhere within this hinterland, the Gelaming. Ponclast's advisors had suggested it was time now for him to start claiming territory further afield, to annex or eliminate the rag-tag tribes that occupied it – before the Gelaming grabbed both land and hara for themselves. There were already rumours of this – phyles disappearing into the mist, either to their doom or to join the invaders.

The intention of Ponclast's travels had been to muster the farthest phyles, in effect to send them to war. The majority of these hara were neither warriors nor politicians. They were farmers, or were becoming so, adopting a rural lifestyle, trading with other settlements. They lived peacefully, in harmony with the land that fed them; once a dream of the human race, or at least some of them. Because it was generally believed the Gelaming could be persuasive, Ponclast's advisors had declared the archon himself must speak to the phyle leaders – reassure them, make them feel important and then unsafe, and finally deliver an order under the guise of a request for help.

When I reached Ponclast's chambers, he received me in his sitting-room, still dressed in the leather armour he'd worn to travel. He was restless, remote. At first, I thought the tribal talks had not gone well. I wondered whether Ponclast had met with opposition to his plans for expansion. This would not have been overt, of course, but excuses can be obstructions in themselves.

'Did your negotiations go well, my lord?' I asked. We were both standing. He had not bidden me to sit.

He fixed me with a stare. 'Everyhar knows what's brewing,' he said sharply. 'Of course they went well.' His voice was chill.

I realised then somehar, in their eagerness to topple me from favour, had got to him before I had. Now I must encourage Ponclast to keep talking, so I could gather information and impressions for a counter-attack. 'How far south did you go?'

For some minutes, I forced this conversation, asking almost meaningless questions, simply attempting, calmly, to relax him, make him speak his mind. I knew this wouldn't be easy. The more he spoke, the more I could sense his repressed anger – and at that point I wasn't even sure at what it was directed. My own fears might be colouring my interpretation.

And then, the moment came. I felt the atmosphere change in the room, as if every atom became aware and alert. 'There was an unpleasant business near the Marsh Thickets.'

'Oh... what was it?'

He skewered me with his gaze. 'The phylarch had some trouble to deal with – a consort, who betrayed him.'

'Such is the danger of taking consorts, I suppose,' I said, my voice carefully neutral.

'Quite so.' Ponclast turned from me, picked up a goblet of wine from his table, turned it in his hands. The danger of intimacy,' he murmured, 'is that it makes a har vulnerable and secrets might be revealed, taken and stored. Used against him.'

'The consort shared secrets with the phylarch's enemies?'

Ponclast put down the goblet without drinking from it. 'He took a lover from another phyle, whose leader is hungry for more power. The consort spoke too freely in bed. It could have been worse, but he was caught early on.'

'I hope the phylarch dealt with the situation satisfactorily.'

Ponclast bared his teeth at me; I wouldn't call it a smile. 'Of course he did. He had the foolish har and his lover drowned. Execution is the only way to deal with betrayal, isn't it?'

I didn't think so, but wasn't about to say that. 'It's important the phyle leaders are safe.'

'Hara are not that different from humans,' Ponclast said. 'Their physical bodies might be superior and their senses greatly enhanced, but they are still petty, greedy and stupid.' He paused. 'I watched those hara drown, one after the other. They executed the lover first, made the consort watch. I suggested this. Let him and all the others of the phyle see the consequences of treachery against their leader. Every phylarch is a har who would die for his tribe; his hara must respect that and be unswervingly loyal. Their survival might depend upon it.'

My heart was beating fast, and I had to regulate my breathing. I mustn't panic. Now, I must be strong, have courage. I drew my shoulders back. 'My lord, is this story meant to frighten me?'

He was for a moment caught unawares by my direct, unsubtle question, but composed himself quickly and murmured in a soft voice. 'Why should I want to frighten you with such a tale, Vashti?'

'Because – as you said – many hara are petty, greedy and stupid. I should have foreseen this, of course.'

He raised his brows at me, as if to say, *go on.*

'You once said to me that I should tell you if I had enemies who might harm me. I believe you were speaking of physical harm, and I've experienced none of that. But there are other kinds, aren't there?'

'Speak plainly,' he said.

'There are those who resent me and are forever alert for chances to undermine my position. While you were away, a har was brought to me from one of the hill phyles. I saw at once he was perfect for your project and decided to prime him personally for this purpose. I was aware my interest in this har might well be misconstrued, and that some hara would waste no time in revealing their assumptions to you.' I allowed a pause.

'What if I said nohar had spoken to me in such a way?'

'I wouldn't believe you.'

There were some moments of intense, stifling silence. I had to force myself to breathe, because without speaking directly I'd set before us both the subject of his feelings. For some moments it was as if a hundred different futures thrust out from Ponclast, like the spokes of a wheel. At the end of some of them I was dead. Then, his choice made, he backed off, not through any physical movement or change of expression; the room simply relaxed.

I realised he wouldn't want to say anything further on the matter, so took up the threads myself. 'His name is Sethra. I believe he could be our breakthrough hostling. I have been preparing him for *you*, my lord. If this pearl is to be a success – and I feel it will – then it should be yours.'

Ponclast smiled grimly, still pinning me to the air with his gaze. 'You're a very *clever* har, aren't you, Vashti?'

'I don't know about that, my lord. But I *am* loyal.'

I could have gone further, spoken obliquely of love and desire, but I knew what he respected and admired and its limits. Neither did I take a step towards him. I waited for him to do that, and he did.

We did not take aruna; he took *me*. Angrily, roughly, because he blamed me for how he'd felt. For a short while, he'd been wounded by his fondness for me. He'd been made aware he'd lowered his defences, let me beyond them, even if only a short way. And it had been a close call for me. If I'd made one wrong move or uttered one wrong word, or allowed a misjudged pause, it could have been Sethra and me drowning in a barrel.

I realised how stupid I had been, how right Sashtri had been. I had chosen my path with free will, and it was a narrow, twisting track – on one side there was a sheer mountain I could not climb, on the other a deadly drop into nothingness. I must keep my eyes to the ground, notice the loose shale that could trip me, avoid it. I must keep on that path to survive and I must walk it alone.

I uttered cries of pain as the archon mauled my body, not because I couldn't help it but because I knew it would make him feel better. I had ground to reclaim before he would be Ponclast to me again.

Dismissed in the middle of the night, I went back to Sashtri, sore and shaken. I still had a key to the apartment and fumbled my way in darkness to his bedroom. He said nothing when I woke him, merely beckoned me to climb into bed beside him. He held me close in silence for quite some time, before murmuring, 'Keep up with the medicine for a while longer.'

Before that point, circumstances in my life had added layers to the personal armour I had taken such effort to construct. Only with Sashtri, and to a lesser degree with Averen, did I ever set that armour aside and be myself, who I hope was a fairly likeable har. But nothing had prepared me for what I had to endure over the next few months. I must shut down feeling completely, do what I had to do to save the har I loved. And I never stopped loving him. Not for a moment, not even when Sashtri's potions made me an empty shell. Not even when Sethra hated me. Love crouched shivering in a dark, shuttered room, too shocked even to weep. To this day I don't know how I maintained that, or even why. I wonder whether death would have been preferable.

He sent messages to me, but I refused to read them. I visited Nethenya and told him of my decision and what I planned for Sethra's future. If that har eyed me shrewdly, and with more than a little despising, I ignored it. I was too exhausted to try and change his opinion.

Eventually, he couldn't help saying, 'You could have been *kinder*, Tiahaar. I hope Sethra's grief doesn't interfere with your plans for him.'

To that har I was like the high keeper of Ashen Weald, using others to help myself. By *kinder* I thought he meant I shouldn't have gratified myself with Sethra's body, shouldn't have made him care for me, should even, perhaps, have sent him away. In Nethenya's eyes I saw reflected a young inexperienced har, whose lust had blinded him to consequences. A selfish, spoiled plaything of Ponclast's. Now, in Nethenya's opinion, somehar else was having to pay for my self-indulgence.

I wanted nothing to do with what must happen, other than give the order, but Sashtri was adamant with me over that. 'Now is the time for your reinvention,' he said. 'You'll be there when it happens. You must. Only then will Ponclast think he can trust you again. For no har could stand by and see that happen to somehar they loved.'

'A har couldn't, no!' I cried. 'But a monster could! Is that what I am, what I've made of myself?' I began to tremble, and turned away from Sashtri to grope my way to the wall.

Sashtri pulled me back before I could weep, turned me round and slapped me hard across the face. A gout of light splashed before my eyes. 'No, Vashti, no! Don't fall apart on me. We're all in danger now, but not from petty events here in this fortress. Beyond these walls, circumstances continually spiral and mesh their way to a climax. It is coming. We all know it. Play your part. Dance. And offer your sacrifice to the har who is our god, with power over life and death.'

'Maybe I don't care anymore about that!' I yelled. 'Maybe Sethra and I would both be better off dead!'

Sashtri shook me, his fingers like claws in my upper arms. '*This* isn't why I brought you here. Pull yourself together. How can we help anyhar if we're weak or dead? And we will *have* to, Vashti. Count on it. And I need to count on *you* when the time comes.' He softened, pulled me to him. I was too dazed to speak further. 'Vashti, Vashti...' Sashtri murmured, kissing my hair. 'I care for you too, you know. If anything, you are the closest to a son I'll ever have. *Do* this terrible thing. It'll be over before you know it, before Sethra knows it. If he hates you forever, that's the consequence of the madness of love. Accept it, release it, and survive.'

I relaxed against Sashtri's body, spoke in a muffled voice. 'Even if I could force myself to bear losing him, I can't bear his hatred, what he'll think of me. The betrayal.' I drew away. 'Can't I just tell him what must happen? Explain? I can't let him think I don't care.'

'You must,' Sashtri said gently. 'It's too dangerous to organise a meeting. You can't risk it.'

'The price is too high. I can't pay it. I can't!'

'I'll help you,' Sashtri said. 'When you administer Azvith's philtre to Sethra, there can be other ingredients in it. This will be some mercy, at least.' He took my face in his hands. 'Maybe in the future there'll be an opportunity for the truth, but not now. His horror, his repugnance, must be genuine.'

I cast off the har I was. I let Sashtri dress me in a costume befitting my position, not to appear like a hostling, or even overtly soume, but contained. The leathers and unruly hair were swapped for formal robes, such as Sashtri wore. I tamed my wild hair, pinned it. When I sat beside Ponclast in public, I would not be a rebellious young har, but an icon of self-control and maturity. My enemies would learn to respect me, for I was capable of horrors. I would become like ice. I would glide like a ghost, a memory of a har. My eyes would be chips of winter, my hands forever cold.

The day and hour were chosen. Sethra was taken to one of the rooms used for quickening, a baroque chamber, with a bed like a sepulchre. Sandalwood incense burned there, and the light was dim.

I met Ponclast at the door, and had brought with me a sheaf of notes, to give my hands something to do, my eyes something to look at.

Ponclast eyed me keenly. 'You've changed your appearance.'

'I thought it was time I was taken more seriously,' I said. 'Do you approve?'

He shrugged. 'If you feel it'll influence hara's opinion of you, dress how you like.'

We went inside the room. Sethra was sitting hunched-up on the bed, surrounded by a shawl of hair. I could see he'd lost a lot of weight. He seemed mindless. It was like looking at a picture. I wasn't really there. Neither of us were. I'm not sure he even realised it was me who gave him the elixir. That was a greater mercy than what Sashtri had bid me add to the mixture.

We had to wait while it took effect, and during this time I spoke to Ponclast of meaningless things. After a while, Sethra vomited and I knew it was time. 'He is ready, lord.'

Then, while Ponclast began the process, I went to stand at the window, attempting to close down my senses, shut myself inside the tomb of my body. Sounds came to me only dimly. Sethra fought the quickening. He fought very hard, to the point where his body battled with what Ponclast and the elixir were doing to him. This must've hurt a great deal. I stared out at the green world and thought of the Gelaming, of thunderclouds shaped like horses that galloped towards Fulminir across the sky. I wanted them to destroy us all.

I had my hara send Nethenya some of Sashtri's medicines for

Sethra, mainly to deaden his mind. I offered no explanation and Nethenya didn't question me about it. After two weeks, Sethra was taken to Azvith's studio. Here, as usual, the Kakkahaar injected his mixtures directly into the pearl, through Sethra's belly. The surface of the pearl would remain soft until it was expelled from his body. Rites were also performed during this time, portals opened to other realms. Azvith again sought to invite an etheric essence to take possession of the pearl. We wouldn't know whether this was successful for some time, but Azvith did see something different in Sethra.

'Wise choice,' he said to me, when he met me later in the day. 'Well done. I have a good feeling about this one. Even the air felt different, and the portals were positively crackling with energy. I tried a new formula I read about. It would have been poisonous to humans, of course, but not to us.'

The fruit of the previous experiment had also been more successful than before. The harling appeared healthy, and wasn't deformed. But after over a month, it didn't or couldn't respond to other hara. Still, Azvith regarded this poor creature as progress. He expected far more of Sethra's son.

I avoided the studio when Sethra was there; always found something important I had to do. Azvith didn't really require my assistance; he had others capable of that. He probably didn't even notice my regular absences.

Ponclast began summoning me for aruna again, perhaps aware of what I had sacrificed for him, perhaps not. One night, he said to me, 'When I've banished the Gelaming from this land, when the Varrs are truly in possession, and our enemies are vanquished, when we begin at last to clear the debris and reshape this world as it should be, then... then you will stand beside me, Vashti, with our son. And if there are more sons, they will stand there too.'

This was the nearest Ponclast could ever get to telling me I would be his consort, if not his chesnari, the founder of his dynasty. It was also unusual he'd mentioned the pearl I'd produced for him already, since the son who had emerged from it was never discussed with me. 'There could be no greater honour,' I said and kissed him as if I meant it.

In another world, I might've been happy. In that world I might have felt something. But there was no world any more, only a stage, and I simply danced mute upon it.

Whatever Azvith did to Sethra it affected the pearl in unexpected ways. Nethenya had the decency to summon me one night because Sethra was suffering violent fits. Although neither of us ever mentioned it, I'm convinced I wasn't the only one wondering whether the medicines I'd provided for Sethra had contributed to his condition now. Perhaps Nethenya wanted to grind my face in the horrific consequences of my actions. I went at once to the room that had become Sethra's, where Ponclast had violated him. In my haste, I had put on only my dressing-gown. What I saw appalled me. Sethra was writhing upon the floor, held by a couple of Nethenya's staff. His long night-shirt was bloody from the waist down.

'What's happening?' I demanded.

'It looks like the pearl is being rejected by his body,' Nethenya said in an even tone, 'but it's not ready to be dropped.'

'Have you called for Azvith?'

'Of course, he'll be here shortly.'

Sethra uttered a groan, then subsided to limp stillness. The room stank of blood.

'The spasms come and go,' Nethenya said. 'I'm reluctant to administer any of the medicines we'd usually use until Azvith advises me. I have no idea how Sethra's body might react.'

Sethra opened his eyes and they seemed completely black. He fixed his gaze on me and said, 'Vashti.' The name was without emphasis or surprise.

I took hold of one of his hands. 'I'm here,' I said.

He simply stared at me, without emotion, which was hideous.

After some minutes, which felt like hours, the Kakkahaar arrived with one of his assistants. He examined Sethra, who at the touch upon his belly began to convulse again.

'Cut the pearl out!' I yelled at Azvith. 'You must!'

He stuck out his lower lip as he considered this idea, eventually murmuring, 'That seems to be expedient. The harling might die otherwise.'

'Fetch a blade!' I shouted at Nethenya. 'Now!'

Nethenya's staff, used to pearl drops, albeit of a more conventional kind, had emergency and standard equipment waiting ready.

'Will he die?' I asked Azvith.

'I've no idea. This is new territory for all of us.'

'We must give him something for the pain, knock him out.'

'Not yet. Being squeamish about this won't help. Ah, thank you.' Azvith took the blade that was offered to him.

The har who had brought it had also had the foresight to offer a wooden bookend for Sethra to bite upon as Azvith cut him open. I'd have let him bite my hand to the bone if they hadn't provided anything else. His own hand, which was gripped in mine, fell slack as the blade sliced his flesh. I feared he was already dead, but then he shuddered slightly, spasmodically, as if through reflex.

The pearl was dragged from his open belly; it looked to me like a huge tumour, trailing bloodied slime. I wanted to snatch it from Azvith's hold and dash it against the wall.

Azvith stood up and had it wrapped in soft cloths, carried by his assistant. 'Take it to the studio,' he said and then turned to Nethenya, holding up his bloodied hands. 'Stitch the cuts and sedate him. That should be safe to do now.' He dipped his hands into a bowl of scented water that one of Nethenya's hara offered to him. 'I'll come tomorrow and see how he's doing, but trust him to your expert hands.'

Sethra was unconscious now. I watched as they attended to the layers of the wound, kneeling on the floor, my hands thrust between my knees. My dressing-gown was splashed with his blood. I'd have to destroy it.

Nethenya spoke my name, several times. Eventually, I looked up at him.

'You should go now, Tiahaar,' he said.

'I would prefer to wait.'

He raised his eyebrows.

'This har is important for the project,' I said. 'He must survive.'

'Go,' Nethenya said, and then reading the truth in my eyes, added in a gentler tone, 'We'll take care of him.'

The pearl was placed in a special bath, which was kept warm. It was fed with nutrients through a tube, along with other substances from Azvith's studio shelves. It swelled like a growing gourd. Sometimes, I'd go to stare it, wondering what its fruit would be.

Nethenya sent me discreet reports on Sethra's progress. Physically, he recovered. His mental health was another matter. For a year afterwards he was kept strongly medicated.

When the pearl broke, I wasn't present, but Azvith sent word to me, excited to share the project's success. The harling appeared normal, although its hair was strangely grey, and in its eyes was an expression I couldn't begin to describe, but the nearest approximation would be unearthly.

Azvith waited for six months before repeating the experiment, wanting to be sure the first harling would survive and thrive. He did. He grew more quickly than a harling usually did, and a harling's growth is hardly slow even under normal circumstances. I wanted to avoid this demon child, but at the same time was drawn to him, because in a strange way it made me feel closer to Sethra. They named him Gavensel. He was a charming creature, yet also weird. He was something other than a har. Something lived in him. And yet he was innocent – for a long time.

He didn't single any of us out for attention, particularly, and was quite self-absorbed, or perhaps self-sufficient. Azvith allowed him to wander around the studio, taking the precaution of having a Vigilant present to keep an eye on him. One day, when I was working alone in the studio, he crept up behind me. His odd, silvery voice made me jump and I staggered against the work bench, making the equipment rattle. 'He said you'd care for me.'

'What? Who?'

'The body said.' Gavensel grinned at me. 'You will too, won't you?'

'We'll all care for you,' I said.

The harling gave me a knowing look that made me shudder. Then he walked away.

They didn't let Sethra see the harling, of course. His part in the process was over. I hoped he would be left alone now, at least for a long while. He wasn't well enough to host more pearls.

Ponclast seemed oddly repelled by the harling – he only had it brought to him a few times. I think he too was unsettled by the otherworldly quality of Gavensel, the presence of a being that was not har inside the body of a har. We didn't discuss it, other than that he would quicken more pearls in the same way when Azvith was ready to continue.

During the next six years, as Gavensel grew, my life progressed in its routine. I worked with Azvith, selected hara for the project, socialised with Sashtri and Averen and their friends, and visited Ponclast when he summoned me. Sometimes, there were gaps of weeks or months when he was away.

I never went to the hostlings' quarters and if Nethenya needed to speak with me he always came to my office, which was annexed to Azvith's workroom. He didn't speak directly of Sethra, but every now and again, said, 'All is well with the prototype hostling. His recovery progresses.'

A recovery of years.

Gavensel was phenomenal. I knew what direction his training would take, and distanced myself from it. That wasn't my sphere. But I heard reports. Eventually, he had brothers who joined him to form a deadly troupe of unharish assassins that became known as the Succubi. While most of their work was kept secret, we knew they used aruna as a weapon, hence the title they'd been given. Seduce a har and murder him while he swooned in the raptures of desire.

Sashtri once said to me, 'Ponclast's ghastly offspring unnerve me. I can't help feeling that one day they might turn on us like rabid dogs.'

We didn't catch sight of these creatures very often now – they had their own quarters. – although sometimes Gavensel came to visit Azvith, the nearest he had to a relative. At these times, he appeared almost normal. He teased Azvith, aware of his own splendour, mischievously flirting. Azvith responded in a fluttering manner to this attention. As for me, Gavensel would occasionally, and pointedly, direct piercing glances towards me. I felt he knew everything about me, and judged me, but not in a sentimental way. He probably thought I was too soft.

Nethenya reported that the Succubi sometimes mixed with the hostlings – I'd hardly call it socialising. Perhaps they were a warning to any who might harbour rebellious tendencies. For some hostlings did. Some died for it.

Over time, the Gelaming let their presence be felt more overtly. We knew they had a base in southern Megalithica and were attracting refugees that included both hara and surviving humans. Ponclast sent out his demon assassins, into the settlements of hara he did not trust and down into the mist itself. They even killed a Gelaming or two, or so it was said. I'm not sure of the truth of that.

The son I'd produced for Ponclast had been sent to Terzian's estate in Galhea, since he'd proved to be an intractable harling. Terzian had a son of his own by then and it was thought that Gahrazel might settle down and behave if he was removed from Fulminir and brought up in Terzian's house, taught by the tutors Terzian had hired for his own son's education. That didn't work out too well. Eventually, Gahrazel tried to defect to the Gelaming and paid the inevitable price. I was proud of him for that, if only secretly. His death proved he hadn't become anything like me. He'd fought back and had been prepared to lose his life for his principles. He hadn't caved in and submitted to Ponclast's demands, made a lie of himself. Poor Gahrazel. I wish we'd been allowed to know each other, but then, if that had happened, he might not have become the har who defied his father. When I heard of his death – and it was from Sashtri, Ponclast never mentioned it to me – I held a small rite beyond Fulminir's walls, such as I'd seen the hostlings at Ashen Weald perform. I went out on the night of a full moon, to the edge of a wood. I did not lie down on the soil and weep, but fashioned a grave of flowers and feathers, sang a song over it.

Ponclast did not appear affected by Gahrazel's betrayal, despite the angry reflex that had impelled him to execute his own son, but perhaps this smothered fury was what made him decide Sethra must host another son, another Gavensel, whose name was so similar to the betrayer's but who did not betray. A son who killed to order in the most abominable of ways. He already had twelve Succubi, now he must add the fatal thirteenth.

Nethenya sent word to me, because he was the first to be informed by Azvith. The Kakkahaar had mentioned nothing about Ponclast's demand. I don't think he kept silent to spare me pain but rather to avoid the chance of a messy confrontation. He never liked mess of an emotional kind.

I asked Nethenya to come to my apartment to discuss the matter, even though I was aware deep down that discussion wouldn't change a thing. 'This mustn't happen,' I said. 'Do what you can to prevent it.'

'You know I can't do anything,' Nethenya said. 'Ponclast is like a volcano about to blow. His son betrayed him, which might've given other hara ideas. And now Terzian is missing.

You know that, of course.'

I didn't. This was shocking news, and Ponclast had kept it quiet. Nethenya must be rooning some important Lordra to get that information.

'He's gone south,' I said. 'I knew of that, but missing?'

Nethenya shrugged. 'The mist took his company. Only a few got out. We can assume the Gelaming have Terzian now.'

Ponclast's best friend and closest ally: taken. This was provocation too far, surely?

'We can't deny him anything at the moment,' Nethenya said. 'Sethra is in a kind of trance most of the time. The other hostlings care for him... It's strange. He's like an icon to them. But anyway, I'm sure he can be kept docile for the procedure.'

'But the wound... it shouldn't be reopened surely?'

'He's har. He'll heal quickly. He'll be fine. The others will make sure of it.' Nethenya shook his head. 'We have no choice, Vashti. Gavensel is the finest of the Succubi, and Ponclast must believe Sethra's responsible for that. He wants an elite force to take on the Gelaming, possibly take out their leaders. Who best but Gavensel's kind?'

'I pray Sethra's next pearl issues up a weaker har,' I said, 'otherwise...' I didn't want to say.

Nethenya knew what I meant though. 'He wouldn't survive that.' He went to my door, paused there. 'We have to hope the time it takes for a harling to mature is too long for Ponclast's purposes. Somehar should persuade him he should act now with what he already has.'

I didn't have quite as much influence as Nethenya believed I had.

There was no way I could risk saying anything to Ponclast. The slightest word from me might break the thin scale of stone that capped the volcano. I could only hope Sethra could withstand bearing another pearl, and that something would happen to prevent him being subjected to hosting again.

Ponclast was distraught about Terzian but couldn't show

this overtly, or talk about it, not even in my company. I knew better than to bring up the subject myself, but I felt his fury and pain when we were together and by then I had no wish whatsoever to assuage his hurts. He wanted to act, take revenge, but lacked the means. The Gelaming hid themselves too well. They had shown him emphatically how powerful they were, yet now did nothing. There was no approach from them in respect of negotiations or demands. Only silence. What were they doing to Terzian? I doubted they would resort to torture, but imagined that they would seek to turn his mind, set him against his tribe. That would hurt Ponclast more than sending a mutilated body back to Fulminir.

Secretly, I was glad about Terzian's capture, because he'd been behind what had happened to Gahrazel, my tragic son about who I couldn't afford to think too much. I hoped Terzian suffered. I hoped the Gelaming would take his son, Swift, too. That wish, at least, was granted, albeit in a way I could not then imagine.

As for Ponclast, I now considered him a wreck of a har. I had thought him magnificent, but all that pomp and glamour had concealed his weakness, his fear and – the result of those traits – the pettiness of his cruelty. He'd been given a son who'd had a mind of his own and had murdered him for it. He'd turned his subsequent sons into beasts and wanted more and more of them to deform. I began to sense fragility in Fulminir, as if Ponclast's will alone held it together, and that was breaking down. Sashtri sometimes appeared wild-eyed, but spoke little to me of his concerns. We were waiting, all of us.

I began praying to the Aghama, the first of all Wraeththu, who was perhaps in truth an idea rather than an actual har. A new god. I begged him to end it all, send the Gelaming to war, save Sethra before it was too late. And perhaps he did hear my prayers, but had his own timetable. The Aghama does not act in haste.

One evening, Nethenya came to my apartment. A house-har let him in. I was preparing to go to dinner with Sashtri at the apartment of a couple of his friends and was half ready. Nethenya came into my dressing-room, and the moment I saw his face I knew why the house-har hadn't announced him or made him wait.

'What is it?' I asked, aware of a wave of icy cold creeping through my flesh.

'You're not like them,' Nethenya said stepping forward. His hands were clasped at his chest, tightly. 'You know that, don't you?'

'Them?' I was so cold I felt sure that soon my jaw would freeze completely and I'd not be able to speak.

'You tried to be, Aghama knows you tried to be, Vashti, and you've survived well. I want you to hold onto this thought now. Don't forget who you are.'

'Neth... tell me.'

He came to me, took my hands, closed his eyes for a moment, swallowed thickly, then said hoarsely, 'Sethra is dead, Vashti.'

I jerked my hands away from him. 'What? No! How? Why?' The words were reflexes. I was ice, through and through.

Nethenya sat down on my sofa and for some moments had to compose himself. 'I told him what had been decided, concerning another pearl.'

I stood motionless, waited for him to continue speaking.

'This was... around a week ago,' he said at last.

'You didn't tell me.'

'No... What point would there have been in that? Could you have gone to him, comforted him? Could you have taken him away? Stupidly, I was trying to protect you.' Nethenya rubbed his hands over his face. I saw then how much he'd cared for Sethra himself. I should always have seen that. 'He took it badly, very badly.'

An image hurled itself across my inner eye; a body falling from the high windows of the hostling house, his robe and his hair swirling around him like smoke. For a moment, I felt an intense relief, gladness even. He was free.

'He didn't take his own life,' Nethenya said, no doubt having picked up my unguarded thought. 'You can't comfort yourself with that. You know what they do to hostlings who are... difficult... don't you?'

'What *you* do?' I snapped. I did know, but I'd suppressed that knowledge, hadn't wanted to consider it, not for my Sethra.

'*I* do?' He stood up again and looked as if he was about to attack me. Then he clearly changed his mind. 'Azvith reported that Sethra refused the procedure, would not submit to it. They drugged him, of course, and handed him to Ponclast. A quickening took place. Because Sethra had been difficult, Azvith confined him in the studio. He appeared quiescent, but this morning he tried to run away.'

Now it was my turn to put my hands to my face, stare only into darkness, not into Nethenya's pain-scarred face.

'They caught him, of course,' Nethenya said, in a resigned tone. 'He didn't take the slightest precaution. He simply ran.'

Down the hill like a hare.

I felt Nethenya draw close to me again, but I couldn't bear to lower my hands.

'My hara – my *real* staff – nurture those in their care, as much as they can. But the Vigilants watch us all and administer discipline when it's considered necessary. You know that. I don't need to tell you. The things they make us do...' He was silent for a moment 'Every one of the hostlings knows what happens if they dare to be defiant. They are terrified. They do as they're bid.' His voice softened. 'Look at me, Vashti.'

I wouldn't, so he grabbed hold of my wrists and pulled my hands away from my face. 'Even once he'd been recaptured he fought. He fought so hard he got his hands on a blade, plunged it into his own stomach. He butchered the abomination Ponclast put into him.'

I uttered a choked cry. 'It wasn't that, not yet...'

'But it *would be*. He destroyed the chamber of creation within himself. He planned to die. He knew he must rather than allow his body to be used to produce those... *things*. He was brave and fearless, Vashti. Could you or I have done that?'

'But he didn't die then, did he?'

Nethenya sighed heavily. 'No... They hung him in the hostlings' lounge. Not one of them hurt him further, despite being ordered to, and were beaten for it. Still, the Vigilants couldn't kill the poor things; they're too useful. I planned to intervene, to end it for Sethra tonight, but...'

I put a hand over my mouth, feeling my stomach heave, but nothing came up from it, only a taste of bile to my throat.

'Sashtri got to him first,' Nethenya said. 'I would've used a blade, but your friend has access to Kakkahaar poisons that can kill a har and do it quickly. It's done.'

There was a moment's blackness, then I found I was on the floor, on my knees. Nethenya knelt beside me, took me in his arms, but I couldn't accept his comfort and remained rigid in his hold. I felt as if I was outside myself, observing the tumble of emotions within me. Sadness and grief didn't come into it; they were emotions too mild. My mind was caught in a wild tide that thrashed against spiky rocks: fury, relief, disbelief, utter belief, a need for vengeance, a desire to scream, to run from that room with a blade in my hand and cut open Ponclast's own stomach, make him face what lay within and how his terror of it made him a murderer. He would pay. One day. I wished him every pain known to this earth.

After a few minutes, I scrambled to my feet. My lips were numb. 'Why did Sashtri give Sethra the poison? He risked himself...'

Nethenya remained on the floor, kneeling, his hands thrust between his knees as if by touching me he'd burned them, but if so it was from the burn of ice. He spoke in a voice that trembled very slightly, as if he were cold. 'You couldn't visit Sethra, but Sashtri could. He's always visited the hostlings. He has free run of the house.'

Sashtri had never told me this. I didn't know whether to feel angry or grateful. 'Will they discipline him?'

Nethenya got wearily to his feet. 'I doubt it. He's Sashtri, also it's accepted that we end such… punishment… when we get the chance, after it's been witnessed. We're allowed that.'

'Did you send word to Sashtri before me?'

'No. Didn't have to,' Nethenya said. 'He has eyes everywhere in Fulminir. He's your friend, your ally. He kept watch on the har you loved.'

'So now you know it,' I said bitterly.

'Always did,' Nethenya replied, 'although you *were* very stupid and careless.'

'I did this to him.'

'No, the Varrs did this to him. Don't flagellate yourself. Reserve your disgust for the regime that condones this and the monsters who enslave us.'

'You could die for those words too,' I said.

'I could, if I spoke them to a har who'd betray me. You won't.'

'You don't know that.'

'I *do*. It's the final straw, isn't it? How can you pretend any longer?'

I couldn't weep, could no longer feel. The tide had drawn back from the shore. *He's free,* I told myself, but it was scant consolation. I couldn't think about the hours before his death.

'We must stick together and wait now,' Nethenya said, 'that's all we can do.'

'Wait for what?'

'You *know*,' he answered, still not daring to speak the name. 'It must be soon. They claim they are just and compassionate. We might not fare too badly.'

I nodded, no longer interested in my own future. I realised I'd harboured delusions of a happy ending for Sethra and me. All this time: so controlled and clever, but deep inside screaming at the unfairness, a terrified harling desperate for somehar to come and make it better.

'Sethra was truly loved,' Nethenya said, 'any one of us in the house would have ended it for him this night. Their mourning now is the deepest I have ever known. You should go to Sashtri.'

'We're going out for dinner,' I said, merely a croak.

Nethenya drew in his breath, as if it hurt him. 'I know Sashtri, and he's strong, but I suspect he might cancel that engagement tonight.'

After Nethenya had left me, I went to Sashtri's apartment. There was a ghastly, grief-stricken atmosphere to the rooms, and few hara in sight. The chambers were cold and silent, as if they'd been shut up, unlived-in, for a long time. Sashtri was in his sitting-room, wearing only a loose robe, his face unpainted, his hair unstyled. I sat down beside him and took his hands. I had no words to break the silence that wouldn't have sounded crass and inappropriate.

After some minutes, Sashtri said in a hoarse voice, 'Averen is away. I must get word to him. He mustn't return.'

'Do you know where he is?'

Sashtri nodded. 'Vaguely. I'll send one of my hara and hope he gets through.'

'What about us?'

'We carry on as best we can, but I feel in my blood that what happened today has set something inexorable in motion. It was the turning of the key and now the door is open.'

'The doors to Fulminir...'

'Not quite. Not yet. There will be cold days ahead.'

We sat quietly again for a minute or so, then I said simply, 'Thank you for what you did.'

Sashtri nodded, his face like a mask. 'At the end, I spoke to him, told him truths. I don't know if he heard or understood.'

At these words I allowed the cataract of emotion to pour from the breached dam in my heart. It was more like retching than weeping. Sashtri said nothing, let me grieve, one hand upon the back of my neck. I vowed I would never love again.

We weren't allowed a funeral rite, of course. Sethra's body was disposed of by the Vigilants. To hold a ceremony of any kind would have been a punishable offence, since Sethra was regarded as a traitor. He had killed a son of the archon. So, we each had to grieve alone. I dreamed of Sethra regularly, never of his torment, but perhaps more painfully of futures that would never happen. I saw him once with the harling he'd been moved to kill, or rather save from being warped and twisted into something terrible. They were walking hand in hand among the ruins of Fulminir, where the green was eating up the vile memories. They were laughing – that deep, deliciously wicked laugh from Sethra – and walked towards a door of light. Before entering it, they turned to wave to me, the helpless observer. I wanted that dream to be true.

Sethra was not the first har to die in that unspeakable way, but perhaps he could be the last. My fey beloved had had a purpose, something I'd sensed in him all along. He'd been doomed but also loved. His death struck deep into the hearts of all who knew him, changed them, kindled resolve. We were all dancers now.

Fermentation

Before the Gelaming slaughtered our land, they made sure Ponclast knew they'd taken Galhea. Terzian's family had defected, and apparently without force, despite the fact their phylarch was still a captive. I wondered what the Gelaming had offered them, which I suppose was fairly obvious. Swift became Immanion's puppet leader in Megalithica later on. The Galheans were lucky Ponclast didn't send the Succubi after them, but events conspired to keep the assassins at home.

I don't really know what I was expecting of the Gelaming; a shining army, perhaps, blowing golden horns of liberation, an army so strong and righteous it could break through Fulminir's diseased walls and destroy the Varrish leaders without a fight. Galhea, after all, had not been damaged. But of course, Ponclast *would* fight, and he had the Kakkahaar to help him. He would not fight cleanly.

The fire came in the night, a strange blue-green wave that undulated over the fields and hills surrounding the stronghold. It flowed over hara too, and then they were no longer there.

I was living back in Sashtri's apartment by then. He'd managed to get word to Averen, or at least believed so, because Averen had not returned to Fulminir. We sat up that night, holding onto to one another at the window, and watched the devouring, cold flame destroy the green, the soft healing growth that had covered up the past. Now the skeletons were revealed again, stark and hideous.

The fire tried to crawl up the walls of Fulminir, but the Kakkahaar were able to dispel it from venturing that close. The withering flames retreated, flowed away, leaving shrivelled ruin behind them.

Our water sources had been contaminated. There was still fresh water in the wells within the fortress itself, but it became clear they would soon run dry. As the weeks passed, our food supplies too began to diminish. Hara who'd lived nearby, and who'd managed to run ahead of the fire, had been given sanctuary in Fulminir, adding to our problems with supplies. Eventually, the animals were killed for meat. Food and water were rationed brutally.

And still we waited.

The Gelaming were no better than the Varrs, I thought. They were the same.

Some tried to escape but, whenever anyhar ventured beyond the walls, deadly flames licked up from the blackened earth and destroyed them utterly. Hara began to call this the Assassin's Flare. So we could either starve to death or burn. Why didn't they attack and finish this?

'There will be a moment,' Sashtri said to me, 'and if we survive 'til then we must help others escape.'

'How?' I snapped.

'I just know we can,' Sashtri answered. 'We simply have to seize the opportunity when it comes.'

I didn't share his optimism. I felt we were all doomed, and our attackers would let us die before they broke the walls. We were weak with hunger.

Ponclast did not summon me during these weeks. I had no desire to see him, not even to try and get information, although part of me was anxious about his silence. He'd shut me out at a time when you'd imagine he'd need comfort or at least the distraction of aruna. Perhaps somehar else fulfilled that function now. I supposed he'd distanced himself because of what had happened with Sethra, and how it had affected the other hostlings. I assumed he must get reports, especially the kind that showed me in a bad light. Perhaps he'd never really believed I'd not loved Sethra. After all, everyhar else seemed to. The siege had deflected attention from all those involved in releasing Sethra from torture, whether through their actions or their refusal to cooperate. Without it, only the Aghama knows what might have happened to us all, especially after the news of Swift's defection came from Galhea.

The Kakkahaar's abilities were no match for the Gelaming. Ponclast's magi didn't know what the deadly fire was, how it had been made, how it was controlled. They were blinded by it, prevented from using their farsight beyond the walls, unable to formulate a strategy for escape. All they could hope for was direct attack, the chance to counter an enemy that stood physically before them. It was rumoured that they urged Ponclast to send out the Succubi, but he would not risk them. He kept them within Fulminir, no doubt in the hope they would help repel the assault when it came.

And eventually it did come.

I suppose the Gelaming had anticipated how long our food and water would last and how long a harish body could survive without them. They didn't intend to kill us, simply weaken us sufficiently.

We lived now beneath a canopy of unnatural storms. The world we'd known had become almost unrecognisable, a nightmare. The water from the continual deluge could not replenish our supply for it was acid. We had to shelter from the downpour; it ate at the stone of our walls.

Then, one morning, the sky opened to the south and lit up with great flashes of white radiance.

They came from the sky.

Sashtri and I went to the window, although we could not see directly south from there. We could see the heavy clouds fracturing and shuddering, heaving with lightning, as if an immense portal had opened up. We had no idea what came from it, and if it *was* an army how large it might be, but we felt certain forces must be massing beneath the sky-breach, a couple of miles from the stronghold.

Presently, more unearthly fire appeared, this time clean and bright. A wall of flame thirty feet high surged towards Fulminir, and I thought for some moments we would soon be dead. But this was the moment the Kakkahaar had been waiting for. The element that assailed us now was not the

Assassin's Flare; it was immense and potent, like a living creature. The Gelaming's weapon – it was more than fire – crashed through the outer walls, utterly demolishing them, and in response the Kakkahaar unleashed their counter-measures. A creature of black flames and oily smoke arose from the fortress and roiled out to meet the enemy. These unearthly forces fought like mythical beasts, shrieking and smashing, splinters of light and flecks of black ash flashing out from their whirring conflict.

Sashtri took my hand. His face was emaciated and hollow in the weird light from outside. 'Come,' he said. 'It's time.'

My hara had joined his household and now we gathered our staff together. Sashtri bid us all dress in Varrish leather armour, which he had prepared for us. I watched him as he shrugged off his robe and stood in his shorts to swathe himself in the costume of a fighter. It was as if he cast off entirely his familiar self and became somehar else, his hair plaited into a rope, his face severe. I felt I didn't know him. He was a Varr warrior now. This tall stranger armed us with blades which he'd no doubt been collecting for this day.

'Don't look at me like that,' he said to me. 'This is who I once was, at all times. Like you, I learned to dance in certain ways.' He smiled at me tightly. 'Are you ready?'

He led us to the hostlings' quarters, to the lounge area, where hara were expected to relax. There were no miscreants hanging on the wall now. Stains had been cleaned away thoroughly every time there'd been a punishment, but to me it was as if Sethra still hung there, his blood running from the ends of his toes to the floor. I had to turn away from that wall, away from the past.

Across the room stood Nethenya and the other occupants of the house, already dressed for travel. What little remained of their supplies was in a couple of packing cases beside them. Clearly Nethenya and Sashtri had been making plans without me.

'We won't be able to simply walk out of here!' I hissed at

Sashtri, forcing him to pause by the door. 'It would be madness to try.'

'We have to,' Sashtri said in an even tone, 'because the Vigilants in this house are now dead.'

The hostlings, then, had had their revenge.

'We'll take the northern exit,' Sashtri said. 'Ponclast's forces will be concentrated at the southern face of the fortress, the direction of attack. We can be careful, pick our way. Any defences or sentries Ponclast has set to the north won't be expecting anyhar to try and escape.'

'But the ground is poisoned out there, the fires...'

The walls had begun to shake, and immense rumbles and crashes, that sounded as if mountains were being hit by meteors, forced us almost to shout at one another. Nethenya had joined us at the door, he too in Varrish uniform. 'If we can get past the guards – and we'll fight if we have to – there are old tunnels that might be safe from the Assassin's Flare,' he said. 'They lead to the old city. If we can reach it, we can hide there for a while, find water and food.'

'From what I've heard of those tunnels, they're impassable now,' I said. 'Ponclast had them collapsed years ago. Also, how can you expect hostlings to fight?'

'You, of all hara, should not dare to say that,' Nethenya retorted. 'You were the one to stand up for equality of aspect and purpose... weren't you?'

Perhaps so, but everyhar in that room was exhausted and famished, a few of them heavy with pearl. They weren't used to fighting. They'd never been encouraged to embrace the side of them that could. There they were, weary yet determined, all staring at us, believing we could lead them to safety. Even if they *were* able call upon the forceful traits needed for survival now, and had killed their Vigilant oppressors, (who'd no doubt been taken unawares), I was sure they were too weakened by hunger to fight their way out of the fortress. Against Varrish warriors? They would be slaughtered. I couldn't condone this plan, however desperate we were. 'Wouldn't it make more sense to keep our heads down and wait for this to be over?' I cried.

'You're assuming the Gelaming will be victorious,' Sashtri said. The floor buckled and he steadied himself against the door frame.

'Well, won't they?'

'Even if they are, we'll be prisoners of war,' Nethenya said. 'They've starved us for weeks. Also, they haven't attacked us themselves; they've sent their sorceries. If that force breaks through the Kakkahaar's defences, what then? For all we know, the Gelaming's plan might be to eradicate every Varr in Megalithica.'

But Gahrazel wanted to join them, I thought. *The Galheans did.* I wanted to believe there was a side to this conflict that was essentially benign.

There were no windows in that room, but I heard an explosion of glass nearby. The hostlings clutched at one another, but I noticed they weren't cowering.

'Vashti, we're not just trying to escape the Gelaming,' Sashtri yelled. 'We're trying to escape *everything*.' Plaster came down from the ceiling in a shower of dust. From outside the room came an appalling, gurgling scream of pain and horror, which was cut off abruptly.

'Forget the old city,' I said impulsively. 'Aim to reach the nearest homestead. You know where they are. There's just as much chance of finding food and water in the hills and forests as in the city ruins and less chance of running into dangers and hostility. Wild animals are unlikely to attack a large group. You should have at least some time to organise yourselves, regain your strength, come up with a stronger plan.'

Sashtri narrowed his eyes. 'It sounds as if you don't intend to come with us.'

It was only at that moment I realised I didn't. Why? I'm still not sure. Perhaps I was convinced the Gelaming would liberate Fulminir, perhaps I just wanted to see what would happen. Or something else held me there.

Wooden panelling on the southern wall creaked as if in agony, then buckled into the room, bringing down a festoon of torn wall hangings.

'If I can, I'll find you,' I said.

'You can't stay here!' Sashtri cried.

'I won't, I'm simply not leaving yet. Now go!'

Sashtri gripped one of my forearms. 'Whatever you're planning...'

I stood on tiptoe to kiss his mouth. 'Be strong. Be fast. Make fighters of them, my magnificent friend.'

He clasped me more strongly for a moment, then nodded. 'Tell them we're leaving, Neth.'

Left alone, I stood for some minutes with my eyes closed in that chamber, which was to me Sethra's sepulchre. He had no grave that I knew of; his body had probably been burned. There was no marker anywhere except in my heart. A ghost of incense perfume haunted the room, whose fabric was disintegrating. I stood in the midst of it, yet it did not touch me. Plaster fell around me in a circle. I bathed in this destruction. I gathered my strength.

Sometimes, there's no option but to allow instinct to guide you. When I left that room, I simply let my body walk, to see where it would lead. I had no plan, despite what Sashtri thought.

I found myself before a door, just as it was being opened. Somehar stood at the threshold, dressed in the uniform of the Succubi, a pliable costume fashioned of strips of cloth that reminded me of bandages, partly covered by a tunic. I realised this was Gavensel standing before me. He was a strange creature; attenuated, with long limbs, his features somehow too large for his face, perhaps because he was starving. His hair was a dusty grey, loose around him. I felt it might lash out and bind me, smother me. I'd not seen him for some time and it was painful to see reminders of Sethra in his face, because that face was not wholly har. Something *else* looked out from it. He stared at me for some moments, and I stared back.

'Why are you still here?' I asked him.

'What have you come for?' he responded.

I held out my hands to him to show I had no weapons, that I came in trust. 'Your hostling was murdered,' I said. 'You should know that, before...' I realised then he was the reason I'd stayed behind.

Gavensel uttered a brief, cold laugh. 'I'm a prisoner here, as much as you, or the unfortunate who spawned me.'

'Yet you will fight for Ponclast, as you always do.'

'What do you want?'

I was silent for a moment, gazing into those eyes. They were harish and yet not. 'The thing they put in you could be free,' I said, 'go back to wherever it came from.'

'You assume I want that. I exist. I have a purpose. There is nothing more.'

'Part of you is Sethra's son, and of course Ponclast's too. Whatever else is in you doesn't belong in this world. How could it be freed?'

'Through this body's death, presumably,' he said.

'You were going somewhere,' I said. 'You opened the door and came out. Where were you going?'

'To my father.' He raised his eyes to the cracking walls. 'He's out there. I can see him, through stone and smoke. He calls for us now.'

I saw that the other Succubi had gathered behind him, shadows in the room.

My words came out quickly, almost babbling: 'Gavensel, find the part of you inside that is Sethra! Kill that monster out there!'

'Which one?' he asked.

'You know which one. The demands of the archon can't possibly matter to you now. This fortress will fall. I don't believe you and your brothers are enough to turn the fight in the Varrs' favour.'

'The enemy uses mighty forces, yes.' He shrugged. 'I am

called. I go. Nothing matters.' He made to move past me and I was aware of the almost gaseous surge of his kin behind him.

'Yes it *does*,' I said, 'because whatever you are, or they have made of you, you're partly har. End this. Do it for your hostling, who was tortured and killed, for *my* son, who was executed, for you and your kin who were twisted and possessed.'

'So *this* is what he meant,' Gavensel said, but he made no further attempt to push me aside. 'When I was still in his body, he said you'd care for me. And so you do. You care about a har who cannot exist, and hara who are dead. You are soft and weak.' He turned to his brothers. 'Come.'

I couldn't stop them. I was terrified. They were beautiful and ghastly, horrific manifestations of something and somewhere I couldn't possibly understand.

There were stairs nearby that led to the roof, where Ponclast and the Kakkahaar undoubtedly conjured their forces. The Succubi headed towards them. On the first step, Gavensel paused and called back to me, 'Up here.'

I followed them.

The sky looked infected, hanging over the world, full of poison. A cruel wind blew. I saw immense braziers and arcane equipment, the Kakkahaar standing in a circle with their arms raised, chanting invocations into the wind, their hair and robes rippling around them. I couldn't see Azvith in the group, but then his function was specifically devoted to the breeding project. Perhaps there was no need for him to be there. Among the Kakkahaar was Ponclast, wearing his red cloak, which billowed about his body like a bloody shroud. I could see that the Gelaming's entity of light was losing its battle, fragmenting amid the oily smoke of the Kakkahaar's summoning.

The Succubi approached their father. He acknowledged them with a brief nod of his head. Then he noticed me behind them. I heard him say, 'Vashti,' almost in wonder. He thought I'd come to support him, perhaps die by his side, if it should come to that. I didn't say anything. I turned my face to the south, tried to take in the impossible sight that did not belong in this world of material things, giants fighting in the sky.

'The Gelaming entity is weakening,' Ponclast said. 'My sons, finish it now and then go to the enemy. Use all of your strength to finish them too.'

Gavensel wasn't my ally, I thought. The Succubi had no feelings. They would simply do as they were ordered.

I saw them change, their bodies shimmering. They would fly. Gavensel leapt up and hovered in the air, his hair floating like an aura about him, leaves of cloth lifting from his body like fins. He blazed before the others, who rose around him. They had no eyes now, only smoking holes that leaked indigo fire.

And then came a sound as of universes shattering. A hot wind gusted against us, sent me staggering backwards. I saw a spire of light to the south, like the furnace of a captured sun. I had to turn away from that blinding radiance.

'What is that?' Ponclast demanded of his Kakkahaar.

'They summon another!' one of them cried. 'Send the Succubi. Now!'

'Go!' Ponclast yelled, flinging out his left arm towards his sons.

The Succubi spiralled upwards. I sank to my knees, unable to stand any longer, holding my hair back from my face. The air smelled of spoiled milk.

Ponclast loomed over me; his cloak of blood appeared to fight to be free of him. 'I won't let them take you,' he said.

There was a knife at his belt and his right hand rested upon the hilt. I hoped he wouldn't use it before he was sure my capture was unavoidable. I looked up into his face as he leaned over me, recognised an expression in his eyes that spoke of the feelings he could never express. In another world... No, I couldn't let myself think it. He was a killer and had murdered love. I stared back at him, hoping he saw within me the hatred I held in my heart. 'I am here to watch you fail,' I said.

He didn't react, just stared at me, and then words were no longer possible.

An immense sphere of energy, like a comet, shrieked towards Fulminir. Ponclast straightened up and faced it. The Kakkahaar's creature of smouldering blackness condensed, drew itself up into a column, ready to soak that assault. It glittered with motes of distant light, as if looking into it allowed me to gaze upon another universe. I could feel its strength. The Succubi must be feeding it. All of this happened in seconds, yet it felt like minutes.

The Gelaming's creature was close. The Kakkahaar entity expanded like the hood of a cobra. It would engulf the light.

The Succubi were a scintillating torrent, whirling around the black fire. I thought they meant to augment it, but then something strange and wonderful happened. The Succubi spiralled around the Kakkahaar's conjuration and bound it in a mesh of shimmering energy. It writhed within this net, helpless before the roaring entity from the south that inevitably crashed against it. Instantly, it blew apart, like somehar throwing a giant pot of ink and smoke against the sky. I saw the Succubi peel off and upwards, scattering. But for one. As the black fire disintegrated, a hard tendril shot out like an obsidian spear and pierced his body through the chest, flung him to the ground. And then time stopped completely.

It was like being caught in a bubble, within which I was turned to stone. I could think, feel and see, but couldn't move. I couldn't breathe but didn't need to. I couldn't blink. Sound was muted. The world was frozen around me, even Ponclast's cloak caught in a violent wind. He was staring out in disbelief. His sons had turned against him; traitors too, like Gahrazel. I would be found here with him, taken for an accomplice. But this didn't matter. I'd stopped him. I'd stopped him! The only thing I regretted was that I couldn't tell him that.

For you, Sethra.

I was resigned to whatever fate the Gelaming decided. I was sure the stasis came from them. Presumably they'd be here soon to take their enemy into custody. As well as holding captives in place, the effect of the stasis was numbing, almost anaesthetic. I felt soon I would drift away into unconsciousness. Nohar would be able to run from this fortress. The victors would find me by Ponclast, and take me for his follower. I thought that perhaps, once we were all anaesthetised, (because they wouldn't be cruel enough to do it while we remained aware), they would simply shatter us where we stood, rid this world of the Varr hierarchy.

Then I became aware of movement around me. I saw long arms, a pair of attenuated hands, and a ghostly face with eyes of indigo flame. A Succubus. He hovered before me for a moment, then lifted me, his hands beneath my arms. The stasis left my body at once. The Succubus did not speak, but in my mind I heard the words: 'Gavensel asked this of me, as he fell.'

I was barely conscious as this creature of ether flew with me from the fortress. I was a limp puppet in his hold, my limbs hanging down. What shred of consciousness remained flowed from me. Perhaps I would fly forever.

When I awoke, I found I was lying on the ground among trees. The Succubus stood nearby, staring at me. He was motionless, his arms hanging loosely at his sides, but almost har once more. I raised myself on my elbows, but couldn't speak. I wanted to know what Gavensel had said to him and his brothers to make them rebel in that way. Or had it even been rebellion? Who knows what impulses moved them. His expression was inscrutable. I think he was only waiting to ensure I'd regained my senses. After some minutes, he simply nodded once and then ran off fast among the trees. I watched him until he disappeared, like a flickering ghost. After this, I lay down again, staring up through the foliage. I must be far away from Fulminir. The leaves were green. This forest was alive.

In fact I was not that far away. The Gelaming had not destroyed land needlessly, and eventually I discovered that the black ruin did not extend more than a couple of miles beyond Fulminir's walls.

By evening I was able to stand and seek water. It was fortunate I was dressed to travel in the uniform Sashtri had given me, and had a knife in my belt, although of course I had no supplies. The sky to the east was clearing now. I could see a mellow sunset, although smoke still spiralled lazily against the thin, peach-coloured clouds.

Distillation

Following the fall of Fulminir, the Gelaming set up a camp for refugees in Oak Hill, a small town around a mile southwest of the fortress. I needed food and shelter and came across this place as I was making my way to what I hoped would be sympathetic hara. I had followed smoke of a more natural kind than that which lingered in the sky. I reached the town mid-morning following the battle. The place was blackened, the roads ashy mud underfoot, hara crouching in ruins being handed food. I was dressed in Varr armour, and realised it wouldn't be wise for this to be seen. Sneaking around the perimeter, observing the groups of survivors, I found a long, thick coat and a flat wide-brimmed hat to steal and with these disguised myself. I went to an area where hara were queuing for food and accepted a bowl of stew, which I devoured so quickly it hurt my stomach.

The Gelaming were as I'd first imagined them, but not simply golden angels. As we'd heard, they were of different ethnic types, all of them vigorous and beautiful. They were sympathetic to the survivors and, from talking with others, I learned they planned to move us south, to their settlement for refugees. This was not the case for Ponclast and his followers. During my time in Oak Hill, I didn't see anyhar I knew from the fortress. I hoped Sashtri and the others had got away successfully. As for Gavensel, I was simply shocked by and extremely grateful for what he'd done. I'd not really expected his help. He'd not sacrificed himself, he'd assumed he'd escape, but even as he'd fallen his last thought had been of me. Whatever Azvith had done to him in his pearl, part of what he really was had survived. I didn't know for sure if he was dead. Who knew what could kill a Succubus?

I suppose there is something in me that attracts convenient saviours. It was no different this time. On the third day, as I sat somewhat apart from a cluster of hara, but ostensibly part of their group, I became aware a Gelaming was watching me. I sensed this attention at first as an irritation against my senses, then raised my eyes and met his. I experienced a feeling of familiarity and remembered Averen, then. I hoped he was safe. The Gelaming was exactly how I'd first thought they'd be, tall, with long, white-gold hair, which he wore loose. This seemed impractical for a warrior, because I thought he must be that. He wore beautiful armour of pearly scales. His skin was mid-way between olive and gold and the contrast of this duskiness against his pale hair was exotic. I risked a smile and he came over to me.

'What are you, a witch of the forest?' he asked, grinning.

I assumed he must mean my costume, which I'd already grown to like. 'If you want,' I said.

'Would you come with me, please?' he said politely

Perhaps I'd been mistaken about his interest.

He led me to a community building that the Gelaming had set aside for administration purposes. Here, hara sat behind desks, processing the refugees. I realised the interrogators must be seeking close allies of Ponclast who might be hiding among the survivors. Now, yet again, I must dance.

My guide took me into a small, separate room, where there was a table with chairs set around it, but otherwise quite bare. I found this sinister. Their suspicions about me must be high since I wasn't to be interviewed in the public room.

'I am Lannarath har Gelaming,' my guide told me. 'Please sit down.'

'What do you want of me?' I asked, trying to sound vulnerable and only slightly outraged.

'This is simply procedure,' Lannarath said. 'We have to talk to everyhar.'

'Yes, I could see that happening in the main room. Why have you brought me here to ask your questions?' I held my coat closely about me, afraid he'd see the leather I wore beneath it.

He didn't answer me but sat down on the opposite side of

the table. The door opened and another har came in. This one was dressed in trousers and tunic of soft green fabric, embroidered with dark purple thread. His skin was golden, his eyes slanted in the Oriental way. He moved with the feline grace of the soume-prevalent, yet was clearly not that. He carried a sheaf of notes and a pen.

'This won't take long,' he told me, sitting down next to Lannarath. 'I am Sea Cloud har Gelaming, and I would like to ask you some questions.' He arranged his pen and papers neatly before him on the table.

I was ready for them by then. I gave a false name – Jacx. The Gelaming wanted to know where I'd come from and whether I'd lived or worked in Fulminir. I lied easily and told them I'd been brought up on a farm and had come south to trade, so had been caught up in the hostilities. 'I should go home,' I said, attempting to fill my voice with the concern of anxious relatives.

'Is that so?' Lannarath said, his tone holding a smile his face didn't show. 'You don't look much like a farmer to me.'

'What do you want me say?' I enquired sweetly. 'That I lived and worked in Fulminir and spent a considerable amount of my time there in the archon's bed?'

His face told me he didn't think I looked much like the kind of har who'd be wanted for that either.

A wave of cold anger went through me, enough to sweep constraint aside. 'You shouldn't interrogate everyhar like this,' I said. 'Fulminir was full of frightened victims who did what they could to survive. They've suffered enough. Some were *waiting* for you.'

'Were *you*?' Sea Cloud asked me. 'When you lived in Fulminir?'

'I traded in the outer markets,' I said. 'I had no reason to wait for you. I believed I had a secure life upon my land, as did the majority of your evil enemies, who are only farmers.'

'We have to be sure none of Ponclast's immediate followers escaped,' Lannarath said.

'And of course they'd hide in plain sight here,' I said scornfully. 'If anyhar did get out, I expect they're long gone.'

'There's no need to be angry,' Sea Cloud said gently. 'We'll do all that we can for you and your hara, but we need to take precautions.' He paused, exchanged a glance with his colleague, and said, 'Give us the details of where you live, then you may return home.'

I gave them the location of Ashen Weald, wondering what they'd think of that little factory if ever they found it. Still, the occupants of the harling farms were free. They wouldn't have to breed in the way they had, and anyway the Varrish military would no longer be visiting them.

The interview concluded, I went outside and stood in the filthy street, seething with weary anger. I wanted to weep and rage, but was simultaneously overwhelmed with exhaustion. I realised Lannarath had emerged from the building behind me. He put a hand upon the small of my back. 'I know that look,' he said softly, close to my ear. 'You're feeling dead on your feet, and your skin is grey, because that's what the stasis does to a har. The only hara imprisoned in that way were those within Fulminir itself.'

'I'm just tired,' I snapped. 'My world has changed so much. I've barely slept or eaten for weeks, the land here has been destroyed, some of those I love might well be dead, and now – hooray! – the Gelaming are our rulers, come to judge us all. Do you really expect me to be bouncing around as spry and happy as a puppy?' Part of me was horrified at these words pouring out of my mouth; it was not a movement of the dance I knew, which generally involved compliance and deceit. Now, I realised I couldn't be bothered to do all that again. This har could take me as I was, or not.

'Come with me,' he said. 'You look like you could use a drink... before you go home.'

He took me to a camp site that seemed to me like a carnival; a temporary town of pavilions. Pennants on poles coiled lazily in the mild wind. Here, Lennarath had his quarters, a one-room yet spacious tent. He had a bed of thick cushions and fleeces, even a table and a couple of low chairs. I sat down on a chair, over which a thick, fringed shawl of dark red fabric was thrown. I felt disorientated. I thought I'd like nothing more than to sink into the fleeces of the Gelaming's bed and sleep for a week. Lannarath offered me a glass of Ferelithian yenayva, a drink I'd never tasted before. I found it bitter in comparison to sheh. But still, it did its job. Warmth spread through me, and an irrepressible sensation of well-being.

Lannarath sat cross-legged on the rug, looking up at me. 'So,' he said, 'what are you going to do now?'

'Go home,' I said, averting my gaze.

He laughed. 'Really?'

I flicked him a glance, but did not speak.

'It's gone, Jacx,' he said.

'No... my farm...'

'Hush. I know you were in Fulminir. I can smell it on you, and recognise the after-effects of the stasis, even if Sea Cloud chose not to see through your little fiction. I'd like to know how you got out, but I'm not going to press you about that now. I can see you're not a bad har and, like you said, Fulminir was full of victims.'

I couldn't trust him, not yet. 'You're more prone to little fictions than I am.'

'Have it your way,' he said, refilling my drink, perhaps in the hope it would loosen my tongue. 'You should come to Imbrilim, our settlement further south. Leave here and find a new life, Jacx. Don't linger in the ruins.'

'What about my land, my hara?'

He didn't say anything to that.

'I *do* have hara who care about me,' I said, thinking of Sashtri. 'They don't know if I'm alive or dead.'

He narrowed his eyes as he took a drink. 'Ah, so some *did* get out before you, then. I wonder why you didn't go with them.'

'Will you just shut up?' I put my glass down on the rug. 'I'm leaving now.'

He didn't stop me.

I couldn't stay in that town, because I suspected I'd simply be carted off to the Gelaming refugee centre; the idea of that was in no way appealing, and I'd gone past the stage of making myself useful to improve my position. I was tired. Perhaps I should follow Sashtri, in the hope I could find him and the others. They might be dead. I wished what I'd told Lannarath was true and I *did* have a patch of land that was mine, a safe place.

The Gelaming set about healing the land they'd damaged. Nature itself cannot be suppressed and soon the green was creeping back, aided by the nourishment the Gelaming gave it. Often, over the next few days, I went to stand at the edge of town and gazed upon the forlorn ruins of Fulminir. It looked to me like a city that had fallen from the sky and broken upon the hard earth. I had no idea what the Gelaming had done with Ponclast and his followers. They wouldn't tell any of us about that.

Lannarath stalked me persistently, manifesting at my side throughout the day to make witty comments or offer me liquor. His efforts to charm me were commendable, I suppose, although I had no idea what interested him so much. I was filthy, bad-tempered, far from my best. I didn't want to go to Imbrilim. I didn't want to be a grubby fragment of a toppled regime being processed by sanctimonious liberators.

'I'm leaving soon,' Lannarath said to me, 'come with me.'

'To Imbrilim?'

He nodded. 'It will be a city one day.'

'I don't want to.'

He laughed. 'Then what do you want, Jacx? Just tell me.'

'Some land, a house,' I said. 'My memories.' I looked at him steadily. 'Can you help me with that?'

He pondered for a moment. 'You'd take others in, others

who didn't want to leave here?'

I frowned. 'No! What gives you that idea? I want to be alone. The only company I want is perhaps that of animals. What do I have to do to make you help me?'

'Not what you think,' he said. 'Perhaps, one day, you'll tell me your story. That will be sufficient.'

We went looking for a house and found one. It was a tumble-down small-holding and Fulminir could be seen from its western orchard, about three miles away. There was a stream on this side of the land, and also three linked pools. To the east was forest, ancient and deciduous, and to the south a Varrish town called Lash Mede. I could barter in this place for anything my land couldn't supply.

To me, this setting was idyllic, almost unreal. I wondered sometimes if I'd died on the roof of Fulminir and had ended up in an agreeable afterlife. The Gelaming made it possible for me to have a home to my liking, or rather it was Lannarath who ensured it. He sent hara to help renovate the old building, which hadn't been lived in since humans had owned it, and to prepare the land for cultivation. They treated me cordially, but mostly I avoided going near them, merely emerging to inspect their work once they'd finished for the day. Lannarath brought me furniture from Imbrilim, which made my home more sumptuous. Eventually a modest amount of livestock arrived: two dogs, two cats, three goats and five black hens. All these things came to me as if brought by a genie in a fairy-tale, although in fact, apart from the animals, were transported through the otherlanes by Gelaming *sedim*, creatures that could travel through the ethers, bearing passengers or cargo. I was secretly pleased so many of the tales we'd heard had been true. This wasn't magic in the literal sense, but a kind of science I didn't yet understand.

Lannarath knew I had a disturbing history. This was no doubt a strong part of his initial attraction to me. I believe he could smell the past on me, hear the faint cries of its ghosts, and was prickling with curiosity about it. But I told him nothing, not for a long time.

After I'd lived in the house for some months, and the hara who'd helped restore it had gone away, Lannarath came to visit me alone. I knew this time things would be different between us. He arrived on the anniversary of Sethra's death, and found my house full of candlelight and woven wreaths of foliage. The air smelled green. Lannarath came into my living room, looking around at my decorations. 'Is this a Varrish festival?' he asked me, taking off his coat.

'Of a sort,' I replied. 'A festival of the dead.'

He stared at me for some moments, then asked gently, 'Who was it?'

These three simple words broke my shell. 'My only love,' I replied, then turned away from him, wanting to hide the tears that stung my eyes.

He walked up behind me and put his hands upon my shoulders. 'One day, Jacx, you *should* talk about it all. You are a bag of grief.'

I laughed shakily. 'My name is Vashti,' I said, 'and that description is not very flattering.'

I turned round and let him embrace me, found comfort in it.

'I can look for your friends,' he murmured, 'if you want me to.'

I was silent for a while. 'They went to one of the homesteads,' I said. 'I'd like to know if they made it.'

'The homesteads?'

I pulled away from him. 'Sit down, Lannarath. Let me make us a meal. This is a long story.'

We came to an arrangement. Lannarath would visit me twice a year at the turning of the seasons. Spring and autumn, such potent times, when memories come like mist from the night, from the ground, from the still waters beside the apple trees.

Megalithica changed. Terzian's son Swift became the tribe's

leader in Galhea, and our tribal name was changed to Parasiel, which was somehow seen as less distasteful than Varr. But we all knew who was in control, whatever Swift and his family believed.

Lannarath did manage to discover the whereabouts of Sashtri and the others – most were safe. They had reached one of the homesteads as I'd suggested and had remained hidden until the Gelaming turned up to tell them they were free. Lannarath found no news of Averen, though. I could have gone to Sashtri, but by the time I found out about him, I had drawn privacy around me like a comforting old shawl. I was glad he lived and was safe, but wanted to be alone; Lannarath's occasional visits were enough to sustain me. We took aruna together for several pleasant days each time, ate and drank well on the gifts he brought me, then he went away for another six months. In the meanwhile, I traded with my neighbours, and farmed my land. In the evenings, I sat on my veranda and smoked my pipe, with dogs at my feet and cats on my lap, gazing at the stark ruins against the northern sky. It wasn't a hard life, not like the lives of those who really worked the land. I was cushioned by Lannarath's position and wealth; once again, really, a pampered subordinate in the house of a powerful har. Still, I couldn't complain. I was lucky.

Lannarath knew some of my history, but not all of it. He knew about my harlinghood and the story of how I'd danced my way to a kind of freedom. He thought I'd always worked for Sashtri. I never went further than that with the tale, not the personal details anyway. He wanted to hear about life in Fulminir and I gave him stories. He was content with that.

Often I wondered what I could have done differently in my life. If I'd stayed at Ashen Weald, eventually I'd have had freedom, but then I discovered that things had gone badly for them there. They'd been attacked by rogue Uigenna who were fleeing into the wildest territories of the north to hide from the Gelaming. The Uigenna had passed through the homestead like devouring locusts, ruining crops, slaughtering livestock, violating the harish inhabitants. Some had died, and some had been damaged irreparably. So I might've lost my life if I'd stayed, or been mutilated in some way.

The Gelaming eventually discovered all the homesteads and did what they could to help the occupants. Lannarath was horrified I'd been born in such a place, but he liked to hear about it, as hara often like to hear horror stories, when they are safe and warm and far from danger. He tried to persuade me to visit Immanion with him, travel elsewhere, see the world, but my house and my land had become my world. I wanted no other.

'It's like you're waiting here to die,' he said to me once, exasperated.

'You have no idea,' I snapped back.

'Then tell me.' He narrowed his eyes. 'You guard your most intimate secrets like a lioness with her cubs. You lick them with your rough tongue and look upon them with love, but they're eating you. Can't you see that?'

'I once lived within a pyramid of lions,' I said. 'I have the scars. You want to look at them, because how I got them didn't happen to you; my wounds are merely your entertainment.'

I'd made him angry. That was an accomplishment in itself. 'You think that? You think that's why I come here twice a year, snatching up the crumbs you throw to me?'

I turned my back on him. 'I'm sure you have others to distract you, Lannarath. I don't believe for one moment you spend most of your time pining for me.'

'You're dead inside,' he said, 'the worst kind of suicide.'

'Get out,' I said.

'No, I won't! Tell me about the lions.'

I turned and stared at him furiously for some moments, then laughed. 'Poor Lannarath. How I punish you. All right. But you might not think the same of me after you've heard this. You see me as a casualty of war who cannot heal; it's more than that.'

'Let me love you,' he said, somewhat abruptly. 'You're

allowed that, whatever happened in the past.'

He was a good har. He did care. I took him to my bed, and afterwards began the real story, the one I'd never told him. I realise he must have taken some of this information back to Immanion and added it to the dossier of Ponclast's crimes, but what did it matter now? He at least allowed me to keep my anonymity.

I could tell it pained him to hear what role Ponclast had taken in my life. He didn't want to think of me intimate with a har he considered to be monstrous. But I didn't spare him. He wanted to know so I told him, perhaps embellishing the gruesome details.

'You were Gahrazel's hostling?' he interrupted at one point, perhaps to stall the discomforting tale for a moment. 'Have you no idea how well-known he is? He's seen as a martyr by your tribe. The Parasilians will want to know this. Vashti... You're part of this land's history. You can't hide away from that.'

'I can, because Terzian's family choose to be Parasilians and not Varrs. It's no longer their business. Now be quiet and hear the rest.'

Later, in the cooling evening, with the scent of the autumn forest all around us, we sat on the veranda and shared a pipe, both drawn inexorably to stare at the past, at the ruins of Fulminir.

'I can imagine it as a toppled sculpture made by giants,' Lannarath said. 'Lions upon lions, only their fangs are broken now, their stone eyes blind. They are just a mass of shattered limbs.'

There was a mellow silence between us, beautiful peace, and then I broke it. 'Where is he, Lannarath?'

He didn't need to ask who I meant and answered almost immediately. 'Confined in a place he'll never escape, somewhere nohar will ever find him.'

I uttered a mordant laugh. 'You're fools. You can't be sure of that. Remember what he achieved, what he was capable of. You should have killed him when you had the chance.'

Lannarath stroked my back. 'That's not our way, Vashti. This is a different world now.'

Coagulation

The years passed. I was content in my house, if not exactly happy. Lannarath brought joy to my life, even if I insisted on rationing it. I know he wanted to see more of me, and this didn't diminish with time, but I feared if I allowed him more access he'd eventually persuade me to leave, become somehar else. His visits, though, gradually became longer.

Sometimes, I'd dream of Sethra, and on waking from such dreams I'd feel like a prisoner who'd just received a visit from a beloved friend. I cherished the dreams and hoped they would never stop. It was rare other hara from my old life appeared to my sleeping mind.

One night, shortly after Lannarath's spring visit, I dreamed of being in a darkened room with a har who was my lover, lying on a bed of lion pelts. I could barely see, but I felt this was Sethra who had come to me. Occasionally a detail became clear; alabaster lips of perfect form, a long slim hand, the shadowed gleam of an eye. What I felt wasn't mere desire: it was craving. I wanted to devour this tantalising creature. When I took him into me, my entire body shivered with bliss.

'My jewel,' he murmured.

We shared breath while we moved together, becoming one being. Then, as my body convulsed in climax, he raised himself, and I saw his face above me. I merely stared at it, numb, as waves of pleasure ebbed away. This wasn't Sethra.

'You foul betrayer!' I hissed, but I was speaking to my own mind rather than to him.

'Aren't we both guilty of that?' Ponclast said.

The dream shifted and I was standing in Ponclast's bed-chamber, fully-dressed, as was he. His mouth was moving and I was aware he was giving me orders of some kind. At first, I couldn't understand his words, as if he spoke in a foreign language. Eventually, I knew he was saying the same thing, over and over, and at last I knew the meaning. 'Find my sons, Vashti.'

'I don't know where they are,' I said. 'Tell me where to look.'

But he could add nothing more to his instruction. I made to leave the room and at the door turned back. The har who stood behind me was quite different to the Ponclast I knew. His hair hung in black ropes to the floor, like Sashtri's once had. He was emaciated, yet grotesquely soume in aspect, dressed in a stained and tattered red robe. His body was stooped; he looked like a hag. I became aware I was dreaming, and perhaps mixing up old faces into one har. Then I woke up.

The dream was so vivid it left me almost paralysed with anxiety. I feared the past was coming back, that the dream was an omen, that Ponclast would break free from his captivity and come to find me, make me do terrible things. How could I take aruna in my dreams, with this har I despised? This was made worse by the fact I'd enjoyed it. Sethra was the har I loved and Ponclast was responsible for his death, even if he'd not killed Sethra with his own hands. How could my sleeping mind do this to me? I was disgusted. Perhaps it wasn't even really my dream, but a sending. The idea of Ponclast thinking about me, wherever he was held captive, filled me with sick dread.

I was so unnerved I was on the verge of going to the Gelaming Listeners' station in Lash Mede to get a message sent through the ethers to Lannarath. I had to go to town that day anyway, to stock up on supplies that were running low. After loading a cart with items to barter, I whistled to my dogs so they'd accompany me, and made my way there. As I walked, I told myself I mustn't go to the Listeners; I'd had a bad dream, that's all, and soon its memory would fade. If I dreamed of aruna, it was because I wanted it and my body anticipated that Lannarath would soon be here to satisfy its needs. That I'd put Ponclast's face on my dream lover was merely coincidence, some strange kind of memory mash. It couldn't mean anything.

I knew many of Lash Mede's inhabitants by name, but they respected my privacy and had never tried to get to know me. Civil exchanges during business transactions and a shallow exchange of gossip were enough for me. I was aware that I was regarded as a rich Gelaming's secret chesnari, who played at having to work the land. I had to be kept secret because I was Varr and therefore somewhat unsavoury, and certainly not a suitable consort for a Gelaming of rank. These assumptions weren't entirely accurate, but I allowed the fiction, because I knew my neighbours enjoyed it and they were grateful for my trade, and what Lannarath purchased from them while he was staying with me.

It was my habit, after I'd concluded whatever business I had in town, to visit the inn and drink two glasses of ale, with the purpose of picking up any news that had found its way there. This was the closest I got to having an interest in the world. The inn had tables outside, shaded by fruit trees, apple and plum. In autumn the air itself became alcoholic. I preferred to sit in the shadowy bar, because hara went up there to order their drinks. Often they would exchange gossip with the pot-har. Sitting there quietly, I could hear it all.

To come across a Kakkahaar in the town was unusual. They'd disassociated themselves from the Varrs pretty quickly after Fulminir fell, and as far as I knew had precarious connections with the Gelaming now, although I couldn't imagine they'd be friends. The Kakkahaar leaders, apparently, had never involved themselves with Fulminir, so it was easy for them to detach themselves from those who had and deny complicity in Ponclast's schemes. When I caught sight in Lash Mede of that familiar attire – the long sandy robe with an enveloping hood – it was a shock. The har was sitting outside the inn with a companion. I could only see his back, but the clothes were unmistakeable. His hood was thrown back and his long dusty hair hung in rags around him. I made to edge past him into the bar, but the har sitting with him looked at me. He was a striking creature, dark of skin and hair with brilliant black eyes. He looked at me and *saw* me. My skin prickled. Maybe I should go home. At that moment, perhaps picking up on his companion's attention to me, the Kakkahaar turned. His eyes widened although otherwise his face remained impassive. It was Azvith. 'Vashti,' he said, 'what a surprise.'

I realised then it wasn't a surprise at all. He was here to find me.

'Hello Azvith,' I said. 'Yes indeed. What a surprise. How are you?'

'Very well,' he said. 'May I buy you a drink?'

What was the point in declining? If I did, he'd follow me home, no doubt, and at least here the meeting-place was public. There was some security in that. 'If you like.'

'Please, sit down.'

I did so, the dogs curling around my feet. I could sense they were wary of these strangers, didn't like what they smelled.

Azvith rang a small bell on the table, and presently the pothar came out to take his order and to remove the remains of a meal.

'So what brings you back here?' I asked.

'Curiosity, mainly,' Azvith answered. 'I take it you've never left this area.'

'No, there are ties to the past, as you know.'

He didn't comment on this. 'I knew things would go badly and got out of Fulminir before the end.'

'Quite a few did, I imagine.' My drink arrived and I sipped it.

Azvith's companion had so far remained silent, and he'd not been introduced. Now he said, 'You are in contact with old friends?'

'No,' I answered and gave him a tight smile. I turned to Azvith. 'You're the first familiar face I've seen since Fulminir fell, to tell the truth.'

'I understand you were there at the end, right next to Ponclast,' Azvith said.

'Really? How do you *understand* that?'

'Colleagues,' he answered briskly. I guessed he meant that some, if not all, of the Kakkahaar on the roof that day had been released by the Gelaming, rather than confined like the Varrs.

Azvith reached into a pocket of his robe and pulled out a leather pouch, which he set upon the table. He pushed this towards me fastidiously, with the fingertips of one hand. 'I know Almagabran currency isn't much use to you here, but I gather you have a friend in Immanion who could spend it for you.' He had clearly researched me well.

'Azvith, how sweet of you,' I said. 'A gift!'

He smiled coldly. 'Not exactly a gift, but a payment for your valuable time, if you would allow me a little of it.'

'Depends how much and what for,' I said.

'No more than a few minutes here,' he said, 'and whatever information you can give me.'

'About what?'

'The Succubi.'

My body went cold and for a moment I was disorientated. The dream... I covered my brief confusion by taking a long swallow of my ale and was eventually able to say in a steady voice, 'What about them?'

'I expect you saw everything that happened that day,' he said. 'Vashti, what about the Succubi? Were they killed? Did they escape? I know Ponclast summoned them to the roof, but information beyond that is vague.'

'I doubt I saw more than your colleagues did.'

'They didn't see much, or so they claim, but I have the distinct feeling there was *something* to see.'

'I didn't see anything.'

Azvith exhaled through his nose. 'You suspect my motives. I don't blame you for that. But if the Succubi, or at least some of them, survive, I intend to find them. They should not be roaming loose, for a start. I mean them no harm, Vashti...' He paused. 'Or perhaps you would prefer it if I did?'

'I don't care,' I said. I had gulped down my drink and now put the empty glass on the table. 'Thanks for that.' I stood up but didn't take the purse.

'Please Tiahaar,' said Azvith's companion, 'don't leave us so abruptly. We've offended you and for that I'm sorry. My friend can be too brusque in his manner.' He gave me a beautiful smile, which few would be able to resist. However, I'm one of the few.

'I'm not offended, Tiahaar, I simply can't help you.'

'Please, one word – did any survive?'

I looked into his beguiling eyes and saw darkness there. He wouldn't leave this matter, I could see. 'Some escaped, yes,' I said.

'Who?' he asked.

'I wasn't on first name terms with them, you understand, so can't give you identities. They all looked very similar to me. The situation was chaotic, but I glimpsed – or *thought* I did – several of the Succubi fly off. I really can't tell you more than that.'

'As you said, the situation was chaotic,' Azvith said, 'but one of my colleagues believes the Succubi didn't in fact obey their father, that they were instrumental in the Gelaming's victory that day. What are your thoughts on this idea?'

'I can't see how anyhar could come to that conclusion,' I answered. 'It was impossible to tell what was going on, and it all happened so quickly. The whole world was light and fire and roaring sound. How could anyhar perceive details in those circumstances?'

Azvith nodded. 'Quite. Still...' He smiled at me. 'You do have to wonder, if the idea is true, why the Succubi would do that.'

'I suppose you do,' I said. 'But of course they might've had their own agenda all along. Have you considered that?'

'Yes I have,' Azvith said. 'The truth is I'm not sure, which is why I'm speaking to whoever I can who was a witness.'

'Unless you speak to a Succubus, I doubt you'll find out,' I said.

Azvith fixed me with a hard gaze. 'You were on that roof

yet you got away. How was that possible? As I heard it, everyhar was imprisoned there by Gelaming sorcery.'

'No mystery,' I said. 'I ran like you did, before it was too late. I cut it fine, but well... here I am. As you no doubt know, everyhar at Ponclast's side were taken captive.'

Azvith nodded. 'Yes. Still...' He smiled. 'I've a feeling you hide a more interesting story.'

'I'm not as interesting as you think. Now I farm my land and am content. I want nothing more than to forget the past.'

Azvith paused for a moment, then said, 'We'll be visiting Fulminir tomorrow.' He indicated his companion. 'I'm sorry, as he rightly says I can be brusque – rude even.' He smiled in a roguish fashion and became again for a few moments my eccentric employer. I remembered I had quite liked him. 'But then we worked together for years, didn't we, Vashti, so you're quite aware of my shortcomings. This is Levvero. He's helping me in my attempt to trace the Succubi.'

I inclined my head, said nothing.

'Would you care to join us tomorrow?' Levvero said. 'Might jog your memory.'

'Nothing would induce me to step foot in that place again,' I said, hopefully in a manner that would convince Levvero, who I suspected might be capable of seeing through solid rock, never mind a feeble excuse. 'I must decline your invitation. Good luck with your search.'

'Vashti, please take the purse,' Azvith said. 'You've helped me enormously simply by confirming my suspicions.'

'I don't need it,' I said. 'Good day.'

They let me leave then. I didn't see them again. But I felt the event was significant, somehow life-changing. For some weeks I half-expected a Succubus to turn up at my door or manifest in my room at night, but this didn't happen. There were no more unsettling dreams.

That year, on the anniversary of Sethra's death I decided I *would* visit the ruins of Fulminir. This wasn't through curiosity, morbidity, or even to undergo a kind of exorcism. I simply felt it would be right to place a wreath there, see how the place felt to me. I'd been restless for months, ever since I'd met Azvith in the town. I'd told Lannarath about it, although didn't feel I could share with him the details of my dream. He had told me I must contact him immediately through the Listeners should Azvith reappear, which I agreed to do. I was looking forward to Lannarath's next visit, which should be soon. He lived and worked in Immanion now. Sometimes, he was detained and had to come late, or would be given a holiday and could visit me earlier and for longer. It was rare he stayed less than three weeks now.

I spent a whole day fashioning the wreath, weaving ivy and oak together, with late roses that grew wild in my garden. I worked my love into it, and also the precious peace that had come to me. I wanted Sethra, wherever he was, to share that.

I felt disorientated as I walked the road to the fortress, a satchel containing the wreath swinging at my side. There was a humming in my ears and my vision became slightly unfocused as if I might faint. But this was not a cursed land. There was birdsong and mellow sunlight, and the scent of apples all around me. Trees grew in the ruins and wild creatures lived there. This could no longer be such a terrible place. I planned to find my old apartment, if it still existed, and picked my way through rubble to reach it. Then I heard voices. I froze, wondering who could be exploring the ruins, but I suppose they were of interest to many hara, being of such historical significance. The sun passed behind clouds for a while and the roofless chamber in which I stood became briefly gloomy. There was a grand staircase, still intact, and movement at the top of it. The clouds shifted, as if right on cue, and sunlight fell on two hara who had begun to descend the stairs. I thought, for a moment, one of them was Sethra. This was not because there was a great physical resemblance. He looked in fact like a Gelaming, with short but artfully tousled, spiky hair and expensive-looking clothes of a silvery grey. But he possessed a familiar ambience and I felt I knew him.

He saw me, and put a hand upon his companion's arm to halt him. There was still some distance between us, and his voice wasn't loud, but still I heard the word he spoke: 'Vashti?'

I approached. Who was this? Somehar who'd lived here at the same time I had? How had he known me? Surely I was changed? I was also wearing the latest incarnation of my favourite clothes – the long coat and wide-brimmed hat. I took off the hat, held it by my side.

'Who are you?' I asked.

'You won't know me,' he answered, drawing closer. 'Well, I doubt it. It was a long time ago, and I... well, I doubt you knew me.'

He stood before me. I felt overwhelmed. That face. Those eyes. For a moment, they shone indigo. 'It can't be...' I said, backing away. 'No, it can't.'

He smiled quizzically, put his head to one side. 'I don't remember meeting you in person, but I've seen you in visions. Does that sound crazy?'

'Few things do to me. Please... who are you?'

'My name is Gavensel,' he said, and gestured to his companion. 'This is Typhis har Aquillon. We're from Immanion.'

I could have reacted in a number of ways, most of which streaked across my mind in pictures, but in actuality I simply broke down inside, even if this didn't show on the surface. Meeting this har put a final, irrevocable strain upon the defences I'd built within me. Sethra's son. I couldn't take it in, couldn't believe it. This was no Succubus, but a har, beautiful... His son.

'I saw you fall,' I said, my words slow and thick. 'You sent your brother to save me.'

He put a hand upon my shoulder. 'Please... I don't mean to upset you, Tiahaar. I fell? What do you mean? I didn't send Melisander here. He *found* me here.'

I managed to pull myself together somewhat. 'Gavensel... I

knew your hostling...'

'I know. What was his name?'

'Sethra. His name was Sethra.'

Gavensel stared at me for a moment. His eyes were still rather uncanny, but not fearsome. 'I know what you did to him,' he said, but his voice held no reprimand. 'I suspect you had no choice...' He took his hand from me and looked at the tumbled stones around us, then shook his head. 'I have little memory of my life here, but what I do remember...' He pulled his face into a scowl.

'How... *Why* are you here?

His expression softened. 'I'm here to discover lost memories, to find out who I am, or was. Would you talk with me about it?'

'Of course. Sethra would want that.' I paused. 'Tiahaar... I'm not sure it's safe for you here.'

'What do you mean?' the har named Typhis demanded.

'Another was looking for... for the sons of Ponclast,' I said. 'A Kakkahaar from the old time: Azvith. He was here earlier this year, with a dubious companion.'

'You know this companion's name too?' Typhis asked me.

'Yes. It was Levvero.'

Gavensel exchanged a glance with Typhis. 'I have nothing to fear from him,' he said, a hardness coming into his voice. 'If anything, quite the opposite was true.'

I don't need to tell you Gavensel's history because he's told it to you already. It was he who encouraged me to write about my own experiences. We realised that in all likelihood eleven Succubi might still be out there in the world, or maybe they had left this realm. I hoped that was the case. Finding Gavensel was a great and unexpected gift, a part of Sethra returned to me.

That day, when we found one another, he asked if I visited the ruins regularly. I explained why I was there and he wanted to be part of this rite, lay a wreath for his hostling. His companion said he'd explore outside, allowing us this time together. I took Gavensel to what remained of the hostlings' quarters, now merely a skeleton of rooms. The ruins here were ugly, mangled, perhaps reflecting the fear and misery that had once lived there.

'Not here,' Gavensel said, grimacing. 'There must be somewhere more appropriate.'

'My old apartment,' I replied. 'Sethra and I were together there, for a short time.'

Gavensel raised his brows. 'You were lovers?'

'Yes,' I said, 'but thwarted. We were torn apart and then... well, you obviously know what happened.'

'Then we must go there,' Gavensel said. 'Lay the wreath where you lay together.'

I was surprised to find my old home was mostly intact; even some of my belongings remained, ignored by looters. I wanted to take nothing away from there.

We stood in silence in the bedroom and I laid my wreath on the bare floor – bizarrely, all the furnishings in this room had gone. This didn't matter. Our love had never been part of this place.

'In my visions, I saw how I was made,' Gavensel said in a low voice. 'And your part in it. Was that before or after you fell in love with him?'

'After,' I said.

I noticed Gavensel wince at this word, but he didn't comment.

'I realise how it must've appeared to you,' I said, 'but I did what I did to save his life. That was a mistake. He died anyway.'

'How wrong I was about you,' Gavensel said in a wistful tone. 'I learned what the Gelaming found in Fulminir, and read the accounts of survivors. When I tried to understand your complicity in that sickening process, I decided you were simply doing what you had to do to survive. That wasn't entirely wrong, was it?'

'No, but it wasn't merely my own survival.'

He nodded, his face pensive. 'I didn't imagine you cared in any way about my hostling. I believed what I wanted to believe, put my own interpretation on the evidence.'

'Everyhar does that,' I told him. 'And visions don't necessarily present the whole truth. We can't deny we've both done terrible things in our lives, but those days are long gone. I've learned it's pointless to punish myself for events beyond my control.'

'I want to know everything,' he said. 'It's why we were meant to meet.'

'Come to my home,' I said. 'I'd be pleased to have you there.'

The har at my side wasn't a Succubus. Somehow, he'd freed himself of the parasite within, and I was just as interested in learning about that as he was to hear my story.

Lapidem Occultum

Yesterday, the voice came again at dawn. I wasn't sure now whether what I heard was real, or inside my own head, or the melding of natural sounds into something meaningful. I lay in bed for some minutes, listening to that insistent whisper. Then I got up, put on my dressing-robe and went downstairs. I opened the front door. Outside the yard was nothing more than a grey, breathless glimmer. I said, 'Come in, Sethra. I'd like to talk to you.'

I turned and went to the living room, convinced I felt a presence behind me, although there were no sounds and nothing to see.

I sat down in a chair. 'I could never tell you the truth,' I said. 'I was prevented from doing so, and now you'll hear why. Before I begin, look into my heart and see the truth that lies inside. I always loved you. Always will. Now listen.'

I imagined him sitting opposite me, yet saw no ghost, felt no phantom hands upon me or even a wisp of breath. But the room was unnaturally still, the air charged.

Spent of words, I fell asleep on the sofa and was awoken a few hours later by my animals demanding food. The front door stood open and the atmosphere in the room was peaceful. Lannarath would be here soon and this time Gavensel would come with him. They have become friends, after Gavensel sought him out in Immanion. Every couple of weeks I go to the Listeners' station in Lash Mede to exchange messages with Gavensel. Threads neatly tied, well most of them. Perhaps in the near future I'll venture from home, seek out old friends, make new ones, try a different life. Perhaps.

Mulling over these thoughts, I put water on to boil for my morning tea and scrambled two eggs for my breakfast. As I turned to lay my plate on the kitchen table, I found that it was covered with a drift of petals – spring blossom – but how could that be? The blossom had already gone from the trees. As I stared at this unlikely sight, wondering, a divine scent filled the room. I almost swooned. 'Sethra.' I held the memory of him to my heart for some moments, then the air cleared, and it was simply a bright and beautiful morning, the smell of the approaching summer filling the house from the open front door. The table was bare. I knew in my heart he'd said farewell.

In the afternoon, my visitors arrived, a couple of days earlier than I'd expected. I'm aware both Gavensel and I now feel we are family; we're becoming more like ordinary hara in this way, rather than damaged freaks. I could have been his father, but I am not. However, the link we share is strong and real. In my most honest moments, I could say that I loved both his parents, but I'm not that honest very often. My feelings vacillate like the surge of clouds. If Gavensel and I ever speak of this, it won't be for a long time.

I wanted to speak to Gavensel alone to tell him about what I'd experienced that morning, but he was excited, clearly sharing some secret with Lannarath. We crowded into the kitchen, and I began to make tea, but Gavensel pulled my hands away from the kettle.

'You must sit down,' he said. 'We have news.'

I did so, expecting to hear about Sashtri, perhaps even that he was coming to see me, and hoping this was so.

'Tell him,' Gavensel said to Lannarath. 'It should be you, since you were the one who made the discovery.'

Lannarath nodded. 'If you like.' He sat down opposite me. 'After Fulminir fell, one of the tasks my department undertook was tracing the sons of the homestead hara.'

I blinked at him. 'I'm not sure I want to know.'

'You do,' Gavensel said, still standing. 'Listen to him.'

'The records were often destroyed or incomprehensible,' Lannarath said. 'Even when the work was done, as much as we felt we could do, I've never forgotten about it. Gavensel has a friend who was a homestead hostling. He asked me if it was possible I could find his sons. Vashti... that har came from Ashen Weald.'

'Are you saying you found out who my hostling is?' I asked, weirdly numb.

'Yes, I know him,' Gavensel said. 'He survived. His name is Grackle.'

'I see. Well, thank you, I suppose.' I stood up. 'Tea, then?'

'Vashti! Gavensel said, grabbing my arms. 'Don't be like this. Grackle's always yearned for his sons – in fact we all thought him a little mad because of it. Then Lannarath managed to find the har who'd been high keeper of Ashen Weald when you lived there.'

'It's taken me a while,' Lannarath said. 'He hid himself well. I could only work on this when I had the time, but I used every means possible to track him down. Once he'd talked and all the information was put together, it became clear. I then talked with Grackle and he remembered you, because he was the hostling who helped you escape Ashen Weald.'

I stood up. 'This isn't real,' I said. 'Too neat, too convenient. I must've died in Fulminir like I've always feared.'

Lannarath gestured with both hands. 'It's real, Vashti. Accept it.'

'I think you should meet Grackle,' Gavensel said. 'Please don't dismiss the idea without considering it. Seeing you would help him a lot.'

I shook myself free of Gavensel's hold 'He can't have been my hostling,' I said, pacing about the room. 'He was weak... I tried to...' I shook my head. 'No, you're wrong.'

'He's not weak,' Gavensel said, in a sharp tone. 'He was severely injured by the Uigenna. He was forever changed by it. You wouldn't even recognise him now. He gave me strength and care when I needed it. I want to give him something in return – the one thing he's longed for over the years. A surviving son. He never believed they were all dead.'

I realised then that earlier I'd given Sethra's son back to him, even if only in my own mind. If his spirit had visited me, he knew that Gavensel lived and was whole and safe. Perhaps all I'd experienced was an omen – of this.

'He doesn't know of your relationship with him yet,' Gavensel said. 'He won't know until you agree to meet him. I know you'll need time, but...' He shrugged. 'What else can I say? It's up to you now.'

I remembered that horrible, pitiful yearning, the hunger in that hostling's eyes. Did I want that in my life? And yet he had helped me when I needed it most. If he'd known I was his son, would he have left Ashen Weald with me that day? If that had happened, how might it have affected all that came afterwards? I remembered that sweet, monkey face, his kindness. I remembered his helplessness, unable to think of any other life than the one to which they'd chained him. 'At the mid-summer festival,' I said impulsively.

I saw Lannarath and Gavensel exchange a glance; conspirators.

'Don't say anything to him yet,' I said. 'I'm not completely sure about this. I need to think.'

Now, I'm sitting on the veranda at the end of the day. The others have gone to bed. This story is ending like a book being closed. What stories lie beyond? The roar of lions is muted now, but *he* is still alive, still out there. The Gelaming believe it is over, that the world has moved on, but I think that such primal forces as I experienced in Fulminir can never be obliterated completely. The pyramid might be demolished, but its ghostly outline will forever haunt the air. And I feel... No. It's done. I am the har who danced his way to the peak of a pyramid of lions. The performance has ended, the applause has died away. The scars have healed, yet tell my story in a trace of spidery patterns. These words I have written. You have read them now.

Glossary of Terms

Aghama (*ag*-am-ah) – the first har of all, regarded as a dehar (god) by hara. While once based upon Thiede, the leader of the Gelaming, the Aghama is now more of a spiritual ideal, separate from the har himself.

Althaia (al-*thay*-ah) – the process and period of change from human to har following inception

Aruna – sexual union between hara that is both spiritual and physical.

Chesna (*chez*-nah) – a close relationship, a chesna-bond can be equated to marriage

Chesnari – a partner in a chesna-bond

Dehar (*day*-har) – a Wraeththu deity (pl. Dehara)

Devastation, the – one of many terms used to describe the final days of humanity, when the world was in turmoil, and there was catastrophic conflict between hara and humans. The days of change.

Egregore – an occult concept representing a 'thoughtform' or 'collective group mind', an autonomous psychic entity made up of, and influencing, the thoughts of a group of people.

Feybraiha (fay-*bray*-ah) – a period of time equating to puberty in humans when a har matures sexually. The term also refers to a day of celebration for this. At the end of his feybraiha, when he is physically ready, a har will take aruna with another for the first time. This is regarded as an important rite of passage.

First Generation – hara who were became Wraeththu by being incepted as humans

Gelaming (*Jel*-ah-ming) – the most influential tribe of Wraeththu, whose tribal home is Almagabra

Har – a Wraeththu individual

Harling – a young har not yet at feybraiha

Hienama (*hy*-en-*ah*-mah) – equivalent of a priest/teacher/healer

Hostling – a har who carries the pearl of a harling, equivalent of human mother.

Househar – a member of the household staff

Inception – the process by which a human becomes har, involving a transfusion of blood.

Kakkahaar – a desert tribe renowned for their interest in dark magic.

Otherlanes – interdimensional, etheric pathways between physical realms.

Ouana (oo-*ah*-nah) – the masculine aspect of Wraeththu

Parasiel – the tribe name taken by the Varrs after Fulminir fell.

Phylarch – leader of a phyle

Phyle – a distinct community within a tribe, a sub tribe

Pothar – har employed in an inn

Pureborn – a har who has been born to harish parents rather than inception from human. A second-generation har and beyond.

Sedim – etheric beings able to travel the otherlanes between realms.

Soume (*soo*-mee) – the feminine aspect of Wraeththu

Spark (v) – to take the role of ouana in the creation of a pearl.

Sulh – a tribe of the islands of Alba Sulh, renowned for their mystical nature.

Tiahaar – a polite form of address (as in Sir, Madam)

Uigenna (ewe-ee-*gen*-ah) – the first Wraeththu tribe in Megalithica.

Unneah (oo-*nay*-ah) – an early tribe formed by disaffected member of the Uigenna. While widespread in Megalithica, the Unneah never had the same influence and power as the Varrs.

Unthrist – a har without a tribe.

Varrs – an early Wraeththu tribe, (deriving from the Uigenna proto tribe), formed by Ponclast and Terzian.

Wraeththu – (*ray*-thoo) androgynous race that came to replace humanity

Alchemical Terms Vsed as Chapter Headings

Song of the Cannibals

A process of alchemical transformation of four stages

Nigredo – 'blackness', sometimes called melanosis. This is the first stage of alchemical transformation and concerns putrefaction or decomposition. From a psychological perspective it represents the 'dark night of the soul'.

Albedo – 'whiteness', sometimes called leucosis. The second stage of alchemical transformation. It involves purification, known as ablutio, which is the washing away of any impurities.

Citrinitas – 'yellowness', sometimes called xanthosis. The third stage of alchemical transformation and involved the 'yellowing' of lunar (silver) consciousness into solar consciousness. The dawning of solar light within the self.

Rubedo – 'redness,' sometimes called iosis. The fourth and final stage of alchemical transformation. The successful conclusion of the Great Work.

Half Sick of Shadows

Components and processes of alchemical work.

Balsam of Soot – also known as Balsamus Fuliginis, this is an arsenic-based salve for wounds.

Caput Mortuum – its literal meaning is 'dead head' and it refers to the non-volatile residue left over in the bottom of an alembic after the process of distillation.

Flowers of Sulphur – the term 'flowers' in alchemy refers to the flower-like residue (or crystals) produced during the sublimation of certain substances. "Flowers of sulphur" refers to sulphur purified by sublimation.

Spirit of Vitriol – Sulphuric acid, usually made by distilling iron or copper sulphate.

Ens Veneris – its literal meaning is "being of Venus", which refers to copper.

Lunafaction – the making of silver, with reference to the moon (lunar).

Mercurius Vitae – Antimony oxychloride; a poisonous and violently emetic white powder made by precipitating butter of antimony with water.

Solifaction – the making of gold, with reference to the sun (solar).

A Pyramid of Lions

A process of alchemical transformation of seven stages (the eighth title here refers to the end product of the work)

Calcination – being reduced by fire to ashes.

Dissolution – the ashes of calcination are dissolved in water to purify them.

Separation – impurities are brought to the surface and removed.

Conjunction – the recombination of the refined elements left after separation.

Fermentation – a process of two parts, the first of which involves Putrefaction, or the death of the hermaphroditic child of Conjunction, followed by its rebirth at a higher level of being.

Distillation – the substance is heated to the point of evaporation. The vapour from this process is then cooled and condensed, followed by the collection of the resulting distilled liquid. Distillation washes away remaining debris for the final stage of transformation.

Coagulation – Coagulation is the summation of the work: transformation into a new and higher being (substance).

Lapidem Occultum – literally 'hidden stone' referring to the Philosopher's Stone, the goal of the Great Work.

About the Author

Storm is the creator of the Wraeththu Mythos, the first trilogy of which was published in the 1980s. However, the influences and inspirations for the Wraeththu world go much further back than that, and continue into the future as she plans more stories for it.

Her other full length works cross genres from science fiction, to dark fantasy, to epic fantasy, to slipstream. She has written over thirty books, including full length novels, novellas, short story collections and non-fiction titles. Her short stories, which she continues to write prolifically, appear in diverse magazines and anthologies.

Storm is the founder of Immanion Press, created initially to publish her out-of-print back catalogue, but which evolved into the thriving venture it is today. Her interests include magic and spirituality, movies, music and MMOs. Among her many occupations, most of which are unpaid, she runs a guild called Equilibrium on the EU servers of World of Warcraft. She lives in the Midlands of the UK with her husband and four cats.

IMMANION PRESS

Purveyors of Speculative Fiction

Para Animalia Edited by Storm Constantine & Wendy Darling

Based on the world created by Storm Constantine for her Wraeththu novels, the stories in this collection explore how various Wraeththu tribes interact with animals, have spiritual or working relationships with them, or have encountered zoological mysteries out in the world. From the wolves of frozen forests, and a har's obsession with spiders, to the snakes of parched deserts and the hunting dogs of what was once the African plains, hara confront a strengthening natural world that is now free of humanity.

'Para Animalia' features stories from nine writers, some of whom are well known within Wraeththu fandom and/or have written Wraeththu Mythos novels published by Immanion Press. Also included are two new stories each by Storm Constantine and Wendy Darling.

ISBN: 978-1-907737-70-1 £11.99, $18.99

Animate Objects by Tanith Lee

There is no such thing as an inanimate object... And how could that be? Because, simply, everything is formed from matter, and basically, at root, the matter that makes up everything in the physical world – the Universe – is of the same substance. Which means, on that basic level, we – you, me, and that power station over there – are all the exact riotous, chaotic, amorphous same. Here is an assortment of Lee takes on the nature, and perhaps intentions, of so-called non-sentient things.

We published the original limited edition of this collection in 2013, to commemorate Tanith Lee receiving the Lifetime Achievement Award at World Fantasycon. It included 5 previously unpublished pieces. This new release includes a further 2 stories, co-written by Tanith Lee and John Kaiine, and new interior illustrations by Jarod Mills.

ISBN: 978-1-907737-73-2 £11.99 $18.99

Immanion Press
http://www.immanion-press.com
info@immanion-press.com